PRAISE FOR
LAURA McHALE HOLLAND

Laura McHale Holland's delightful *Shinbone Lane* captures echoes of San Francisco's Summer of Love, with a few surprising twists. Set in a quirky corner of the city peopled by old friends, new friends and one very lonely – and rather chatty – magical pigeon, Holland's novel reminds us that despite kind intentions, utopias often mask a dark underbelly.

— RAYNE WOLFE, AUTHOR OF *TOXIC MOM TOOLKIT* AND FORMER *NEW YORK TIMES* REGIONAL STAFF WRITER

I haven't got a clue how Laura conjures such mysterious locales, but she has surprises in store for me when I get there, and it's always a fascinating ride.

— BARBARA TOBONI, AUTHOR OF *LIGHT THE WAY* AND *THE BUNNY POETS*

Shinbone Lane is full of charm, humor, and memorable characters. In a delightful blend of magical realism, mystery, and social commentary, the author explores themes of friendship, family, and the search for truth.

— REBECCA ROSENBERG, BESTSELLING AUTHOR OF CHAMPAGNE WIDOWS NOVELS

I'm impressed with how well Laura created so many interesting and delightful characters who all had their own special stories, and how she wove those stories together.

— EDIE BARAN, TEACHING ARTIST, ARTS FOR ALL WI

Laura McHale Holland's strong prose riveted me through three books, and I'll be returning for more.

— MARY ELLEN GAMBUTTI, ADOPTEE ADVOCATE AND
AUTHOR OF *I MUST HAVE WANDERED*

SHINBONE LANE

SHINBONE LANE

A NOVEL

LAURA MCHALE HOLLAND

Publisher's Cataloging-in-Publication Data
Names: Holland, Laura McHale.
Title: Shinbone Lane : a novel / Laura McHale Holland.
Description: Rohnert Park, CA : WORDforest, 2025 | Summary: On San Francisco's Shinbone Lane in 1974, sixteen-year-old runaway Maddy finds refuge among a spirited group of wanderers, artists, and dreamers. Taken in by elderly Clara and her neighbor Ted, she discovers a place where magic blends with reality—and secrets emerge to heal, haunt, and transform lives.
Identifiers: LCCN 2024922663 | ISBN 9781733668385 (pbk.) ISBN 9781733668361 (pbk.) ISBN 9781733668378 (ebook)
Subjects: LCSH: Runaway teenagers – Fiction. | Secrecy – Fiction. | Friendship – Fiction. | Resilience (Personality trait) – Fiction. | San Francisco (Calif.) – Fiction. | BISAC: FICTION / Magical Realism. | FICTION / Historical / 20th Century / Post-World War II. | FICTION / Women. Classification: LCC PS3608 055 2025 | DDC 813 H—dc23
LC record available at https://lccn.loc.gov/2024922663
Book cover design by Ebook Launch

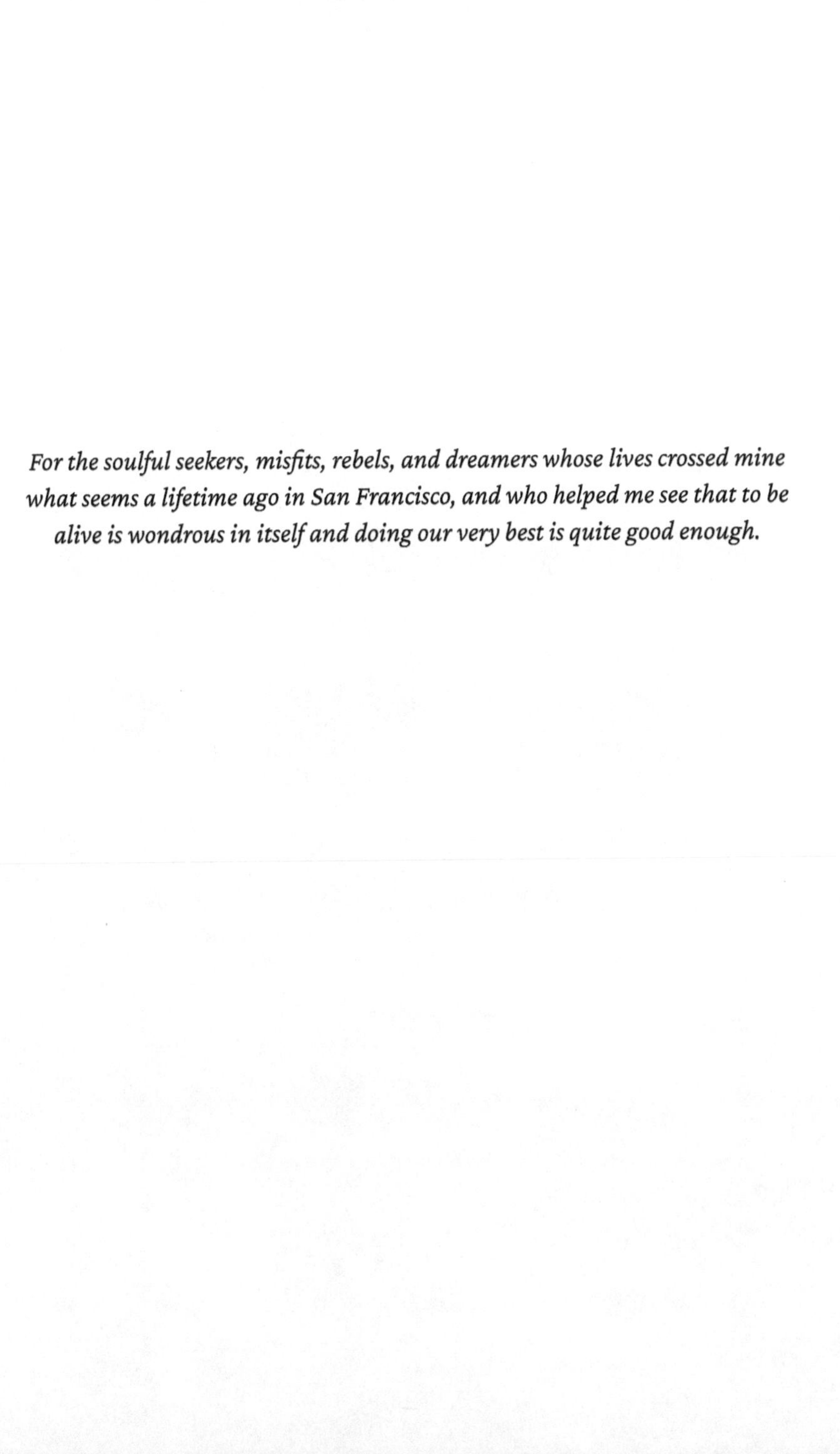

For the soulful seekers, misfits, rebels, and dreamers whose lives crossed mine what seems a lifetime ago in San Francisco, and who helped me see that to be alive is wondrous in itself and doing our very best is quite good enough.

PROLOGUE

At the kitchen table, she couldn't complete the simple task of paying her bills. How could she, the way they watched her every move?

Like parents who'd caught their child in a lie, they peeled her soul with their eyes. They could punish now or hold the threat at bay. Even when she closed the blinds and turned her back, they assaulted the life she'd begun after her mother's sudden demise. A heart attack. In middle age.

They'd been close, the child born during the Great Depression and her single mom. Until the big mistake. The unforgivable act. The one that caused mother to banish daughter to days and nights of bedpans and Melba toast for a simpering great aunt, and diapers and Gerber meals for a squalling baby she never wanted. She spent seven years cooking, scrubbing, rubbing while the elder shriveled and the child grew. Fresh air rarely touched her skin.

Then, a Special Delivery package: a note scribbled in her mother's final moments, train fare, keys. Freedom. At the funeral, the sole row of mourners didn't recognize her. The toll of indentured servitude now worked to her advantage. She was twenty-five and looked thirty-five. She wouldn't have to lie about where she'd been, and why.

With a tidy sum her mother had hidden in a hat box, she rented a cheerful, sunlit place near her careworn childhood home. She had plans. It was 1961, a young decade with hints of change in the breeze. She would start over. She would make curtains and hang plants in the windows. She would throw them open to salt air in the mornings. She would be normal, live alongside people for whom she'd been a clump of fennel growing unbidden on the hillside, not a treasured rose planted with care. People who had no clue who she was.

But the day she moved in, she saw them perched like royalty on a gilded balcony. They studied, judged, choked her hope. Every hour, every day, they reminded her she was unworthy.

With anger sizzling her blood, she swept the checkbook and stack of bills off the table. Something had to change. She had suffered enough. Done her time. The lofty tormentors must go. She needed help. Someone to sneak in and ravage their roost. And that someone was right under her nose.

CHAPTER

ONE

With a backpack full of dreams slung over her shoulder, Maddy entered the weathered Greyhound station. She took in the sweat-and-patchouli air as Keeley's parting words swarmed her mind. "Nothing lasts forever. Look at the Beatles. No more songs from them, mind-blowing as they were. That's how life is, cupcake."

Maddy merged with the rumpled crowd and slinked forward. Fear clogged her throat as she slumped into a vacant seat. Head cast down in the City of Saint Francis, the storied City by the Bay, she brushed tendrils of her thick brown mane from her face, pulled out a sketchbook, and drew a few lines in charcoal.

Boots shiny as black sapphire came into view, followed by a swirling lavender hem. A woman plopped with an oof! beside her. "Hello," the stranger said, her voice layered with years of joy and sorrow.

"Um, hi," the youth mumbled. She flipped to a blank page.

A few yards away lurked a paunchy man with gold front teeth. He'd tried to pull Maddy toward him when she'd exited the bus. She'd batted him with her pack and fled inside, where she'd thought of pleading with an agent for a free ticket home, but then she remembered. She no longer had a home.

Soft as a good-night prayer, the woman hummed the melody to "Moon River" while Maddy sketched her skirt. It struck the budding artist how easy she'd had it since she'd run away eighteen months ago. Her fifteenth birthday.

She'd slipped through her bedroom window, hugged a tulip tree that had heard her every whispered hope, and sprinted past remnants of smashed pumpkins and scattered candy wrappers to Highway 68. There she stuck out her thumb. Within minutes, a van of dropouts from Antioch College, where her dad worked as an administrator, pulled over. They'd just set off to visit friends scattered across the country and said she could come along.

Keeley, who at age twenty had already published a children's book, took Maddy under her wing. They baked bread for a commune in the Smoky Mountains, sang and passed the hat on Philadelphia street corners, made sandwich boards for a theater in Kansas City, cooked breakfast for a dude ranch near Tombstone, sold jewelry in campgrounds across North America—anything and everything to get by under the table.

But then Keeley fell in love with a glassblower in Los Angeles and joined him on a journey to Machu Picchu in Peru. No one else invited. One by one, others in the group pulled away to follow divergent stars.

Maddy panhandled and caught a Greyhound north. A guy she met in the Rockies had scribbled his phone number on a matchbook. "Come to San Francisco sometime. I'll take you around my hometown," he'd said. He could spin a yarn better than Arlo Guthrie, and his voice was resonant as a Martin guitar. But his eyes were midnight pools of sorrow. Maddy never thought she'd actually call him. Her companions were family, after all. Ha! What a jolt to see the truth. No one was family. He'd seemed okay, but what if he wasn't? He might try to force himself on her. Or he might be looking for love. She was the wrong person for that. Stupid love. It's always trouble.

Now, on a windy May morning in 1974, in the city that stole Tony

Bennett's heart, sixteen-year-old Maddy pondered what to do next. No more Keeley. No more protector. And only a handful of hippie stragglers left in The Haight. She stopped drawing to brush her bangs aside and rub her itchy brow.

"Goodness me." Fingers with clean, clipped nails twisted a gold wedding band kept in place by a swollen knuckle. "Is that what my bottom half looks like?"

"I'm not that skilled." Maddy filled in shadows along the ribbing of a turquoise sweater. "I do this when I'm sorting things out."

The woman looked her up and down, and Maddy bristled, preparing for unwelcome advice or comments. But the elderly lady unclasped her mint-green leather handbag and pulled out a bright fuchsia wallet. "I'd like to buy that when you're done."

"You must be kidding." Maddy studied the woman's face and found a weathered version of Glinda the Good Witch of the North in *The Wizard of Oz*. She wasn't all sparkly, waving a wand, she didn't have apple-red cheeks, but she exuded the kind of grace that lifts spirits.

"I most certainly am not kidding," the woman replied as wrinkles crinkled around her eyes. "I'm Clara, by the way, Clara Tremblay."

"Maddy. Pleased to meet you." She gave a quick smile and returned to the drawing, eager to capture the moment. Clara sat still while Maddy outlined and shaded the woman's torso. Next Maddy sketched her shoulders and finally her face, which was framed by wisps of white hair that had escaped from a bun at the nape of her neck. When Maddy finished, she ripped out the page and handed it to Clara.

Clara rubbed her bottom lip as she looked over the drawing. "My, my, this is remarkable. How much do I owe you?"

"Nothing. It's yours."

"You should be paid for your work." Clara pulled a five-dollar bill from her wallet and pressed it into Maddy's hand. "Buy yourself a little something special."

Maddy tried to wave her off, though sorely in need of money. Long gone was the $166 she'd emptied from her piggybank.

Clara held her ground. "I insist."

Maddy gave in, thanked her, and stuffed the money into her pocket.

Clara glanced at her watch. "Ah, it's time for me to go." She stood up and hovered over Maddy. "Would you mind helping me outside? Ted should be here now. He's my neighbor, a true godsend. My Packard's on the fritz yet again. That's why I rode the bus." She grabbed two overstuffed canvas bags. "There's so many people to wade through, you know."

"Sure. I should get going anyway." Maddy tucked her pencil and sketchbook away, hiked her pack over her shoulder, and took one of Clara's bags.

Gusts of diesel wind lifted Clara's hem as they stepped outside. She batted her skirt down. At the curb, a slender man, with shoulders slightly stooped and eyes the color of new violets, pulled up in a maroon pick-up truck and tipped his tweed fisherman's cap at Clara. A piece of history brought to life, the vehicle had curves like chocolate-covered cherries and wide, black running boards.

A bird shot up from the truck bed, which was rimmed with wooden slats. It resembled a pigeon, but with bold coloring like a kingfisher or parrot and a longer body and tail. The bird, which had one normal claw and one that appeared to be a spring, maneuvered from the slats into the cab and pecked at the collar of the man's flannel shirt.

"Here's Ted, always right on the button. Comes from his days at Southern Pacific Railroad. Best engineer they ever had." Clara opened the passenger door. From Ted's truck wafted a potpourri of leather, sawdust, lemon oil, rose petals, and weathered books, which caused Maddy and several passersby to sigh as though sniffing perfume they couldn't afford.

Clara smiled at Maddy's reaction to the scent. "Isn't it lovely?"

"Just a second," Ted said. "I'll come around and help you up."

"It's okay. Maddy will help." She winked at the girl and stepped onto the running board. "In fact, you're coming over for a cuppa tea, isn't that right, dear?"

"Better hop in quick." With a calloused hand, Ted motioned them forward. "We're not supposed to linger here."

Maddy could have said no thanks, closed the door after helping Clara inside, and waved them off. But she felt like a punctured tire losing air fast. Then she spotted the man with gold teeth only a few yards away, leaning against the building, watching her. Why not pause for a little while, pretend all was well before figuring out where to go next? Clara slid over to make room for Maddy and patted the seat.

TED DROVE the truck through streets busy with buses, cars, and bicycles angling for space, yet traffic flowed with friendly, small-town ease. People came and went from warehouses, auto shops, run-down hotels, old Victorian homes, and apartment buildings. Dusty storefronts housed restaurants, bridal shops, check cashing services, beauty salons, artist cooperatives, mom-and-pop groceries, and dime stores.

As they wended along, they passed colorful murals covering entire sides of multi-story buildings. Signs in Spanish advertised businesses as *mercados*, *panaderias*, *carnicerías* and *lavanderías*, which Clara pointed out were markets, bakeries, butcher shops, and laundromats. Before long, Ted turned onto a boulevard with palm trees lining the median.

"Look on the right, and you'll see Mission Dolores, built in 1791," Ted said.

"It's one of the oldest structures in the city," Clara added.

"And here's Dolores Park," Ted swept his arm to an open green space that spanned about two square blocks. "Lots of things going on there."

Looking out the window, Maddy grinned. "It's full of people—sunbathing, jogging, picnicking. Oh gosh, look at that gorgeous Irish setter. It just leaped way high to catch a Frisbee."

"Too bad the Ed Sullivan Show's not still on TV," Clara said. "That dog would be a hit."

As they continued past the park, Maddy remarked, "It looks like all the buildings are kind of squished together. No lawns, no side yards."

"That may be so," Clara replied, "but you'll find many a sanctuary in our backyards, and just look at all the flower boxes bursting with color."

"Not to mention our famous painted ladies," Ted said.

Maddy cocked her head at Clara. "Painted ladies?"

"That's the Victorians painted so beautifully," Clara added.

Absorbed in the passing scenery, Maddy's tummy fluttered as they drove up and down hills that by San Francisco standards were far from steep. The conversation lulled. After a while, Clara, who never sought the spotlight but knew every Broadway hit by heart, lilted the first line of "Wouldn't It Be Loverly." Maddy and Ted joined in with off-key harmonies, which made them all laugh. Captain, the wild-colored pigeon, tapped his beak against the dashboard in time to the beat.

They turned off Dolores Street onto 29th Street and headed uphill. Like other streets in the area, it was packed with a mix of Victorian and Edwardian homes and apartments. Shortly after they passed a church with school buildings Clara identified as St. Paul's parish, the incline grew so steep it seemed to Maddy they were driving straight into the sky.

At last, Ted turned onto Shinbone Lane. Immediately, an open, green space at the top of a graceful upward slope came into view. Warm sunlight illuminating manzanita, bougainvillea and other greenery cast a rose-gold glow all the way down the lane. Maddy gaped, and blinked her eyes, as the truck passed homes large and small. Some even had side yards sporting a joyous riot of colors.

Two pocket-sized, dark-green structures with flat roofs set uphill and far back from the road caught Maddy's eye. A long, winding path dotted with rose bushes in a multitude of colors led to them. "What are those?"

"Earthquake shacks, or some folks say cottages, built after the big quake in '06 for folks who'd lost their homes," Ted said.

"The O'Grady brothers moved them up here around '08. A few

generations of their progeny live there now," Clara noted. "You'll see a gaggle of kids in uniforms pile out and file down the hill on school days."

A few moments later, they stopped in front of Ted's three-story Italianate Victorian at 346, three houses before the lane ended at the foot of the lush hillside. Ted's lifelong home sat directly across from Clara's smaller and simpler Edwardian at 631, the addresses a reminder that early residents took liberties when numbering homes along their unpaved lane, which stretched roughly two-and-a-half blocks. But who could say for sure? Shinbone had no side streets.

Meanwhile, the monthly meeting of Shinbone Friends was in full swing at The Farmhouse, the first structure built on the lane. Abandoned in the 1940s, it was purchased and refurbished for community use in 1960 by Shinbone Friends. The group had formed because neither Glen Park nor Noe Valley, the two closest neighborhoods, would claim Shinbone as its own for various reasons—the main one being they found the lane's name gruesome.

Eloise Watkins, a middle-aged dance teacher whose family had lived on the lane since the 19th century, looked into her compact mirror. She applied crimson lipstick as she listened to her neighbors discuss the dilemma.

"It seems to me," said Rosie, a petite woman with puppy-brown eyes, "we could at least consider a name change." Silver bracelets on each arm jangled as she tucked her chin-length red waves behind ears adorned with silver hoop earrings.

Most members regarded Rosie with approval. She was well-liked for her welcoming smile and for the bargains she provided at her sidewalk sale every Saturday on Sanchez Street.

But Eloise puckered her face at Rosie as though she'd been offered a plate of moldy cheese and stale crackers. "What would you know?" she demanded. "You don't even live on Shinbone, being as that your home —rented, I might add—is on the far corner facing 29th. I guarantee you won't be here long." She tossed her makeup into her purse and patted Coco, the toy poodle snoozing in her lap.

Bea and Barb, identical twins with blond hair and almond-shaped eyes, who shared a room at 346, cried out in unison that Eloise wasn't being fair. The man seated next to Eloise elbowed her and admonished that Rosie was as much a part of the lane as anyone else. Murmured words of agreement echoed through the room.

Eloise put Coco on the floor, stood, and straightened her butter-yellow skirt-and-sweater set with a couple of good yanks. "Our name and the story of how we got it belong to us. We can't just cast it aside. But I have more important things to do than this." She put a hand on the man's shoulder. "Why aren't you helping me find my Julianna, hmmm?"

"Kids these days—she'll turn up," he replied.

Coco skittered across the room and out the door. Ever the ballerina, Eloise *chasséd* after, her well-worn slippers barely touching the floor. "Come back here, sweet Coco, little love." Outside, she stopped abruptly and squared her shoulders at the site of Coco yipping and wagging her entire body at Ted's truck, which sputtered, creaked and pinged before growing silent.

Coco sniffed Maddy when the youth stepped out and she wagged her tail at Captain, but when Clara emerged, the dog leaped into the old woman's arms and licked her face. Eloise glared from across the unpaved lane before strutting over to rip Coco from her elderly neighbor's arms.

Rattled, Clara clutched her purse to her chest, looked down at her boots and hummed the first bars of Barbra Streisand's hit song "People." Ted reached an arm around Clara's shoulders and pulled her in for a quick hug.

Eloise scanned 346 from ground level to the roof and back. "It's time you do something about this aberration, Ted Yates. It steers kids the wrong way, turns them against families that love them."

"Good afternoon, Eloise." Ted took off his cap and ran a hand over his crew cut. He chuckled, for what his home was, or was not, depended on who was looking. Not to mention time of day, density of fog, and other factors that are difficult to measure. A small number of folks claimed on "general principles" that 346, rumored to have once been a house of ill repute, remained a bad influence.

To many, 346 was merely old Ted's ramshackle eyesore, with bull thistle, fennel, and calla lilies choking the backyard, fungus-weary rose bushes clawing the rickety fence, and bougainvillea enveloping windows and doors. Curiosity drew others in. They lingered while on strolls or errands to admire the exterior paint in shades of green, mauve, off-white, and gold. They fawned over the flower boxes with oversize petunias and pansies forever in bloom. Many secretly envied the tribe of free spirits clad in repurposed hand-me-downs dashing in and out at all hours.

To the band of people who called the place home, 346 was a refuge. Soft, golden light filled the rooms; a soothing hum spread from rafters to nooks and crannies at sunrise; paint on the walls emanated appeal, as though a final coat of love had been applied.

And the backyard was a revelation. A path unfolded like a cozy mystery, to reveal a slender creek lined with fruit trees, vegetable patches, and a waterfall. Cottages made from scavenged materials nestled beneath tall pines and oaks. These served as studios for art, music, and other creative pursuits. Nobody could explain how all of this fit into what appeared from the outside to be an ordinary San Francisco backyard.

Eloise poked Ted's chest. "I must inspect the place. You can't guarantee that my Julianna isn't hidden in some alcove in back. She could be lost in there for all you know. After all, the place is always changing."

Ted could not deny that 346 constantly transformed in ways difficult to fathom. It had been that way as far back as he could remember. But after a quick consultation with his pigeon friend, Captain, who was fluent in English and sent advice directly into his mind, Ted remained confident Eloise's daughter was not in his midst.

"How can you be sure Julianna didn't take off on that trip around the world she always talked about?" he asked. "She said she'd go when she turned eighteen."

Eloise scoffed and shrank from the kindness beaming from his violet eyes as though it were a twisted scarf tightening around her throat. "I know my Julianna—that's how."

She shook off the fear and focused on Maddy, who stood mesmerized in front of a tree, which had pale-blue bark cracked like birch and covered in places with a dusting of moss. Its rippling, heart-shaped leaves reflected light in variegated colors the way crystals do.

"Nabbing another lost one, I see." Eloise's pinched face radiated disdain. "Look at her, head in the clouds, perfect for your band of riffraff, the very reason no neighborhood will claim Shinbone Lane as its own."

"What an amazing tree." Maddy patted the trunk, and a tingle ran through her, which brought to mind the tulip tree that had comforted her in childhood. "The ripples and light and this faded blue trunk ... I could watch all day." The leaves chimed faintly as a breeze ruffled by.

"We should rip that no-good ripple tree out." Eloise poked at her hair, which hugged her skull like a bathing cap and then broke into a frizz of curls on the ends. Plastic combs and hairspray kept all strands in place—a look straight out of the early 1950s. "But nobody listens to me."

Eloise huffed, whipped around, and beelined diagonally across the lane toward her home, which perched far above the road at the end of a set of rickety wooden stairs. But instead of climbing the stairs she swerved and headed up Shinbone hill.

Ted clucked his tongue. "Never mind her," he said to Maddy. "It's just her heartbreak talking. She can't even bear to be at home since Julianna left."

"That's too bad." Maddy leaned against the tree trunk, and a soothing sensation ran up her spine. "Why would anyone name such a beautiful place Shinbone?"

"There are different stories about that," Ted replied, then addressed the bird. "Right, Captain?"

The pigeon waddled past Maddy. This gave her a good view of his variegated golden, fuchsia, turquoise, deep-purple, red-orange, and burgundy plumage, as well as his mismatched feet—one normal and one fashioned from a spring—before he bobbed his head, flew up to Ted's shoulder, and nibbled on his ear.

"And I have good news about that," Ted continued. "We have a volunteer to transcribe Ida's version of how Shinbone got its name."

"That *is* good news!" Clara, whose shoulders loosened for the first time since Eloise's onslaught, turned to Maddy. "Ida was the last of the generation that raised Ted and me. She passed on six months ago at age 105." She sighed, recalling how much she missed Ida's voice, took in a deep breath, and recognized a welcome smell.

The scent of scones fresh from the oven at Star Bakery, located several blocks downhill, permeated all the way up the lane. The treats had a one-of-a-kind glaze—a secret recipe. It tasted of butterscotch and maple, with a hint of apricot.

Once a week, the bakers made an afternoon batch for a canasta club that met in an apartment above their shop. The late-day pastries had grown so popular, they started making extra batches. With stomachs growling, all remaining attendees at the Shinbone Friends gathering tabled their business and hurried off to grab some of the coveted goods before they sold out.

"Follow them, please, won't you, dear? I'll have tea waiting when you return." Clara waved toward her home across the lane and handed Maddy another five dollars. "Get half a dozen and drop a couple off for Ted and Captain on your way back."

Distracted by the smell of baking scones, Lark ripped a page of poetry from her Smith Corona portable, crumpled it into a ball, and tossed it toward the wastebasket. It nicked the rim and landed on the floor.

Leaving her desk, she crossed to her third-floor bedroom window. The ripple tree's heart-shaped leaves sent shadows cascading around the room. She listened for their whisper-soft harmonies, but the leaves held their silence. They chimed only when it pleased them. She heard laughter instead. On the path below, someone Lark hadn't seen before nodded to Clara and ran after a group loping toward Star Bakery. The poet cringed at the sight of the newcomer's lithe figure and impossibly thick mahogany hair falling below her shoulders.

Lark had tried to achieve lush locks like those before giving up on her stringy, dishwater blond mane. She'd finally opted for a pixie cut, a style that may have flattered Mia Farrow but only drew extra attention to Lark's thick-lensed, tortoise-shell glasses.

The urge for big bursts of buttery flavor was an undertow difficult to resist. Lark's mouth watered, but her thighs, tummy, and breasts, which she deemed flaccid, bulging, and heavy, kept her feet in place. Her body, she opined, must be what had caused her heartthrob, Dave, to bail on her. What else could it be?

Now, if queried about this, not one person on the lane would fault Lark's body for not being as thin as a two by four. Indeed, many neighbors thought she was Marilyn Monroe's doppelgänger, only studious and with better curves and hair more beautiful due to its natural tones. But they didn't share their thoughts with Lark, concluding, correctly, that she wouldn't have believed them. So she stewed on about her lost love.

Both insomniacs, Lark and Dave had often sipped chamomile tea together in the kitchen of 346, where they both lived. She'd even inspired his latest song. "In the Deep" he called it, meaning the wee hours when most people are dreaming. She should have known an up-and-coming folk-rock musician would be as hard to hold as a butterfly.

Lark returned to her desk and tapped a portable cassette player that held Ida's rendition of how Shinbone Lane got its name—a far-fetched tale, she thought. Lark wanted to transcribe the recently deceased old-timer's story before the annual Shinbone Fair, but hadn't been able to concentrate on that, nor had she been able to write more than the beginning line of one poem. Her mind kept chewing on Dave. How many times had they spent the entire night in the kitchen and hugged at dawn before parting ways on the landing?

She recalled telling him about her MFA studies at San Francisco State, how he, a gentle tide titillating her, had pulled her from the shores of solitude. With a quavering voice, she'd read him her poems, then whispered painful truths, describing the day her parents went on a six-month sojourn, leaving her, eight years old, in the driveway with a nanny while their cab to the airport grew smaller and smaller in the distance. She remembered how Dave would often arrive too wound up to sit still after a high-energy performance, how he said her voice soothed him, centered him, helped him open up. He spoke of his small-town upbringing, his tour of duty in Vietnam, how he stood across a creek from a Vietcong for the first time, locked eyes with him for what must have been mere seconds but seemed like forever, and pulled his trigger, killing someone who looked more boy than man. He'd confessed it was empowering to know how strong his survival instinct was. But those eyes—too many nights they haunted him.

This very morning, Lark and Dave had lingered at the landing, hugging longer than usual. Lark, on tiptoes, kissed him first on his cheeks and forehead and then on the mouth. He kissed her back, then took her hand and led her to his room.

If only she'd kept her mouth shut and let their hearts and bodies lead them, she might still be with him, basking in newfound love. Instead, the scene in his room played over and over in her mind's eye, starting with when he pulled his T-shirt over his head, and she said, "I was right to wait for you."

"Mm hmm." Eyes half closed, he reached over to help her slip out of her robe.

Suddenly realizing all she had left on was a flimsy nightgown, she said, "You'll be gentle, won't you?"

He held one of her hands and kissed it.

She quivered at his touch. "It's just that I waited so long for you to show up."

He pulled her closer to him. "But I moved in here way before you did."

"Insomnia brought us together."

He kissed the top of her head. "I can't argue with that."

"I want everything to be just right."

"Um, what are you getting at?" He unfastened his ponytail, letting his walnut-colored hair fall to his shoulders.

"It's like a crescendo has been building, um, toward this very moment of, of ... true love."

He sat up straighter. "You know the band's taking off, recording contract, the whole nine yards. I'll be on the road a lot. I'm not ready for love with a capital L."

Her heart beat with a new urgency. She gripped his hand. "But today's the day, the day I've been—."

He pulled away. "What's gotten into you? It's like you're not you anymore."

She fidgeted, hands in lap. "I've heard it can hurt—"

"You mean you've never—"

"But I'm ready, really ready to give myself to you."

He rubbed his chin. "Let me get this straight. You're a smashing gal with loads of friends, a wild way with words, and you're a darling at the Poetry Center at SF State, but you've never, you're a—"

"Virgin, yes, but don't look at me like it's some kind of affliction."

Dave shot up from the bed while putting his T-shirt back on. "This was a bad idea. It's way too heavy, too much. The fact that you've waited till you're twenty-two—"

"Twenty-one. I'll be twenty-two next month."

"I care for you. I really do. But I should never have ..." His voice trailed off, his face the picture of pity.

Lark wanted to blast him into outer space. She grabbed her robe and fled like a bird flushed from a bush.

The scene continued to play out in her mind that afternoon. Those words—I care for you—stung like a snake bite. With venom of shame. She couldn't face anyone, let alone Dave. She'd thought of asking Clara if she could rent her recently vacated attic studio across the street. Then she wouldn't be Dave's housemate anymore. But looking out the window, she had a hunch Clara already had a new tenant in mind, the nubile arrival who could probably eat a dozen scones without gaining a feather of weight.

Sooner or later, Lark would have to leave her nest. But not yet. And not for scones. She snatched her crumpled work from the floor, peeled it open. The paper held only four words: *The quest is over.*

Unrequited love called her to the keys.

CHAPTER

TWO

Clearing a path through his mother's spare bedroom, Ricky shoved aside newspapers and junk mail piled on top of boxes stuffed with clothing, games, knickknacks, and other castoffs, none of which he recognized. After tossing a few throw pillows aside to make room for his pack, he carried a stack of weathered *True Detective* magazines to the kitchen and plunked them on the table.

His mom, Natalie, wiggled her chubby body into a chair. She could be straight out of a Reubens painting hung in a museum, except for her purple polyester pantsuit, the bright, geometric-patterned rayon scarf around her neck, and the phlegm she hacked up while holding a lit cigarette with nicotine-stained fingers.

He put a hand on her sturdy shoulder. "I don't know why you keep these, but they're in the way, along with random stuff piled everywhere, all of it breeding who knows what sort of grunge." His words accused, but his smile teased.

"Like you care how I live." Natalie scrunched her face into a sneer, but it didn't hide the glimmer of hope his homecoming brought.

He sat beside her. "Is this how it's going to be?"

She poked at the thinning permed hair at the crown of her head. "I'm no fortune teller."

"I don't know why I bothered to come back," he said, drumming his fingers on the chipped kitchen table. "Do you?"

Natalie blew smoke rings in his direction and then chortled as he waved them off. "Sissy—that's what you are."

He pushed his chair away from the smoke. "Could you stop with the attacks?"

"Haven't been here more than a day, and you're itchin' to leave me alone again. I can tell."

"I was in VISTA, remember?"

"Havin' a gay old time."

"It's Volunteers in Service for America. Service, get it?"

"There's plenty of work to do right here. You didn't have to go all the way to Kentucky and leave me high and dry."

"I was doing something worthwhile for once."

"Only for a year. Then you took a whole 'nother year, takin' your sweet time to get home, not that you were even home when you were here. I know who you really are, Ricky Pine. Your soul's as dark as your indigo eyes."

"It's not my fault social services took me away." He searched her face for some acknowledgment of the truth.

She turned away. "Don't give me that look, that well of sadness so deep it throws me off. There's no call for it." She faced him again. "You know very well you didn't have to go after them pigeons." As she spoke, the tip of her nose gleamed.

"You told me to."

"Never could take a joke."

"I was eight years old."

"People saw you runnin' away, couldn't even finish the job." With her index finger now glowing red, she tapped ash from her Camel filter into an overflowing ashtray.

Ricky put his hand on the table and immediately withdrew it. "Jeez, it's hot; you're radiating heat again. Better relax or pretty soon we won't be able to breathe."

She took a puff on her cigarette. "You haven't even told me how long you're stayin'."

He stood up and walked to the back door. "I gotta get some air."

"I always was too much for you, kid, but never enough at the same time. I shoulda washed my hands of you from the get-go. I shoulda turned tail and run like the dickens, but I had no spine. So I wore a big scarlet letter that didn't belong to me."

"You're talking nonsense. This is 1974, not 1674. We aren't Puritans."

"You don't know. You really don't know. I accepted my fate the best I could. And now, here you are all grown up, handsome as all get out, and you're no use. If you were willing to play along, we could use your looks to our advantage. You could sweep women in Pacific Heights off their fancy little feet if you wanted. Think of all that we could pull off."

"Sure, Ma, sure." Ricky scuffed onto the back porch and up a set of stairs to a neglected rooftop deck lined with pots full of dead plants. On Castro Street, it afforded a bird's eye view of where 29th Street met Shinbone Lane. The enticing smell of Star Bakery scones filled his nostrils as a swarm of people burst from the lane and promenaded down the hill. Among them was a sylph-like girl with thick brown hair darker and prettier than any locks in a Breck shampoo commercial. She looked familiar, but he couldn't recall from where.

He returned to the back porch, opened the door a sliver, and peeked into the kitchen. "Glad you calmed down; it was starting to feel like an oven in here."

She scowled at the stack of magazines on the table. "What am I supposed to do with these?"

"I gotta go. We'll talk later."

"Of course you do. It's too much trouble to think about what I want for a change."

"I'll bring some scones from Star if they have any left."

"Bottom of the barrel, that's all I ever get."

Ricky closed the door and sprinted toward the crowded queue, which was now backed up a block outside the bakery. The young woman with the gorgeous hair was about a quarter block ahead of him. When she stopped in line near the bakery's entrance, he ducked into a market across the street and watched from the storefront window, feigning interest in a copy of *Road and Track* magazine.

After what seemed an interminable time during which the clerk at the cash register eyed Ricky with suspicion, the girl entered the bakery. It wasn't long before she reappeared carrying a white bag. He slapped the magazine back on the rack and followed, adjusting his pace to match hers, never getting close enough for her to notice him tailing her. Every time a car passed, she skulked close to the buildings like a fugitive seeking shadow. With each step, Ricky grew more certain he knew her.

PERCHED atop a set of shelves in Ted's garage, Captain cleaned his feathers with beak and tongue poking up and down, in and out, up and down, in and out. Meanwhile, his best friend, Ted, was back after helping Clara carry her shopping bags home. The spry retiree with an ample pension hung his cap on a peg and got busy. When not lending a hand to neighbors and housemates for all manner of projects and conundrums, Ted spent his days fixing broken and discarded toys, appliances, and tools; painting and polishing them until they looked better than new; and then giving them all away.

"So, the girl?" Captain's gravelly rasp came directly into Ted's mind. "Do you think she'll stay the night?"

"You know Clara, how irresistible she can be to restless souls."

"So that's a yes." The bird fluffed himself up and stretched out his wings.

"I wouldn't bet against it." Ted grinned, creases forming at the edges of his eyes and mouth.

Captain flew down to Ted's work table and watched calloused

hands sand a jewelry box designed like a set of drawers. "Why are young humans so footloose nowadays? Why don't they settle down, make a home? Isn't that what people do?" The bird asked, half to himself.

"I can't speak for the baby boomers, don't know why so many are on the move. Things were different when I came up. We had to work for everything at the dawn of this century." The conversation lulled while Ted recalled a world without cars, automatic dishwashers, refrigerators, vacuum cleaners. "Heck, I didn't see a TV until I was sixty." He leaned down and blew fine dust off the jewelry box.

"If I had a family, I wouldn't leave."

"If you had a family, my friend, maybe you would."

Captain squawked, bounced on his spring foot and went a couple of feet into the air and back.

Regretting his remark, Ted rubbed the pigeon's chest with his index finger. "Look, if you always have something, you take it for granted. That's all I was trying to say."

Captain tapped his beak on the table. "It's about time I go looking again."

"How many quests have you gone on now? Fifteen?"

The bird pecked Ted's pinkie with his beak.

Ted jerked his hand away. "Each time you return, alone, your feathers are thin and disheveled, your eyes dull, you can barely eat. It takes weeks for you to be able to talk to me again. " Ted returned to sanding.

"If it bothers you, I don't have to come back."

"I hate seeing you in pain is all." He paused to look Captain in the eye, then resumed. "And maybe it's not worth it."

"She's out there somewhere. I need to find her. I wasn't meant to be alone."

"What would be so wrong with one of the street pigeons?"

Glowering at his friend, the bird looked like he'd just seen Ted shrink to half his size. "They can't think in words, for one. How could I mate with a bird who isn't multilingual?"

"Sometimes it's better to accept that what you've been longing for will never be and move on."

"Like you did, giving up on love before you even knew what it was."

"That's a low blow."

"What's a low blow?" Maddy stood at the open door, pastry bag in hand. "Who are you talking to?" The garage workshop smelled like Ted's truck, only stronger, with more sawdust and leather in the mix, and fewer hints of rose petals, lemon oil, and weathered books.

The bird's rumbly, ragged voice came into the teenager's mind: "He's talking to me!" She tucked a strand of hair behind her ear and looked from Captain to Ted.

The bird shifted his weight from natural to artificial leg. "You heard me," he said to Maddy.

"Well, well, this is quite unusual." Ted put down the sandpaper and blew dust away again. "Captain doesn't talk to just anyone."

"I'm ... I've ... I don't ..." She cleared her throat. "I've never met a talking bird. Well, it's not exactly talking, is it?"

Captain puffed up his feathers. "If it isn't talking, I certainly don't know what it is."

The youth stepped into the workshop to get a better look at Captain. "I like all your colors."

"Thank you, Miss Maddy." The bird dipped down and waved one wing from his breast to his side in a mock bow.

"He comes from a long line of versatile birds, going back to ancient times. He's a hybrid, most likely a mix of band-tailed pigeon and the extinct passenger pigeon. Not sure from where." Ted slid the tiny jewelry box drawer into place. "Germany or thereabouts, I think."

Maddy took a step backward. The tulip tree outside her former home had seemed to understand her, but she could easily have imagined that. This wide-open communication with Captain would take some getting used to. "I feel like I'm in a dream."

The bird focused on the white bag in her hand. "I would like mine now, please."

With trembling fingers, she put one scone down next to Captain, who instantly attacked it, crumbs flying. Then she held out the bag to Ted.

"Thanks." He reached in and took one. "Mmm, it's still warm."

"I'd better get to Clara's so she can have a warm one, too." Maddy hurried to the open garage door, then looked over her shoulder. "Are you really talking, Captain?"

"Come back soon," the bird answered.

WARM, golden sparkles permeated Shinbone Lane as residents scurried home, bulging bakery bags in hand. They hurried to unlock doors to buildings hugging together like long-lost friends, a few homes with wide lots and lush side yards being the exception.

People coveted their scones, not only for the delectable mix of flavors, but also because biting into them brought back fond memories buried by time. The scenes inevitably faded as quickly as they'd come, but they left behind a sense of well-being. This was true even for grumbly folks who insisted their lives had been cruel and bruising from day-one. Radiance infused every room, alcove, and cranny along the lane. In Clara's living room, Maddy and Clara sat at a little round table tucked into a window nook.

"It's like the houses all have halos." Maddy nibbled her scone. "And this is ... wow!" She took a full bite. "These could be more addictive than potato chips." Maddy suddenly felt as though she were two years old again, playing with a toy telephone on the family room rug while her parents held hands on the couch—and from the phonograph came Gene Kelly crooning "Singin' in the Rain."

Clara chuckled and filled the youth's cup with tea. "There you go." She bit into her scone and recalled a day when she was a young mother pulling her daughter, Tilda, up the 29th Street hill in a red wagon. Despite the steep incline, Clara felt light as an angel.

Maddy's memory vanished as though she'd never experienced it.

Yet she felt uplifted while she stirred honey and milk into her cup and took a sip. "This tea might be addictive, too."

Clara's fond memory of Tilda faded as well, but it left her with a lingering bittersweet feeling. "It's from the community store down the hill. Some call it the 'hippie store.' They sell things in bulk—grains, loose tea, nuts, even henna for body decorating and reddening hair. I think it's all the rage with you youngsters."

Maddy took another taste of tea. "I feel kinda silly bringing this up, but did you know that Captain, uh, kind of throws his voice into your mind?"

"He's spoken to you?"

"Yeah, when I stopped at Ted's."

"I dare say that's quite an honor. He doesn't speak to just anyone."

"I bet he doesn't talk to the woman with the little poodle."

"Eloise?"

"She seems a little ... on edge?"

Clara swallowed several times. "That's certainly one way to put it."

"Is she—"

"Oh, goodness." Clara shot up from her chair with the vigor of someone twenty years younger. "I'll be right back."

She darted to the kitchen and rummaged through a cabinet drawer. She returned to Maddy, who was leaning back, eyes closed, while a memory of running barefoot through tender grass faded.

"I forgot to bring out my special occasion chocolates." Clara lifted the lid and held the candies out for her guest.

Maddy opened her eyes.

"These are eighty percent dark chocolate."

The teen took a piece and bit off a small chunk. "Mmm, groovy. I've never tasted chocolate this ... strong."

"Your parents must not have adventurous palates."

Maddy looked out the window at the glimmering lane and its mix of earthy hues. Shades of gray, brown, and beige intermingled with blades of grass poking up here and there to form a rustic, uneven canvas. "It's odd," she said, "that the street isn't paved."

"Oh, Shinbone Friends would never hear of paving our lane. There's history in every chip, every bump and rut, and every attempt to fix it."

"Makes sense." Maddy smiled at Clara. "You know, I was wondering about how the lane got its name. Didn't you say people have different versions of the story?"

Clara settled back into her chair. "Ida's version is probably the best, but I'm partial to what I heard at my pa's knee. I suppose we're all like that. The stories we hear in childhood take root and sink deeper with each passing year." Clara stirred her tea. "Check with Ted. He did say he found someone to transcribe Ida's version."

"You've known Ted a long time?"

"All my life."

"Must be nice to have roots like that."

"You don't have family?"

"I'm all on my own."

The two sipped tea in silence for a while, each absorbed in her own thoughts.

"Could you just tell me your dad's version? I'd love to know the story before I go."

Clara's cheeks reddened. "Dear me, I am no storyteller." She patted the bun at the nape of her neck, pulled out a couple of loose hairpins, then slid them back in.

"I guess I won't find out how Shinbone Lane got its name then, since it's about time for me to shove off. I've got someone to look up."

"Someone?" Clara's eyes twinkled with amusement. "How well do you know this someone?"

Maddy hesitated, then confessed, "Hardly at all."

Clara pointed out that fog had rolled in while they were talking and the wind would soon be strong enough to gust straight into a person's bones. "It'll be dark in a wink. I'd feel much better if you spent the night here and looked up that someone tomorrow."

The girl took a last gulp of tea while her heart thrashed like a rat in a trap.

"I have just the place for you." Clara described her recently vacated attic studio. "My last tenant, an aspiring actress, lovely girl, ran off with a mushroom farmer just last week. It's all aired out and sparkling clean now. You must have a look."

Maddy resisted at first, uncertain whether she could trust this elderly woman whom she'd met only hours before. Was she too good to be true?

Clara reached across the wobbly table and put her hand on Maddy's. "I'm worried about you racing off to find some lad you don't know in a city you don't know, wondrous as it is. ... Besides, I have more than enough food for dinner."

The runaway considered her options. Phone a guy she'd met only in passing and ask to come over or stay with Clara on the most peculiar little street she'd ever encountered. "I guess I could check it out."

"This way, my dear, and bring your pack so you can freshen up before we eat." Clara showed Maddy to the interior staircase.

Upstairs, like Goldilocks finding Baby Bear's bed, Maddy lay down and rested her head on a pillow. It smelled of ocean spray.

CHAPTER

THREE

Lark, the resident poet of 346, awoke to sunshine and a Steely Dan jazz-rock tune coming from her bedside radio. Banter between KFRC's Dr. Don Rose and a guest, whose name she wasn't quite awake enough to grasp, followed. She considered slapping the snooze button but held off, having promised Barb and Bea that she'd check out the Tai Chi group that met three mornings a week on Shinbone Hill at the end of the lane.

The twins had a soft spot for misfits and underdogs, for they'd weathered difficulties of their own. They'd been labeled freaks throughout childhood for their honey-hued skin and crescent-moon eyes framed by thick, straight, white-gold hair.

Then, in their second year of high school, they learned they were part Chinese. This was when a stranger named Ron Li phoned and claimed he was their dad's cousin. "Our grandmother is on her deathbed," he said, "and she wants to make amends."

Their father doubted this was true. His mother had died young, and his dad said she was Armenian. But out of curiosity, the twins' father and mother, who was descended from the Sámi, the indigenous reindeer stewards in Sweden, met the woman claiming to be his grandmother. She showed them a black-and-white photo of his parents

29

standing arm in arm. His mother had eloped with a man from Finland, a "ghost" her family called him, instead of marrying the Chinese boy they had in mind for her. For this, they had disowned her.

After this revelation, the twins felt betrayed by their father, though he had merely repeated what he'd been told about his ancestry. They also felt out of place when visiting their newfound relatives. In time, however, they grew fond of Ron Li, a Tai Chi master who practiced daily in Chinatown's Portsmouth Square. They joined him on Saturdays, gradually felt more at home with their multicultural identity, and forgave their dad. Intrigued by their enthusiasm, their parents began attending, as well. When the twins moved to 346, they shared the art of Tai Chi with their neighbors.

Now, the twins had their sights set on Lark. She'd resisted their efforts to engage her in conversation at dinner yesterday and avoided eye contact with Dave, who sat across from her at their long dining room table. She'd also only picked at the lasagna on her plate. Lark would usually have two hefty helpings and then, looking woeful as a waif in a Keane painting, would unfasten the top button of her jeans, complaining they were too tight. So, while the three women later washed and dried dishes in the kitchen, the twins invited her to join them for Tai Chi, claiming it does wonders for a person, brings you to the present, gets your mind off things.

Snug in bed the next morning, Lark was having second thoughts. She had poetry to write and Ida's tape of Shinbone's origin story to transcribe. Besides, she liked watching Tai Chi, but wasn't sure she could do it. Slow movements took balance, and then to do them gracefully, well, she'd never been known as lithesome. She stretched, considering her options. But the Jackson Five came on the radio, and the beat got into her. Bouncing to the music, she tore off her PJs, threw on her sweats and Puma sneakers and went out the door, using her fingers to comb her short hair.

When she reached the grassy area, a half-dozen neighbors were already following the twins' flowing movements with ease. Rosie waved her over. Lark took a spot beside the petite redhead and tried not to compare herself to Shinbone's queen of sidewalk sales, whose eclectic, vintage wardrobe always looked custom made for her.

"Welcome," Barb called to Lark. "Good to see you." She, like her sister, wore a name tag to make it easy for neighbors to differentiate them.

Lark muttered a quick thank you and did her best to copy what the others were doing.

"Remember to breathe in at the start of a movement and out as you move toward the end," Bea said.

Lark wobbled in her attempts to follow along.

The twins walked around the group, making slight corrections to participants' stances when needed. Barb touched Lark's back to adjust her posture with fingertips light as ladybugs. "Don't worry about being perfect. Don't hold your breath. Let it flow naturally," she advised.

While leading the group, the supple instructors worked in mentions of chi and meridians, concepts Lark had run across before but hadn't paid much attention to. She tried to hold a ball shape and then bring chi to her heart while breathing in and out at the right times and moving her feet just so, but she became flustered and shook out her hands in frustration. It seemed everyone else did these strange movements with ease, even Waddles Fenton—Waddles, who was in her eighties like her lifelong friends, Ted and Clara.

When a half hour of guided Tai Chi was over, Eloise arrived with Coco in tow. "It's about time you clear out. I must dance for my Julianna, try to conjure her home. Are you sure none of you have seen her?"

After an awkward silence, Bea said. "We'll keep our eyes out for her."

Most of the others gave vague words of encouragement and hurried off. Lark watched, mesmerized, as Eloise improvised her own brand of modern dance with Coco mimicking her moves.

"Coco would be better at Tai Chi than me," Lark said to Rosie, who was also watching.

"You're too hard on yourself." Rosie pulled a necklace made of beads, charms, paperclips and other found items from her purse, which she'd stashed on a bench with other students' belongings during class.

"Eloise is something else," the poet said.

Rosie leaned closer to Lark. "I've heard she and her best friend, Tilda, were amazing when they were teenagers. They even spent a summer in New York studying with Martha Graham, the great modern dance pioneer. Back in the day, everyone on Shinbone thought they'd both be famous by now."

"What happened?"

"Life, I suppose." Rosie said. "The ones we all think are most likely to succeed aren't always the ones who do."

The two young women walked down the hill together and stopped on the flagstone path that served as a sidewalk in front of 346.

"So, do you think you'll come back?" Rosie hovered like a hummingbird.

Observing Rosie's wiry build and fine curls framing her heart-shaped face, Lark wanted to leap away at jack rabbit speed. "I don't know. Maybe," she said, though she had no intention of returning.

IT WAS WELL past noon when Clara's new guest, Maddy, padded downstairs. She'd slept through the night fully clothed on top of the bed covers. The stairway door opened to a hall that stretched from the front foyer all the way to the kitchen at the back. Maddy stood across from a bathroom divided in two: toilet on one side of a wall, bathtub and sink on the other—a novel arrangement to Maddy that was routine for many a long-time San Franciscan. She heard a familiar melody and walked toward it. She found Clara in a storybook room with mint green cabinets, flowered curtains and tablecloth in shades of blue, green, and yellow. The elderly woman was bent at the open oven, potholders in hand, sliding something out while singing "On the Street Where You Live" with a hint of giddy anticipation in her voice.

"Mmm, smells good in here," the teenager said.

"It's turkey meatloaf." Clara put the hot dish on a trivet. "I hope I got it right this time. It has tiny cubes of Macintosh apple and Dijon mustard to add flavor."

Maddy inhaled the aroma. "I've never had turkey meatloaf."

"It's Waddles' recipe. We've had a little cooking competition going since we were kids, believe it or not. And somehow, we can follow the exact same recipe—using the exact same ingredients—and my dishes never taste as good as hers."

"I'm sure it'll be delicious."

"Can you mash potatoes?" Clara pointed to a pot on the stove. "They're all cooked and drained."

"I guess you're inviting me to lunch?" Maddy took a hair tie from her pocket and pulled her thick brown mane into a ponytail.

"It's too late for breakfast, my dear. There's butter and milk in the fridge, salt and pepper in the rack behind you. I'll rustle us up some salad."

With the meal ready and the table set, the two fell into easy conversation while they ate. As they finished up, the doorbell rang. Clara went to answer it. Maddy stayed to clear the table. When Clara returned, she said that Ted had stopped by before heading off for the day with his fishing buddy, Harold Ramsey. He brought good news about Shinbone's origin story: Lark had begun transcribing Ida's tape and would have a couple of pages done that day, but she needed someone to proofread for her.

"Young girl like you must have sharp eyes," Clara said.

"I'll be out of your hair by then. I just need to make that call."

Clara pointed to a wall phone. "You can use that one there. ... It's a boy, am I right?" Her eyes twinkled with mischief.

"It's not like that." The young traveler pulled the matchbook Ricky had scribbled his number on when the two had met in passing in Colorado. She turned it over in her hand a few times and marched to the phone. She dialed the number and waited until a woman growled out a hello. Maddy almost hung up, but then responded. "Hi, um, Ricky gave me this number to call if I came to San Francisco and ... Yes, he asked me to call. ... I didn't mean to ... No, this isn't a crank call. ... There's no Ricky there? ... There is a Ricky there? ... What? ... Is this 415 —? ... Oh, the number's none of my business? ... And you know Ricky? ... Okay, so, that's not what you said? ... I'm confused. ... Do—"

She hung up the phone, wiped moist palms on her jeans, and slid back into her seat at the table. "Some lady hung up on me after going all *Exorcist* on me. She said she'd trace this number and come get me. And she snarled. She really did. It even felt like the phone was heating up in my hand. Freaked me out just like when I saw the movie."

"I never saw it; demonic possession isn't my cup of tea."

Maddy brushed away a few strands of hair that had slipped loose from the tie. "I couldn't tell if she knew Ricky or not. I guess I have to regroup."

"You're welcome to stay here while you sort things out."

"I don't know. I don't want to impose—"

"Nonsense. You can proofread Lark's pages. And I want to get a few things out of the built-in cabinets in my workroom. It's getting hard for me to reach up where I need to."

Maddy glanced from floor to ceiling. "I can see why; the ceilings are really high in here."

"Why not go upstairs and have a nice, long shower? There's soap and shampoo, toothpaste, and towels. There's also peach-vanilla lotion from a shop on 24th Street. The gals who own the place make it themselves. And when you're all refreshed, open the drapes and you'll see sliding doors to a deck big as this kitchen. A great place to dry that beautiful hair of yours. Plus, the table and chairs would be a great place for an artist such as yourself to sketch."

"I'm not really an artist."

"Could be you're a little too young to know what you are, but you have great potential. Great potential. I'm certain of that, my dear."

Maddy felt a twinge of grief well up at Clara's tenderness. She couldn't recall the last time a grown-up had encouraged her. She took a deep breath, trying to shake the feeling off. "I guess I'm really in no hurry. It's not like anyone's expecting me." She rose, pulled her hair from the tie and shook her head, letting her brown locks cascade past her shoulders.

"I'll let Lark know. ... Oh, and you'll find clothes in the closet that might fit you. They're not new, but I hear vintage is all the rage these days."

"It's like you knew I was coming or something."

Clara laughed. "I'm not psychic, just prepared."

ROSIE SETTLED into a turquoise armchair and looked out her living room window. Late afternoon fog blew down 29th street, chasing sunshine downhill to the Mission District. With her youngest, Lucas, down for a nap and daughter, Heather, rearranging furniture in a dollhouse Rosie had found in a dumpster and refurbished, she relished the thought of some quiet time.

She opened a chapbook Lark had given her and read the poet's signature and note on the title page: "To Rosie—the consummate lemons-to-lemonade queen." Not all lemons make good lemonade, Rosie thought. She turned the page, eager to read, but couldn't concentrate. She thought instead about what Eloise had said at the Shinbone Friends meeting, how Rosie wouldn't be in the neighborhood long. The comment stung because there was truth in it. She and her husband, Wayne, had been rootless for years. Now with two children, a nomadic lifestyle had lost its appeal for Rosie, but not for Wayne.

Rosie gave up on reading, leaned her head back and closed her eyes. Just as she drifted into sleep, Wayne's truck, a former Entenmann's bakery delivery truck, clattered and groaned to a stop in the driveway.

He strutted through the door and stood tall in his battered cowboy boots, jeans, and blue work shirt. Black, horn-rimmed glasses slid down his nose. His brittle sun-bleached hair, not the least bit tamed despite a bandana wrapped across his forehead and tied in back, stuck out in all directions. "Come see what I've got for you and the kids! Come on. Chop! Chop!" His voice blared like an auctioneer's.

"Shhh, Lucas is sleeping," Rosie said.

"Come outside." Wayne swaggered back to the truck. A handyman, he kept an eye out for castoffs Rosie might be able to sell.

Heather bounced with enthusiasm behind him. Rosie hauled herself up and followed, feet dragging. She found Wayne unloading three cardboard boxes of assorted clothes and household items.

"You wouldn't believe all the stuff this guy had to clear out." Wayne rubbed a finger across his bushy mustache and grinned. "His mom was a real packrat. He hadn't seen her for years before she kicked the bucket."

"That's sad," Rosie said.

"If not for me, all of this would have gone straight to the dump."

Rosie opened the first box. "Oh, la la, look at these scarves!" She held up a shimmering silk in shades of purple and orange.

Wayne pulled out a puzzle and handed it to Heather. "For you, Heather-o. It's wooden, not cardboard—and it's a castle."

"Wowee zowee!" The girl grabbed the box and shook.

"Careful," Wayne said before reaching back into the van to retrieve a pull-toy dog. "For Lucas," he said to Rosie.

Rosie looked up. "Oh, that's good. Since he just took his first steps, he'll need toys like that." She returned to sifting through the new wares. "I think some of these clothes would be great for dress-up. Maybe I should donate them to Happy Days."

"That co-op is too wild. I don't want Heather going back there."

Heather cried out, "But Daddy—"

"Don't you 'but Daddy' me. If I say you don't go, you don't go!"

Heather burst into tears and threw the puzzle down. The lid came off the box and pieces scattered across the cracked sidewalk.

"Better pick that up, young lady, or you'll regret it," Wayne barked. "That's no way to treat a gift."

"He's right about that, honey, but his delivery is sorely lacking."

"Sorry," the child said. With mouth turned down, she knelt, gathered pieces, and began working the puzzle.

"You trying to undermine me here?" He glared at Rosie. "Then maybe you don't deserve this." He tossed a jewelry box at her.

She caught the box but delayed opening it. "Believe it or not, you're not lord of this family. You and I are equals—or supposed to be."

"Yeah, yeah, okay, you and your women's lib stuff."

"Here I thought you were an enlightened guy, but you're as old-fashioned as they come." Rosie lifted the lid and gasped at a gleaming Swarovski necklace, bracelet, and earrings set. She slipped the bracelet on and held her arm up in the muted sunlight. "I can't believe you found this."

He pulled out a metal box with a handle and cartoon characters on every side. He cranked the handle and out popped Winnie the Pooh instead of a traditional Jack-in-the-box. Heather came close. He put it down in the driveway. Rosie and Wayne watched Heather play with the toy until a belching Volvo sedan chugging up 29th Street caught their attention. Dented and scraped, it looked straight out of a junkyard as it turned onto Castro Street.

"Yuk! I can smell that exhaust from here," Rosie said.

Wayne squinted at an approaching VW van. "Look what else is coming. What's on that thing?" Wayne took off his glasses, wiped them with the tail of his shirt, and put them back on.

Heather jumped up and down. "Fruits and veggies, fruits and veggies all over." She pointed as the startling vehicle sputtered past them.

"How cool is that?" Rosie said. "It's got plastic apples and oranges and cucumbers and carrots and costume jewelry, and what are those? Oh wow! They're those little glass animal figurines."

"Too flashy," Wayne grumbled.

"Look at the paint swirls, colors of the rainbow—and a mural on the back, too, of a tent cabin in the redwoods, could be Big Basin. Amazing," Rosie said.

The van turned left onto Shinbone.

"Can we do that to Daddy's truck?" Heather begged. "Can we? Can we?"

"What a stupid idea," Wayne snapped at her.

Heather backed away, then ran inside the house.

Rosie kicked a stray stone into the gutter. "Why are you so hard on her?"

"All you do is baby that girl." He put his arms around his wife.

She tried to pull away from his python grip.

He held her closer and kissed her neck. "How much do you want to bet that spectacle on wheels is going to 346?"

UP AND DOWN THE LANE, people peeked from their windows at the VW bus parked in front of Ted's. They'd seen similar vehicles in recent years with peace signs, rainbows and flowers painted on the sides, but none came close to matching the colorful riot of paint, emblems, plastic fruits and vegetables, beads, toys, and other curiosities on this one.

"It's like a 3D collage," Clara said to Maddy, who sat beside her on the front porch, sketch book in hand.

"It's a traveling art museum," Lark, the poet, said to a cat that had followed her home one day and never left.

"Aren't they ever going to get out?" a member of a women's collective asked her housemates, who all squeezed together to peer outside.

In Ted's workshop, Captain flapped his wings and grumbled. "Another bunch of hopefuls, no doubt. Dave Deely moved his entire band in. Used to be they'd rehearse here, and afterward, everyone except Dave went home, but now the whole lot bunks here. Then there's Bea and Barb, and Lark. That's on top of the half-dozen or so other hooligans living here. Where could you possibly put more?"

"Just hold on a sec." Ted shook his head and chuckled. "We haven't even met them yet. We don't know why they parked out front."

Eloise, hoping the newcomers might have news of her daughter, Julianna, was the first to step outside to get a better look.

Inside the bus, Chip stretched in the driver's seat and gave a groan laced with skepticism. He'd driven to the home of an old guy named

Ted on an unpaved lane called Shinbone—all because a former rocker named Russ, who now goes by Abbudin and directs a Sufi choir, convinced him to come look up his former band mate Dave, who apparently lives here. Oh well, Chip thought, if we don't like the vibe, we can check out Project Artaud. He brushed aside a curtain of beads separating the front and back of the van and called to his little sister. "Oh, oh, Sunrise, Sunrise, wake up, wake up."

A four-year-old girl rolled over and rubbed her eyes. "I'm hungry."

Chip searched through a crinkled shopping bag for the Tupperware container of sesame-cashew-honey bars he'd made while visiting a commune in Laytonville about 150 miles north of San Francisco. He found the snack and looked through the window to see Ted walking a classic red-and-white Schwinn to the flagstone path in front of 346. The bicycle brought back memories of a blue Schwinn Chip rode while growing up in Oklahoma. He used to clip baseball cards to the spokes, creating a motorized sound when he pedaled. "Those cards would be worth a fortune today," he muttered.

"What would be worth a fortune?" Sunrise asked.

"Oh, sorry. I was just thinking out loud. Baseball cards. They used to be a dime a dozen, but those old ones like I had as a kid got really valuable."

Sunrise climbed to the seat next to Chip. He handed one of the bars to her, as a father and son trotted up to Ted, dribbling a basketball. Soon the boy was pedaling down the rough macadam road of tightly packed stones with splotches of other materials used to fill potholes. The father, cradling the basketball under one arm, pulled out his wallet. Ted shook his head and waved him off.

"That must be Ted," Chip said. "Let's get out."

Everyone who had a good view watched a man with a slender, runner's build, come into sight from the driver's side of the van. His bell bottoms flapped at his ankles, and muscles rippled under a tie-dyed T-shirt with a big heart in front with the message, "Make love, not war." His flawless skin was deep olive. Shining black ringlets bounced almost to his shoulders. Right after him came a little girl who looked like a tiny, female version of him. She clung to his legs and giggled. He tripped on the flagstone and dropped the container of snack bars—much to the delight of Captain, who hobbled with great speed toward the fallen treats, his artificial foot not slowing him down in the least.

Chip chuckled at the bird. "Looks like someone likes sesame, cashew, and honey snack." He grinned, revealing a gap between his two front teeth.

"Captain'll eat anything," Ted said.

Braver now, Sunrise stepped forward. "Is he a pigeon? He's kinda too big."

"He's a different sort of pigeon: band-tailed, for sure, probably some passenger blood in there, too—unfortunately, they're now extinct—and some long-gone ancient varieties never seen around here. He's definitely longer than the rock pigeons that waddle down sidewalks everywhere."

"Wild colors, too," Chip said. "He's gorgeous, even with that strange leg of his."

Captain puffed up his chest and declared what only Ted could hear. "He's a good one, my friend."

The pansies and petunias sporting eye-popping hues of purple, yellow, and mauve caught Chip's eye. "These flowers look drenched in extra color and smell like ambrosia—or how I imagine ambrosia smelled to the Greek gods." He touched a petal with the reverence of someone holding a fragile family heirloom. "Sure wish I had a green thumb."

"We all have something to contribute." Ted pulled a rag from his back pocket and rubbed grease from calloused fingers. He extended a hand to Chip. "Name's Ted. I can see you two are related."

Chip clasped Ted's hand. "I'm Chip. And this is my baby sis, Sunrise." Touching Ted, Chip had a sense of greeting an old friend, though he'd never laid eyes on him before.

"What's wrong with his foot?" Sunrise crouched to get a better look at Captain.

"That's a long story, little missy, maybe for another day." Ted pulled a root beer-flavored lolly pop from his pocket and handed it to her. "Here's something for today."

Sunrise grabbed it and pulled off the wrapper.

"What do you say?" Chip asked.

Sunrise blushed. "Oh, thank you."

"So what brings you to 346?" Ted asked Chip.

"We were headed for Project Artaud in the Mission district. A friend of a friend has space in this amazing loft she made there. But we met this guy on the road. Abbudin. He's an old friend of a guy who lives here. He has a band. His name is ..."

"Dave," Ted interjected, "from Dave Deely and the Frogs. You're in luck. They're out back rehearsing right now."

CHAPTER

FOUR

With wonder guiding her hand across the page, Maddy rendered versions of the scene unfolding across the street. Viewed from Clara's front porch, the wild van parked by the ripple tree fit the lane like a missing piece of a jigsaw puzzle snapped into place. The man and child who exited the eclectic work of art appeared to float more than walk toward the front stairs to 346. Their dark ringlets swirled when they turned in unison at the sound of Eloise's voice.

"They look so much alike," Maddy said to Clara, who sat in a wicker chair beside her. "They must be father and daughter."

Clara took a sip of lemonade. "That's a likely conclusion, though he seems mighty young, from this distance anyway."

Eloise closed in, calling to Ted. She stopped inches from him, holding a defiant stance, and began her interrogation, which was so familiar to residents watching from their windows and porches that they knew what Eloise was saying almost word for word. It was a new experience for the two who stood beside Ted and watched Eloise gesture like a rousing band leader. While the dancer pressed for information about her daughter, Coco maneuvered around the people's feet, yipping, wiggling, and nipping at sandal straps. The child crouched down and hugged the dog, who responded with nuzzling nose to nose.

"That one looks about the same age as Rosie's little girl, Heather," Clara said.

Maddy sketched the girl and the dog until Eloise gave Ted a dismissive wave. He and the new arrivals continued into 346. Eloise, clutching Coco to her chest, stormed away, angry as Myrtha, the queen of betrayed spirits in the classical ballet *Giselle*. Maddy did a quick sketch that captured Eloise so well, the drawing appeared to move on its own. The artist turned to a new page and focused on the van, an explosion of colors and kitsch on wheels. As she filled in what looked like a grape vine running along the edge of the roof, a sense of homecoming she both yearned for and feared added a layer of complexity to the sun-dappled day.

While Maddy drew on, Clara pulled a knitting project from a canvas bag embroidered with two well-worn ballet slippers. The click-clack of her needles permeated, along with a faint scent of lilacs and vanilla, the result of the women's collective a few houses down the lane, who often experimented with homemade sachets.

Lark broke their concentration when she opened her bedroom window and called from across the lane. "I've got a little over three pages done."

"Bring them over, doll. We're just admiring the view after all the excitement of that amazing bus," Clara replied.

Shinbone's resident poet soon arrived with the pages, a red pen and a paper with proofreader's marks. She put them on a little wicker table at Maddy's side. "I really appreciate your proofing for me."

"Did you meet those people Ted brought inside?" Clara asked.

"Yeah, he introduced us in passing. They're a family. Chip and Sunrise. A brother and a sister, a big age gap there. Ted's already asked them to stay for dinner."

"Ah, I didn't imagine them as siblings," Clara said.

"Me neither, but then you did mention he looked pretty young," Maddy replied.

"Early twenties, I would guess," Lark said.

Maddy picked up the page of proofreader's marks and scrunched her face. "I have zero experience at this, you know. These look like hieroglyphics."

"You'll get the hang of it in no time, dear, I'm sure," Clara said.

"Especially since it's really just typos and spacing problems you'll have to spot," Lark added. "I didn't type Ida's ums and stumbles. I took out a couple of asides, too, where she answered questions from people who were listening. It's pretty clean."

Maddy clutched the red ballpoint and clicked it in and out a few times.

"No rush either," Lark assured her. "I've got to spend the rest of the day finishing a paper on Adrienne Rich's poetry collection, *Diving into the Wreck*, that I was supposed to turn in weeks ago. My extension runs out next week."

"That sounds intense," the teenager said.

"It's fascinating, really, sort of metaphorical exploration of personal and social issues, you know, feminism, self-discovery, the search for truth."

"My job sounds a whole lot easier all of a sudden." The teenager tapped Lark's pages with the pen. "I'll do my best."

"Thanks," Lark said. "It's back to the typewriter for me."

As Lark darted back home, Clara asked, "Could you read it out loud first, before you think about corrections? It'll be like having Ida back for a little while."

Maddy took a long guzzle of lemonade and then began the story.

A LONG, long time ago, when adventurers from across the globe rode, marched, clawed, borrowed, and thieved their way to California after gold was discovered at Sutter's Mill, Gunter entered his grandfather Otto's apothecary shop in Boston's North End. Threadbare clothes hung from the teenager's slight frame as he made his way past assorted remedies in bottles, tins, and boxes.

Gunter approached Otto, who stood near a shelf stacked with potions, salves, and other remedies at the back wall. Candles flickered. Smells of herbs permeated, as usual, but Otto was not the same as the day before. Instead of standing firm, the old man swayed like a sapling in the wind. His usually wild white hair lay limp against his skull.

"Opa, what's the matter? You don't look good."

The old man greeted Gunter with a craggy voice. "Don't look so shaken, my son. You knew this day would come."

"But there's so much more to learn." Gunter bent down to pick up a penny on the floor and put it on Otto's table.

"Your uncle arrives this afternoon, my only surviving son. He knows I am failing fast and will take over my affairs. But he is cruel. He will cast you out, though you already know more about remedies than he ever will." From a shelf at the back wall, Otto pushed aside a small chest, and from behind it, he pulled down a flute made from a human child's shinbone. "He will also turn the place upside down looking for this." He held the instrument out to Gunter. "I told him it was lost on the journey to America when your dear parents and grandmother succumbed to cholera. You almost died, too. I said I was too ill myself to keep track of it. He's never believed me."

Gunter knew the lore about the flute. It had been passed down in the family for generations from a time when animals and people conversed, inanimate objects moved on their own, and stones told stories to those willing to listen. In that era, there was a village girl who had a voice so beautiful people came from far and wide to hear her sing. This made her sister jealous, for no one noticed her at all. So one day, the jealous girl convinced her sister to have a picnic on a ridge high above a nearby river. Once there, though, as they admired the view, the jealous girl pushed her sister over the edge. The songstress tumbled to the water, hitting rock upon rock, and was washed downstream.

Certain everyone would now come to hear her sing, the jealous sister lied about what had happened. But when the jealous one tried to sing, instead of music, frogs came from her mouth, so everyone knew she'd had a hand in her sister's disappearance. And, though people searched for the girl, her body was never found. Far downstream where word of the tragedy had not spread, one of Gunter's forefathers found a child's shinbone on the bank. With reverence for the life it once carried, he whittled it, smoothed it and fashioned it into a flute. His family, already known for their healing remedies, discovered the flute had healing powers and used it discreetly in their work.

Otto wiped dust from the flute with his sleeve. "Take this and use it only to serve others. And guard it well. In the wrong hands, it can do harm."

Gunter had seen Otto play the flute only once in what is now Austria. It was shortly before they'd left for America ten years prior. Otto had been called to a landowner's home where the first-born son was gravely ill. The healer closed everyone out except for Gunter. He burned sage, rubbed the young aristocrat down with a rosemary tincture, and then played the flute. As sounds of innocent beauty filled the room, a sparkling, multicolored mist enveloped the youth. Vitality gradually returned to his body. The next day, he was fully healed. The only payment Otto accepted was food for his and Gunter's journey home.

Gunter bowed his head at the thought of accepting the flute. "I am not worthy of such power."

"I cannot let my greedy son get hold of this. It would bring only tragedy."

"I don't know how—"

"Take it, and use it sparingly, only for those who deserve it. And don't let anyone see you play, except for an apprentice you may choose someday." Otto handed Gunter the instrument, coughed, and struggled to his cot in a corner of the apothecary. "I've paid your passage on a ship that leaves Boston this morning for California by way of Cape Horn at the bottom of South America. It will take months to get there. It's said gold is everywhere for the taking, and fools believe it. The captain is expecting you. You'll calm seasickness and other maladies as part of the arrangement. Many will need your help to survive on the journey and afterward. You'll find your gold in what I've taught you, not in mining."

"I don't want to leave."

"This is the way of life. It's inevitably too soon when these passages arise."

Gunter rubbed the flute as sorrow flowed through him. "Boston's my home now. How will I get by?"

"You are a smart boy with a gift for language. Listen well on the ship and you'll learn new tongues before you reach your new home." The old man motioned to the table where Gunter had watched him mix remedies for years. "Take my medicine bag and put on the clothes and footwear I set aside for you. Take Mystery, too. He'll advise you and help keep the flute safe." Otto nodded toward a type of pigeon with a golden-brown body and head, long purple wings and tail, with yellow and turquoise markings around his neck and on his wings.

"But he doesn't talk to me."

"His voice will come to you when the time is right. Go quickly. Your uncle will be here soon."

MADDY LAID the pages on the table, stretched her arms, and yawned. "I really want to know what happens next."

"Looks like you'll have to stay a while." Clara picked up her knitting and, as her needles softly clicked, she hummed "Where is Love?" Her voice carried Oliver Twist's aching sorrow, yet it also warmed the room with hope.

WHILE SHINBONE WAS abuzz with talk of the new arrivals and their outlandish van, a couple of blocks away, Truman Raddatz parked his rattling Volvo sedan on Castro Street. Natalie stood in her underwear, about to try on a neon-green kaftan she'd found at the Salvation Army thrift store. She heard the car wheezing and smelled burning brakes. Glimpsing out the window, she wondered why a person would park in front of her home and sit inside without coming out. Perhaps someone was looking for a fixer-upper to buy. Everything about the place sagged, from the roof and gutters to the empty flower boxes at the windows, to the front stairs and door with peeling paint. The abode had never been a candidate for *Better Homes and Gardens*, even when Natalie lived there as a high schooler, given her now-deceased mother's penchant for lounging, inebriated, one eye half-open, on the living room couch.

Finally, Truman slid out of the car. He shook out his long limbs but didn't attempt to smooth his wrinkled suit, which gleamed with wear at the elbows. Natalie recognized him instantly. She slipped the kaftan on and fastened it. He passed fennel flourishing along the front perimeter and stepped onto what remained of the front walk, which, like the adjacent overgrown driveway, was barely visible, overcome with Scotch broom, cape ivy, ice plant, and other weeds. Natalie leaned against the front door. His footsteps hammered on the rickety stairs. A cat meowed and skittered below the boards.

Natalie's heart thumped with such force she feared Truman would feel it through the door. She considered her options: do not answer; open the door a crack, give him what-for and slam it in his face; or open it wide and fall into his arms. The first choice would be the safest for now, but knowing Truman the way she used to, she figured he'd keep coming back. She bristled at the thought of embracing him; he didn't deserve it. That left option two. She waited, not about to answer right away; that would seem too eager. All these years, she'd managed without him. She didn't need him now.

Truman knocked. Natalie shifted her weight from one foot to the other. The floor creaked beneath her.

"Dammit," she muttered under her breath.

"Natalie, is that you?"

Struck by a wave of fear that made her struggle to breathe, she crouched and counted to ten, while he tried to peer in through the door's sooty stained-glass window.

Truman knocked again. "Natalie? You there?"

She stood still, rage rising to scald memories of puppy love.

She listened as his footsteps receded down the stairs and clomped around the side of the house to the weed-infested backyard. She ran to her bedroom in the back of the house and watched him lift the lid on the trash can and mutter something she couldn't make out.

He climbed up stairs so full of dry rot one of them almost gave way under his weight. Knocking on the back door, he called, "Natalie, Natalie, you there?"

Panicked because the door was so warped the lock no longer caught, Natalie opened her armoire and pulled out a shotgun. It wasn't loaded, but Truman wouldn't know that. She leaned down, slid the window open a few inches and shoved the barrel of the gun outside. "Get outta here before I call the cops." She growled the words.

"Ah, I'd know that voice anywhere. Come on, you're not gonna do that. You hate any sort of authority, just like me. We got that in common."

"Go away." Her voice cracked, weakened by his familiar tones of flirtation. She retreated and sat on the bed, shotgun in hand, uncertain whether to let him in.

He tried the door. It creaked open. He walked to the bedroom and leaned on the doorframe. "Natalie, Natalie, it's been too long." He stepped into the room. "Um, I could sure use a cup a coffee."

Their eyes met. Natalie let out a little gasp and put down the weapon. "You gotta be kidding me. You come by after all these years for a cup a coffee?"

"Never had the guts to stop before."

"What's so different now?"

"Maybe just a pull to know how things turned out for you."

She shook her head. "Time for that's way past."

"Do you want me to go?" He backed into the kitchen.

She stood up. "I got one of those fancy Melitta things my son gave me."

"You have a son?" His rheumy eyes widened.

"Don't look so surprised. Why wouldn't I?"

"An old man, too?"

"That's none of your business." She burped, then bumped him aside on her way to the kitchen.

~

FBI INTRUSIONS PERSISTED like a mosquito buzzing in the dark for Penny Ferguson. Why did they keep coming back? Why did they always march through the door as if they, not Penny's parents, owned the home? She gripped her wheelchair and snuffed in frustration at the hovering agent. Barely able to see since the accident that had almost ended her life, she saw him in shades of black, white, and gray—all color drained away. Jutting out her strong jaw in defiance, she squinted at her mother's lace curtains fluttering at a window cracked open. The smell of flowers in the spring breeze didn't lift her spirits; May 20, 1974, was just another day she couldn't enjoy.

"I've told you all I know," she hissed. "It'll be three years next month, and still you grill me. Why don't you bring news of Blossom?"

"No need to get on your high horse," he said. "That won't bring your daughter back."

The FBI visits began right after Penny came out of a coma. In pain, bandaged and disoriented, she struggled to see, breathe, move. Yet the barrage began. What did she know? Who was involved? Did she help make explosives? What did they use? Where did they get materials? What did she see, and when did she see it? Who lived in the building? How many were Weathermen? What names did they go by? What were they planning next? They didn't believe she knew nothing of the violent intentions brewing around her.

Penny rolled her chair away from the agent clogging her life with suspicion. Her story stayed the same through every encounter because it was the truth, she maintained. Couldn't he see that? She leaned her head back, remembering the last day she could move freely, see clearly. How tightly she held her toddler. The soft tread of her desert boots on cracked pavement. Children playing jacks in a driveway. A neighbor watering geraniums on her porch. Penny's plan on that sun-drenched day in June 1971 had been to tell Bill she was done. She was through. Her prince, a college boy who loved Joe Cocker, *Bonanza*, Woodstock, and the Apollo program; her soulmate, who used to write songs about world peace and tender love while she cooked spaghetti on long winter afternoons; her best friend since they'd met at a folk festival, she merely seventeen, and he nineteen; the father of her daughter, her mate for life, so she'd thought, had become a lizard, tongue darting to catch and crush all dissent. How he'd shifted from peace marches in 1968 to secret meetings in 1971 eluded her like the solution to a quadratic equation. But it no longer mattered. Tired of longing for love no longer there, she had decided to pack up. Call her parents. Move on. That afternoon. Then everything changed.

Penny rocked side to side in her wheelchair and moaned.

The agent's partner, a woman, fidgeted at the threshold to the living room. "Come on. That's enough. She's had enough."

"For now," he said, disgust flying from him like dust from a shaken rug. "You'd think the Greenwich Village townhouse that blew up and killed three of 'em would have been a wakeup call, but no, not these deviants ... and this one, almost obliterated in the Portland blast, won't lift a finger to help put a stop to the insanity."

The agents strode to the front door, where Penny's mother stood with squared shoulders, ready to usher them away.

Penny rolled to the foyer just as the male agent blasted outside. His female counterpart leaned in toward her mom and said, "She's got to face the truth someday."

"God forbid you have a child suffer such a trauma and some know-it-all like you comes along telling you what to do."

"Good day, then, Mrs. Ferguson," she said before jogging to catch up with her partner.

Penny positioned her chair next to her mom. "What did she mean about telling me the truth?"

"Some platitude about how lying creates more pain and suffering in the end than coming out with the truth, no matter how hard it is to bear. She's been on me about that so much she's like a broken record."

In an adjacent room, Penny's dad sat in a hospital bed, paralyzed on one side and unable to speak. His shaking hand gripped a piece of chalk; his lap held a slate board. His attempts to form letters were illegible, but he persisted.

The phone rang, sending Penny's mom running to the kitchen.

Penny followed. "Maybe it's Truman."

"You think that every time it rings," her mom said.

"Yeah, but he left for San Francisco weeks ago, and still no word."

"Hello? ... No, I'm afraid my husband is no longer conducting investigations. ... So am I. ... He retired ... for health reasons. ... Yes, he was training Truman, Truman Raddatz. ... He's finishing up one case for us. ... He left Portland weeks ago to pursue a lead. ... Frankly, I can't recommend him. He's not a licensed private investigator. ... Yes, he's too new to the field. ... Okay, give me your number. I'll pass it on, but do try to find someone with more experience."

Before her mother signed off, Penny muttered, "He's finishing up one case for us?" She maneuvered the chair to her room and closed the door. How could her mom refer to finding her own granddaughter as a case? She leaned back and silently begged for relief from her drab world, from endless limbo, tortured waiting. She begged for clear sight, mobility. To get word from Truman. To hold her daughter. What happened to Truman's prime lead in San Francisco?

She closed her eyes and saw a flash of her elderly neighbor's geraniums from that awful day. She could feel Blossom sliding from her arms as she watched her tiny feet touch the bottom stair. No! Stop! Rewind. Penny's eyes popped open. She would not, could not, live through the blast again today.

IN THE PHONE booth outside St. Paul's Market at 29th and Sanchez streets, Truman drank Schlitz from a can and placed a collect call. Penny's mother accepted the charges. Truman pictured her sitting on the floral-patterned couch in her Portland living room. She spoke softly, hoping to shield the conversation from her daughter, he assumed. But Penny must have heard the hushed tones her mom reserved only for Truman, because he heard mother and daughter exchange words, and then Penny was on the line, berating him.

Truman kept his conscience at bay with beer while the young

woman's frustration sputtered through the line. She railed on about a recent visit from the FBI. When she paused to catch her breath, he reminded her that his assignment had nothing to do with locating the bombing culprits, that he couldn't influence the FBI if he tried, and he was making progress on finding her daughter.

"Don't worry so much. I'm on it," he said. "I've got it right this time. ... The intel is solid. This is the place. ... The fact that I'm from here is merely coincidental. ... Convenient for what, exactly? ... Yeah, you could say that, but it doesn't amount to a hill a beans. ... I know I'm under the gun here. ... That's why I've taken extra time and measures to track this lead down. ... I don't appreciate all this pressure, bad for my health. ... I absolutely am not dragging this out. This is the real deal. ... What about the photos I sent? ... You're not sure. Okay, so you want more? ... No problem. I can do that. ... No, don't cry. ... I sure wish your dad was still on the job. ... He gave me direction, mentored me. There's nobody to do that now, no more wind in our sails. ... How's his recovery going? ... Aw shucks, please don't cry."

Truman listened for an extended time, sweat beading on his forehead and soaking through his shirt as he doodled with ballpoint pen on the phone book chained to the booth. Penny alternately sobbed and raged at him. Finally, she quieted down and the conversation resumed.

"I didn't mean to upset you," he said. "I'm sorry, kid. ... I know, I know how hard all this is on you and your mom. ... How is she, by the way? ... Still your guardian angel, I bet. ... Suffocating? She's suffocating you? Now, now, you must remember she almost lost you, and now your dad. It's all so touch and go. ... I really am right this time, though. ... I won't let you down. Things have to run their course, takes time. ... Here? ... You want me to bring you here? ... That is a bad idea. Your dad would never go along with it if he could weigh in. ... That's pushing it. ... I need more time. ... I know I said I'm sure. ... I am sure, but we gotta do this right, dot all the i's and cross all the t's. ... If we move too fast, we could blow the whole thing. These people are slippery. Everything I've done for the past couple of years, all the tracking, all the calls, it could all go kaput. Don't you get that? ... All right, all right. ... I'll work faster. ... Look, I'll get some help, just to double check all the bases. ... I get it. ... You need to get off my back. ... I'll do right by you, like I promised your dad. ... Yeah, yeah, we'll wrap it up. End of summer? I don't know about that. ... Look, I'm no slouch. ... I swear, we're almost there. ... Yeah, I'll call again after I send more photos. ... You really can count on me, kid. ... Bye."

Truman returned to his beat-up Volvo sedan and kicked the dented door several times before opening it and getting inside. He chugged the rest of his beer and wiped his mouth with the edge of his tattered sleeve. Why did old man Ferguson have to go and have a stroke? He'd know what to do right now, how to wind it all down. Truman saw no finish line. He'd have to keep improvising. If Penny weren't so set on coming to San Francisco, he wouldn't feel so much pressure. He put the key in the ignition but didn't start up the car. He opened his window a crack, lit a Marlboro and watched people come and go. A woman in a navy blue spandex outfit trotted by with a husky that was off leash. A boy on a skateboard zoomed toward them. The dog darted ahead, barking, and leaped on the boy, knocking him off balance, but he managed to stay on the board. The woman and her dog trotted off as though nothing had happened. Lucky kid, Truman thought, I'll stay upright, too, just like him, one way or another.

CHAPTER

FIVE

Tapping out a rhythm on a set of bongos, Lark watched from her window as members of the Tai Chi group passed by on their way home from their morning exercises. When she was sure they'd all gone, she strode uphill, drums in hand, and found Eloise and Coco dancing. She sat on a patch of grass and put the bongos between her crossed legs. She'd learned to play two years prior while camping on a beach in Morocco, where every day, travelers joined a group of Moroccans to play drums as the sun set over the Atlantic.

That was when she first thought of improvising poetry to bongos, but she hadn't had the courage to do it back then. Now, her feelings tumbled like tickets spinning in a raffle before a hand reaches in and grabs one; she needed an outlet, a way to let go. Echoing the dancers' rhythms, she tapped the drumheads, adding a crisp, immediate flavor to their movements. Coco stopped prancing with Eloise and poked her nose against Lark's jeans.

"Coco, don't interrupt. It's not polite." Eloise said.

Lark scratched Coco behind the ears and looked up at Eloise. "She can interrupt me anytime. I was hoping to add some percussion and words to your choreography. I'm amazed at what you do and how you get Coco to dance, too."

"It's not me. It's all Coco. You should have seen that dog pirouette with my Julianna before she took off. We were quite the group. Reminded me of when Tilda was here.

"Tilda?"

"Thick as thieves, we were. We planned to dance around the world, my best friend and I."

"What happened?"

"Everything falls apart in the end." Eloise dismissed the question with a wave. "Carry on, will you?"

The poet tapped a couple of beats; the dancer took a few steps in response; the dog followed. All three clicked into sync. Lark's fingers flew, and her words flowed: *Today is a bloom day/ a rock candy sweet day/ today/ but I am a plain metal door/ today/ travelers pass me by/ today/ no one knocks on me/ today/ oh/ no one knocks on me/ who will cross the bridge/ today/ to my heart/ today?/ who will notice/ today/ there's more beyond the door/ oh yes, there's more beyond the door/ today?/ Oh, today, please roar/ today/ like a lion inside of me/ today/ so no one can deny/ today/ no one can deny I can do more/ today/ than wait, wait/ today, today/ for my time to come.* Lark paused to push up her glasses.

"Have you thought of getting contact lenses? Those monstrous rims and thick lenses get in the way in more ways than one," Eloise said.

"What's the use when you're frumpy as I am?" Lark replied.

"You're as frumpy as you think you are—ponder that, hmmm?"

"That would send me smack into some kind of existential crisis." Lark picked up the pace of her drumming.

Eloise dipped, jumped and spun, improvising new staccato movements, sometimes coming to a halt, every part of her still except for one body part at a time isolated, starting with her hands twitching to punctuate Lark's rhythms. Coco came to a halt, too, circling one paw at a time in tandem with Eloise. The ripple tree down the hill even responded, heart-shaped leaves swaying in time.

Lark sped up: *Today/ today is ripe strawberries, sandalwood incense/ today/ saffron folding into rice/ today/ today/ lizards sunning on rocks today/ today/ yet I cannot reach alone through metal/ today/ today/ cannot reach alone through metal/ today/ bring me/ today/ a key/ give me a story-book/ today/ rich in lore/ today/ rich in trials and victories/ today/ rich in the promise of just one glance today/ today.*

Eloise shifted gears, using large movements, her whole body involved, mirroring Lark's varied rhythms and speeds. Captain flew up and landed on a nearby rock. He bobbed his head to Lark's rhythms, too.

Lark burst out laughing. "Even Captain is getting in on it." Then a group of clouds covered the sun momentarily. A chill ran from her limbs to her core. She tried to shake it off and continued: *The sun leaves/ now/ today/ no time left/ today/ I sink in fading light/ today/ oh, the colors of pain/ today/ are exquisite/ today/ divine/ today/ today/ but the cold dark claims my rusty hinges and locks/ stuck in place/ today/ monotonous, monstrous today/ I wish all useless hope away, away/ today/ I wish the day away/ today.*

Eloise stopped, breathing heavily. "I believe you have a dark side." She patted her chest. "I'm a tad out of shape."

"You're doing better than I ever could," Lark said. "You're like the queen of dance."

"Martha Graham is the root from whom all branches flow. I'm forever a disciple. In one short summer, she changed my life."

"She, uh, created modern dance, right?"

"My Julianna will click with you when she returns; you're unlike most of those unsavory characters at 346."

"Unsavory? No way. Ted takes in good people. He has a sixth sense or something."

"Including the ones in that van that pulled up—when was it—last week?"

"Chip and Sunrise are really nice."

"You never know. They could be holding my Julianna against her will, hmmm? She might be gagged in that strange VW bus of theirs as we speak."

"That's some crazy talk. Why not join us for dinner sometime? You can see for yourself what they're like."

"That's not up my alley." Eloise took out the compact and lipstick from her handbag and smacked her lips after applying deep red color to them. Then she primped her hair, tucked her makeup away, and turned to Coco. "Come along. We've got things to do."

"I'm gonna try reading some poems the night of the Shinbone Fair. It's coming up fast, July twentieth. You could join me. The crowd would go wild."

"I don't cotton to that fair, drawing attention that way, all those strangers poking their noses where they don't belong."

Eloise and Coco ambled downhill. Lark continued drumming, eyes closed, words spilling out in spurts. At her feet, Captain spun on his prosthesis, his natural claw propelling him in rhythm to the beat.

COVERS TUCKED up to her ears, Maddy peeked around the attic room. The slanted walls, cubbies, built-in bookshelves, dresser, and four-poster bed beamed personality. Even the tiny bathroom, with its old-fashioned toilet and elevated tank that flushed with a chain, delighted her. The whole room made her feel at home, which she took as a sign she should move on as soon as possible. Attachments could be deadly. Maddy washed up, dressed, and padded downstairs. On the kitchen table, she found a note from Clara, who'd already gone out to read stories to a wiggly tribe of youngsters at Happy Days Preschool. On weekdays, the school occupied much of the ground floor of The Farm-house community center situated between Clara and Eloise's proper-ties. Clara's note mentioned fresh poundcake and sliced strawberries for Maddy's breakfast.

After a quick bite to eat, Maddy set off for 24th Street, where she window shopped, poked around a couple of clothing stores, and stopped at the Acme Cafe's bulletin board. She perused ads for harmonica lessons, strange kinds of body work called Feldenkrais and

Rolfing, a couple of households looking for roommates, poetry readings, flyers for all kinds of events, a piano for sale, a few job offers. Then she went to the counter to order. The long list of available teas made her hesitate. She couldn't decide which one to try.

Behind the counter, a young man with a long blond ponytail scrunched his brow in mock concentration. "Hmm, you look like the adventurous type. Why not try lopsang souchong? It's got a smoky flavor."

"Smoky tea? That would be different. Okay, I'll try it."

When he rang up the purchase, he handed her a slip of paper with a phone number on it along with her change. "Name's Garret, by the way."

Maddy tried to hand the paper back to him, but he explained it wasn't his number. "I saw you taking notes at the bulletin board and thought you might need work. My friend Paul's looking for an assistant, basically someone to mail packages for him a few times a week, maybe keep a few records."

"I don't think so, but thanks." She left the paper on the counter and sat down at an empty table to sip tea and draw.

When she readied to leave, Garret called her over. He was on the phone and held his hand over the mouthpiece when he spoke. "Paul's on the line and said if you could work just a couple hours today, that would be an enormous help. He's a little odd, but he's perfectly safe." He thrust the receiver at her. "He really needs help."

Exploration was in her plans, not mailing packages for someone she didn't know, but she'd observed Garret greet every customer who'd come in after her like an old friend. He seemed like a stand-up guy. She accepted the phone and said a tentative hello. Paul's desperation came through the line. He promised it would be for a couple of hours, max. Plus he lived only a few blocks from the cafe, and he was willing to pay her fifteen dollars for two hours' work. The thought of having fifteen dollars in her pocket that afternoon swayed her. She asked for directions.

"I can't believe I'm doing this," she muttered under her breath as she walked out the door and headed to Paul's home on Vicksburg, half a block up from 24th. She arrived in under five minutes and rang the bell. A dark-haired man, skinny as a finish nail, opened the door.

"You must be Maddy. I'm Paul, Paul Mellick." He ushered her inside. "Thanks for helping me out."

He motioned for her to follow him down a dim corridor. Glimpsing a room with door ajar and a ray of muted light coming from inside, she paused to see shadows dancing on the walls. In the center hummed a projector, sleeker and more complex than any she'd seen in a class-room. It faced a screen on the far wall, its reels spinning steadily as images flickered across the room. Nearby, alongside a machine she couldn't identify, an array of reels lay scattered on a table, some empty, others full, their silver surfaces gleaming under the low light. Maddy inhaled the sharp, acrid scent of chemicals, the air thick with unnatural warmth.

Paul stopped at a door several feet from where Maddy stood. "Don't worry about all that stuff. It's for production. I need you in the office."

He disappeared into the room. Maddy rushed to catch up. Inside were a pile of padded envelopes, stacks of film reels, a postage meter, a desk, and a metal filing cabinet.

"Do you know how to work one of these?" He patted the meter.

"I've never seen one before." Maddy bit her bottom lip, fearing he would escort her right out the door.

"Don't worry," Paul said. "It's easy." He showed her how the meter worked. Then he instructed her to hand address fifty envelopes, stuff them with the right films, which were identified by names tags taped to the canisters enclosing them, and affix the correct postage. "You gotta work fast, because all of these have to arrive before Memorial Day weekend," he said.

She sped through the work, and when she was done, she helped load the packages into the trunk of his car to take to the post office. Before he got into the driver's seat, he paid her more than they'd agreed on: $20 for what turned out to be less than two hour's work.

"I could use your help again next Tuesday, maybe make it a regular thing, two or three days a week. It won't be as rushed as today."

"Sure." Maddy gave a quick nod. She could always change her mind, she reasoned, as she resumed meandering along 24th Street. The air was crisp, the sunlight a storybook hue; vibrancy brewed in shop windows and footsteps everywhere. And a job that paid more per hour than she'd ever earned had fallen into her lap. Was it meant to be? Since leaving home, she'd never stayed long in one place, not even in magical New Orleans or the breathtaking Rockies. Would it be safe here? Could she stay on after she proofread the Shinbone story? Maybe enough time had passed. Maybe nobody was looking for her.

ROSIE WINCED as she sat on the rainbow-painted stairs leading to Happy Days Co-op Preschool's outdoor play area in The Farmhouse's back-yard. Usually pleased with the cowrie shell necklace, bracelets and earrings she'd chosen to wear, she was now irritated by the feel of them against her skin. The Tylenol with codeine she'd taken about fifteen minutes before hadn't kicked in yet. Pain stabbed with each movement; tender places on her torso and arms throbbed, a testament to what a demon-drunk Wayne was. Chip stepped outside and joined Rosie on the stairs. Rosie eased back on her elbows, hoping her children hadn't heard the beating that morning. She closed her eyes, sun soothing her freckled face.

Rosie's daughter, Heather, and Sunrise, Chip's little sister, whispered and giggled by a rope ladder that led to a playhouse nestled in a loquat tree.

"The kids are having so much fun here," Chip said, "but I don't know if I could pitch in for all the required hours during the school year. Plus I have zero experience working with a bunch of preschoolers. It could be overwhelming."

Rosie reassured him that there were regular education meetings and plenty of experienced parents and the director ready to help newcomers. "And at this age, it's basically all about keeping them engaged and safe." As soon as she said "safe," Rosie feared what would happen to Heather and Lucas if Wayne kept drinking. How long would it be before one of them set him off? She put her palms against her temples.

"Is something wrong? You seem kind of down." Chip reached for her arm.

Rosie pulled away. "Just a little under the weather, that's all."

"I saw some aspirin in the kitchen pantry. I could get it for you."

"No thanks." Rosie forced a smile.

Several tots blasted outside. Beloved neighborhood elder Clara, ensconced on a couch in the school's cozy area, had just read them a story about children living in a flying house. The youngsters were now bent on taking their playhouse in the yard on an adventure into the sky. They packed in and urged Sunrise and Heather to join them for lift off.

"Has Sunrise gone to preschool before?" Rosie asked.

"No, but it looks like she really likes it here."

"Wayne says nursery school's just a high falutin' luxury. He likes to point out that we never went to preschool and did fine in school, but I think he's wrong."

Swept into the flying adventure, the girls shrieked and cried out at each imaginary obstacle and collision. A few kids pretended to fall out, screaming as they slid down a curved metal slide. They feigned injury, and the game shifted to a rescue operation with tykes climbing down to play police officers, bystanders, and EMTs.

Uplifted by the children's antics, Rosie said, "You and your sister are really close, huh?"

"I've loved her since I first set eyes on her, a squiggly, squalling little ball of light, and sharing the van with her has been a blast. Being on the move all the time is getting old, though, and Sunrise is curious about school."

"Wayne and I did a lot of traveling, but when we came over the Golden Gate Bridge and saw San Francisco, it was so ... magical, yes, magical, the way the city gleamed in the sunlight. It felt to me like we'd come home."

Another parent stepped onto the deck and called out, "Snack time!" She held the door open with her foot and clapped her hands several times.

Some children dropped their games right away. Others lingered, favoring play over food. Heather grabbed Sunrise's hand, and the girls ran inside. The rest of the children soon followed. Chip went down to the yard to pick up a doll and ball that had been left behind. Rosie, walking gingerly to minimize pain, checked all possible hiding places to make sure every child was inside. Satisfied the yard was in order, they entered the building. As they neared the snack area, children were devouring miniature blueberry muffins and apple slices brought in by the family on snack duty that day, one of the responsibilities parents assumed in San Francisco's growing co-op preschool movement.

Rosie and Chip pretzeled into chairs at a child-sized table. Rosie's T-shirt rode up, exposing a sliver of bruised flesh. She jerked it down and tucked it in, relieved Chip was looking at a row of toddler paintings drying on easels.

"I WAS BEGINNING to think you'd gotten lost somewhere," Clara called from her easy chair when she heard Maddy come through the front door. The youth bounced into the living room and grinned, revealing a set of matching dimples. Clara put down her knitting. "It's great to see you smiling. You must have had a grand walk."

Maddy flopped onto the couch. "Did I ever!" Enthusiasm pushed out a sun-shower of words as she filled Clara in on how she got paid twenty dollars for helping a guy named Paul get a slew of packages ready to mail. "He wants me to come back in a few days to help him again ... so I guess I have landed a job?"

"My, my ... without even looking for one."

"I was thinking maybe I need to get some money together before I move on, so can I live in the attic studio for a while, is the offer still open?"

"I've been hoping you'd stay on." Clara gushed, for she saw no need to hide her delight that the teenager was going to be around longer than expected.

"I can pay rent."

"Your help around the house and yard would mean more than any money you could pay. And the Shinbone Fair is coming up in July. I could use your help getting ready. You could sell some of your drawings, too." She picked up her knitting and began working again.

"You think so?"

"Your ripple tree sketches would sell better than those mood rings everybody under thirty is crazy about. ... Oh, I almost forgot. Lark stopped by." She nodded toward a few typewritten pages next to the latest *Redbook* magazine on the coffee table.

Maddy picked them up. "Want me to read aloud again?"

"Please do." Clara continued to knit.

Maddy skimmed the pages, then began the next segment of Shinbone's origin story.

GUNTER BOARDED the ship for California minutes before it pulled up anchor. He carried the flute, medicines and, on his shoulder, the hybrid pigeon, Mystery. The sea slapped, roared, and jolted with uncommon fury throughout the journey, as though monsters in the depths were at war. While nauseated himself, he treated several passengers for seasickness, a few for dysentery, and, when he was at a loss for how to treat a poor soul suffering delirium, Mystery's gravelly voice came into his mind, telling him what he'd seen Otto do in such cases. Finally, they reached San Francisco, until recently known as Yerba Buena, where the lust for gold had taken over. Shacks and shanties cluttered the shoreline and dotted the hills. All but two sailors abandoned ship, hoping to stake a claim and strike it rich.

Gunter spent several days blending into shadows, listening to what people said about routes, supplies, and streams full of gold. With possibility in the air everywhere, he thought he could be both healer and prospector. Some might say it was foolish of him, but the boy had to make his own decisions now. He purchased basic supplies and a mule with gold coins Otto had left in the pockets of his hand-me-down clothes. Then he set off for the Sierras, where gold was said to still be plentiful. He trekked along. At one point, he stopped at a shotgun town that had sprung up. There he met a Nissan shaman, whose tribe had been wiped out by gangs of gold seekers who'd arrived by wagon train from Missouri. Gunter shared a ritual for easing troubled spirits he'd learned from Otto; the shaman showed him several local plants with healing powers.

Farther along his journey, he met Maeve, an Irish woman whose husband trapped for a fur company while she raised their children and ran a booming boarding house. Also a healer, she said she was descended from the goddess Airmed, whose tears over her slain brother's grave gave rise to the world's healing herbs, some of which Maeve grew in her garden. Her home was also a haven for birds drawn to her from all corners of the earth. Some were pigeons colored just like Mystery. Two males and three females fluttered to Gunter when he was preparing to move on.

"Would you allow them to come with us?" Gunter asked.

"It's not up to me. They come and go of their own free will."

So Gunter left with a flock of six instead of Mystery alone. A few days later, at a fork in the Yuba River, Gunter heard groans coming from the side of the road. There he saw a bulky man prone with eyes swollen shut and blood oozing into the dirt.

"Lark sure left us hanging this time." Maddy slapped the pages down.

"Goodness me," Clara replied. "I'd be a tad impatient, too, if I didn't already know how the story goes."

"Shoot!" Natalie hunched forward at her kitchen table and attacked letters in a crossword puzzle book, muddling the simple task of erasure. She brushed away bits of rubber and lead, exposing a gray blob instead of clean squares and pressed harder, tearing through the paper. She threw the pencil and book down. A smattering of dust motes flitted up to her ankles and floated back to the floor. "Damn crosswords. Who needs 'em anyways." She lit a Camel filter cigarette and took a long drag, slackening to the smell as much as to the taste and feel of smoke.

The doorbell rang. "Go away!" She took another drag. Who could it be? Nobody ever came to visit; Ricky, now back home for who knows how long, had a key. There was Truman. Would he be back again so soon? She didn't think so. Must be some kind of salesperson. Crews of young people sold Colliers Encyclopedias door to door a few years ago. She'd taken great pleasure in leading them on, listening to their full pitches when she was about as likely to buy a set as she was to join the Dolphin Club and swim in the Bay. Those college kids had learned not to come around anymore, though. Some Avon lady up the block stopped by every few months trying to make a sale. Natalie always invited her in, made small talk while she looked through the latest catalog, but she'd placed only one order for a pearly pink shade of lipstick—five years prior.

The bell sounded again. Thinking it was likely the Avon lady, Natalie decided it would be fun to toy with her. She stubbed out her cigarette and shot down the hall, slippers slapping against her heels, nightgown fluttering behind. Better try to look decent, at least, she thought. She ducked into her bedroom, quickly changed into a yellow-and-white tent dress that could cover a tomb full of ills, kicked off her slippers, and slid into a pair of white flats. The bell rang again.

"Okay, okay, I'm coming," she said. "Jesus Christ, why is everyone in such a hurry these days?" At the door, she peeked through the small window and coughed at the sight of a young man. She opened the door just a crack. "What d'ya want?"

"Are you Natalie Pine?"

"Yes, I am. What's it to ya?"

"I have a delivery for you." He tried to hand a nine-by-twelve manilla envelope to her through the opening. "You'll have to sign for it."

"I don't have to sign for nothin'; I'm not guilty."

She pushed the door to close it, but he blocked it with his foot. "This isn't a summons. You're not in trouble. It just means the document inside is important."

She opened the door a little wider. "Oh yeah? Lemme see, then."

He held it up so she could read the return address.

"The law offices of Malachi P. Burnside, Esquire? Why would my landlord be sending me anything? I pay my rent just like everybody else living in the dumps he owns."

"You know he passed away last month, right?"

"Yeah, they made a big deal of it—all over the news. Big gadfly. It's got nothin' to do with me."

"Listen, I just run errands for the firm. I'm not in on their meetings, but the word is that these packets are going out to his heirs. There aren't many, and you're one of them."

"Impossible!"

"Why don't you open it and see? It won't obligate you to do anything. I swear."

"How would you know, being as that you're not a lawyer?"

"What do you have to lose?" He pushed the envelope farther through the opening.

Natalie snatched it. "All right. All right. I'll take it just to be rid of the likes of you." She signed to acknowledge receipt and thrust the paper in the young man's face. "We done here now?"

"Yes, that's it. I'm sure it's good news."

Natalie closed the door and made her way back to the kitchen, where she sat back down and tore open the envelope. Inside was a short cover letter requesting that she meet with Burnside's estate lawyer, who would explain the three-page document enclosed. She skimmed the pages and gasped before stuffing the document into her purse.

THE CALENDAR SAID MID-JUNE, but the wind that swept under Maddy's collar and cuffs snapped like Jack Frost as she huffed up Shinbone Lane. Head down, she hunched her shoulders and patted the twenty-dollar bill in her pocket, her payment for helping Paul pack up the latest batch of films for clients across the country. Good money. The work wasn't as frequent as he'd promised, but she had enough to get by since Clara wasn't charging her rent. She pictured sinking into a hot bath when she heard someone call her name. Drawn from her daydream, she spotted Lark crossing the lane, typewritten pages in hand.

Out of breath, the poet greeted Maddy and got in step at her side. "This is a long one," Lark warned, handing Maddy the pages. "I hope you're up for it."

"Sure, I'll be happy to read these when I'm inside, where it's toasty —some weird summer we've having."

"Nothing all that unusual for San Francisco," Lark replied. "We'll get a whiff of real heat in late August and September. But there's balmy weather right now all around the Bay." She mentioned she was heading for a poetry festival in San Rafael, where the temperature was eighty degrees. "I can't wait to peel off some of these clothes." She lifted her poncho to reveal a light jacket over a shirt with tails draping over baggy cargo pants. "I've got a tank top and shorts under all of this."

"Looks like you're prepared for anything," Maddy said.

"Layering. That's the secret to comfort here," the poet said. "Say, why not come along? You could sketch the crowd while enjoying the warm sun on your face."

Maddy, eager for quiet time, declined. She bid Lark farewell and proceeded to Clara's front door. She could have taken the back stairs, which afforded privacy. However, Clara's voice invariably gave her a little boost of optimism, just like the harmonies of Crosby, Stills, Nash & Young did. She always came through the front and used the interior stairs to reach the attic. Once inside, the young artist found her bene-factor asleep in the living room, faint snores chirping. She placed a pillow under the old woman's head before peeling off her jacket, making a pot of tea, and settling in to read silently.

GUNTER KNELT beside the man and found his barely perceptible pulse fading rapidly. Rather than administering a laudanum tincture to ease the man's last hours and moving on, Gunter decided this spot, where passersby were rare, presented a perfect opportunity to test whether he could use the flute in the same healing way Otto had long ago in Austria. He set up camp, washed the man's many wounds, and ate a simple meal of salt pork, stale biscuits, and water. Then he waited. At nightfall, by a small fire and the only sound the man's shallow breathing, Gunter pulled out the flute.

He hesitated until Mystery's gravelly voice entered his mind. "You can do it," the voice said. Gunter looked up at Mystery perched with the other pigeons on pine branches above. Heartened, he took a deep breath and blew into the flute for the first time. The sound that came out was angelic, much like the sound when Otto had played. Gunter's muscles relaxed, each note to him the sound of hope.

In the morning, the stranger's swelling was down; his breath flowed freely. Gunter watched over him throughout the day as he slept on. Late in the afternoon, the man grunted, opened his eyes, and looked around the simple camp.

"Thought I was a goner," he said as Gunter offered him a cup of water. The man winced when he reached for the cup. "Thank you." He took a sip, swished the liquid in his mouth, and swallowed. "Four guys attacked me out of the blue. Took everything I had—my mule, supplies, took it all." He tried to rise but fell back against the boulder.

"Today you rest, tomorrow you stand," Gunter said.

"Name's Arvel, by the way. Arvel Yates. You must be some kind of miracle worker."

"I'm just Gunter, doing what I can with remedies from home."

"Where's that?"

"Boston and before that Vienna."

"All the way in Europe? You sure came a long ways. I just came down from Oregon. My dad and mom got a farm going there, but it's not doing so well, too many mouths to feed. I set off to seek my fortune."

The pigeons flew down and pecked the ground near the campfire. "What's with these odd-looking birds?" Arvel asked.

"They're traveling with me, keeping an eye out for me," Gunter said.

"You some kind of animal trainer, too?" Arvel asked before drifting back to sleep.

When night descended, Gunter played the flute again until he, too, fell asleep.

The next morning, Gunter made coffee to go along with a meager breakfast of salt pork and stale biscuits.

"Thanks." Arvel took a swig of coffee, then stood up with ease. He was a good six inches taller than Gunter.

Gunter dipped the end of a biscuit into his mug. "Looks like you're strong now, so I'll be moving on."

"Where to?"

"Downieville."

"I buried some nuggets a little ways from here, was saving to go I don't know where, maybe San Francisco one day, set myself up with a general store. Now I'll have to use my stash to start all over again. It's half a day's journey out of your way, but we could team up and keep watch in case those ambushers come back. Then we could go to Downieville together. I can get supplies there, and I can vouch for you, tell everybody how you saved me. You could really cash in."

"I never charge for healing. I ask for no more than a little food and lodging for a few days to rest up. I do hope to find a good claim one day, though, and settle down."

"Hey, buddy, anything goes here. ... Anyways, I'd like your company."

Mystery's voice came to Gunter. "Go your own way. There's ruin upstream."

Gunter considered Mystery's warning but thought he could handle any travails in his path. "Half a day isn't too much to lose," Gunter said.

So the two set off, with the pigeons coming and going above.

"Them birds bothered me at first," Arvel said, "but now they seem like guardian angels."

Toward the end of the day, they came upon a camp where four miners, gasping for breath, lay on the ground. Gunter recognized signs of cholera, for he'd witnessed his parents and grandmother succumb to the disease on the way to America. The disease had almost claimed him, too.

Arvel wanted to steer clear of them. "We'll all get sick and die. You gave me new life. I don't want to risk it now."

But Gunter believed he could help them. He administered herbs from his medicine bag. At night, he gave everyone a calming drink after supper, and with the others sedated, he pulled out the shinbone flute. Soon ethereal tones permeated everyone's dreams. All breathed easier except for Gunter, who concentrated on his playing long into the night.

At first light, the miners rose from their bedrolls as though born anew; two even felt well enough to resume work. In gratitude for saving their lives, they told Gunter and Arvel about a place a few miles upstream where they'd found gold still visible in the water, like in the early days of the Gold Rush.

"We was about to move camp up there, but after this misery, all we want is to go back to our families in Nebraska," one of them said. "When we finish panning here, we'll have enough gold for our journey home. And thanks to you, we have our lives."

"You'd have done the same for us," Gunter said, packing up his mule. "But I can't accept your offer. I do my healing work for free."

"This is a land of free enterprise. How can you turn down gold you can grab just like that?" Arvel asked.

"We could both use a good claim, but—" Gunter coughed, a deep rattle that brought up blood, and fell to the ground.

"No!" Arvel rushed to his side.

One of the miners handed him a tin cup of water. He tried to get Gunter to drink, but the water just dribbled from Gunter's mouth.

The young healer struggled to speak. "Take my belongings. Whatever you need. But whatever you do, safeguard the flute, and listen to Mystery when he speaks." Gunter swept his arm toward the pigeon who'd been with him since he left Boston. "Keep the flute hidden, a secret shared rarely. Guard it with reverence, always. Use it only for healing. Never show it off."

Arvel ran his hand over Gunter's damp hair. "You must be delirious. I don't know what you're talking about. And I know nothing about music."

"Cherish the instrument, never use it for personal gain. The flute will play itself."

"What do you mean?"

Gasping and with long pauses between words, Gunter told Arvel about life as an apprentice in his grandfather Otto's apothecary, how the shinbone flute came to be, and how Otto warned him to never abuse its power.

"Why go on about some stupid flute?" Arvel's voice cracked. "You're not gonna die now. You're gonna be a big healer in Downieville. You're gonna make a killing."

"Sure, sure," Gunter mumbled to Arvel, whose worried face was the last thing he saw in this world.

. . .

CLARA NAPPED ON. With scenes from the story vivid in her mind's eye, Maddy tiptoed upstairs and sketched, so absorbed she lost track of time.

AS JUNE TICKED SWIFTLY into July, Ricky had little cash left from his last job. In Seattle, he'd canned salmon for a few months before returning to San Francisco. He'd answered ads in the *Bay Guardian* for any and every job he felt the least bit qualified, including Xerox machine installation and service person; ticket and refreshments seller at the hip Roxie Theater; handyman for a real estate management company in the Tenderloin; apprentice arborist in St. Francis Woods; member of a tie dye garment collective; teacher's aide for an after-school arts program; and Noe Valley ghost walk tour guide. The woman who interviewed him for the tour guide position said his strikingly sad blue eyes might help set a spooky mood for participants. But she never called him to follow up. As a last resort, he shambled, head down, into Bell Market on 24th Street, where he'd worked before joining VISTA.

"I'd say you're a day late and a dollar short, fella. The world doesn't just stop turning 'cause you want to get off." The balding store manager looked over the rim of his reading glasses. "Why should I hire you back?" With a Bic pen, he tapped Ricky's application, which rested on a thick stack of other applications on the desk.

Ricky shifted in his seat, taking in the windowless office. It was barely big enough for the desk and two chairs it housed. The gray walls were dreary as a dead sparrow. "I, ah, well, um ... I think I did a good job here before. You were happy with me—or you said you were."

"And then, funny thing, you left. It was not too long after we got you all trained. Do you think I consider that a good investment?"

Ricky rubbed behind his ear, wishing he could disappear into a scene in the manager's wall calendar of horses grazing in a sun-kissed meadow, mountains rising in the background. "Guess not, sir."

"You didn't even give a day's notice, just showed up at your shift time with a pack slung over your shoulder and said you were joining VISTA for a year. Then a year goes by and zip. Not a word from you."

Ricky met the man's eyes, then looked away again.

"Don't gaze at the wall. Say something."

After a silence that seemed to stretch far longer than the few seconds it was, Ricky confessed he couldn't take the way everybody looked at him; nobody was willing to give him a chance.

"I have news for you. Nobody's paying attention. Everybody's too busy with their own dramas. What looms large in your memory is long forgotten by most. Who would even know you, all grown up now, are the one who set that fire? Exactly no one."

"It was the whispers, the looks," Ricky managed to choke out.

"Nobody on staff spoke ill of you, even after you told Carlo—who still works here, by the way—what got you placed in foster care. We had a staff meeting after that, remember? I said the deck was stacked against you from the start with that mom of yours. And that social worker Harold Ramsey vouched for you, said you'd thrived in foster care, turned your life around. That was good enough for me, and every single person you worked with said it was good enough for them, too."

"It was the customers. They complained."

"The only person who complained about you was Eloise Watkins from up on Shinbone. And, my God, son, she didn't single you out. She didn't recognize you. She complains about everything and everyone. Our fruit is bruised, our lines too long, our service too slow. She even barged in here yesterday with her little dog and accused us of having her daughter, Julianna, in the freezer."

Ricky couldn't help but laugh. "Eloise should meet my mom. They'd probably get along."

"Natalie never mentioned Eloise and Tilda? They all went to school together. I was a couple years behind them."

"She's never said boo about them. The way she talks, it's like she was born full grown and smoking a cigarette."

The manager chuckled and pushed his glasses to the top of his head. "So what have you been up to and why are you here?" He leaned back in his chair.

Ricky filled him in on his travels after his year with VISTA. "I thought maybe I'd find some place that clicked for me, where I could dig in, relax. I thought I could break free of the past, but I found out we all bring our stuff with us, our own brand of garbage, wherever we go and ..." His voice trailed off as self-doubt gnawed him. "The truth is I couldn't decide on any place else. The answer to where I belong never came. And I gravitated toward home."

"That doesn't sound like much of a commitment, son." The manager sat up straight.

"I guess the past will always dog me as long as I'm here." Ricky moved his feet, accidentally hitting the bottom of the desk. A photo fell off the edge and into his lap. He lifted it up. It was of the manager, and his wife holding a baby. He put it back on the desk. "You have another kid?"

"Yes, unexpected. Two kids in college, and now it's like starting all over in middle age, but there's real benefits to commitment, sticking through thick and thin."

Ricky brushed moist palms on his jeans. "Um, I don't think you want to hire me. Why should I waste your time and mine?"

"Did I say I don't want you back?"

"No, but—"

"Okay. Let's try this. What did you learn when you were in VISTA?"

"All kinds of stuff." Ricky rubbed his temples with his fingertips.

"Just give it your best shot. Wow me, why don't you?" The manager shrugged, smiling.

Ricky took a deep breath and then described his experiences at VISTA starting out with working at a food bank, where he helped with stocking donations, organizing the huge warehouse, filling bags and carrying them to people's cars, making deliveries to homebound people, learning about community organizing and door-to-door fundraising. He even helped with cooking because the folks at VISTA were always having big meals with wealthy donors and people from the community.

"Some of that doesn't translate from the nonprofit world to our world here, but it looks like you've learned some good things, especially about relating to people. How about your time afterward when you were traveling?"

"Well, sir, I could write a book about that."

"I suppose you could."

"So, I'll just be—"

"Hold your horses, kid." He handed Ricky a W-4 form. "Fill this out and come back tomorrow. And don't ever think nobody will give you a chance again."

ON THE FOURTH OF JULY, Maddy, Clara, Ted, and several other Shinbone residents took a day trip to the Marin County town of Tomales, where they enjoyed a small-town parade and a picnic along the coast. They returned to the city in time to gather on The Farmhouse's roof and watch fireworks bursting over the Bay with their neighbors, a patriotic bunch who, idiosyncratic as they were, vibrated with love for the U.S.A. They shared snacks and drinks as the sky lit up. But for them, this was a prelude. The event they all looked forward to most was the Shinbone Fair, coming up on the third Saturday of the month.

A few days later, Lark finished transcribing Shinbone's origin story just before dawn. It wasn't long before lights came on in Clara's living room. Throwing a robe over her nightgown, Lark charged outside and across the lane to deliver the final pages. Maddy, yawning, opened the front door. While pulling her robe snug around her body and tightening the belt, Lark apologized for coming so early and held out the pages. Maddy rubbed her eyes and then took them.

"I had a bunch of stuff to do and only got back to this yesterday," Lark said. "I want to fix any typos you find and take the whole story to my friend Gordon. He said he'd typeset it and print a couple hundred copies—for free. Then I'll assemble booklets in time for the fair."

"That's cool."

"It's a far-fetched tale, for sure. Just the thing to entertain fairgoers."

"It'll be like a keepsake or souvenir."

Clara emerged from her room and saw Lark and Maddy at the door. "Goodness, my dear, invite Lark in."

"Thanks, but I can't. I just came to drop off the last pages." Lark turned and rushed down the porch stairs.

"Are you ready to hear the rest of the story?" Maddy asked.

"I certainly am," Clara said.

Juggling cups of apricot-flavored black tea and plates of bagels with cream cheese and olallieberry jam, the two took seats at the kitchen table. The teen, eager to find out what happened to Arvel and the flute, cleared her throat and began, red pen in hand.

After burying Gunter in the shade of a dogwood tree, Arvel wanted to respect his friend's last wishes, but he doubted the power of the flute entrusted to him. He thought Gunter's final words were those of a suffering man who'd lost touch with reality. Arvel tucked the flute away and located the claim the other miners had described. They'd exaggerated how much gold gleamed in the stream for easy picking, but he found a good vein and worked it. Then, out of boredom one lonesome night, he took out the flute and brought it to his lips. He couldn't believe how easily the music flowed, and how enchanting it was.

Mystery pecked at Arvel's boots and projected his voice into the man's ear. "Stop! Stop right now!" Arvel shook his head, believing, at first, he was imagining the voice. But when the bird responded to comments Arvel muttered to himself, he realized Mystery was indeed communicating with him—in English. Startled as he was, he continued to play the flute. He could not stop himself, so enraptured was he by the melodies winding through him.

In the following months, Mystery and Arvel developed a good rapport in the daytime, telling each other jokes and philosophizing, but Arvel's anger flared nightly when he played the flute, and Mystery urged him to put it away. "I'll catch you and cook you if you don't shut up," he threatened. Despite this, Mystery continued to warn him, becoming each evening like water dripping slowly, relentlessly onto his head.

Arvel occasionally camped with other people while on the road. Travelers often told stories and played musical instruments around campfires. Ignoring Mystery's ever more insistent warnings, Arvel joined in with the flute. People were charmed, and he continued to dismiss Mystery's misgivings. When campers parted ways with Arvel, they would leave him gifts, usually just surplus coffee or biscuits, but sometimes he'd find money and jewelry tucked into his saddle bag. Gunter entered Arvel's dreams at night, telling him to be wary of the flute or great sorrow would eventually consume him. Arvel paid no heed. He thought the people he met on the road were incredibly generous, and he was generous with others in return. The money and valuables he was given enabled him to leave the mining life and move to San Francisco sooner than he'd dreamed possible. When he arrived, he had enough saved up to establish a general store and buy a strip of hillside land at the edge of what had once been Jose de Jesus Noe's Rancho San Miguel. Arvel's sliver of land later became known as Shinbone Lane.

Arvel married Lucille, the daughter of a schoolteacher and a teacher herself. He built her a home (eventually transformed into The Farmhouse) and continued to run his business. She grew vegetables, had several cows, and started up a cheese business. While tending their farmstead, she gave birth to a son, Arvel Jr., and then a daughter, Georgette. Occasionally, Arvel would gather with friends at a bar to play music. Patrons would linger, enchanted by his flute. And so the Yates family prospered. Arvel doted on Georgette, who warmed his heart like no other. He brought home ribbons and trinkets, dolls and fancy dresses, and shoes galore for his little darling. Arvel Jr. received only a few coins or pieces of candy. Gunter continued to visit Arvel's dreams, warning him that tragedy would strike if he didn't hide the flute away, for he was ignorant of how to use its power. Mystery, too, warned him in increas-

ingly strident tones. Arvel ignored them, though a creeping feeling of dread took hold that became difficult to shake, even during the best of times.

One summer, Arvel journeyed with friends to a large swath of redwoods in Siskiyou County near Mt. Shasta that they intended to purchase and harvest for lumber. Mystery and several pigeons from the growing flock went along. After surveying the area and working out the logistics, the men signed a contract for the land. They made their way home, absent a few pigeons who liked the area so much they decided to remain. But when Arvel returned home, he learned that his beloved Georgette had died from complications of scarlet fever. She'd been taken so swiftly, it was a shock to all. Arvel collapsed upon hearing the news and took to bed, aching all over, crying out in pain. Lucille called in the local doctor, who tried all the remedies at his disposal. Nothing helped. His condition became grave. The doctor said there was nothing more he could do. Arvel had lost the will to live. As he lay dying, he told his wife and the doctor about Gunter and the flute. He mentioned the warnings Gunter had given him and described Mystery's voice in his head, sounding the alarm. Convinced the flute was what had caused his and Georgette's demise, he begged Lucille to bury it deep in the ground where no one could retrieve it. Then he passed away.

At the dead man's bedside the doctor looked at Lucille's face, which had lost all color, and escorted her to a chair in the living room.

"What am I to do, doctor? Are we cursed? Is his flute really made from a child's shinbone? What a horrid thing."

The doctor patted her hand. "It's just the ramblings of a delirious man. I've seen this sort of malady many times. Nothing to worry over."

Shortly after Arvel's burial, Lucille found the flute among the few things he'd brought back from his trip to Siskiyou County. She thought the notion of burying the flute ridiculous and put it in a curio cabinet. She confided to her closest friends that the flute had been one of her husband's finds and was supposedly made from a human shinbone. The doctor spoke of it, too. And tales of the flute's powers spread, but to everyone who heard and repeated the story, it was mere folly, meant to entertain. No one believed it was even made of bone. And so the story lingered—enough for the lane to land a mention in Bancroft's Tourist's Guide to San Francisco.

One day, when Lucille was old and infirm, an archeologist came to visit and asked about the flute. She hobbled to the cabinet and brought it to him. He confirmed it was hewn from the shinbone of a child seven or eight years of age. Aghast, she hid it away, and when people asked about it, she said she must have misplaced it. She never told anyone where it was, not even Arvel Jr., fearing her husband's bedside rantings were true and her son might succumb to its powers. She needn't have worried. Arvel Jr. wanted nothing to do with the flute or the lane named after it. When Lucille passed away, he made enough money to build a home in Pt. Reyes Station by divvying up the farmstead for people thirsting to live on a hillside with stunning views no matter what it was called. Eloise's great grandfather was among them. So was Frederick Yates, Ted's grandfather and first cousin of Arvel.

Some particulars of the tale have changed through the years, but as far as anyone alive knows, nobody ever found the shinbone flute. Mystery and several other dazzling pigeons stayed on, though, all living longer than birds possibly should. Captain's the only one of their descendants left now.

MADDY LET THE WORDS SETTLE, then turned to Clara. "It's wild, really wild. ... Captain's right here on Shinbone. ... so ... the story's still alive in a way, don't you think?"

"That's it exactly." Clara raised her cup. "I could use a warmup, couldn't you?"

CHAPTER

SEVEN

At sunrise on the third Saturday in July, the fog enveloping Shinbone Lane bloomed with iridescent colors that swiveled, shimmered, and swirled before slowly burning off. An auspicious sign, according to most residents. Their usually quiet two-and-a-half-block lane—a textured mosaic of stones, smoothed and worn by countless footsteps, wagon wheels and later cars—would soon pulsate with people trickling in from around the city for the annual Shinbone Fair. Amateur vendors arranged makeshift displays showcasing new creations and neglected castoffs: chapbooks typed and stapled the evening before, a local band's concert tapes, velveteen vests stitched by hand, refurbished antiques, homemade pastries and sweets aplenty, and jumbles of junk and hidden treasures heaped onto folding tables.

Amid palpable and growing anticipation as opening time drew near, Captain waddled into Ted's garage turned workshop and watched his friend rub a cloth over the gleaming base of a 1940s Waring blender. The bird flew up to a shelf at Ted's eye level and sniffed in the familiar mix of leather, sawdust, lemon oil, rose petals, weathered books, and other earthy smells. But another scent was in the air, one that caused Captain to fidget. He moved his head side to

85

side and conveyed that he was hungry directly to Ted's mind. Then he opened and closed his beak, turned in a circle, tapped his spring leg on the shelf and looked beyond the open garage door.

Ted followed the bird's line of sight to Chip, who was arranging pastries he'd gotten up at four o'clock that morning to bake. As morning unfolded, an enticing smell drew the residents of 346 from their beds and into the kitchen, where they nibbled the samples Chip had set out. The taste, they all agreed, was like dormant hopes given life on a breeze. Captain had yet to have a taste. He'd been busy dive-bombing a coyote that had slinked into the yard and threatened to wreak havoc at the fair. Captain finally drove the coyote off, but by then, the samples were all gone.

"It's unjust," Captain said.

"I'm sure Chip will let you have a taste later." Ted resumed polishing the blender.

"I was defending the lane. That should count for something." The bird jumped up and down, hopped from real to artificial claw, spun around, and repeated the syncopated sequence with the abandon of a drummer doing a solo on stage.

This caught Chip's attention. "You want something, Captain?" The young man's black curls bobbed as he put the finishing touches on his display of homemade baked goods and punch.

"He was busy this morning chasing off a coyote, so he didn't get a chance to taste your pastries," Ted said.

Chip, who like most people couldn't hear Captain, chuckled and said, "We'll have to do something about that."

Captain flew from the shelf to the low branches of the ripple tree by Chip's table. The heart-shaped leaves danced in the wind. The bird craned his neck and peered at a plate of brownies. If he could have growled, he would have when he saw Eloise approach.

"What are you selling here, young man? I couldn't stay away. The closer I got to your table, the more my heart fluttered." Eloise bent down and scrutinized each tray of pastries. "How did you do this? Their aroma rivals Star's scones, and that's saying something. No one else has the touch."

Chip shrugged. "Beats me. I'm just happy to be able to bake. I've never done it before. I always wanted to, but my parents wouldn't allow it. My job was yard work with my dad. Period. After Sunrise came along, she was in the kitchen with Mom."

She pursed her lips and squinted at Ted. "Are you sure this lad didn't put some sort of drug in here? I wouldn't put it past anybody living at 346."

"Nice to see you, too," Ted said to Eloise.

Eloise reached into a box that held free treats, for it was a tradition at the fair that everyone selling goods designate some items to give away. She took a bite from a chewy cookie with a blob of apricot jam in the center. "Oh, this is a surprise, out of this world! I feel young and lithe again. Star doesn't sell anything like this. Maybe they'll pay you for the recipe, or hire you, hmmm? They just lost one of their girls. She ran off like you young people do all the time these days, like you don't have families who care about you."

"That's enough, now," Ted said to Eloise. "Chip didn't run off with your daughter. Nobody here did. You know that."

"Someone knows where she is, though. I don't suppose you've thought of that. No, of course you haven't. You're not a parent." She squared her shoulders, did a demi-plié, and lifted one leg into an arabesque pose. Then she sniffed, lowered her leg, and stormed off.

Chip turned to Ted. "She's really got her dander up."

"She hasn't heard from Julianna in quite a while. Nobody has."

"At least she cares." A palpable sadness wrapped around Chip's words.

Ted returned to polishing, and Chip tossed a cookie to Captain.

"Finally," the pigeon muttered. As soon as his beak touched the treat, he envisioned a female pigeon with plumage even more striking than his own. She sat on a branch, alone and lonesome.

～

As fairgoers gathered at 29th and Shinbone, volunteers found creative ways to keep people from entering before the nine o'clock opening time. A yodeler, a magician, a clown, and a balloon artist took turns entertaining the crowd. The flaxen-haired Barb and Bea, whose beautifully tapered eyes expressed a universe of emotion, showed off their improvisation skills, giving folks a taste of what was in store for the evening show.

Meanwhile, Maddy arranged and rearranged a card table with sketches and notecards she'd created since deciding to live in Clara's attic apartment, at least for a little while. Vending for the first time ever made her jumpy as a girl about to give her first piano recital. In a box marked "Free," she placed one of her favorite scarves; a dog-eared copy of T. H. White's *The Once and Future King*, a bestseller released only a few months prior; and a patchwork shirt fashioned from squares resembling the American flag and others in a floral design. She'd found the scarf and shirt at Rosie's sidewalk sale, which had become a must-do Saturday activity for her.

At the adjacent table, Clara hummed a medley of show tunes as she arranged hats, vests, afghans, and scarves. Despite her advanced age, her nimble fingers had been busy. For the last month, after knitting or crocheting on her front porch during the day, she'd continued working in front of her black-and-white TV in the evening. She, too, set aside a few of her favorite belongings to give away.

"I still can't believe that fog, all those colors." Maddy pulled up a folding chair and sat down. "There must be some explanation for it, right?"

Clara explained that the fog has been magical on the third Saturday in July for as far back as anyone could remember. People would watch in awe from their windows and porches but never did more until Dave arrived at 346 six years prior. "As it burned away, he climbed the hill and let loose a mandolin improvisation that brought everyone out into the street, dancing and singing. That lit a fire under us, and we each spontaneously ran inside to retrieve something special to give away.

Long into the evening, we exchanged gifts and shared food and drink. It changed us, made us better."

"You've done it every year since?"

"My, how it's grown. We sell things now, too, but we always set aside a few favorites to give away. It wouldn't be the Shinbone Fair if we didn't."

Laughter drifted their way as parents from Happy Days preschool set up a temporary children's area in Clara's ample side yard. Those with a theatrical flair pitched a tent for telling stories to tots. A few parents manned an arts and crafts table. One mom with a steady hand lined up paints and glitter so she'd be ready to fashion flowers and hearts and stars on children's faces. As Clara and Maddy watched their neighbors scurry about, Lark stopped by to hand each one a copy of Shinbone's origin story in booklet form.

"This looks mighty nice," Clara said.

"Our very own lore is now preserved." Lark backed up, ready to leave, but then Maddy's notecards caught her eye. She thumbed through them. "I absolutely love these. You've captured emotion, you know, even what the buildings are feeling ... and your ripple tree renditions are ... transcendent. I see it now in a new light."

"Thanks." Eagerness tickled Maddy's gut at the thought of making her first sale.

Lark thumbed through more cards. "You know, I was green with jealousy over your hair the day I first saw you, by the way, but then you jumped right in to help me with proofing, and I got over that. But now I'm green with envy over your artwork."

"I'll never write poetry," Maddy offered.

"I want to buy some cards, for sure." Lark ran a hand through her pixie cut. "But I have to go help Bea and Barb finish making scenery for tonight's show. They roped me in yesterday. I'll come back later."

"That would be nice." Enthusiasm waning, the teenager pretended to brush dust from one of her sketches and then skimmed a program distributed by members of Shinbone Friends. "Where are you in the lineup?"

Lark pointed to the program list. "I'm right there."

"Deely and the Frogs?" Maddy would dance on her back deck whenever she heard the band practicing. "Dave plays so many instruments. I love the mandolin best, I think. ... So you're one of the Frogs?"

"No, no." Lark pointed again. "I'm one slot above them. I love Dave's music, too. ... I've had a crush on him since the first time I watched him play."

"I can see why," Maddy said.

"It's kinda hard living in the same house as him. The proximity ... it's ... I thought there was something special between us, but whatever it was lasted about a minute. Now he barely knows I exist."

"Give it time," Clara interjected. "Girl as pretty and talented as you? He's bound to notice."

"I'm, oh, I didn't mean to dump my woes on you two. I don't know what got into me." The twins waved to Lark from across the lane. "I gotta go. They need me now."

As CLOCKS and watches along the lane ticked and clicked toward opening time—some lagging behind by a minute or two, others speeding ahead—Rosie finished arranging and rearranging second-hand clothing, satisfied with the look of the tables she'd hauled out from her garage. In her free box, sat a lime green cashmere cardigan, a fleece vest, a meerschaum pipe, and several enticing bracelets, brooches, and earrings. She would be able to sell them all easily at a routine Saturday sale, but in keeping with the spirit of the day, generosity was uppermost in her mind. This was true for the other vendors, too, all of whom took great care when picking items to give away. All except for Eloise, that is. The dancer's home sat far uphill near the back boundary of her land. Her views were rumored to be spectacular, but it had been years since she'd invited anyone beyond the dance studio on her ground floor.

Rosie looked up at Eloise's and imagined enjoying the view from the wraparound porch, but she didn't expect to ever be invited up there, given how often Eloise criticized her. Rosie rolled her eyes and berated herself for not standing up to Eloise—or Wayne, for that matter. Then, with beaded bracelets and earrings jingling like wind chimes, she sprinted uphill. Lucas bumped in a pack on her back. Heather trotted by her side. Exchanging brief hellos with neighbors as she passed, Rosie didn't stop until she reached 346, just as Sunrise plowed down the front stairs. Heather ran squealing to Sunrise, then peppered Chip with questions about his pastry display.

"Are you sure it's not too much trouble?" Rosie asked Chip.

"Are you kidding? The girls will keep each other occupied. You're doing me a favor." His deep brown eyes beamed with reassurance. "I can walk them across the lane to the children's area. A couple parents from the preschool said they'll keep an eye on them for a while. And when they've done all the activities there, they can poke around here with me and Ted. There's tons of fascinating stuff in Ted's workshop."

"I really appreciate it." Rosie took Chip's hand and squeezed. "Heather would be bored spending the day at my tables when there's so much to see here. And Wayne can't help. He took a last-minute job clearing out a seriously cluttered spare room for somebody or other."

Chip squeezed Rosie's hand in return. "How about if we bring you some lunch later on? I've heard there's a potluck buffet set up at lunchtime at The Farmhouse. Is it as good as everyone says it is?"

"Yep." Rosie broke into her first smile of the day as she described dishes brought the year before: Ted's spaghetti with tangy sauce and garlic bread, salads and desserts of all sorts, and sandwiches galore— Waddles Fenton's turkey meatloaf being the favorite by far. "So, I'd like a meatloaf sandwich, for sure. Heather will probably go for a PBJ. Even those are better at the fair."

"Like camping, you know? You grill chicken over the fire, and it tastes way better than when you cook it in your kitchen."

"You're right about that." Rosie glanced at her watch. It was eight fifty-five, time to get back to her tables before the crowd swarmed in.

She gave Heather a last hug before Chip handed each of the girls a bite-sized brownie.

They tittered with delight as they bit into the treats. Then Chip ushered the girls away from his table. "Let's go. It's almost time to make masks from paper bags." The girls raced ahead to the children's area to claim bags and chose supplies from bins of pipe cleaners, tissue paper, beads, feathers, crayons, charms, and assorted odds and ends.

Rosie reached her table just in time to greet a young man she hadn't seen before. He was looking at crystals she'd hung from a display made from driftwood.

"Hello," she said, wiggling Lucas out of the backpack and putting him on a blanket scattered with his favorite toys.

The stranger looked up and smiled, but his blue eyes held a penetrating sorrow that suggested the movie *Love Story*, when Ali MacGraw's character, Jenny Cavalieri, died. Rosie turned away to catch her breath.

CHAPTER

EIGHT

When Shinbone's '74 street fair was in full swing, fairgoers lingered with pleasure at residents' displays. Pecking along at their feet, Captain made the rounds, snatching morsels dropped by people who nibbled homemade fare while seeking the perfect bargain—the one brilliant find they could bask in for years to come. They inspected merchandise, poking and haggling, more for sport than penny-pinching, since prices were already low. Captain sampled tidbits up and down the block instead of sticking close to Ted, where he felt safe from felines stalking and people gawking.

For Captain, Ted was all the good in the world condensed into human flesh and bone. The man had saved his life. That was when Ricky, who lived with his mom next door to 346 for a short time when he was a boy, scaled the fence with destruction in mind. He then climbed to the loft where Captain was a fledgling in a thriving flock and set fire to them all. Ted and several other residents rushed to save the birds. Of the half dozen they managed to wrest from the flames, Captain was the only survivor. One of his feet was burned so badly, the vet had to amputate it.

Captain lay on the edge of death in a lonesome cage at the veterinary hospital when Ted confronted Ricky's mom, Natalie, at her house. Ted later described Natalie's gruff welcome, with no small talk and no seat offered when he stepped over the threshold and relayed what the boy had done.

In response, Natalie shouted so loud her words rang in everyone's ears up and down the lane, as well as in Captain's ears several blocks away. "That's nuts, nutso, nutty! Not my Ricky. No, no!"

"Ma'am, I saw him drop a blowtorch right before he jumped back over the fence into your yard. Others saw him start the blaze," Ted said.

"Did not," the boy said, voice trembling as he peeked out from behind her skirt.

"How dare you accuse my son! You and your like and those horrid birds on this precious lane of yours, always thinkin' you're better than us. No time for people sufferin' right nearby." She turned red orange. Her body expanded, her skin taut as a balloon stretched thin. "Wait till my husband comes home. He'll burn your entire house down. See how you like that, you busybody, sticking your nose in where it doesn't belong." She lifted a vase full of irises and took aim.

Ted bolted seconds before glass broke against the closing door. Her threat was empty, however. No one on Shinbone had ever seen her husband. And before week's end, mother and son snuck off in the night.

Years later, Captain rarely thought of the boy whose cruelty had left him without a family and with a wire prosthesis where one of his claws should have been. But he did remember Ricky's smell, and when he got a whiff of his former tormentor, he stopped gorging and followed to the source: a young man with dark brown hair falling just above his shoulders. Wearing faded bell bottoms, tie dyed T-shirt, beaded necklace, and Birkenstock sandals, he blended into the crowd. The pigeon followed Ricky as he made his way up the block. He complimented a budding fashion designer on her patchwork jackets, admired a display of kites fashioned in bold colors, spent a long time talking with a family selling used books, and bought a vial of patchouli from a woman hawking essential oils and incense. Ricky uncorked the oil, took a long whiff, and continued strolling.

At Ted's garage workshop, fairgoers, elbow-to-elbow, checked out the free, refurbished goods. Out front, Chip's pastries, considerably thinned out, continued to tempt everyone who passed.

"Hey there, what's in this drink?" Ricky asked.

"Trade secret, I'm afraid." Chip grinned, his gapped front teeth on full display. "Want a sample?"

"Maybe later."

"Don't wait too long. People can't get enough of it. This is our last batch."

Ricky lifted an arm to take another whiff of patchouli. The bird swooshed forward, grunting, and bit his big toe.

"Hey, what is this?" Ricky shook his foot, trying to loosen Captain's grip.

The vial slipped from his grasp and fell into the punch bowl. The drink's fruity scent mixed with patchouli smelled so bad people in line to purchase a cup all gagged and turned away. Ricky dislodged Captain and grabbed for him, but the hybrid pigeon flew to Ted and landed between his protector's feet.

Ricky glared at Ted. "My toe's bleeding. I should sue you!"

"That guy dropped something in the punch," Chip said.

Ted squinted at Ricky. "It's just a little scratch you have, but Chip's punch is ruined!"

"It was an accident, for cryin' out loud," Ricky said, lips quivering. "You're just a bitter old man with a grudge. And that bird should be in a cage." He slapped the punch bowl before quickly folding back into the crowd.

"You know him?" Chip asked.

"I didn't think so at first, but then I recognized his woeful eyes. He and his mom lived next door for a short time, less than a year. He must have been around eight." Ted said. "Looks like he's still got some growin' up to do."

Smarting from the wallop Ricky had dished out during their tussle,

Captain hobbled to the backyard where two rock pigeons pecked the ground for crumbs. He winged up to a loft Ted had made for him and watched the pair below. He felt a familiar twinge of longing for companionship with one of his own. There had to be others like him out there somewhere. With that thought, Captain drifted into sleep and dreamed of gliding in a wide circle above an oak in the wild, calling and fluttering his wings while coming in to land.

AT DAY'S END, many fairgoers carried bags with small treasures and sleepy children with painted faces toward nearby homes, cars, busses, and streetcars. Others brought blankets and camp chairs to the open, grassy top of Shinbone Hill, content to wait for the evening show to begin.

Clara sipped from the glass of lemonade she'd been nursing all afternoon. Fatigued after hours at the table, she rose from her chair and fanned herself with a program. "Whew, it's been quite a day." She smiled at Maddy, amused to see the youth guzzle her fourth bottle of Calistoga water for the day.

Maddy threw the empty bottle in their shared trash bag and lamented that she'd made only two sales. "I was hoping for more. ... Oh, well, at least there's Paul."

"You can do better than mailing packages for some fly-by-night film operation."

"It's part-time, totally flexible, and he pays me under the table. What's not to like about that?"

"The fair's not really about making money anyway." Clara didn't say more, fearing her skittish tenant would clam up if she offered too much advice. She stretched toward the sky to loosen her joints and get blood flowing.

A puff of wind ruffled items on their tables just as Ricky stepped from the dwindling crowd, picked up one of Clara's berets, and turned toward Clara. "Are you doin' that hatha yoga or something?"

Clara brought her arms down. "Goodness, no—just trying to wake myself up." She pointed to the hat. "Berets are all the rage now, especially multicolored ones like that, or at least that's the word on 24th Street where those boutiques have cropped up."

Maddy eyed the hat. "Those shades of blue, green and purple play off of each other like—"

"Here." Ricky put it on her head. "Looks great on you."

Clara agreed. "Like it was made for you."

"How much?" He reached into his pocket and pulled out a roll of bills.

The teen ripped off the hat and threw it on the table. "I, I can't accept. I didn't come here for—"

Ricky let out a low whistle. "Easy now. Who says I'm giving it to you?"

Maddy flushed. "Of course. How silly of me." She wiggled in her seat and appeared to study the passing crowd.

"Anyway, it's good to see you again," he said to Maddy, who stood up abruptly, knocking over her chair in the process.

"You okay, dear?" Clara asked.

"I'm fine, just fine." Maddy bent down and righted the chair.

After an awkward pause, Ricky asked Clara, "So how much is it?"

Clara asked for two dollars. While Ricky peeled two singles from his roll, Maddy bolted inside the house. Clara accepted his payment and tucked it into her cash box.

"I was just kiddin' around with her. We met in Colorado. Never thought I'd see her again." He looked over Maddy's sketches and paused at one of Captain. "Stupid bird," he groused.

"What?" Clara asked as she wrapped the hat in tissue paper and put it in a small paper bag.

"I can't believe he's still here," Ricky said.

She studied the young man's face, sensing something familiar about him, but she couldn't figure out what it was. "You from around here?"

"You could say that. My mom used to know your daughter. I just found out."

With a knot of emotion clogging her throat at the mention of Tilda, Clara looked away, coughed a few times, then looked up.

He thrust the bag at her. "I think she should have this."

She held up her palm and shook her head. "You'll have to do that yourself."

With his mouth downturned, he said, "Thanks for nothing, I guess."

"Are you giving up just like that? She wouldn't want to know a quitter. I'm certain of that."

He rubbed a finger across the letters MM that served as Maddy's signature below Captain's peg leg, then picked up the book in the budding artist's free box. "Hey, I've heard good things about this. It's supposed to be a great book." Ricky tucked the novel in the bag. "Tell her thanks," he said, and walked away.

It wasn't long before Maddy slinked back to her seat. Clara wondered why a little bit of flirting would rattle the teenager so, but sensed Maddy wouldn't be able to answer if asked.

"That boy says thanks for the book. He likes you, you know," Clara offered.

Maddy reached down and slid a cardboard box from under her table and slammed a drawing inside.

Clara packed her wares with care, glancing sideways at Maddy's frenzied motions. "You're like a wild horse, corralled," she said. "I don't think he's out to hurt you."

THE TWILIGHT SKY glimmered gold and bronze, and puffs of wind ruffled greenery along Shinbone Lane while vendors tucked unsold treasures safely away. Everyone—except for a few whose energy had flagged— joined the growing audience on the hilltop. Opening acts for the evening show engaged the crowd, including a nine-year-old ventriloquist whose goal in life was to get on the Johnny Carson show, eight O'Grady children in traditional Irish dress dancing to the beat of a bodhrán, and several tone-deaf members of a glass-blowing collective who studied harmonica with a member of Dave Deely and the Frogs.

When Maddy arrived, avocado sandwich in one hand and picnic blanket in the other, Lark waved her over to a group seated in a semi-circle. She hesitated, her longing for friends at odds with her need for privacy. Curiosity about the neighbors she'd been observing from afar won out. She approached the group.

"Hey, sorry I had to go before I could buy any of your cards," Lark said as she helped Maddy find a spot next to Chip.

The artist waved it off. "It's okay."

Chip held out a hand. "I've been looking forward to getting to know you."

Maddy clasped his hand. "I love your van. I've sketched it a lot."

"I'd like to see them sometime," Chip said. "People here named it Crazy-Wild."

"Before you settle in, let me take you around to meet the gang." Lark said. "Come over this way."

They walked around the circle, where Maddy met people she'd nodded to in passing, including a jewelry designer who sold necklaces made of lupini and navy beans dyed bright colors and strung on fishing line and a husband-and-wife clothing design team about to open a boutique on Cortland Avenue. They mentioned needing help in the store soon. Maddy demurred, doubting they would pay as well as Paul did. Next, Lark introduced two women who belonged to a women's collective two doors down from 346. They'd recently opened a cafe on Church Street. They, too, were hiring and said every worker got a free meal each shift. Maddy agreed to think about it but didn't seriously consider the offer.

Lark was just about to introduce Maddy to the twins, but they headed for the stage before she caught their eye.

"Oh, I forgot," she said. "They're up next—and they have no script. Isn't that just the bravest?"

Maddy had to agree. "I can't imagine getting on stage."

They returned to their spots just as Captain waddled over. He poked the teen's ankle as she sat down. "It's about time you stopped hiding from everybody." His voice came into her mind.

Maddy put an elbow against her knee, leaned her chin on her fist, and stared at the bird. "I haven't been hiding, not really," she finally whispered.

"If you say so," Captain replied, then flew to a gaggle of children surrounding Rosie and Wayne, who were making s'mores at a hibachi.

Taking the stage, the twins immediately captivated the crowd. They morphed into a variety of characters in response to audience suggestions. They went from Billy Jean King and Phyllis Diller doing the can-can, to a couple of gum-chewing teenagers trying to fashion their hair like popular actress Farrah Fawcett, to characters from *All In the Family* and *The Waltons* getting into fist fights over whether anyone should be called "Meathead."

After several more acts, Lark drew the audience in as she read several poignant poems from her chapbook. Deely and the Frogs followed her and introduced new folk-rock originals that got everyone up dancing. As people moved about, a warm white light spread among them, each person's aura mixing with the others until the entire audience and the musicians on stage were immersed in it, feeling weightless and free.

From a balcony of her home above the gathering spot and far removed from the rest of the houses, Eloise scanned the scene with binoculars for signs of Julianna. "Someone in there must know something," she said to Coco, who slumbered on her lap.

At the edge of the crowd, Ricky stood rigid by a kerosene lamp placed at the perimeter. His eyes returned again and again to Maddy, whose lush brown hair swayed with the beat. Longing to dance with her, he dipped a foot toward the light but swiftly retracted it. His knees quivered at the unfamiliar feeling of circulating joy.

NINE

Approaching Vicksburg Street on the last day of July 1974, Maddy carried a Just Desserts slice of coffee cake and a cafe latte for her employer, Paul. After the fair, like many others on Shinbone, she'd settled into a rhythm of work, creative pursuits, and small adventures. Everyone agreed it was a smashing success—except for Eloise, of course, since Julianna did not show up. As she strolled along, Maddy reveled in how well her first real job was going. She hadn't even babysat for neighbors back in Yellow Springs. She spent all her time outside of school with her mother and little brother, Tyler. This meant keeping her eyes on a rambunctious little boy and a woman whose grasp on parenting was as weak as a paper chain.

Now Maddy had time to herself and a small stash of cash tucked into an embroidered box she'd scored at one of Rosie's sales. She had a wardrobe of offbeat clothes and scarves that suited her spirit. And her sketches filled the walls of her room, a sanctuary, something she'd never dreamed of, let alone had.

She turned a corner onto Vicksburg, but instead of the quiet street she was used to, the block was ablaze with activity. People gathered on the sidewalk, forming a ring around something unfolding in front of Paul's place while three men in dark suits kept onlookers at bay. Maddy reached the group just as a man in a navy-blue suit escorted her boss out the door, his hands cuffed behind his back.

Maddy gasped and dropped the bag. The coffee cake bounced onto the concrete. She gripped the cup until some of the contents spurted onto her hand. "Ow!" she cried out and dropped that, too, splattering coffee on her shoes.

Some of the liquid sprayed the loafers of a woman standing next to her, who scrutinized Maddy. "Say, don't you know this guy?"

Maddy backed away. "No, you're mistaken." Maddy turned and ran.

The woman called out. "Sir, sir, there's a youngster running away who knows something. I'm sure of it."

Without looking back to see if an agent followed, Maddy turned onto 24th Street and ran full speed down the block. When she reached Real Foods she slowed down, her sides heaving and heart galloping. She slipped inside and feigned interest in an aisle full of soaps, shampoos, and lotions. Calmer now, she went up and down the aisles, never putting anything into her cart. At the produce section Maddy stopped in front of the apples. Her mind wandered to Keeley's parting words: "Nothing lasts forever. Look at the Beatles. No more songs from them, mind-blowing as they were. That's how life is, cupcake."

A worker adding oranges to a bin near her pointed to a display. "Try the pink ladies. They're really good."

Maddy picked one up. The smooth skin felt good in her hand. "I think I will," she said. "Thanks."

She kept an eye out for men in dark suits when she left the store and fretted her way home. What am I going to do for work now? Is this a sign that I should move on?

THE MORNING the FBI hauled Maddy's boss away, middle-aged Eloise *chasséd* up Shinbone hill, lithe as a fawn. She reached the lane's prized coast coral tree, which sported red flowers year-round, and stretched fingers toward the clouds. The tips of her toes barely touched the ground before she lowered her heels and arms and sat by the tree. The lane was unusually still. She leaned her back against the trunk and closed her eyes. Then, exaggerating the expansion and retraction of her chest, she rocked her head to one side, then the other.

Coco sat beside her and rocked her head, too. Eloise repeated the motion, gradually letting more of her body move, starting with her neck and collar bone, then the shoulders, and down the spine until she was moving from her waist. With hands on knees and elbows jutting upward, Eloise let her body lead the gradual changes as she had done long ago with her best friend, Tilda.

She extended an arm and flexed a foot, relaxed, then did it again, continuing to let the movements evolve as she recalled the grand plans she and Tilda once had. Her memories of the summer they flew to New York to attend Martha Graham's dance school when they were seventeen arose fresh and visceral. She felt the studio's wooden floor, the hot air against her skin, the proximity of other dancers. She saw Tilda's sweet smile as they whispered in their rented room and made grand plans. Inspired by Graham, they would take their own version of modern dance around the world. They had pushed one another daily to do more with their bodies, certain they'd become world renowned one day. But reality obliterated that dream, dashed by Tilda's parents, Clara and Matthew.

Coco rolled onto her back and slow-motion pedaled her paws in the air. Eloise reached behind her back. With arms straight, she clasped the tree and rose a fraction of an inch at a time to a standing position. Then she slid down. Without pausing, she angled up again, grabbed the trunk, and leaned away from the tree, stretching more than seemed humanly possible. Then Eloise let go and rolled down to a ledge, where she perched, legs dangling.

She surveyed the lane, so quiet in the late morning. She wished Lark had joined her, for when the poet let loose on the hillside, her beauty shone through, despite her overbearing glasses and baggy clothes. Seeing that beauty lifted Eloise's spirits. She felt a short burst of kindness for the bedraggled youngsters who continued to pass through the city despite the Haight-Ashbury's fading star.

Losing Tilda hurt like silence in a room that once held laughter. After that, she danced out of habit—no more hunger, no more joy. She'd done one tour with Martha Graham but wasn't asked to join the company. Heartbroken, she returned home to form a troupe that gained support among friends and neighbors but received tepid reviews from the *Chronicle* and *Examiner* newspapers. So she found purpose in teaching dance to children. She followed the career of Marin County choreographer Anna Halperin. She even danced barefoot beneath redwoods at her far more successful contemporary's studio. And then came the affair with an exquisite male dancer, an Adonis, who didn't want to be tied down. From that came Julianna, her Julianna, who danced with Eloise on the hillside all her life, first watching from her baby carriage, then toddling along, then quickly inventing moves Eloise had difficulty following.

Julianna. Eloise had locked up the dance studio on the ground floor after her daughter went missing. She couldn't bear the sight of the barre, the mirror wall, the wooden floor polished to perfection, let alone conduct classes there. Where was Julianna? Someone must know something. Eloise had an uneasy feeling the answer was hidden on the lane, but where? Frustration propelled her into a series of jagged, warrior-woman moves. She would find her child somehow, wouldn't she? Out of breath, she sank down again. Coco, panting, crawled into her lap.

Eloise scratched her companion behind the ears while Maddy trudged up the lane like a prisoner on a forced march. "That child lives in the attic that used to be Tilda's." The dancer gnashed her teeth with rage. "If she only knew what had happened, she'd run from Clara as fast as she could." The dog nuzzled her hand.

❧

MADDY SLOGGED up the front stairs and onto the porch. Clara, seated on a wicker loveseat while stitching multicolored yarn into a vest, sensed something amiss. She put her knitting down and opened her arms to the teen, who nestled in and recounted the scene that had unfolded outside of Paul's. When she finished, one tear escaped her eye. She wondered aloud what she could do now. A sense of loss bigger than a lost job bled from Maddy to Clara. Stroking the girl's hair, Clara began "Climb Ev'ry Mountain," a quaver growing in her voice as she sang. The teen's eyes closed, her breathing slowed.

Across the street, Chip plopped on his bed, eager for a nap after spending hours in the darkroom in the back of Ted's workshop. Ted, meanwhile, repaired an antique rocking horse while envisioning some tot riding it on adventures yet to be imagined. Sunrise, Rosie, and Heather played Twister in Sunrise's room. All three giggled when they lost their balance as they tried to place their hands and feet on the mat's colored circles without touching any white space. In the kitchen, several residents discussed current events while a pot of homemade vegetable soup simmered on the stove.

Then Dave Deely's inimitable guitar licks burst from the backyard and spread expectation all along the lane. To most folks on Shinbone, Dave was a virtuoso on par with Carlos Santana. Maddy and Clara sat up straight and listened. Residents of 346 stopped what they were doing and headed out back. Neighbors joined them. Folks rarely spoke of the yard behind 346, which stretched beyond ordinary limits without affecting surrounding properties. They did not attempt to explain the inexplicable. They went with the flow. On their way to the music, they followed a trail that wended through foliage and trees. They passed a hut used by ceramic artists, a yurt where people did yoga and practiced meditation, and entered the insulated, A-frame structure where musicians gathered.

As the building filled, Lark tucked into a corner, making herself as inconspicuous as possible. As Dave and his band conferred about what tunes to practice for their next gig, a bearded man in loose fitting white pants and tunic called from the entrance. "Dave Deely, you son of a gun!" The man tightened a fuchsia sash at his waist and strode forward. Following him were a dozen other men and women dressed the same, except each wore a different color sash.

"Russ?" Dave's eyes brightened "Is that you?"

"It's Abbudin now."

"You're one of those—"

"Sufis, yes."

"Whirling dervish and stuff. I wondered what happened to you, man."

"Spirit happened." Abbudin waved the white-clad group to the stage.

"No more music?"

"It's music all the time now. We show devotion through melody, harmony, note upon note," he said. "We came to the city yesterday to do a workshop and thought we'd drop by to see how you're doing. I've heard good things."

The white-clad group gathered around Abbudin and hummed. Dave stepped aside as harmonies filled the room. Abbudin conducted with hypnotic motions, his back to the gathering crowd. The music, an amalgam of influences from around the world, brought balm to even the most guarded hearts in the room.

After the first piece, everyone clapped, and Dave said, "That was amazing."

Abbudin nodded to Dave, and with a wide sweep of his arms, asked, "Join us?"

"Sure, but not too long. We've got a tour to prepare for," Dave said.

"I remember those days," Abbudin replied.

Dave and the band added their voices, guitars, and drums to the mix as Abbudin and the chorus broke into polyphonies and cadences that were ever more intriguing. Soon everyone, even Lark, took part in creating music that penetrated deep into their psyches. They danced and swayed, and in that moment, there was nowhere else they wanted to be. In time, Abbudin gradually slowed the chorus down and brought the music to an end. In silence, those gathered sat still, keenly aware of their breath in a new way. Abbudin and Dave embraced.

"I've missed you, man," Dave said.

"You know, we live in Sonoma County off of a winding road. It's isolated, peaceful. On the ridge you can see for miles. It's the quietest place you'll ever find." He pulled a business card from the pocket of his flowing pants and handed it to Dave. "You're welcome anytime. There's a little town nearby called Ripplewood, too, and rumor has it there used to be a grove of trees with heart shaped leaves like the one you have out front. That's how the town got its name, old-timers say, but I've hiked all around there and never seen a tree like that until right here today."

"Interesting," Dave said. "That could be where Arvel Yates, the first settler to build a home here, found it. He brought back a dozen or more, so the story goes, but the one out front is the only survivor."

The two hugged again, and Abbudin headed for the door with the chorus right behind him. He spotted Lark in a corner, watching the crowd. Abbudin stepped over, squeezed her shoulder, and leaned down. "The divine flows through you," he whispered. "You'll go far."

Lark thanked him, hoping he was right. Then she dashed to her room to jot down the beginning of a poem that had come to her during the unusual performance.

Abbudin and his followers shared hugs with people as they wended their way out of the yard, through the main building, and out the front door. Behind them were Bea and Barb, whose improvisations had delighted the crowd at the recent fair's evening show. And when the group boarded their refurbished school bus, the twin thespians from 346 boarded, too.

CHAPTER

TEN

Maddy drifted to Rosie's Saturday sidewalk sale after dawdling the morning away. She perused racks, stacks, and bundles, but nothing caught her eye until she dug through a box of books. She brought her intended purchase to Rosie, who furrowed her brow at the calligraphy manual in Maddy's hand.

"No scarf for you today? I've got a new batch." Rosie pointed to a woven basket replete with silks, cottons, and wools in vivid colors.

"Not today." Maddy took a dime from her wallet. "I lost my job. I'd just gotten into the groove of it. Then poof! It was gone."

"Sorry to hear that. What kind of work do you do? Maybe I know of something."

Nervous, Maddy chuckled and brushed her long bangs from her eyes before explaining she'd had a part-time girl Friday sort of job for a guy who made bootleg movies, not knowing what he did was illegal.

"Was it that guy over on Vicksburg? I read about the raid."

Maddy feigned interest in a pair of socks on the table.

"You weren't there, were you, when the FBI came?"

Maddy gave a flicker of a smile. "No, but if they'd come a couple minutes later, I would have been."

"You shouldn't mix with shady people like that."

"He wasn't really shady. He broke the law, but it's not like he was distributing pornography or anything close to that. He sold classics, you know, *Casablanca*, *The Big Sleep*. Every now and then he'd get a recent one—like last month he was copying *Young Frankenstein*. He had a gazillion customers; one of them must have turned him in. I don't know what I'll do for work now."

"Looks like you're already moving on." Rosie gestured toward the calligraphy book and mentioned a woman living up on Clipper Street who did a brisk business addressing wedding invitations.

"I was thinking I might try it." Maddy had seen a flyer offering calligraphy services on the Acme Cafe bulletin board. More than half the phone-number tabs at the bottom were torn off. "This is ten cents, right?"

Rosie shook her head. "Take it. No charge. I'm selling whole bags of books for a dime today."

"You sure?"

"Absolutely." Rosie turned toward a young man looking at an antique waffle maker. "It works," she said to him.

Book in hand, Maddy meandered to Color Crane, the art store on 24th Street, where she picked up two calligraphy pens. Then she checked out the bulletin board at the Acme to see what was new. Amid all the batiking and Aikido classes, support groups, roommates wanted and all sorts of things for sale, she saw a poster for a job distributing flyers. She passed it over at first but then tore off a phone number tab from the bottom and tucked it into her pocket.

Back at the attic, she unpacked her new tools. And when she opened the instruction book, the rafters vibrated, creating a soft hum that filled her with optimism. But after practicing until her right hand ached, she looked at her efforts and found her letters lacking. She feared her calligraphy book would end up stuffed into a trunk at the foot of her bed, where she'd already stashed a dulcimer kit she'd ordered from the *Whole Earth Catalog* and had yet to open, along with a half-completed cable-knit sweater she'd ripped apart several times and given up on because she kept dropping stitches.

Maddy closed the book, capped her pen, and flopped on the bed. Realizing it would take longer than she thought to get up to speed with calligraphy, she pulled out the phone number she'd ripped from a flyer. She lifted the receiver of the pink Princess phone Clara said was hers to use as long as she didn't run up long-distance charges. She dialed the number while carrying the phone to her desk, grateful that it had a long extension cord. The rafters, still humming, buoyed her as she sat down and heard a male voice say, "Hello."

After an awkward pause, Maddy said, "Uh, I'd like to know about distributing flyers. The poster at Acme Cafe?"

"Glad you called. I was beginning to think nobody would. I'm overwhelmed with posting." After he explained the basics of the job, he said, "You've got a bike, right? That's how I get around."

"Sure," she said, though she had no bike and not enough money to buy one.

ON A DAY that many San Francisco residents would call balmy, Natalie grumbled under her breath about the heat, though it was only seventy degrees and breezy. She checked her Timex every half block or so as she strode along 24th Street from Noe Valley through the Mission. After she crossed Bryant Street, she slowed, checked her reflection in a storefront, primped her hair, and smoothed the front of her pink-and-green striped kaftan before pausing at the door to St. Francis Fountain. As soon as she walked inside, Truman waved from a booth in the back. She strode forward and slid in across from him, noting he wore the same rumpled clothes he'd worn the day he dropped in on her.

He pointed to a chocolate soda at her place. "It's still your favorite, isn't it?"

"What is this? You callin' me, sayin' it was urgent that I meet you here."

"You sure look fine, doll."

"Wish I could say the same for you." She unwrapped her straw and folded the paper into a mini accordion shape before jabbing the straw into the soda and taking a sip. "Mmm, it's good." She looked around the old-fashioned stop. "Jeez, I haven't been here since—"

"Graduation, 1953."

"I coulda come after that. Lotsa times. What do you know? Zip."

He took a bite of a chocolate sundae. "Nothing beats these."

"Just get to it."

"Lighten up, will you? I can see you gussied yourself up."

"A woman can't walk out the door in her housedress." She took a long, slow draw and quivered with delight at the taste before leaning forward, squinting. "Why are you trying to butter me up, meeting like this at—"

"Our spot, where we first kissed."

Natalie jerked back, her head thumping against the back of the booth. "We're too old for that flirting business."

"Middle age is not old."

"What's so important? Some sort of scam?" She squinted again.

"Not exactly. I mean, it wasn't meant to be one, but ... you know how these things can go."

"Some things never change." She took another slog of soda.

He scooped in several bites of his melting sundae. "I went straight after the joint, you know, but this job, the one I got goin' now, it's getting outta hand, way too complicated."

"What's in it for me?" She stuck a long spoon into her glass and fished for a dripping blob of ice cream.

"I have this client who's expecting results, but I need more time. The broad's in a hurry, though, wants to see for herself what I've dug up. I need help with legwork, finding plausible details."

"You've been stringing her along and she's called your bluff, right? Like I said, some things never change."

"Her dad's the one who roped me into this. I'm just trying to find a good way out for all concerned."

"Speaking of dads. Have you seen yours since you arrived?"

Truman squirmed in his seat, his discomfort palpable. Then he blurted that his father had died.

"That mean bugger kicked the bucket, huh?"

He gulped down the rest of his sundae, lifted the dish and licked it clean. "He disowned me, so he said, when I went to San Quentin. We never talked after that, not even once. But he left me his savings in the end. Feels good to have some money in the bank for a change."

"Funny, I just got some unexpected inheritance, too."

He leaned forward. "Really? What sort of inheritance?"

She tightened her lips and stirred her straw in the dregs of her soda. "So tell me how I figure into plans with this so-called client of yours."

"When she comes to town, she'll need a place to stay while I orchestrate things."

"When's that?"

"Sooner than I want."

"Why bother when you got this nest egg from your dad and all?"

"The thing is, the whole job was a wild goose chase, a sham invented by her dad to keep her from cracking up while she's healing from some pretty heavy injuries. And I guess you could say it's gotten out of hand. See, there was this explosion. A whole building— smithereens—and people died, kids died, her little girl gone ... but she doesn't know she's really gone, you know, dead. She thinks her daughter was kidnapped. That was her dad's idea, and now I'm stuck keeping the ball rolling. On the bright side I can keep earning money and give her something to sink her teeth into here, something to satisfy her urge for results until the inevitable can't be put off any longer."

"You're sure in the thick of it now." Natalie smirked and dabbed a napkin to her lips.

CHIP PULLED HIS VAN, Crazy-Wild, to a stop in front of 346 and jumped out whooping. The sound brought an abundance of Shinbone residents to their front windows. Some thought he'd landed a job, others insisted he must have scored some potent pot, some believed the young man with bouncy black curls was just a little exuberant by nature, which was fine with them. None of them guessed he'd just found a deal on mirror squares in the *Bay Guardian* classifieds and bought enough to fill an entire wall of his room.

Chip had already painted his walls deep pink, a color his parents had called "girly" and forbidden him to use when he was growing up. They hadn't allowed him to pursue photography, either. Now a Nikon F2 camera Ted had fixed up for him swung from his neck. He lifted the camera and took a few shots of Clara's home across the street, happy to be pursuing one of his primary passions at last. Maddy waved to him from her attic window.

He waved back and broke into his gap-toothed smile. "Come on over," he called to her. "I'm gonna do some redecorating."

Maddy hesitated but then put her charcoal down and headed downstairs.

"This is my place, my time," Chip said to himself as he opened the van's sliding door. He lifted a box of one-foot square mirrors with adhesive on the back.

A few roommates who'd been milling about in Ted's garage ambled over to help carry boxes up to Chip's room. Maddy grabbed one, too. Roused from a nap by footsteps on the stairs, Sunrise followed the noise to Chip's room, where roommates and neighbors gathered, propelled by curiosity. Lark was the last to squeeze in.

Chip pointed to a blank wall across from his waterbed. "This is the best place for the mirrors. I don't want them behind the bed."

Maddy circled the room, studying the options. "You're right. It's the only spot that'll work. I mean, there's built-in drawers and shelves everywhere else, except where the bed is."

"You can't cover the pink." On the verge of tears, Sunrise spit out the words. "We picked it out together."

"Not to worry, pumpkin," Chip said. "It'll still show on the other walls. Plus, you can dance in front of the mirrors. Won't that be neat?"

Sunrise's lower lip protruded while she thought it over. Then she plopped on the bed. "Okay, I guess."

Stacks of photographs toppled over, and several slid off the bed as Sunrise landed. Lark, who'd been standing nearby bent down and picked up the fallen photos. The shots were from the fair's evening show. "I'm not sure I've ever seen photos this good." She handed one to Maddy, who had come over to help. It was a close-up of Dave singing. His lips almost kissed the microphone. Raw emotion rose from the paper. "These could be in a gallery show."

Lark asked Chip, "How did you do this?"

Chip shrugged as he finished opening a box of mirrors. "I really don't know." He crossed the room to Lark, who usually reminded him of Éowyn, the victorious warrior maiden in the Lord of the Rings trilogy. But today, she looked deflated, like Eleanor Rigby in the Beatles song. He hugged her and said, "I bet you can't explain how you do poetry, either."

"But these portraits are incomparable," she replied.

"I think it has more to do with the subject than with me."

"I'm surprised he's not here right now," Lark said, more to herself than to Chip.

"He's on the phone with his grandfather. The old man took a spill a few days ago. Dave's really worried about him, calls him a couple times a day."

"That's too bad. His granddad got him into music really young."

"I think it was ukulele when he was three or something—along with Hank Williams songs. And music is what saved his sanity when he returned from Vietnam," Chip confided.

Lark's eyes swelled with surprise. "He's talked with you about that?"

"Yeah, some."

Rubbing a finger across Dave's face in the photo, she said, "What a gift you have. I used to think I had something special, but that was long ago. I don't think my poetry will ever be as arresting as your photos."

"You're all of, what? Twenty-two? There is no long ago for you, and there are no limits either."

"Yeah, no limits, Lark." Maddy waved her arms in the air.

"No limits for any of us," Chip called out. "No limits, even when we get old."

"Like when we're sixty-four?" Lark, buoyed by their enthusiasm, chimed in.

Several others in the room sang a few bars from the Beatles song "When I'm Sixty-Four," an age that seemed eons away to all of them.

Whether it was the times, which showed signs of optimism with the Vietnam War's end; the women's movement; and underground music, magazines, and movements of all kinds; or whether it was the nature of 346 and the people mingling there; no one knew or cared. They were all certain the future would be brighter for everyone because they would make it so. Laughter and banter continued while Chip inserted a tape of Deely and the Frogs, and bowed in front of Lark, inviting her to dance. She stalled, pulling down her T-shirt to cover her thighs, then took Chip's hand and danced the old-fashioned jitterbug. Soon everyone let loose, trusting that no one there was judging their movements, a contrast to the restraints of far-flung homes where they'd been raised.

ELEVEN

Looking forward to meeting friends at the Day Park playground, Rosie held tight to Heather as they entered the crosswalk at Sanchez and 29th streets. One-year-old Lucas bounced in a pack on her back. Heather, in tears because Rosie had refused to buy treats at the corner store, yanked and twisted, trying to break away. "I want an IT'S-IT, Mommy! I want one!"

With her free hand, Rosie patted a bulging woven bag slung over her shoulder. "We've got snacks right here, remember? And we can make our own treats at home. We've got Bud's vanilla in the freezer. Fresh, home-made cookies, too. No IT'S-IT can beat that."

Appeased, Heather fell in step with her mom. Halfway across the intersection, Rosie recognized Maddy and Lark bicycling downhill. She ushered Heather to the curb just as a black-and-white puppy romped into the street, chasing a cat that jetted out from under a car. "Oh, no! That harebrained puppy's off leash again."

Maddy and Lark both braked to avoid the pup. Lark leapt off her bike, landed hard, and twisted her ankle. Her bike fell sideways and slid several feet. At the same time, the rear wheel of Maddy's bike flipped up. She leaned forward. Tumbled headfirst over the handlebars. Slammed onto the pavement. The bike landed on top of her, wheels spinning in the air. Just then, Chip pulled to a stop in Crazy-Wild on Sanchez, turned right, and accelerated up 29th.

While Maddy struggled to sit up, a Chevy Vega barreled toward her, its horn blaring. Chip screeched to a halt, leaped from the van and rocketed toward Maddy. The Chevy swerved and smashed into a parked motorcycle, sending it flying toward the fallen teen before the Vega crashed into a weathered Volvo sedan with a *bam! clang! clunk!* that reverberated up the block. The stench of burning rubber permeated. Maddy howled when the motorcycle landed on her leg. Chip managed to free her from the motorcycle and carried her to the corner where Lark now sat at the curb.

"I'm scared, Mommy," Heather said.

Rosie hugged her daughter. "You're safe, honey. You're safe. Let's see if I can help." She ran, with Heather at her side and Lucas blubbering on her back, to her friends. Maddy, eyes half-closed, was still in Chip's arms.

Rosie put a hand on Lark's shoulder. "You okay?"

"Oh man. I feel awful. Ted just gave us the bikes to test drive. I mean, really, just a few minutes ago. Maddy's got some job she needs a bike for, and I was supposed to help her, you know, get used to biking here. Now look at what happened. I shouldn't have led her down such a steep hill first thing."

"It was an accident, plain and simple, not your fault." Rosie poked through her bag for change before stepping into the nearby phone booth to call for help.

Neighbors crowded around, intent as seagulls stalking tourists' French fries at the zoo. Truman, in a soiled shirt, rumpled suit jacket, stained slacks, and frayed fedora, left the market with a pack of Camels in hand. He saw the mangled cars and groaned.

A stocky teen appeared, shaking, from the Vega. "Oh man, I'm screwed!" he cried out, sweat beading on his pimpled face. He ran to the corner. "I wasn't gunnin' for you guys. Honest." He looked from Lark to Maddy. "The brakes, they didn't work."

"It's okay," Lark told him. "You only hit a car."

While Truman muscled through the small crowd toward the youth, Chip carried Maddy to the van, where he nestled her in with pillows before loading the bicycles in the back. He then insisted that Lark get checked by a doctor. She protested that she'd only twisted an ankle. He persisted, and she finally consented. He helped her into the passenger seat, and they headed for San Francisco General Hospital.

Meanwhile, Truman confronted the lad. "That's my ride you just smashed up." He stood chest to chest with the youngster and pushed him backward. "I bet you don't have insurance. You're not even old enough to drive, by the looks of you."

"Don't answer him, and don't fight back," Rosie said to the youth. She pointed to a patrol car pulling up. "Just talk to them."

"Well, look at you, little miss busybody. What do you know?" Truman challenged.

Rosie, intimidated but determined not to show it, narrowed her eyes. "You'd be surprised."

Truman scoffed and lit a cigarette.

The police questioned the young driver and several witnesses. Then they situated the driver in the back of a patrol car and drove off.

Lucas whimpered and squirmed. Rosie sat on a nearby stoop, wiggled the pack from her shoulders and prepared to breastfeed.

Heather sat down and leaned her head on Rosie's arm. "Will they be okay?"

"I'm sure they will, honey. The worst is over."

"Can I have an IT'S-IT? Please, please, pretty please?"

Rosie sighed and pointed to her bag. "Take a dollar bill from my wallet and be quick."

WORD of the accident jolted folks into action. Clara dropped her knitting, pulled out her Shinbone Friends membership list and made calls. Waddles sped to Clara's to help, waving in passing at Ted, who was making sure his truck was in top working order in case he was needed to ferry anyone or anything. While nobody knew the extent of the young women's injuries, Shinbone residents erred on the side of too much action. They never wanted one of theirs to be laid up without hearty meals and pleasing treats to get them through.

Rosie donated two woven baskets for gifts that were already arriving at 346's front door. Star Bakery bagged up cookies, doughnuts, and brownies; the German store on Church Street donated bottles of Kneipp herbal bath; Verona's offered a gift certificate for two large pizzas, no expiration date. A neighbor who made soaps and lotions provided samples for each basket; a student of traditional Chinese medicine offered acupuncture treatments, something most residents had never heard of. Gifts continued to arrive, and somehow, without appearing to expand, the baskets squeezed every donation in.

Eloise refused to contribute at first. "Nobody is helping me find Julianna," she huffed and hung up the phone when called. But at the last minute, she thrust two hastily scribbled gift certificates into each basket. They guaranteed three months of lessons at her dance studio, even though it was closed due to Julianna's disappearance.

By the time Lark emerged from Crazy-Wild, with an Ace bandage wrapped around her ankle and gripping Chip's arm for support, one apparently bottomless gift basket and a slew of homemade meals were already on 346's kitchen counter. A matching set was also at Clara's.

Once inside, Chip and Lark confirmed that Maddy wasn't coming home yet. She had a concussion, a sprained wrist, and various scrapes and bruises in addition to the burn from the motorcycle.

"A concussion could be serious." Ted left at once to tell Clara, who was on her porch puzzling over why Maddy hadn't arrived along with Lark.

Upon hearing the news, Clara made for her stairs with the focus of a greyhound chasing a rabbit. "Poor girl. I must go there. Someone has to be with her."

Ted followed and put a hand on her shoulder to slow her down. "I'm not sure that's—"

She stopped and faced him. "She has no family, or that's what she believes. I'll tell them I'm her grandmother."

"She's in good hands, I'm sure."

"She doesn't know a soul there. You must take me right now. The old Packard's on the fritz again, otherwise I'd drive myself." She backed up one stair and wobbled. Ted held tighter to help her regain her footing.

"I need to grab my favorite pillow. Then I'll be fine."

"Clara, you're eighty years old—"

"I know very well how old I am, and what I'm capable of. You, of all people, should know that."

Ted gave in, chortling. "Okay, I'll pull the truck up and take you and your pillow to Maddy, Grandma."

On the way to the hospital, they passed Ricky, who carried a bag of groceries up the 29th Street hill toward his mother's Castro Street home. He noticed what looked like a daypack in the gutter and crouched to get a better look.

RICKY PACED 28th Street between Church and Dolores streets. Each time he reached a three-story building with a small rose garden in front and attached garage, he paused, ran a hand through his shoulder-length locks, and blinked his deep-blue eyes. Memories he couldn't tamp down swirled.

The ornate yellow Victorian with off-white and cranberry trim was a source of pride for people on the block. Every December the owner, Ted's friend Harold, decorated it with an ever-growing collection of lights, angels, stars, glittering trim, reindeer, a working model train, and more. On Christmas Eve, Harold dressed up as Santa and, with the help of teenagers dressed as elves, handed out candy canes to young and old alike who dropped by. Ricky, who had once been among those helpers, peered up at the apartment above the garage, recalling the warm light that filtered into a room where he'd spent many hours in his troubled youth.

After lingering more than half an hour, Ricky crept to the apartment's slender door. He pressed his face against a dusty square of glass, with hands cupped on either side so he could see in. A familiar staircase with a few bags of books cluttering the right side came into view. Pulse kicking up, he stepped back and rang the bell.

A man with white hair and mustache opened a window and leaned out. "Hey, Ricky, it's been a while. I'll buzz you in."

The lock released with a wheeze. Ricky opened the door and bounded up. Harold gave him a warm smile and hug when he reached the top. The young man leaned away, socked by emotions that took him by surprise.

Harold dropped his arms. "So, what's up?"

"It's not a problem, is it ... that I came?"

"I said when you turned eighteen and I'm saying now, you can call on me anytime."

"People say lots of things they don't really mean, just to soothe things over, or whatever."

"What good does bitterness do?"

Ricky swiveled to face the stairs. "I should go."

Harold tapped the young man's shoulder. "I just made a big pot of chili. You hungry?"

Ricky's stomach grumbled at the thought. "Like you used to make on Saturdays? Nothin' beats that."

"Come on, then."

Harold waved toward the kitchen. Ricky followed, the throb of impossible longings pressing just beneath his skin.

"There's shredded cheddar and soda in the fridge." Harold pulled utensils from a drawer. "And you know where the napkins are." After placing two spoons on the table, he lifted the lid from the pot simmering on the stove, took a good sniff, and stirred the chili with a ladle. "Mmmm, grub's ready. I'll dish it up."

At Harold's 1950s Formica table, the two dug into the meal, swiftly finishing two bowls apiece. Harold patted his stomach with a satisfied sigh.

Ricky guzzled a Coke, put the can down, licked his lips and cleared his throat. "So, well, I'm back at my mom's."

"That's the last place you need to be. I thought you'd be all set after VISTA."

"Who's going to take care of her if not me?"

"She's no good for you, that woman."

"She's my only family."

Harold threw up his hands and leaned back in his chair. "Nothing I say will get through to you, not when you're with your mom."

"I guess that's that, then." Ricky stood, jaw tight, and started for the hallway.

"Why did you come by? Must have been a reason."

Ricky stopped, a trace of hope almost within reach, and spun around to face Harold. "I found something that doesn't belong to me, and I don't want to give it back. I'm kind of on the fence."

"Did you tell your mom?"

"No."

Harold gestured toward the vacated chair. "Talk to me, son. All you'll lose is a little time."

Ricky picked at his teeth while deciding whether to confide in Harold, then returned to the table and opened up about finding Maddy's backpack. "I know she's hiding something. I could stir the pot with that. I probably shouldn't, but I want to."

"Darn right, you shouldn't."

The two debated, their voices rising and falling as their remarks shifted from congenial to heated and back. The afternoon crept by. When sprays of late-afternoon fog slopped over Twin Peaks, Harold picked up the phone. He placed a call to a household of young adults who were doing well after aging out of foster care. He asked if they had room for one more.

TWELVE

Maddy flitted through time in fitful dreams that blended pieces of the present, past and imagined future into a confounding brew. One moment sidewalk-sale Rosie was at Maddy's eighth grade graduation, walking next to her in cap and gown. Moments later, Maddy walked with her parents through a violet-colored mist—Dad with a gas-pain smile, Mom staring up at clouds while holding her second-born child, Tyler, in her arms so tightly Maddy thought his eyes might pop out of his head. Then she drifted to her bedroom and watched herself stuff a backpack. In went a change of clothes; her sketchbook and pencil case packed with charcoals; $166, her life savings wrapped in a bandana; a troll from Oliver, her first and only crush. He'd treated her to an ice cream cone that day, her birthday, walked her home, kissed her lightly on the lips at the door. Her first kiss.

Then he'd asked her to the movies. "Wanna go see *Sleuth* tonight?"

"Um, my dad says I can't date yet, you know, really date, date."

"Meet me there, then. Say you're going with Dorrie. That's what best friends are for, right?"

Smitten with him from the moment they'd met at a pool party on Labor Day, she couldn't say no. "Okay, yeah. I'll do it."

But instead of meeting him later, she'd opened her bedroom window and left her childhood behind. In her dream state, though, she didn't hit the ground. She landed in a bathtub full of hot, soapy water. She sank below the surface, kicking and thrashing, desperate to get back inside and run to the living room where her father was lying to the police. She fought to the surface and gulped in air before submerging again. She wanted to stick up for herself, tell the truth. There must be evidence pointing straight where it belonged. At her mother.

Maddy flailed in the water. She'd promised to stay home, keep an eye on things, but how could she have guessed what would happen? Why did he expect her to act like an adult? And why did he want her to say she'd drowned her own brother? She'd been wrong to leave the two of them alone. But this punishment didn't fit the crime.

The bottom of the tub dropped farther and farther below. She tried to rise. Strong hands pushed her back. Up, down, up, down, up, down, she went until, exhausted, she stopped resisting and fell, moaning, onto a floor. A voice came through, scaring her more than the water:

There you are. Yes, it's time. Fun time. Come, come, honey-bun, bright eyes. Ready? Let's see. Bath crayons. Bubbles. Little blue boat. Yellow ducky. Warm water flowing. Is it hot? Too hot? Let's test it. Oh, it's fine. Your bitty toes will love it. Where are you, little one? Ah, behind the hamper. You little sneak. No time for hide and seek. Water's nice and high. Too high? No, no, no. Just right.

Come, come now. Off with your T-shirt, your pint-sized jeans. Down with your undies. There now. Look at you, naked angel. See your toys? See how they float and bob? Don't you just love them? I know you do. In you go. Splish splash. The water's just right now. Not too hot like last time. We're good, aren't we, little child of mine? Precious one. Stop that squirming. See me pour the golden shampoo into my palm. It's magic. No tears if it gets into your eyes. Oh, child, don't look so worried. There's nothing to fear.

No slapping. Don't knock my hand away. Do not—oh, look what you've done. Shampoo's in the water. Wasted. Money doesn't grow on trees. What'll I do with you? What'll I do? Wait just a minute, there. Are those tears? Stop your blubbering. There's no call for that. It's just a bath. Quiet down. Quiet. Don't, don't make a scene. It's just a bath, a little bath. Stop it. Don't try to stand up. Don't make me hold you down. Watch it! You're soaking me. You mustn't do that. Never, never get me wet.

Shhh. Enough. I said enough. Okay, you asked for it. Dunk time. One potato, two potato, three potato, four and ... up. Shhh. You know better. Let's dunk again. Settle down. You give me no choice. One potato, two potato, three potato, four potato, five potato, six potato and ... up. Stop that wiggling. Down you go again. No counting this time. Just. Stop. Wiggling. Relax. No more fighting. That's it. There you go. No more troubles. No more tears. You're happy now. Peaceful. So beautiful. My child.

Maddy floundered, breathed in water. Was she channeling Tyler in his last moments? Or was she the one drowning? It hurt like someone stubbing out cigarettes in the lining of her lungs. If only she'd gone straight home that afternoon, kept an eye on things. If her puppy love for Oliver hadn't drawn her away, Tyler would be pestering her to play hide and seek, whisper secrets by their faithful tulip tree, or snuggle up with his favorite book, *Corduroy*, at bedtime.

She floated again, a limp sack of regret. Then another voice rippled through. Was someone singing that song from *The King and I*, the one about whistling a happy tune? Trying to rise, she stroked through water now thick as sludge. The voice grew louder. Who was it? So kindly. More than she deserved. Maddy gripped some sort of cloth. A sheet? Was she on her back? Where was she? She opened her eyes to white walls, insistent beeps, harsh cleaners masking decay. Had her father locked her up? Had the past year and a half not happened? Was she back in Ohio?

Clara patted her hand. "Thank goodness you're awake. You were thrashing to beat the band."

Maddy flinched at first, not sure what was real. Then, slowly, Clara's touch cut through, and her body softened with relief. "Clara? Are you real, *really* real?"

Clara leaned forward and whispered, "Best call me Gramma, for now. I had to use a little white lie for them to let me stay here."

"Them?"

"You're at San Francisco General. It's about 5 a.m., and if all goes well, you'll be coming home soon."

RICKY TURNED up his coat collar against winds spiked with ocean salt. Half a block ahead, his mother's home shimmered, a sign she was plotting something. Coming up her front walk, he passed a beat-up Volvo sedan in a driveway so overcome with weeds, it was almost impossible to distinguish from the gnarly lawn. Wondering what his mom was doing with a car since she didn't drive, he scaled the steps and opened the door in slow motion to avoid creaking in case she was napping. He heard her voice when he strode the hall, boards groaning underfoot. At the kitchen doorway, he stopped.

Natalie snapped her head in his direction and sneered before returning her gaze to a man seated with her at the table. "Well, lookie here. It's the prodigal son himself."

The man, dressed in a suit that looked like it came from the free box at the local community store, took a drag on a cigarette and blew smoke rings while regarding Ricky with bloodshot eyes. "You don't say."

"I'm not prodigal," Ricky said, defensive.

His mother glowered. "Mind your—"

"Just because I decided not to live here doesn't mean I abandoned you." He slid the groceries onto a stand by the stove. "You've got that Bible story all wrong."

She shrugged and gestured, palms up, toward the man. "See what I'm up against? He's got no respect."

"I'm gonna pick up a few things I left behind and get outta your hair, so you and this bum can get back to whatever you're cooking up."

"That's no way to talk about our friend Truman here."

Ricky snorted. "Truman, like that dude Truman Capote? You gotta be kidding. That's not a real name, I mean, for a guy who's not famous. It's like a stage name."

Natalie's nose reddened, nostrils flaring. "Why ever did I keep you, you ungrateful brat?"

"Yeah, ten years in foster care. Great job on that, Mother of the Year."

"Never woulda happened if you hadn't set that fire at 346."

Ricky held up a hand in protest. He pointed out that she'd egged him on, that the whole thing was her idea. She countered that he was more trouble than he was worth. He blasted that she left him alone, sometimes for days, when he was small. She growled that she kept him housed and fed, and that was enough. He snapped that the real problem was she never loved him. She trembled with rage. Her nose reddened. Her temperature crept up as they continued trading barbs.

"Listen, Nat, you've got to cool off. Breathe, will ya?" Truman said.

She brushed a few crumbs from the tabletop onto the floor and mumbled, "That was the beginning of the end."

"Like I'm the cause of all your troubles."

She gave her son a withering glare but breathed deeply. "If you only knew."

Ricky struck again. "You're probably behind on your rent, too."

"I won't have to pay rent here anymore. I'm an heiress now."

Ricky snickered. "You? Fat chance."

Truman took a drag on his cigarette and blew out. "Hold your horses, kid. I know your mom here can be a handful, but you gotta respect your elders."

"Yeah, get off your high horse. He's got an offer for ya," she spat out.

The man lifted a couple of fingers in a mock salute. "Truman Raddatz at your service."

"He grew up right on Cortland." Natalie beamed camaraderie at Truman.

"How come I've never met him before?"

"He got called away, so to speak." She tapped the torn vinyl seat of the chair next to her. "Come on, hear him out."

"Thanks but no thanks. I've got a job now, a good one."

"I suppose your new roommates are glad Bell Market took you back. They need you to make the rent. Bunch a Moonies is what they are, livin' all packed in together. When they gonna marry you off?"

Ricky gripped the back of a chair. "They're not Moonies," he said, though he suspected a couple of them might be. "Didn't you host a seance here last week with some fake medium? Like you even know what a seance is. I bet you snookered a few, though."

Natalie doused her son with impatience. "Give him a minute, for Christ's sake. If you don't like what he says, just leave like you always do."

Truman stubbed out his cigarette on a chipped saucer. "So I'm in this here business of private investigations, been a little down on my luck lately—"

"Big surprise." Ricky looked Truman up and down, grabbed a frayed fedora from the table, and spun it around his finger. "That's your beater in the driveway, too, right? One side all dented in." He flung the hat off his finger.

Truman caught it, put it on Dick Tracy style, and smirked. "Never mind that, kid. I cut this break, got a big job. And I need help to wrap it up."

"Like I said, I'm employed now."

"Stacking shelves again. Whoop dee do." Natalie's grin exposed incisors jutting out from receding gums.

"I've got three shifts a week at Bell now."

Truman pulled a crumpled pack of Camels from his pocket and tapped out another cigarette. "This won't interfere—work, school, nothin'. You can do it in your spare time. I'll pay ya a couple bucks an hour under the table to take some notes, snap a few photos, and if you deliver, the money'll be real good."

"How good?" Ricky pulled the chair out and sidled onto the seat.

"Thanks for looking after me all week. I've been really blotto." Maddy sipped tea from one of Clara's mismatched china cups and savored the taste of orange spice.

Clara opened a tin of Salerno butter cookies. "Think nothing of it, dear. I'm just glad you're recovering so well from that terrible spill." She slid the tin across the table toward Maddy. "Do you like these? My brothers and I would put our little fingers through the holes in the center and wear them like giant rings until Mother told us to settle down and behave." She chuckled at the memory. "When I became a parent, I did the same."

"You have children? Do they live around here?" Maddy asked.

"I had one child, a daughter." Fast as a spark, the color drained from Clara's face in the late morning light.

Maddy rubbed a finger along her cup's gold trim, uncertain what to say next. "This cup might be my favorite. Where did you find them all?"

Clara gazed out the window as though in a trance.

Maddy blew bangs from her eyes and reached for a cookie. "I've never had these." She took a bite. "Mmm, this is good." She nibbled and chewed in silence.

Clara put a hand to her heart and took a long breath. "The best." Her cheeks gradually regained color as she turned toward Maddy. "But, of course, you kids today don't want plain old cookies anymore. They're old hat. You like those brownies with marijuana and carrot cake. My goodness, every birthday party these days has carrot cake. People think it's healthier, but I'd wager it's got more sugar than any chocolate or vanilla cake."

"The frosting, though—you have to admit buttercream on a carrot cake is the yummiest."

"You can put buttercream on anything."

"Like butter cookies?"

Clara's eyes glistened with unspilled tears. "My Tilda would smear them with butter if I let her."

"I'd like to meet her."

"I'm afraid that's not possible. She's no longer among the living." Clara finished her tea and, with trembling hands, poured another cup.

"I didn't mean to upset you."

Clara loaded her tea with cream and sugar and stirred, concentrating as though she were learning a difficult crochet pattern. Then she put the spoon down and mustered a weak smile. "I shouldn't have brought her up. She's always on my mind when her birthday draws near." Clara gazed at a chandelier flickering above. "I should get that light checked out."

Maddy looked up, twisting several strands of hair around her finger before she reached for her teacup. She sipped in awkward silence, her foot tapping a staccato rhythm on the floor. Then she bent down to open the portfolio she'd leaned against a table leg and pulled out a poster. "I did this as a favor to Eloise. She stopped by the hospital when you went to grab a bite to eat with Ted. I mentioned I'd tried calligraphy but was giving up on it. She encouraged me to keep at it and asked me to do a flyer about Julianna." She handed Clara the flyer.

Clara examined it, lips pursed. "This is quite good. How did you do it with your wrist out of commission? You are right-handed, aren't you?"

"I'm ambidextrous."

"You're a girl full of surprises." Clara handed the flyer back.

"I'm sorry I brought Eloise up. I shouldn't have."

"You did nothing wrong. It's just that—" Clara's voice cracked, but she continued. "It's just that my Tilda and Eloise used to be best friends. They danced on the hillside the way Eloise does with Coco now. They thought they'd start a dance troupe and travel the world one day. It was like I had two daughters and then, well, it's all my fault, really ..." Clara glanced at her wristwatch. "Oh my, look at the time. We must get you to your follow-up appointment. We must make sure that pretty noggin of yours is okay." She stretched and groaned. "For me, everything creaks."

"I could go alone, take a cab maybe."

"I won't hear of it. You are my granddaughter, after all." She gave a conspiratorial smile. "And I just got the Packard running again."

CHAPTER

THIRTEEN

Making her way up the hill, Clara knew just where to step to avoid wobbles in the flagstone. It was the twenty-fourth day of August, nineteen hundred and seventy-four, and instead of humming a happy tune, which she often did, she huffed out a tiny groan with each breath. She reached a row of vine hill manzanita and sat on a bench dedicated to her daughter, Tilda. A golden fog wrapped her with the scent of Je Reviens, Tilda's favorite perfume. One by one monarch butterflies flitted to her, alighting on her head, shoulders, chest, arms.

Tears filled Clara's eyes as she reached into her coat pocket and pulled out a silver box with a mermaid on the lid. She lifted a silver bracelet with charms Tilda had collected: ballet slippers, a rough coated collie, a globe that spun in its holder, a dime, an empty heart locket, the Eiffel Tower, a Model T Ford, a pair of dice, an apple, and a teacup.

Clara brought the bracelet to her lips and kissed it. "My darling daughter, if only I'd—" she choked up. "You suffered, and I wasn't there."

She rubbed fingertips to her temple, and though she made no sound, her anguish carried to her sleeping neighbors. Each tossed and turned as grief wove into their dreams, and when they awoke, they shook off something they couldn't quite pinpoint. Meanwhile, Clara saw Tilda in her mind's eye. The vision of her vibrant daughter as a young woman warmed her, easing something deep inside. She got a stronger whiff of perfume, and her sense of Tilda's presence grew stronger.

"Happy Birthday, my darling girl. How I wish you were really here, that I could see you, hear you, touch you, even for only a moment. It's cruel torture. I must settle for hints, impressions, notions that may all be in my head. I wish I could feel grateful you were mine for eighteen years. Then—"

Tilda's words came directly to her mind, the way Captain's messages reached those who could hear him. Her voice was clear and mellifluous, just like when she was alive: "Enjoy the butterflies come to greet you during their annual migration, Mama, and forgive yourself for what happened. You are not to blame. You did your best."

"It's just like you, darling daughter, to not blame me." Clara blubbered and fished out a handkerchief to dab at her tears. "Others aren't so kind."

"Focus on the miracles in the moment and stop all that worrying over Eloise. She's in more trouble than you know."

"What kind of trouble?" The scent of Je Reviens began to fade. "Tilda? Tilda? ... Oh, darling, have you gone already? ... I will try, my girl, to stop letting the past chew me up inside. I will try to 'be here now,' as the youngsters say. I will try."

Clara waited for some time, hoping to hear her daughter's voice again, but to no avail. The butterflies flitted about her and formed a heart shape in the air before alighting on the manzanita branches. As the sun grew warm upon her back, Clara put the bracelet back in the box. She grasped a ring made of golden ribbon thin as string that her husband, Matthew, had braided for her when they were teenagers. "Matthew, my love, might I be able to forgive us both after all these years?" She replaced the ring, closed the box, and stood up.

Crouched behind a bottlebrush shrub, Eloise held Coco and accidentally knocked some pebbles downhill.

Clara looked over her shoulder. "Eloise, it must be you there, probably snickering at my attempts to commune with the departed. But I'm going to try not to flinch at your feelings and talk to you instead. Remember the parties we used to have on August twenty-fourth? And again on your birthday, the twenty-fifth? Wouldn't it be grand to bring the laughter back? Focus on the good, not the bad? Perhaps that's a way to lessen life's load for both of us. ... Tilda seems to think you're in trouble of some kind."

Eloise kept silent, jaw clenched at the notion of accepting any advice from Clara. Coco barked, wrestled free, and ran to Clara.

Clara scratched the back of Coco's neck. "Good girl, good little girl. Go tell your mom I'm too old to play hide and seek, too old to go on like this. Soon enough, I'll be too old to climb this hill." She straightened her back and began her descent.

Eloise watched from behind the bush. "Traitor," she muttered to Coco when the dog returned to her side, but she lifted the dog and held her close.

"You mean I can still have the job?" Maddy stood by her desk and twisted the extension cord in her fingers. "I can't believe the guy you hired quit on you. ... I can start on the first week of September, for sure." She declared this despite her doctor having advised her to ease back into strenuous physical activities slowly to ensure she fully recovered from the bike accident. Maddy hung up the phone and moseyed downstairs, wearing patchwork pajamas Clara had stashed in the attic dresser days before Maddy's arrival. The teen found Clara puttering and humming to herself in the kitchen.

Clara looked up, eyes puffy but bright. "You want some tea? I made a pot of Earl Grey."

"I'd love that."

While they chatted at the table, Maddy mentioned she would start posting flyers the following week. Clara questioned whether that was a good idea, but Maddy was determined to go ahead with the job.

"Will you at least rest for a few minutes at each bulletin board and quit working if you feel dizzy or have other unusual symptoms?"

"Sure, sure I will." Maddy took a sip of tea. "Speaking of unusual symptoms, well, this wasn't a symptom, but it was odd. I had my window open earlier, and I swear perfume was in the air. Did you smell it?"

"Je Reviens. Your mother might have worn it," Clara said. "It was quite popular with the generation between us. Now I guess Chanel No. 5 is all the rage."

"I've seen ads for that on TV. 'Every woman alive loves Chanel No. 5.' I've never heard of Je Reviens."

"My Tilda used to wear it, was her favorite. She would have been thirty-eight years old today, same age as Eloise. Their birthdays were one day apart. We had two celebrations back to back. The girls had sleepovers, so it was like one long party."

"That sounds like fun." Maddy ran her hand over the tablecloth as though smoothing wrinkles, but there were none.

Clara reached over and patted Maddy's hand. Their eyes met, and then they smiled.

"It's okay, dear," Clara said. "I was thinking of making a cake, for old time's sake, and giving it to Eloise even though we've been estranged for years. I've got a Duncan Hines devil's food cake mix and a can of double chocolate fudge frosting in the pantry. She used to be mad for chocolate."

"Once a chocoholic, always a chocoholic, right?" Maddy stood up, giggling.

Clara rose, too, and the pair busied themselves. Soon they slid the cake pans into the oven.

Clara sat back down at the table and sighed. "I need a little help with something else."

"What is it?"

"I've got a wooden chest in my bedroom closet. It's too heavy for me to lift. Can you bring it to the living room? I'll meet you there."

Maddy found the chest and carried it to the living room. Mahogany with gold bands, it reminded her of a treasure chest.

Clara opened the lid, pulled out a framed photo of Tilda, and handed it to Maddy. "That's my Tilda."

"She was beautiful," Maddy said.

"Indeed she was, dear—and a gift from God. We'd given up on having a family, and then in our forties, we conceived." Clara retrieved a few more framed photos and put them on the coffee table, her fingers lingering just a moment longer on one frame, as if tracing the past. "It's time I bring these out from hiding. She was much more than her tragic end."

As the cake baked, the two sang "Happy Talk," their voices buoyant as palm fronds in a warm island wind as they placed the photos around the room. In a few photos, Tilda stood alone; Clara, Matthew, and Tilda crowded together in others; several showed Tilda and Eloise arm in arm, heads together. Maddy put photos on the mantle and on book-shelves. She hung some on the wall in the foyer. And with each photo placed, the home shimmered with what Maddy likened to the light of love. It filled Maddy with a craving that left a bittersweet taste in her mouth.

A timer went off, and she took the pans out of the oven to cool. When she returned, she mentioned an open mic coming up at Moon-rise Cafe the last Friday of the month.

"Lark's gonna read. Want to go with me? I haven't been there yet."

"My, my, an evening out, and to an open mic, to boot. I've never been to one. I'll have to think on it."

While waiting for the cake to cool, Maddy sketched the mantle, and Clara finished knitting a yellow scarf. Afterward they frosted the cake together, with Maddy licking up plenty of frosting in the process.

When they finished, Clara sat down again and repinned a few wisps of hair to tidy up her bun. "You remind me of Tilda, your zest for life, how you take time to bring things out we might not otherwise notice, the feelings that come out of your work. I knew when I saw your drawing at the bus station that you had it."

"Uh, wow, um, thank you."

"Why not go to school? San Francisco Art Institute or maybe San Francisco State?"

"I don't have any college credits," Maddy said. "I don't even have a high school diploma."

"Smart girl like you. Why not?"

"Uh, I ..." Maddy stared at the cake and picked at a pimple forming above her eyebrow.

"Never mind. You'll tell me if and when you're ready." Clara got out Tupperware for the cake. "This should do the trick."

Relieved, Maddy transferred the cake to the container and headed for Eloise's.

MARCHING TOWARD ST. Paul's Market at 29th and Sanchez streets, Wayne almost plowed into Ricky, who was writing in a notebook while exiting the corner phone booth. "Watch where you're goin', man," Wayne grumbled as he sidestepped out of Ricky's path.

Captain sat on a tree branch high above the booth and shifted his weight back and forth from real to prosthetic claw. Inside the store, Wayne purchased IT'S-IT ice cream treats, a local favorite, for Heather and Rosie; a banana for Lucas; and a six-pack of Schlitz and the *San Francisco Examiner* for himself. Leaving the market, he saw Ricky taking photos of people passing by. Wayne paused near the doorway to push up his glasses. Ricky snapped him, too.

Wayne stomped forward. "What are you doing taking pictures like that? Who do you think you are?"

"Cool your tool, buddy." Ricky backed away from Wayne. "I don't mean anything by it."

"Something's fishy about this. You'd better—"

Captain swooped down and landed on Ricky's head. The young

man cried out, attempted to bat the pigeon away, and dropped his notebook in the process. The ragtag group of regulars who consumed too much alcohol to do more than gather, wobbling at the corner, hooted and cajoled while forming a half-circle around Ricky. Not one of them helped him disengage the bird.

Meanwhile, Wayne grabbed the notebook and scrambled away. At his repurposed delivery truck, he put the newspaper and bag of snacks inside, leaned against the front of the vehicle, and thumbed through pages of notes about local people. Many centered on folks who lived on Shinbone Lane. Some were about Wayne and his family, including detailed notes from Rosie's sidewalk sale earlier that day. Anger ricocheted through him.

Ricky freed himself from Captain just in time to see Wayne slip the notebook into his back pocket. With several strands of Ricky's hair in his claw, the bird flew to the eaves of the corner building and peered down. Ricky, rubbing his head, caught up to Wayne, who was about to get into his truck.

"You planning to make off with my property?" Ricky yanked the notebook from Wayne's pocket.

Wayne gave Ricky a look that could wilt a cactus. "What are you up to anyways, taking photos, making notes on everybody? It's invading our privacy." He got behind the wheel.

Ricky wiped a dribble of blood from his forehead. "I could be the next great American novelist for all you know."

"Stay away from my family or you'll regret it." Wayne started up the engine and sped home, slowing at stop signs but not coming to a halt until he was in his driveway. Once inside the house, he thundered straight to the kitchen, where Rosie and Heather, in matching flowered, granny dresses, shared a flurry of laughter while stirring cookie batter. Lucas sat on the floor banging an assortment of pots, pans, spatulas, and spoons.

Wayne plunked the bag of snacks onto the table. "We have to talk," he said to Rosie, then motioned to Heather. "Take your brother. Go watch a cartoon or something."

"But Daddy, we want to see what you got."

"Do what I said—now." The last word jolted like a slap.

Heather grabbed her brother's hand and ushered him away.

As soon as the children were out of earshot, Rosie asked, "Jesus, why do you have to be so hard on her?"

"You always think I favor Lucas, but I can't deal with that now. We have bigger worries."

"Life is good. You wouldn't believe all that I sold today. The morning air smelled like a lovely perfume, put everyone in a dreamy mood."

"That guy Ricky who's been hanging around—you know him?"

"I've seen him a couple of times."

"He was taking photos at the corner store and then got into a scuffle with that pigeon or dove or whatever it is."

"Captain?"

"Yeah, and he dropped this notebook. Man, he's taking notes on everybody, and I mean everybody, even Heather and Lucas. It's not right. He knows our habits, where we go, what we do, who we know. ... Nobody should be up in our business. It's time to move on."

"Why not just keep an eye on him for a while?"

Wayne scanned the tall corners of the room. "I'll miss these high ceilings." He reached for the bag, took out his beer and opened it.

Rosie spoke slowly. "Let's not be rash. We're building a life here."

"You know better than to push me, doll, don't you?" He took a long slug and sighed with audible satisfaction.

LARK'S SHOULDERS relaxed when she entered Moonrise Cafe for the first time. Three mics stood in front of an upright piano. A selection of hand-held percussion instruments sat in a basket nearby. The eatery created by Shinbone's women's collective looked to Lark like a welcoming place for budding musicians and performance poets. She took in the rest of the room. A few feet from the counter where customers placed orders, Maddy and Clara waved her to a table. She sidled through a sea of patrons, most of whom dressed in what looked like Army Navy Surplus and second-hand Thrift Town garb.

Maddy slid a cup toward Lark. "We got you a Mexican hot chocolate."

"Thanks." The poet hung her jacket over the back of a chair and sat down. "It's really packed."

"Some big name in women's music might be here," Maddy said.

"Women's music?" Clara asked.

"I read about it in this leaflet here." Maddy slid a flyer across the table to Clara. "All these amazing feminists like Holly Near, Linda Tillery, and Ida Lou Evers, they're proving that men are fine, but we don't absolutely need them to make great music."

Clara chuckled. "You youngsters think of the darnedest things."

Lark ran a hand through her short, dishwater blonde hair and took a sip of hot chocolate. "Mmm, this is tasty."

"We knew you'd like it." The teenager inclined her head toward four women talking and laughing at a table near the entrance. "I heard they're forming a band."

"Maybe you should join them," Lark said.

"Me?" Maddy shook her head. "I'm no musician. I could see the twins joining a band, though. When they improvised songs at the fair, they sounded great. I bet they'd love it here. ... Come to think of it, have you heard from them?" she asked Lark.

"Nope, but their mom phoned yesterday. Bea and Barb haven't checked in since they took off with Abbudin's chorus. She and their dad are worried because they usually call or stop by a couple times a week. It's not like them to be out of touch."

A member of the collective came from the kitchen and strode to the makeshift stage. "Welcome to our Friday night jam, where professionals and novices mingle and share music, poetry, and maybe new mixes never seen before," she said. "First, we have an open mic, then to my absolute delight, Belle Ely will blow us all away." She nodded toward a woman seated to her right who sported black hair resplendent with multicolored beads, a fuchsia satin pantsuit, pink silk shirt, lime-green necktie, and three-inch platform shoes. A gasp went through the crowd as Belle stood up and flashed an effervescent smile.

"After that, Belle will pick some of you to jam with her, and who knows how long you'll go?" The emcee held up a straw hat and stepped into the crowd. "I'll walk the hat around one more time. It's your chance for ten minutes of glory."

Lark slipped in a folded strip of napkin with her name on it when the emcee came by just before the open mic began. The first performers to take the stage were the women Maddy had pointed out earlier. They sang original songs in haunting harmony and accompanied themselves on guitar, piano, and banjo. Lark's thoughts drifted to Dave and how she wished he would notice her again.

Maddy tapped Lark's arm, "Earth to Lark. You're up."

"Oh, I spaced out." Lark pulled a spiral notebook from her pocket and tried to look calm as she approached the mic. Sweat beading above her upper lip, she muttered a quick hello, cleared her throat, and dove into reading. Shaky as a fawn at first, she gradually gathered power as she swayed and dipped with the words. The audience swayed with her. The lights above got in the act, too, twinkling to her undeniably musical cadence. Then, as her spirits soared and the audience was completely taken in, she threw the notebook down.

Lark performed poems from the heart, ones she hadn't quite worked out yet, letting them take shape in the moment. Listeners leaned in. She slowed down and improvised a poem she'd begun but hadn't been able to finish. After the first line, a haunting melody came to her, and the song flowed freely:

THE QUEST IS OVER; there is no Romeo for me
I never was much like Juliette anyway
And now my fine hair is graced with gray
The quest is over; there is no Romeo for me

. . .

Restless mirage of feelings finally stilled
  If only my heart had spilled and filled again
  But then I'm tired of waiting, wondering
  When, oh when, oh when?

The quest is over; there is no Romeo for me
  I didn't like playing Juliette anyway
  And now my fine hair is graced with gray
  The quest is over; there is no Romeo for me

When she finished, the room was silent as the pause when a baby takes in air before wailing. Then applause rattled the walls. Lark returned to her seat in a daze and consumed the rest of her hot chocolate in one gulp, hoping to calm her thrashing heart. She slowly relaxed as the open mic resumed with a variety of musicians, poets, and storytellers. Finally, Belle let loose with blues and gospel originals that in turns brought folks to tears and got them on their feet clapping and stomping.

After three encores, the show came to an end. While people milled about, Belle approached Lark and asked her to stay for the jam. Lark's heart pounded again.

Clara rose from her seat. "Give it a go. I'd stay and cheer you on, but it's way past my bedtime."

"Yeah, go for it," Maddy took hold of Clara's arm to help her navigate through the crowd. "But don't forget our bike ride tomorrow. We've gotta get back on the horse, as they say."

As the jam unfolded, Lark swayed to the music. Words came to her, and she surprised herself by singing responses to lines Belle threw out.

When the jam wound down, Belle handed Lark a piece of paper with her address and phone number on it. "A few of us are rehearsing tomorrow afternoon, about three o'clock. We're getting ready for a tour, a couple of spots north of here."

"You mean you want me to work with you?"

"You'll fit right in." Belle patted Lark on the back. "And I love to collaborate."

Back at 346, Lark leaped up the stairs to her room. Down the hall, light glowed from the bottom of Dave's door. She tiptoed forward, thinking she might share her joy with him. She put her ear to the door and heard murmurs. Bedsprings creaking. At 2 a.m. A bitter jolt ran through her. She fled to her room, pulled the door shut behind her, and sobbed a litany of pent-up woes into her pillow.

CHAPTER

FOURTEEN

At first light on the last day of August, Captain tapped on Ted's bedroom window, flounced his wings, and called in his gravelly voice, "Ted, my man, get a move on!"

Ted sat up in bed, stretched, and groaned before crossing a blue area rug to the window where Captain bobbed on the ledge. He opened the window.

The bird fluttered in. "Took you long enough. I've been calling to you."

"I am old now, my friend. I don't expect to have your kind of longevity."

"Didn't do my family any good, snuffed out in an instant."

"A tragedy that brings us all sorrow."

"I can't stand seeing that Ricky coming around here now. What right does he have to bring it all back? Why couldn't he stay away?" Captain fluffed up his feathers and shook from crown to claw.

"For a wise old bird, you're certainly on edge."

Captain pecked at Ted's thumb.

"Ow! That hurt!"

"I got him the other day, just couldn't stand the sight of him, big as you please, in the phone booth by the market. Scratched up his scalp pretty good and got some hair before he batted me off."

"Why are you all worked up? This isn't like you."

"Sorry I nipped at you." He rubbed his head against Ted's thumb. "It's just that I need to search again. It's time."

Ted sighed, wringing his hands. "You always return more upset than when you left. It takes such a toll. You were skeletal last year."

"She's out there somewhere. I know it." He cocked his head and searched Ted's eyes.

Ted looked away. "It's just been so hard on you to come up empty handed time after time."

"Pffft! None of that giving up for me. I want a family."

"So I can't talk you out of this?" He turned back to Captain and rubbed the bird's chest.

"No, indeed, you cannot. But keep rubbing." He quivered with pleasure. "That feels nice."

As Ted continued to stroke his chest, the bird's breathing slowed. He closed his eyes and hummed the first bars of the song "My Girl."

"Ever hopeful, you are. Just guard your heart, will you?" Ted gave a weak smile but couldn't keep his eyes from watering.

"Don't look so sad. I'll be back—with a mate this time." Captain hopped back to the ledge, then took off. He circled around 346 several times, gathering courage for the journey.

Ted watched his friend fly off, then readied for another day in his workshop. Fixing the discarded was something he could control.

High above, the determined pigeon readied for the unknown. He winged to Dolores Street. There he visited a flock of screeching, red-headed parrots that had escaped captivity and found one another. They flitted from frond to frond in palms populating the median. The parrots didn't interact with the common rock pigeons that roosted in the eaves of homes lining the street, but they always welcomed Captain. That morning they warned him to be careful; they'd glimpsed raptors skulking on their migration to warmer climes. Songbirds were on the wing, too, which the parrots found irritating, but

Captain enjoyed their music and wished he could embody their beauty.

When he'd heard enough parrot talk, Captain flew to the Panhandle where people walked dogs, strolled from Haight Street with coffee cups in hand, waited at bus stops, or gawked at a band of Hare Krishna devotees chanting and dancing in dappled sunlight coming through a Monterey pine. He sat on a branch and vibrated to the sound of tambourines before heading farther into Golden Gate Park. Captain dipped his head into the waterfall at Lloyd Lake and noticed a woman with purple hair pointing at him.

"Look, at you, a big ole wild-colored bird with a spring for a leg. You should come live with me. I'll take care of you." She stepped toward him, lost her balance on a slippery rock, and plunged into the water.

Captain lifted off. He landed briefly in pines at the Presidio before soaring over the Golden Gate Bridge and angling westward. He followed the coastal range, stopping occasionally to forage for acorns and berries. He steered clear of southbound hawks, falcons and such. Once he caught the eye of an osprey, so he plunged into dense under-brush and waited, motionless except for his thrumming heart, until he heard the snorts of rooting wild pigs. He flew northward again. On and on he went until he reached a forest with an assortment of fir trees and smatterings of redwoods, spruce, tan oak, big leaf maple, and western hemlock. The smell of the place heightened his yearning for kinship and intensified his desire to hear a deep, owl-like whoo-hoo echoing through the trees.

~

UP EARLY ON the day Captain left on his quest, Maddy grabbed a light jacket, tiptoed down the stairs in case Clara was still asleep, and slipped outside. She breathed in lavender scented air both bracing and soothing and tingled head to toe, as did other residents on the lane welcoming the new day. She stretched, and in a corner, she spied her daypack sitting on top of what looked like a picture book. "Eee gads," she said to the pack. "I thought you were gone for good." She unzipped it and found a few dollars and change still in her wallet. Her old school ID remained under a flap where she'd hidden it. She slung the pack over one shoulder and picked up the book. It was the first *Madeline* story, the one introducing the little red-headed girl in a Catholic boarding school who becomes ill and has her appendix removed, the child Maddy had been named after. She dropped the book, not wanting to think about why it was there. Shaking off an unsettled feeling, she made her way to Ted, who was lifting the creaking garage door.

"Hey, Ted. Nice morning, huh."

"The air is mighty refreshing."

"Is Lark home?"

"Far as I know. Door's unlocked." He gestured toward the entrance.

She bolted up to Lark's room. Finding the door closed she called to her friend.

As slow as a banana slug, Lark stretched, eyes closed, then sat up. "Come on in."

Maddy opened the door and poked her head in.

Lark greeted her and patted the mattress next to her. The eager teen sat down and reminded Lark of their plan to ride bikes together to get over any lingering fears from the accident.

Lark frowned. "I'm so sorry. I completely forgot."

"How late did you stay at Moonrise?"

"I got home around 2 a.m. I was too wired to sleep. ... Belle Ely invited me to rehearse with her band and collaborate with her. I guess I'll work on lyrics and stuff."

"Gosh, you had the best night ever!"

"I was really stoked about it until I got home."

"That doesn't sound good."

"Let's just say I've lost every tiny remaining shred of hope I had for me and Dave."

"A bike ride might get your mind off of him."

"Can I take a rain check? Belle wants me to come over today."

"Sure. No problem." Maddy stood up, chewing on her thumbnail. "I'll have to go it alone when I post flyers. I may as well go it alone today." She leaned down to hug Lark before heading to the workshop, where Ted was surveying a row of hand tools hung on a pegboard. When Maddy arrived, he looked over his shoulder, his violet eyes beaming, and nipped to a row of bicycles. "I fixed up a nice one, looks made for you." He rolled out a purple American Eagle with gold trim. "It's a ten speed. Might take some getting used to."

"That's a dream bike."

"I knew you wouldn't stay grounded for long."

Ted wheeled the bike to Maddy. She thanked him and took off, coasting to where Shinbone met 29th. Instead of heading downhill, she walked the bike up to Diamond Street, then pedaled toward 24th. As she approached Clipper Street, she heard someone call her name. Ricky came into view, waving as he stepped from the curb. She braked, out of breath, her heart speeding.

Ricky looked at his feet before clearing his throat. "Um, hey. Glad to see you're riding again. I heard about your spill."

"I'm not as scared as I thought I'd be, but then I haven't tackled a steep hill yet."

"You'll get the hang of it." He gave a quick smile. "Um, I've been meaning to come by and see if you want to go to Golden Gate Park with me. This friend of mine's out of town for a while and asked me to take care of his Yamaha. I can ride it as much as I want."

"You mean a motorcycle?"

"Uh huh."

Maddy had ridden on the back of a motorcycle when she was traveling with Keeley and her gang. The thrill of wind on her face and in her hair was stronger than her reservations about Ricky. "That sounds like fun."

"I can swing by your place today, about two o'clock, after I finish my shift at Bell."

She hesitated, thinking maybe she should talk it over with Clara first. "Do you like working at a supermarket?"

"There's good people there," he said, "so yeah."

She warmed to his voice, which was resonant and pleasing, and wondered what she was getting herself into. "Okay, then. See you later." She shoved off, doubts buzzing like hungry mosquitoes. Why had she agreed, and so quickly? She turned onto Clipper and gripped the handlebars in fear as she coasted down, down, down. Grateful to encounter no cars at the cross streets, she stopped at Church Street to catch her breath. Her thoughts returned to Ricky. Oh, well, no matter, she decided. It was only a ride, nothing more. He'd better not be expecting some sort of relationship with a capital R.

Ricky headed for work, surprised she'd agreed to spend time with him, but expecting she'd run from him as fast as she could if he told her what he knew.

"SAY, stranger. What cha got for me?" Truman swaggered like a swashbuckler down the Bell Market aisles and stopped inches from his mark.

Ricky turned from a crate of spaghetti sauce he was stacking on a shelf. Truman tipped his stained fedora and grinned as though he'd just won the Irish Sweepstakes.

Ricky shook his head. "Hey man, not here." He returned to his task.

Truman closed in, forming a wall of menace. "You should have intel for me, I believe."

Ricky pivoted and jabbed a finger at Truman's sternum. "I said, 'not here'!"

The private eye brushed Ricky's hand away and smirked. "Is that any way to treat a customer? Come on, your mom mentioned notes."

"She says a lot of things." Ricky set his jaw and continued stacking jars. He placed the last one on the shelf and lifted the empty crate. "You can't be bugging me at work." He turned his back on Truman and took a few steps.

Truman pursued, and with the toe of his scuffed wingtips, he caught the back of Ricky's sneaker, pulling it off the heel.

"Back off!" Ricky jerked around, dropping the crate, and knocked the aggressor off balance.

Truman hit a section of pasta. Packages of linguini, spaghetti and vermicelli fell to the floor just as Chip wheeled a cart into the aisle with Dave at his side. Chip whistled low through his gapped front teeth and gripped tighter to the cart.

Dave put a hand on Chip's shoulder. "Hey, man, you okay?"

"Yeah, yeah, but something's off with all this stuff scattered—"

"Nothin' here you need to worry about, fellas." Truman raised an eyebrow at Ricky. "Right, son?"

Head down, Ricky crouched to fix his shoe and put the scattered pasta back on the shelf.

"We'll take one of those." Dave pointed to the linguine. "He's gonna teach me how to make clam sauce."

"How sweet, the local photographer and rising folk rock star in the kitchen together," Truman said, "like two little girls in home ec."

"Some folks are born assholes," Dave muttered to Chip.

Ricky tossed the pasta to Dave, who caught it and dropped it into the cart.

"Nice catch," Ricky said. "I guess those fingers are good for more than strumming."

Truman advanced on Dave, hovering a few inches away. "Better watch what you say, pretty boy, or those fingers will be good for nothing."

"Get away, creep." Dave backed up. Then, to Chip and Ricky, he said, "Can you believe this guy?"

"Unfortunately, yes." Ricky lifted the crate again and headed toward the back of the store.

"Hey, I'm not done with you!" Truman chased after Ricky.

"Let's split," Dave said to Chip, who was glaring after Truman. "Chip?" Dave snapped his fingers in front of Chip's nose.

Chip shook his head. "Oh, sorry man. Yeah, let's go."

Truman pursued Ricky to the employees-only section and tried to follow him inside, but a worker pushing a dolly loaded with canned vegetables blocked him.

"You can't go in there," the young man said.

Truman leaned against a refrigerated display, crossed his arms, and waited for Ricky to come back out. Ricky, whose shift had just ended, took off his apron and name tag, and left through the back door, eager to forget Truman and pick up Maddy for their motorcycle ride.

Chip and Dave checked out and loaded the groceries into Crazy-Wild.

As they pulled out of the parking place, Dave asked, "That guy bugging Ricky—what a creep, not that Ricky's all that nice, from what I hear."

"I hear ya," Chip said. "I've had a bad feeling about that man since I first saw him after Lark and Maddy crashed their bikes."

"We've got to be more under the radar." Dave said. "I don't need harassment, especially since I'm not sure I'm ... you know ... and the band. They're depending on me. It could get sticky."

"Whatever," Chip muttered. "Nobody's forcing you into anything."

MADDY TIED her jean jacket around her waist and leaned against a bay tree in front of Clara's. When Ricky roared up on the Yamaha, she tugged at the bottom of her T-shirt, then brushed her long locks behind her ears. "Hey," she said.

"Hi there." Fine dust rose from the road as Ricky's boots hit the ground. "Ready for Golden Gate Park?"

"Sure am."

Several residents of the lane looked on, surprised to see Maddy straddle the motorcycle and wrap her arms around Ricky's torso. Eloise clucked her tongue and patted Coco, who snored in her lap. "She's just recovered from that horrid bicycle accident, and now she's clinging to some hooligan on a motorcycle," she said. "That girl has no sense."

Waddles called Clara and said, "How could you let her ride off with that no-account? Captain laid into him at the fair, so he's got to be bad news." Clara paused before responding, "Maddy has a good head on her shoulders. It's not my place to interfere." And so the conversations went.

Maddy tried to quash a thrill ruffling her insides when Ricky accelerated, let out a whoop, and sped them off. He drove up hills with gorgeous vistas, past landmarks he pointed out, though she could barely hear what he said. In the park, they reached Martin Luther King Jr. Drive, motored past the Children's Playground and Carousel, and continued westward. When the road veered, they made a sharp right and whooshed by the California Academy of Sciences, around the Music Concourse, past the DeYoung, and got back to MLK Drive. They came to a stop near Stowe Lake and dismounted.

Ricky suggested they walk around the lake. "We can stop at the concession stand and get soda and pink popcorn, maybe even rent a paddle boat."

"Sounds good," Maddy said.

They strolled along, talking about current events. They speculated about where kidnapped heiress Patty Hearst might be hiding.

"She could be holed up at the Granite Lady," Ricky joked.

"What's that?"

"The old San Francisco Mint building at Fifth and Mission. It survived the 1906 earthquake."

Laughing, Maddy said, "No, no, no, she's a waitress at that German deli—"

"Speckman's?"

"Yeah, hiding in plain sight, hair bleached blond and in a beehive, and body padded thick, so you'd never guess. Glasses too, you know, the kind with rhinestones and corners that curve up."

They continued joking while taking in the ducks and geese, the waterfall, the people boating, the shadows dancing on the bridges. They stopped when the Chinese pagoda came into view.

"That was a gift from the people of Taipei," Ricky said. "There's a legend that goes with this lake, too."

"Really? Tell me."

They sat by the water, and Ricky began the tale. "Okay, um, there was this young mother who grew tired while pushing her baby in a stroller. So she sat on a bench, you know, just to rest for a bit by the water with the stroller right next to her. While she relaxed, an older woman joined her, and they got to talking. It had been a while since the mother'd had a good conversation, so her spirits lifted as they spoke. She turned toward her companion and became so absorbed that she didn't notice when a gust of wind put the stroller in motion."

"Uh oh." Maddy clenched her fists. "I hope a passerby saves the day."

"No such luck. The baby rolled away and fell into the lake. The mother was so spellbound by the other woman that she didn't hear the splash. After a while, the woman said she had to be going and left the bench. The mother turned her head and shrieked at the empty spot where the baby and carriage had been. Panicked, she looked back to seek the woman's help, but she had vanished, too. The frantic mother raced around the lake, asking everyone she met, 'Have you seen my baby?'"

"Just like Eloise, always asking, 'Have you seen my Julianna?'"

"I hadn't thought of that, but you're right. Anyway, all afternoon and into the evening she questioned people, 'Have you seen my baby?' But nobody had seen a thing. When darkness closed in, and she was all alone, she accepted what she most dreaded. Her baby had rolled into the lake. She dove in." Ricky gestured toward the shimmering water. "Nobody ever saw her again, not alive anyway."

"What do you mean?"

"People say that weird things happen if you come here at night, like the poor mother comes up from the bottom of the lake, dripping wet, skeletal, you know, with long, long fingernails and hollowed out eyes, and she asks you, 'Have you seen my baby?'

He paused for effect; Maddy held her breath.

"If you say yes," he continued, "she'll let out a piercing scream that will haunt you for the rest of your days. But if you say no, she'll pull you into the lake and drown you."

"That's scary." Maddy stared, owl-eyed, at Ricky. "I don't want to be here at night."

"It reminds me of a story Ernesto, a kid I knew in grammar school, told me. It's 'La Llorona,' about a peasant woman who drowned her kids in the Rio Grande."

Maddy squirmed. "I've heard that one, gives me the willies."

He smiled, a glint in his dark blue eyes. "I guess I shouldn't be surprised you know it, Maddy Macken, or should I say Madeline?"

"What?" She jolted up. "How do you know I'm not Madison or Madonna or even Magdalena?"

He cringed, wishing to take his words back. "Look, I didn't mean anything. I just want you to know you're not alone."

"Why, you—"

"Sit back down, will ya? Please?"

"You're the one who had my pack. You found my old ID." She glared at him. "I have to go."

"Hey, I'm, I'm sorry. I shouldn't have said—"

"Now!" She sped away like an antelope.

"Okay, okay. Wait up."

Out of breath, he caught up to her at the motorcycle. They mounted and rode in silence, their bodies touching but a breach as wide as the universe between them. Maddy let go and sprang off when Ricky slowed down at Clara's. She scrambled toward the front door without looking back. Certain Ricky had an ulterior motive, she was mortified that she had the urge to run back and kiss him.

CHAPTER

FIFTEEN

"I can't believe someone gave these up." Rosie shook out a pair of bell bottoms adorned with embroidered flower chains and an assortment of appliqués. "There's just one little rip in this seam. I can mend it, easy peasy, and they'll be good to go."

Lark shifted her weight in a threadbare but comfy stuffed chair a former resident had left behind. She brushed a hand through her short hair and looked at Rosie, who sat on the bed, a sewing basket by her side. "Thanks for helping me. I'll only be gone one night, though. It seems like a lot of fuss. I doubt Abbudin and his people would have a problem if I arrive just as I am."

"You're a performer now, and your wardrobe needs flair to match your soul."

"I don't know about that." Lark rubbed her thighs. "Two of you could fit into one leg of those jeans."

"Skinny as a coat hanger is what Wayne calls me," Rosie lamented. "I guess he's right."

A hush of tenderness rose within Lark, soft and unexpected. "More like a beautiful hummingbird," the poet said.

Rosie gave a shy smile. "Gosh, why is it so hard for us to love our bodies? We're all beautiful in our own way, aren't we?"

"It's so easy to forget that. It reminds me of a poem." Lark shot up from her chair and walked to her bookshelves. She scanned rows of books. "Ah ha! Here it is! *Crossing the Water*, a collection of poems by Sylvia Plath." She returned to her chair and leafed through the pages. "Here it is. 'Mirror.' It's from the point of view of a mirror. There are different ways to interpret this, but I think it's about the struggle to see your true self." Lark read the poem aloud, and the two friends sat silent for a short time.

"That's deep," Rosie finally said. "But I don't see how it relates to how easy it is to forget how beautiful we are."

"I think Plath was focused on aging, having to accept that, accept what the mirror sees. But someday I'd like to write a poem about how hard it is to face the beauty that's there, not just the aging."

"I get it. Well, I think I do. I hope you write that poem." Rosie dug into a box by her feet, pulled out a purple tank top and handed it to Lark. "You'll need this. It's going to be hot up north at Abbudin's, a lot hotter than the city."

"Am I doing the right thing, going to check on the twins?"

"It's more than the right thing. Just don't get stuck there, okay?"

"Don't worry. Nobody's gonna hoodwink me." Lark noticed the tank top's label. "Yikes, it's Capezio. Stylish. Not what I'm used to, not at all."

"Remember high school, how much it mattered what you wore?" Rosie asked. "Now girls can wear slacks to school. Even jeans in some places."

"It took a lawsuit to do it, but 'the times they are a changin.'" Lark broke into the Dylan song.

Rosie joined in, and when they finished, they started in on "I Am Woman," Helen Reddy's hit song that had become a feminist anthem. Their energy built until they were belting out tunes, stomping in rhythm, and howling with laughter as they circled the room.

Dave came down the hall and leaned on the doorframe. "You sound fantastic, ladies. You should form a duo—or grab a couple more and form a girl band."

Startled, they stopped dancing, breathing heavily. Then Rosie grabbed his hand, inviting him to dance along, but he pulled back. Rosie let go and sat back down on the bed. Lark moved to her chair.

"Yeah, maybe we should form a band," Rosie said to Lark. "We could go on the road with Belle Ely."

"Belle Ely?" Dave asked. "That's like trying to go from zero to a hundred right away."

Rosie looked at him with pity in her eyes. "You missed the boat, buddy. Lark's already helped Belle with some lyrics."

"Looks like I'm good enough for one local star," Lark muttered.

Dave edged toward her. "It's not personal, Lark. Spoken word doesn't fit with what the band does. We have to please the audience or we'll be toast."

Lark tried to stare him down but couldn't hold his gaze. Though she knew he meant well, a twisted knot of emotion pulled her focus to the floor. Dave leaned down and touched her shoulder. She flinched. He drew his hand back.

"She really could become Belle's opening act, and sooner than you think," Rosie said, her voice carrying a new current of confidence.

"I'm happy for you, Lark, whatever you decide to do." Dave said, then headed for the door.

Lark gulped and blurted, "I know you're into somebody else."

He spun around. "We never promised—"

Lark held up her hand, traffic cop style. "Forget it, okay?"

Dave rubbed his hands together. "Well, then, uh, good luck. I really mean it. Let me know if you need anything." He strode down the hall.

Lark sank a little lower in her chair.

"Are you okay?" Rosie moved in to give her friend a hug.

"He didn't lead me on, not really. I misinterpreted things and got strung out."

"We've all been there in some form or other," Rosie said. "Or we've gotten together with the wrong person, didn't see what was coming." Rosie shook out a patchwork vest from a box and tossed it to Lark. "This is perfect for you."

Lark put the vest on and walked to the full-length mirror on her closet door. "I love it!" She swiveled to see the vest from different angles. "I swear I see a glimpse of my true self in there."

DURING THAT BLINK-AND-YOU'LL-MISS-IT time when the fog lifts, the sun blazes, and San Francisco heats up, Clara placed a glass of iced coffee and a copy of *Redbook* on the table by her living room window. She sat down and opened the magazine but couldn't even skim the table of contents. It was past noon. Not one board had creaked upstairs. Worry wrapping her thoughts, she put the magazine down and paced the hallway several times before opening the door to the attic stairs. "Maddy, dear, are you okay up there?" she called. "I didn't hear a peep from you all morning. Are you ill? ... Hmm, this is a bit of a pickle. I don't want to disturb you, but I am concerned."

Met with continued silence, Clara dithered in the doorway before deciding to act. "I'm coming up." She gripped the railing and climbed. At the threshold, she peered into the room, which was chilly despite the rising temperature elsewhere in the home and on the lane. The walls, floor, and everything inside seemed washed with gray. Maddy lay on the bed, covers kicked to her feet, tiny goosebumps on her skin. Clara approached, leaned down and tapped her shoulder. "Dear girl, what's wrong?"

The teenager shrank from Clara.

"Come, come, child, you've got me worried. Even the room seems upset."

"I just want to sleep," Maddy mumbled.

Clara reminded her that they'd both signed up for booths at a fair coming up in Dolores Park, and the deadline for a juried show that featured unknown artists' work was looming. "You've got a portfolio to organize. There's much to do." A stack of flyers on the desk caught Clara's eye. "Looks like you've got flyers to distribute, too."

"I can't do it."

"What do you mean?"

"I just ... I can't do any of it. I have to leave."

Clara sat down on the bed. "I thought you—"

"I love it here. You are wonderful. This room is wonderful. Everyone on the lane, everyone's just the best."

"What is it then?"

Maddy, choked with emotion, swallowed hard. "You really are the grandmother I never had." With that, tears slid down.

Clara pulled the young woman to her bosom. Maddy resisted at first but soon leaned in like a lost puppy and sobbed.

"Get it all out, get it all out."

Her grief subsiding, Maddy sputtered, "I'll always remember you." She burst into tears again.

Clara rubbed Maddy's back and asked, "What could be so bad to cause all this?"

"Ricky knows."

"That boy who's sweet on you?"

"He knows who I am."

Clara held Maddy at arm's length. "It seems you've got something to get off your chest."

Her tenant looked away. "No, not here, not you."

"Rushing off isn't going to solve anything."

"I don't want to complicate your life."

"Goodness gracious, you're talking nonsense." Clara narrowed her eyes and did her best to look imposing. "I'm not getting off this bed until you tell me what's going on."

Maddy looked around the room. "Geez, it's gloomy in here. I've even ruined this place."

"I'm waiting," Clara said.

Maddy grumbled and straightened her back. "You're not gonna be happy to hear this ... but I ran away from home. It'll be two years on November first, my birthday. I'll be turning seventeen. So, you see, you're harboring a runaway from Yellow Springs, Ohio."

Clara rubbed Maddy's arm. "You must have had a good reason."

"I slipped out my bedroom window while my dad was talking to a police officer, blaming me for something I didn't do. Something big, something awful."

"Dear Lord. Whatever could he have been thinking?"

"There's a Green Tortoise, goes to Los Angeles. I'll leave this afternoon."

"That hippie van? You'll do no such thing."

"I have to. The police are looking for me."

"What do they think you did?"

Maddy rubbed her teeth on her bottom lip. "I can't talk about it. I'm leaving. I have to."

Undeterred, Clara stood up and insisted Maddy get dressed and come downstairs for a good meal. "Then we'll figure out what to do— together. You don't have to explain anything, but I hope you know by now that whatever you say, I won't breathe a word of it."

Maddy glanced out the window, where all was still as though the entire lane were waiting for an answer. Her tears slowed.

Clara reached into her pocket for a tissue and handed it to Maddy. "I'm simply not leaving until you agree."

"Okay." Maddy said, dabbing her cheeks.

Clara made her way to the stairs. At the bottom, she called up. "One BLT with coleslaw and potato chips on the side coming up."

RICKY'S FOREHEAD gleamed with perspiration as he extended the arm of a duster to reach cobwebs in Natalie's kitchen corners. When he finished, he stomped to the back deck and shook out a cloud of dust as repellant as exhaust from a junker.

"Why don't you ever clean this place yourself?" Ricky asked, returning the tool to the utility closet, which was stocked with cleaning supplies, light bulbs, garbage bags, and other items Natalie never touched. "I reorganized this for you. The least you could do is make an effort."

"These walls are sixteen feet high. I'm five-two. How am I gonna reach?" She cinched the belt of her red-and-white striped wrap dress, though no amount of tightening could make her thick waist look slim.

"You always have some excuse." Ricky closed the closet door. "What's there to drink? September heat always throws me for a loop." He rummaged through the refrigerator and pulled out a carton of molding cottage cheese and a dozen expired eggs and threw them into the garbage can under the sink. "Why ask me to get you eggs if you aren't going to eat them?"

"Don't start with me. I'm your mother. Don't you forget that."

He returned to the fridge and spotted a pitcher of lemonade. "Has that creep Truman been around lately?"

"Speak of the devil." She cracked a coy smile. "He's opening the door right now."

"You gave him a key? Mom—"

"Stop your bellyachin' and get us some drinks." She tilted her head toward the counter. "There's some Danish in the bag, too, from Star— the ones you like with that jelly inside, and some cheese."

Ricky considered leaving through the back door, but since he'd have to deal with Truman sooner or later, he arranged pastries on a plate and poured three glasses of lemonade.

Truman entered the room and sat down. Ricky handed him a drink.

"So you gave me the slip the other day. Pretty slick, kid," Truman said.

Ignoring him, Ricky brought the pastries to the table and sat down while Natalie lit a cigarette. "Do you have to do that?" He brushed smoke away from his face.

"Listen to him," she said to Truman. "You'd think he was the parent." She coughed, chest rumbling like a go-cart.

"Are you gonna tell me what you have, or what?" Truman asked Ricky.

"Don't come to my work again." Ricky put his spiral notebook and a disposable Kodak camera Truman had given him on the table. "Nobody's up to much on Shinbone or anywhere near either."

Truman swept the notebook and camera to the table's edge, pocketed the camera, and opened the notebook. "You mighta seen something and not realized it. I need observations, not conclusions." He took a bite out of a sweet roll and looked through Ricky's notes. "Well, well." He slapped the notebook down and tapped a page with his index finger. "This here's mighty interesting." He took an index card from his pocket and scribbled.

"You got dirt on somebody already?" Natalie asked.

"Not exactly dirt, but possibly useful." Truman put the card in his pocket, closed the notebook slid it back toward Ricky, along with five $10 bills. "Good job. Keep watchin' these people."

"I'm done," Ricky said. "I don't like this line of work."

Natalie let out a hyena laugh that hung, teasing, in the air. "I suppose you've found your calling stacking shelves at Bell."

"You can't back out now." Truman snapped.

Ricky grimaced. "You think you're the mafia or something?"

"Okay, okay, take it easy, kid." Truman gestured toward the pastries. "Enjoy the bounty and see what happens."

"It's the least you can do." Natalie gulped lemonade and spit some of it up. Liquid dribbled down her chin. "Truman gave you an opportunity. You gotta see it through."

Ricky grabbed a napkin. "Look at you, can't even drink without making a mess." He reached over and wiped her face.

"Nice boy you got there, lookin' after you," Truman said to Natalie.

"Better than you ever did," she spat out.

"That's a low blow. We were kids—what? Eighteen years old—"

"Always chasin' after some girl that didn't want you. I was never enough."

A sour taste flooded Ricky's mouth. "You two were ... an item?"

Truman waved his hand as though erasing Ricky's comment. Then, exuding indignation, he leaned toward Natalie and declared it was she who had dumped him. She insisted it was the other way around.

"I was in San Quentin. What could I do? You never came to see me. You never even wrote."

"How dare you!" Natalie's face reddened. "You had all the girls doting on you," she sputtered, "and you, you enjoyed every minute, no matter the consequences."

Ricky stood up.

"Where do you think you're going?" Natalie pounded a fist on the table.

"You're gonna have an explosion." Ricky pocketed the money from Truman and headed for the hallway.

"Come back here," Natalie demanded.

"Let him go," Truman said. "He'll be back."

Ricky charged down the hall and onto the front porch, slamming the door behind him. The sound cracked the air like a thunderclap and pulsed throughout the house.

"How would you know? You ever raise a kid—on your own to boot?" Anger rolled through her, wave after wave.

"Settle down, will ya?" He reached for her.

She shot up and ran to the sink. Truman followed and tried to take hold of her, but she wiggled away. Around and around the kitchen they went, the whole room shaking with her fury until he got a good grip and held her against his chest, despite the searing heat she gave off. She railed against him. An array of old photos shook against the wall. Pots and pans hanging above the stove clanged. The table and chairs rattled.

"There there, Natalie. My sweet, sweet little Natalie." He tightened his hold, her tears melting into his already soaking shirt.

CHAPTER

SIXTEEN

As San Francisco's short September heat wave subsided, Captain's absence niggled Shinbone residents like blisters on tender skin. Eloise lamented to Coco that she missed the bird's syncopated way of dancing. Clara mentioned to Maddy that Ted's shoulders slumped a bit more and his eyes grew weary every time someone asked where Captain was.

"It's such a shame," folks would mutter when discussing the pigeon's new quest. They were all certain he would return bedraggled, skinny, struggling for breath, and depressed. And they brainstormed for ways they might help Ted and the bird get through when the time came. A few thought the unthinkable: Captain might never return.

Far north of the Golden Gate, Captain often thought of turning back. He was hungry, tired, despondent. And he missed his best friend, Ted. He missed all the goings on at Shinbone Lane. He even missed Eloise, who did nothing but complain. Losing hope, he nibbled an acorn, wondering how long it would take to get home in his depleted state. But then he heard a low, owl-like whoo-hoo, a sign his kind were near.

Then he spotted her. A female pigeon perched alone in a Douglas fir. Scanning the surrounding trees, he thrilled to the sight of numerous pigeons, in pairs, at their nests. They sported color variations brilliant as San Francisco's ornate Victorians. Captain circled the solo female's tree, drawn in by her feathers of bright green, purple, mauve and gold. She sat still.

Around, around, and around he flew ramping up to give a wheezing, guttural call. Then he fluttered his wings and glided toward her. He landed with ease, clutching the branch with his one good claw. There, he stuck out his neck and raised his feathers, which made him appear larger than he was. Then he lowered his head and spun in a circle, maneuvering with grace despite his spring foot. Next, he puffed up his chest and neck, and with tail lowered and spread, he cooed. This caught her attention, and when she saw his jerry-rigged foot, she didn't look away. She turned her head to the side and revealed that she was missing an eye.

Neither backed away in disgust, as other potential mates had done in the past. Captain did his courting sequence again. They drew closer to each other. He cooed to her; she cooed back. His coos pitched higher and speeded up as he created a song just for her. She sang back. Their voices harmonized as they leaned against each other, each basking in the other's company.

He brought his bill near her face; she opened her beak and accepted his horny plates with affection. Then they switched, and he explored her. He shared his English-language name, Captain, and she shared hers, Bonbon. By the time stars flickered in the night sky above, he had mounted her, and they were mates, gently preening one another's tail feathers and wings.

Over the following days, he foraged, bringing her seeds, berries and bugs, and they shared pieces of their struggles and joys.

"There was a big wind. A sharp twig flew into my eye. That's what blew it out," Bonbon told Captain. "My mother said not to get my hopes up. Nobody would ever want to mate with a bird that could see only half the world at a time."

"I will help you see the other half, my love," Captain said.

"I never expected you'd come along. My family puts up with me, barely. That was all I could expect."

"I used to have a family long ago."

"What happened?"

"A fire took them all, my foot and part of my leg, too," Captain said. "I've been alone since then; that is, if you don't count my human friend, Ted, and a few others who are safe."

"Ted?"

"I live in his backyard on Shinbone Lane in San Francisco."

"He's human? You're friends with humans? They're dangerous."

"Ricky, the one who set the fire that maimed me was, but some of them are quite nice."

"Do they know you know language?"

"Less than a claw-full."

"Please don't tell any humans that we're here." She scrunched her head down and flattened her wings against her body.

"Not to worry. I want to take you home with me, start a new family there."

"Why not start a family here?"

"With those who have practically ostracized you?"

"It's beautiful here, safe."

"My home is a special place, too."

She pulled away from him and spun around so he saw only her backside. He tucked his beak into his chest and shivered at the thought of returning home with a heavy heart once again, just as Ted had feared.

IN THE LIVING room of her parents' home, Penny slouched in her wheelchair. "Why Truman?" she muttered. "Why did my dad pick him, of all people? Weeks go by and no word." She squinted at the television screen, ashamed that she'd succumbed to the lure of *As The World Turns.* She could hear the dialogue well enough, but her blurred world was still all shades of black, white, and gray, including TV shows everyone else saw in color.

She popped a Reese's peanut butter cup into her mouth and quivered as flavor cradled her tongue. But then a recurring, waking nightmare stole her body and mind. It twisted her perceptions, took her back to the moment she put Blossom down on the bottom stair. A boom reverberated around and through her. Ears ringing, she flew into the air, her mind melting. Blossom, snatched by the force of the blast, collided with an airborne cheese board before sailing into a cloud of thick, black smoke.

Shards of lives interrupted—a tricycle wheel, hiking boot, banker's lamp, twisted silverware, blackened sun bonnet, long-stemmed roses —rained down with bricks, glass, burning papers, and wood. Neighbors ran screaming from the building. The smell of singed hair and burning insulation permeated the air.

Something sharp jutted into Penny's back when she landed. A burning photo album slapped her thigh. Blinking at grit that blinded her, she mewled, hot with fury. Spit drooled from her mouth.

A strong hand gripped her shoulder.

"You're okay." The deep male voice sounded distorted, as though it came from under water, but it penetrated like winter rain.

Penny lifted her head, winced, and struggled to speak. "My Bluh-Blossom? My da-dau—" She collapsed, head banging the sidewalk.

"She's right here," the voice said.

Penny rose, weightless. Searching the blur of rubble and blood below. She fought to stay above, to see her girl. But she slammed down, spirit rejoining flesh. Her cries merged with a growing din of misery. She couldn't move.

"You're okay," the voice repeated. "You'll be okay."

A surge of anger brought Penny back to her mother's living room, where the latest batch of pictures from Truman rested in her lap. She sorted through them. One of the men looked like a pot and amphetamine dealer who'd often come around the apartment. Was it his voice she'd heard that day? She'd have to see him in person, hear him speak to be sure. Who else could it be, though? It had to be him. Yet here it was already mid-September, and Truman kept delaying her trip to San Francisco.

A spasm of pain ran from her lower back through her legs, and she flipped to the past again. Five months pregnant with Blossom, she licked S&H Green Stamps and pasted them into a book. She was saving up to redeem them for CorningWare.

Bill came into the room, a sour look on his face. "Green Stamps? You're kidding me."

She showed him the cookware in the catalog.

"How square you are. Anything you need, you can get at the Salvation Army or Goodwill, or in the free box at the co-op." He sauntered out of the room.

A gunshot reverberated from the soap opera on TV, jolting Penny back to her parents' living room. She opened her eyes a crack and closed them again, her mind filling with visions of FBI agents insisting with each visit that she knew what was going on.

Sure, she'd told them, Bill had carried a copy of Mao Tse-tung's little red book in his shirt pocket; other books like *The Wretched of the Earth* and *The Morning Deluge* appeared on the dining room table, along with the Weather Underground's manifesto. But she'd never read them, preferring *Between Parent and Child, Parent Effectiveness Training* and good old Dr. Spock. She'd also adored her dog-eared copy of *Jonathan Livingston Seagull*, which Bill and the others had called "nutty" and "banal." She admitted she'd often heard them arguing in the living room, but the door was closed to her. She'd never imagined they would make bombs.

The doorbell rang. Penny spun away from the TV, peeked out the window and, though she saw the woman only in shades of gray, she knew by her full figure and proud stance it was her childhood friend Courtney. She opened the window and called out, "Come in. It's open."

When Courtney entered the room, Penny turned off the TV and said, "Just a little something to pass the time."

"Don't be embarrassed. I watch that one, too."

They both giggled, then Penny asked, "So, what brings you here today?"

"I want to take you to Ashland, to the Shakespeare Festival."

"I don't know. I mean, I'm getting better at using that thing." She flicked her wrist at a walker in the corner. "But I can't rely on it yet, and that's a long way to haul somebody in a wheelchair."

"Why not let me worry about that? It would do you a world of good. Think of all the fun we could have."

"Mom would probably have a cow if, you know ... she's already so worried about Dad after the stroke. She won't want me to take risks. I should probably—"

"But where's the girl who snuck out at night with me and the gang, who went pool hopping and looking for all the best parties? What would she do?"

"She's long gone."

"Nonsense. Not that I want us to revert to our delinquent days. But you can't spend all your time in here with your mom fretting and your dad laid up like he is."

Penny sat up straighter as an idea struck her. The old Penny would do more than go to Ashland with Courtney. She'd have Truman meet her there and drive her to San Francisco. Her mom wouldn't know until the deed was done. She could confront the drug-dealing child thief Truman found once and for all. Penny grinned at her friend. "Mom'll object at first, but if I can get my doctor on board, I think I can convince her."

After Courtney left, unintelligible sounds from Penny's dad echoed down the hall to the foyer. It must be so hard on Mom living with the two of us, Penny thought, as she rolled to her father's room. He grunted and waved a pen in the air. She drew her wheelchair closer and leaned down so she was just inches from a pad of paper on his lap. "Wow, Dad, you've written some letters that are actually legible. Let's see. It looks like STOP. Is that right?"

He lifted his head but then wobbled to the side.

"Stop what, I wonder," she murmured.

He groaned and dropped the pen.

WITH THE HEAT WAVE OVER, Shinbone denizens dressed in their favorite layers and prepared to shed jackets, sweaters, hats, or vests, depending on where they planned to go, given that each neighborhood had its own microclimate. On the lane, Maddy pulled weeds from Clara's flower boxes while Clara swept the front porch. Chip cleared gum wrappers, stray toys, and other odds and ends from Crazy-Wild. His little sister, Sunrise, drew with chunky chalk on the sidewalk. People came and went from Ted's garage workshop. Some sought advice from the calmest person on the lane; others needed a little companionship before moving on with their days. They all experienced a twinge of sadness at the empty shelf where Captain often perched to watch Ted work. Across the street, Eloise flitted about her bedroom, stuffing a child-sized patent leather suitcase with a nightie, toiletries, and a change of clothes.

Lark ran outside, a macrame shoulder bag that looked large enough to hold Sunrise hung from her shoulder. She greeted Ted, who was polishing a 1957 red-and-white Chevrolet he'd recently restored and parked in front of 346.

"Be safe," he said, handing her the car keys.

Lark thanked him and got into the driver's seat, put the key in the ignition and adjusted the rearview mirror. She was about to start the engine when Eloise strutted up. Balancing her poodle, purse, suitcase, and Betty Boop lunch box precariously in her arms, she rapped on the driver's door. Lark rolled down the window.

"I hear you're going to that Abbudin's place," Eloise said.

"Word sure travels around here."

"Somebody there might know where my Julianna is. I must accompany you."

"But—"

Coco leaped from Eloise's arms and sailed through the window onto Lark's lap.

"See, Coco's decided," Eloise said.

Ted approached. "Two could be better than one on a mission like this."

Eloise sniffed and squared her shoulders. "It's about time you agree with something I want to do."

"Eloise, Eloise," he replied, shaking his head.

"Oh, why not?" Lark shrugged, then motioned to the dancer. "Come on in."

Eloise loaded her gear into the back and folded into the passenger seat. Coco sidled onto her lap.

BLISS WHOOSHED through Captain's body as he winged with Bonbon, toward home. Unsure whether it was love causing his heart to boom or age catching up with him, he landed on a pine branch to rest near the Lost Coast in Humboldt County. Bonbon alighted beside him.

He beamed his thoughts to her. "My heart's going so fast. I think it's my joy at finally convincing you, my darling, to come home with me." He nuzzled his beak into her neck.

"Mmm," she replied, nuzzling him back.

The bright-feathered birds took flight again, stopping for nibbles of acorns, and then again at a beach adorned with row after row of sea urchin shells. A human couple cleared an area of broken shells, stones, and driftwood to spread out a blanket for a picnic. Captain landed in the sand about three yards away.

Bonbon shivered as she landed. "What are you doing? You're putting us in danger."

"Have no fear, my love. They're safer than that raptor over to the east."

She turned her head and spied what she hadn't seen before due to her missing eye. A falcon eyed them, as though they were a feast dropped from the clouds. She snuggled up to Captain in the sand. And thus began her first lesson in human behavior.

"Some like us, some don't," Captain said. "You can usually get out of the way fast if it's the latter." He took a few steps toward the blanket.

Bonbon followed. The woman smiled at the birds. "Look how beautiful they are," she said.

The man cleared his throat and spat into the sand. "Some strange sort of pigeon, looks like."

"Look at their brilliant colors. They should be in a zoo or sanctuary where they can be studied." She broke something into little pieces and threw it at the birds. "There you go, peanut butter cookies."

"Don't encourage them," the man said. "They might bite."

Captain stood taller and sniffed in indignation.

"I swear that one looks like he understands us. And look at his leg. It's a spring! I bet he's got stories to tell."

"Don't go anthropomorphizing again," he said.

Captain strode forward, snatched a chunk and then dropped it at Bonbon's feet. He grabbed another piece and nibbled it down. "Mmm. Good. You should try it."

His mate stared at the foreign substance on the sand.

"The trick is to not eat too much, just enough to give you some energy. Humans tend to overfeed us. And since our loft at Ted's is still a long way off, we can't get bogged down."

Trusting her mate, Bonbon nibbled and savored this new taste. She felt a surge of energy as she watched the human creatures consume strange things that Captain identified for her: tuna salad sandwiches, potato chips, dill pickles, peaches and cream, roasted peanuts. They also guzzled liquid from cans. Captain identified that as Coca Cola, a drink popular with humans. The raptor, meanwhile, continued to eye the pigeons. The people packed up their blanket, put their leftovers in a cooler, and trudged through deep sand toward a parking lot. The pigeons waddled behind and hid in a dense thicket while the couple drove off.

"The falcon won't come after us here. Too many people." Captain said.

A few minutes later, the predator flew north. A truck pulled out of a parking space and headed to the exit. One red taillight flashed.

"They're going south," Captain said, noticing the bed had a tarp over it, but it was loose. "Follow me. We can catch a ride."

He flew to the tailgate and held the tarp open for Bonbon. She lifted off just as the truck pulled onto Highway 1, pointing toward San Francisco. She bumped into Captain as she landed. Both fell into the cargo bed. "I hope we made the right decision," she said, quivering as the truck rumbled along, "to leave the wilderness and settle in some man-made loft."

CHAPTER

SEVENTEEN

Dust gusted up, sprinkling a tan layer on the Impala's whitewall tires and lower body as Lark steered along a winding mountain road. In the passenger seat, Eloise scratched her wrists, pulled out a bottle of calamine lotion, and rubbed it on her skin. The itching had begun early in their journey when they crossed over the Golden Gate Bridge. Several wrong turns and hours later, the car reeked of smoky menthol.

"Are you sure it's not the dog that makes you itch?" Lark asked.

"Coco? She's a poodle. They're hypoallergenic. You must know that. Some breeds have hair that grows much like human hair. They don't cause reactions like dogs with fur."

"Well, whatever's going on with your skin, that stuff isn't helping."

"Now you're the skin expert, hmmm?"

Eloise fanned herself with a map of Sonoma County they'd gotten from the one-pump gas station/general store in Ripplewood, the closest town to Abbudin's. The hamlet, once known for trees like the ripple tree at 346—with heart-shaped leaves that glimmered and danced in sunlight and even chimed on rare occasions—now had none. Droves of people had tramped in, dug up saplings, chopped mature trees down, and stripped the leaves from others for souvenirs.

It was rumored, though, that some ripple trees survived deep in forested land, hidden well by the steep hills and majestic fir and redwood trees.

"I guess Arval Yates was one of those who ruined the forest," Lark said. "I heard he planted them all along the lane."

"Shinbone's founder should have left them where they were."

Lark and Eloise bumped along in silence. Then they rounded a steep curve, and a dome came into view uphill to the left. "Look! There it is, the dome just like Abbudin described," Lark said. She drove up a dirt driveway that led to a compound in a clearing surrounded by towering evergreens. All the structures were forest green with golden trim.

When she pulled to a stop, a man in a white robe and sandals came out of a large, low-slung building and strode toward them. An iguana sat on his shoulder. Eloise stuck the map on the dashboard and opened her door. Coco leaped out, ran to the man and circled his feet. The dog yipped; the iguana hissed.

"Come back here this instant," Eloise demanded.

The dog continued circling the man and kept up the noise.

"Don't worry," he said. "I can tell your pooch means no harm." He put the iguana down on the edge of a burbling fountain and scooped up the dog. "Nice little girl you have." He kissed Coco's nose. The dog wagged her tail.

Eloise rushed up, rubbing her arms and wrists. "I'm so sorry. Coco doesn't usually make such a fuss." This, she knew, was a lie. She took the dog from him and pointed to the iguana. "Does that thing bite?"

"Dixie's never bitten anyone here."

Lark stuffed keys into her backpack as she came forward. "Not exactly reassuring."

The man nodded to her. "Hi, my name's Barry."

Eloise gave a stiff nod. "I'm Eloise." She patted her dog. "And you've met Coco."

Lark stuck out her hand. "I'm Lark. I saw you when the chorus came to Shinbone."

"What a lovely time we had." A smile of recognition warmed his face. He gestured toward the building he'd just left. "Everyone's in meditation right now in Peace Hall. Everyone except me. It's my turn to greet people who stop by, which is usually pretty boring because hardly anyone ever comes here."

"We're looking for the twins, Bea and Barb," Lark said. "They boarded the bus with you and nobody's heard from them since. It's concerning."

Eloise put Coco down and rifled through her purse to pull out a picture of Julianna, whose angular features resembled her own. She handed Barry the photo and flinched as though she'd just stepped on a thorn when she told him her daughter was missing.

She stood on tiptoes and leaned forward, scratching her elbows, while he studied the photo. Then he handed it back. He didn't recognize her. She was welcome, the young man offered when he saw Eloise's sad eyes, to ask around when everyone came out for supper. He then put the iguana back on his shoulder and asked the women to follow him to the low-slung building. They did, with Coco trotting beside Eloise as they entered the dining hall.

"This is Right Way Hall," Barry said, "where we have all our meals. I hope you like lentil stew. Abbudin picked up the recipe on a trip to Greece a few years ago. A family in Thessaloniki told him it heals everything but heartbreak."

"Oh, is that what I smell?" Lark looked up at him. "I've never smelled anything quite like it, nor have I heard of stew with such healing power."

"It's got onion, garlic, carrots—lots of good stuff. We serve it with fresh flatbread." Barry escorted them to a couch against a wall. "Have a seat. There's some information about what we do here if you're interested."

Eloise continued to scratch, her skin reddening. "If only a stew could stop this infernal itching."

"We make a salve that will clear that all up," Barry said.

"Not likely," Eloise muttered.

"I'll get you some. You'll see." He handed each of them a leaflet from a side table then ambled to double doors across the room, pushed one open, and disappeared.

Lark and Eloise leaned back on the couch and skimmed the literature. Coco hopped up and snuggled between them. A gong sounded. Vibrations filled the room. All three closed their eyes and drifted into sleep.

~

HUMMING THE SONG "MY FAVORITE THINGS" from *The Sound of Music*, Clara tied off a lavender Angora scarf. She held it up to warm afternoon light dancing through the living room windows and smiled with satisfaction. Seated on the couch, Maddy brushed bits of charcoal from a drawing of an antique sewing machine in a corner of the room. The doorbell rang.

Maddy tiptoed to the window and peeked outside. "Oh no!" She slunk back to the couch. "It's that cad Ricky. What if he told someone?"

"It's been a week since you went on that unfortunate motorcycle ride. No authorities of any kind have come around. I think you're safe." Clara stood up. "I'll see what he wants." She advanced slowly to the door and opened it. "Hello, young man. What brings you here?"

"I really need to talk to Maddy." From behind his back, he pulled a bouquet of wildflowers. "These are for her. They're from my mom's yard."

Clara hesitated, rubbing a spot behind her earlobe for a moment while thinking that if his blue eyes had been light and sparkly and not so incredibly dark and sad, he would resemble her sweet Matthew on their wedding day. But then, he was far from the first dark-haired lad who'd brought Matthew to mind.

She took the flowers. "I guess there's no harm if you stop in." She ushered him inside. "You'll have to turn right around and leave if she doesn't want to see you."

Clara made for the living room; Ricky tagged behind.

"You didn't. I can't believe it," Maddy grumbled at seeing Ricky's tentative smile.

"I'm a sucker for flowers." Clara handed the bouquet to Maddy. "He picked them for you."

"This is unreal." The budding artist squeezed the flower stems.

"Let's just see what he has to say. ... I can be a buffer between you," Clara offered.

Maddy sighed. "Oh all right, since he's here already." She thrust the flowers onto the coffee table.

Clara settled into her favorite chair.

Ricky wrung his hands as he spoke. "Okay, I admit it. I found your pack and kept it for a while. At first, I just wanted to find out who owned it so I could return it. But I found a student ID for a high school in Ohio."

"Yeah, I figured that out, Sherlock," Maddy snapped.

"The ID said you were a sophomore in the 1972-73 school year, so that got me—"

"Clara already knows I'm a runaway."

"Has she seen the story in *The Columbus Dispatch*? I found it in microfiche at the library."

"I most certainly have not." Clara's eyebrows furrowed. "What story?"

"Heck if I know." Maddy looked down and rubbed her cuticles.

"Then you don't know what happened after you left," Ricky said.

"You had no business prying into my life!" Maddy declared.

A brew of emotions hung in the air as the three eyed one another. Finally, Ricky said, "You're right. I was out of line, but the story in the paper was so thin, just a few paragraphs about your brother drowning, you disappearing, and your dad being quoted saying he was at his wit's end. I wanted to know more, so I called the paper, but got nowhere until finally I wheedled out the number for your dad's office and hit pay dirt."

"You talked to my dad?"

"He was out of the office, but the gal who answered the phone had a lot to say."

"Betsy. She loves to gossip."

"Will it upset you if I go on?"

"I'm already upset, so you may as well tell us what you know." Maddy locked eyes with Clara. "I was gonna tell you at some point."

Both women regarded Ricky. He looked away. Then, silence. Three heart beats raced. Finally, he continued. "So Betsy told me about your mom's history of mental illness, and being institutionalized twice before she drowned your brother, Tyler, in the bathtub."

"She did what?" Clara asked.

"It gets worse," Ricky said. "There were even rumors that she attempted to do the same to Maddy when she was small."

Maddy let out a tiny yelp, then exclaimed, "They don't think I did it anymore?"

"Your dad broke down and told the truth the same night you left."

Clara took in a sharp breath and then said to Maddy, "So that big, awful something your dad ... your dad blamed you for on that night you ran away"—her voice caught—"was ... drowning your little brother? And he knew—he knew your mother had done it?" Clara rose and paced the room.

"If only I hadn't gone off with Oliver that afternoon. I left Mom alone with Tyler." Maddy's eyes glistened with tears unspilled. "I'm a walking billboard for stupid things people do when they think they're in love."

"Betsy told me it was your birthday, to boot," Ricky said. "Why shouldn't you have been able to celebrate? The sympathy in your hometown is all with you."

Clara sat beside the teenager on the couch and put an arm around her. "My goodness, what a burden to carry all on your own."

"Yeah, what dad tries to get his daughter to take the rap for a murder she didn't commit?" Ricky asked.

Maddy wiped her eyes with the back of her hand.

Clara handed her a tissue. "You should never have been responsible for your mother. It's clear from what Ricky says that she was a danger to the family, and your father knew that."

Maddy dabbed her cheeks, then wadded the tissue into a ball as she spoke. "At first, I thought he was right, that I should take the blame. But when I went to my room to find my shoes, I panicked. They were waiting for me in the dining room, with my mom soaking wet right by my dad. And once I had my shoes on, I didn't want to lie. I didn't want to take the blame. But it would be his word against mine. I went out the window instead, probably made me look guilty as all get out."

"I bet you weren't expecting your young tenant was running from a murder rap," Ricky said to Clara.

"I knew something bad had happened, but I wouldn't have guessed this." Clara glanced outside, then at the troubled teen she'd grown to love.

To Maddy, Ricky said, "The upshot is that your dad was suspended from his job for a few months, your mom's in some institution now, and your classmates have plastered yellow ribbons all over the high school. ... It was messed up of me to say I wasn't surprised you knew about La Llorona."

Maddy looked down and kneaded the damp tissue in her hand. "What do I care what you say or do now? No police are looking for me. I suppose my dad could try to haul me back to Ohio if you told him where I am."

"I would never do that," Ricky said, his voice stiff with hurt.

"You'd better not," Maddy replied. Then she turned to Clara and said, "I'll be seventeen in November. Just one more year until I'm free of him. Till then, he's a loose end."

"You can stay here as long as you like. I'll deal with your dad if it comes to that," Clara said. "And don't go thinking you'll take that Purple Tortoise again."

Maddy smiled. "Green Tortoise. You already talked me out of that." She picked up her sketchbook. "I have to capture that look on your face. You look luminous—like Yosemite Falls at first light."

"You've seen it?" Ricky asked.

"Why would I tell you?" Maddy's combative tone told him to leave.

Wincing at her rejection, Ricky strode toward the door, then turned back. "I'm a jerk, no denying that ... but I want you to know your secret's safe with me."

~

Rosie's coin bracelet clinked melodiously, the sound delicate and bright, as she stirred a pot of chicken stew in her cozy 29th Street kitchen. But her thoughts were heavy, simmering like the stew itself as she worried about the future. She couldn't believe Wayne kept insisting they uproot themselves—again.

"I'm telling you, I've decided. I won't move this time." Rosie's stirring speeded up. "We've got a good thing going here."

Wayne wobbled in his seat at the kitchen table. "Nod anymore, we don'." He grunted, finished off his Schlitz, and crunched the can in his hand.

"I suppose it won't do any good to tell you to slow down. You're unsteady, slurring your words." Rosie took the can from his hand and put it in the trash under the sink. "There are programs, you know. You could get help."

"That Ricky guy shouldn a been snoopin' around."

"You must think he's spying for those creeps in Arcata. But that can't be, right? You said they just wanted to scare you away, that the thousand dollars you owed wasn't worth their time."

"True enough."

"Was there some other drug deal gone bad, somebody else you pissed off?"

"How am I spose ta remember every jerk thas got an ax ta grind? You just better start packin' up. Thas all I'm sayin'." He took a joint from his pocket and lit it.

Last time he'd forced them to flee, Heather was two years old. They were renting a home in Arcata and planned to settle down there. She babysat for a few families with children close to Heather's age. Wayne worked as a handyman and sold pot on the side, claiming his operation was small enough to stay under the radar of big dealers and authorities alike.

But one afternoon he barged through the front door looking jumpy as hot corn kernels. "Caruzo's after me!" His eyes bulged. "Drop everything and pack up quick."

"But—"

"He said he'll break my kneecaps if I don't pay up, and unless you've got a grand stashed somewhere, we've gotta scram."

Within an hour, they sped away in the bread truck he'd won in a poker game. No plan for the future. They soon ran out of cash. Rosie sold their belongings at sidewalks in towns and rest stops along highways.

They discovered she had a knack for matching people with gently used things they fell in love with. Wayne scoured everywhere for discarded items that could be cleaned, refurbished and sold. She branched out to sell in campgrounds and at swap meets, bringing smiles to countless faces. But they were always on the go, never part of a community. Rosie didn't want that life for her growing children.

Seeking to quell the anger brewing in her gut, Rosie opened the oven door and concentrated on the comforting smell of baking bread. If she raised her voice, he'd be triggered. She didn't want to go to bed with fresh bruises. "Mmm. Garlic bread's done." She pulled the loaf out and put it on top of the stove.

Wayne took a deep toke, then coughed. "Strong stuff."

"It's gotten old, being a nomad, especially with two kids."

His stomach growled. He took another drag on the marijuana, then held the joint out to Rosie. "Want some?"

"This is how it starts, Wayne. This is how it starts."

"Aw, you're no fun." He took another drag.

"I swear if you get locked up again, on a 5150 hold—"

"I'm just plannin', thinkin' ahead."

"You promised this time. You promised me you wouldn't get out of control with your drinking and drugging and paranoia—and abuse."

"Come on, sweet thing. I always know when is time ta go."

"I don't get it."

"Aren' you my midnight moon girl, my skinny-dippin' love bug? Don' you wanna be free?"

"That is not romantic anymore."

Wayne rose from his chair and stumbled to his wife. He pressed his bulk against her rear, his breath pulsing against her neck and up into her soft red waves.

Rosie pulled away and returned to stirring the stew. "Give me some breathing room! I was trying to talk to you, have a real conversation about our future. Here. In this house. With friends. A community to rely on."

"Some weird-ass community if ya ask me. We don' need it." He flopped back down at the table.

She stirred, staving off tears, then lifted a spoonful and held it out to Wayne—as if flavor could render their love tender again. "Want a taste?"

He stubbed out the joint. "See, look. I'm in control."

"Was that a yes or a no?"

"Oh sure, sure."

She held the spoon to Wayne's mouth, and he slurped from it.

"Thas delish. Could use a liddle salt."

"I'll add more tamari." She opened the refrigerator and grabbed the condiment.

"Say, git me a beer while yur dere."

"In control, huh?" She looked into his bloodshot eyes. "You were doing so well. Now look at you, bumbling, sliding back."

"I'll jus get it mahself." He tried to stand but then lost his balance and plopped back into the chair. "Damn Ricky, busybody."

"It doesn't matter what that guy does."

"You don' know dat," he said, then raised his voice. "You really don' know whad yur talkin' 'bout."

"No need to get worked up." She added tamari to the stew and stirred, then tasted it. "Mmm, I think it's perfect now."

"Mommy?" Heather stood in the doorway. "Me and Lucas are—"

Wayne lifted his head. "Dere she is. A great big, gian' miztake." He leaned forward and rested his head over folded arms on the table.

Heather's bottom lip quivered. "Mommy?"

Rosie held a finger to her lips."Shhhh." Then she tiptoed to the doorway and gave her daughter a hug. "Daddy's about to fall asleep," she whispered. "He's been talking nonsense. It's not about you." She kissed the top of Heather's head, then held her at arm's length. "Go on back to the living room, hon. I'll bring our meal there."

The child turned just as a cloud crossed the sun, blocking the light and warmth that had been beaming through the kitchen window. Rosie shivered, watching her daughter walk away in shadow.

LAUGHTER LIKE WIND chimes and savory smells curling through the air pulled Lark from a dream. She opened her eyes and saw Coco, all wiggles and yips, begging for scraps at a long dining table. At Lark's side, Eloise snored and mumbled in her sleep.

Lark tapped her companion's thigh. "Eloise, wake up." She surveyed the room. Barb and Bea sat at the far end of a row, carrying on like dolphins at play. Lark tapped her companion again. "Look! They're here, and they look just fine."

Eloise stirred. "Julianna?"

"Sorry, not Julianna. The twins." Lark helped Eloise sit up straight.

Eloise called to Coco, who trotted over with tail wagging.

Seeing the travelers awake, Abbudin ambled over, greeting diners along the way. Some reached for him with easy affection; others held themselves tight, like deer sensing an eerie stillness in the woods. "I hope you had a good rest," he said when he reached the guests. "You must have been exhausted."

"Or you did something to us, hmmm?" Eloise accused.

"People often become so relaxed when they visit that they nod off at first. You've only been asleep for about twenty minutes."

Eloise pulled out her crinkled photo. "Have you seen her? My Julianna?"

Abbudin studied the photo. "I'm afraid I don't recognize her. I doubt she's been here, but you're welcome to ask around after supper. We've saved a place for you across from the twins."

"They're here?" Eloise asked.

"I just pointed them out to you." Lark stood and smoothed wrinkles from her taupe seersucker shorts.

Abbudin pointed to the serving area. "Our meals are cafeteria style, and there's plenty for all." He helped Eloise stand and walked with her toward an array of colorful, fragrant dishes, including the lentil stew and flatbread Barry had mentioned, along with fresh cheeses made in the compound's own creamery.

Eloise leaned down to sniff the buffet. "Smells quite peculiar."

After the guests filled their plates, Barb and Bea called out in unison, "Hey, Lark, Eloise! Over here."

The two unlikely traveling companions joined them and chatted all through the meal. When asked why they hadn't called home lately, the twins explained they'd written a letter to let their folks know they'd be out of touch for a while.

"Your mom sounded fit to be tied when she phoned," Lark said.

"She's just a worrywart," Bea said.

"Someday you'll be a mother, and you'll never talk like that again," Eloise said. "You should have more respect."

After an awkward pause, Barb said, "We'll write again tomorrow."

"And I'll call her when we get back to 346 to let her know you're okay," Lark said.

With that settled, the conversation moved on to skits the duo were developing. Lark cleared her plate while encouraging them in their creative explorations. Eloise pushed food around hers, taking only a few bites. Then she excused herself, pulled out Julianna's photo, and went from table to table, asking everyone if they'd seen her.

One woman took a long look at the photo. "I saw her. Yes, I'm sure I did. That long hair down to her elbows, and that gorgeous beaded necklace."

"She made that herself. She's got talent, my girl."

"It wasn't near here, though. ... I saw her in San Francisco a couple of years ago. Come to think of it, it might have been at one of those cool fairs on Shinbone Lane where everyone gives stuff away."

"Are you sure?" Eloise leaned in, eyes fixed on the woman's face. "Sure you haven't seen her here?"

"It was definitely in the city."

"That was before she went missing, so you're no use to me."

"Sorry I couldn't help," the woman answered sincerely.

No one else at the compound recalled seeing Julianna. Eloise said no more; she just slid the photo into her purse as though it were a love letter too dear to read again.

Later, reassured that the twins were okay, Lark and Eloise bid farewell to the group.

Abbudin and Barry accompanied them to the Chevy where Barry handed Eloise a jar of salve. "For the itching," he said.

She thanked him and fumbled her way into the passenger seat.

Lark put the car in gear, and they headed for the coast, where a cozy motel room awaited them. It had a hot tub with a panoramic view of waves lapping the shore.

Barry turned to Abbudin. "Those two were mighty suspicious at first, especially Eloise."

"There's something unsettling about that one," Abbudin replied, a stoic glint in his eyes, "like she has barbed layers better left alone."

EIGHTEEN

After they adjusted to navigating in low light in a speeding vehicle, Captain and Bonbon poked through paraphernalia in the truck bed. They found boxes of papers, clothing, small appliances, fringed lamp shades, a crib-sized mattress, boards, and other trappings of human life. Then they came upon a crate with two large pigeon hybrids whose feathers were primarily yellow, tan, and violet with touches of aquamarine.

Roused from a state of torpor when Captain and Bonbon drew near, the captives opened their eyes, clapped their wings against their bodies, and crept forward to peek through spaces in the crate's wooden slats. The birds stared at each other, all four still as fossils until Captain shrugged and dipped his head in greeting. One by one, the others followed.

Captain took a chance and beamed words to the strangers. "I'm Captain, and this is my mate, Bonbon. Who are you?"

The male of the pair replied in kind. "Our master calls us Sonny and Cher. He chortles when he introduces us like we're some kind of joke. But before we were captured, I was Stormer and my wife," he nuzzled the pigeon beside him, "was Misty."

"Well, Stormer and Misty, pleased to meet you," Bonbon said.

"Do you know where this truck is headed?" Captain asked.

"Some place called Fort Bragg," Stormer said. He explained the man's wife had just kicked him out of the house in Ferndale, so he was going to stay with his parents for a while. "At least that's what we understood from their horrid arguments," Stormer said.

"Their anger spread through everything, even us, like skunk stink," Misty added.

The truck went over a big bump. The crate banged into a box and then slid back toward Captain and Bonbon, who struggled to keep their balance. They hopped on top of a rolled-up rug just as the crate came to a stop where they'd been standing. Misty and Stormer poked and preened, each making sure the other was okay.

"Does he always keep you in this crate?" Bonbon asked.

"Yup, unless we're tethered to a perch," Stormer replied.

"Then you must come with us to Shinbone Lane, where you'll have no master, and you'll come and go as you please," Captain said.

"He won't let us go. He says he's going to sell us for a fortune now that he needs money, because we're so unusual," Stormer said.

"He doesn't know the half of it, does he, like you can use language when you want to?" Captain said.

"He doesn't have a clue," Misty replied.

Bonbon poked around the crate, her beak and claws darting and pulling. She pointed out that the lid was tied with leather. "We can chew through it from outside," she said. "We can get you out."

Stormer fluttered his wings in excitement. "Yes, yes, and we'll all fly up and away when he lifts the tarp."

"Ted's certain to be surprised when I come home, not just with a mate but with two new friends. We're going to start our own community." Captain puffed up his feathers with pride.

"We must work fast," Bonbon said. "We don't know how much longer before he stops."

"Who's Ted?" Misty asked.

"We'd best get into that once you're out of the crate," Bonbon said.

Misty backed away a few inches.

"That doesn't sound good." Stormer made a guttural sound and backed up, too. "Are we going from one trial to another?"

"Ted's a human, but he's my best friend in the world. He'll protect us; you'll see."

Stormer and Misty leaned into each other, murmuring. Then Stormer said, "Okay, we'll take our chances with you. Wherever we land has got to be better than this cage."

BENEATH A BLUE SKY with scattered clouds as white as sugar moon roses, Lark turned the Impala onto Shinbone Lane.

"Seems this trip was nothin' but a waste of time," Eloise said as the car chugged toward 346. "I'm no closer to finding my Julianna."

Lark glanced at Eloise. Her companion's face had taken on a grayish tone, and her usually impeccable lipstick was smeared, giving her a wilted look, like a washed-out clown after a final curtain call.

Concerned, Lark aimed to reassure Eloise. "You found out she hasn't been to Abbudin's. Only one person thought she'd seen her before, and it was right here on the lane. That's something."

Hearing the V8 engine humming, people looked out their windows. Some later commented that chartreuse sparks shot from the exhaust pipe; others said that was pure folly. Members of Shinbone Friends debated the subject but, as with many other issues, they agreed to disagree in the end.

Sunrise, Chip, and Ted were already outside when Lark parked the car. "I'm just gonna stop here first to check in real quick." She patted Eloise's hand. "Then I'll drop you off."

"Don't be silly. It's less than a stone's throw away."

"Since you practically bought out that consignment store in Point Reyes Station, you'll need help with your bags. And honestly, you look like you might be coming down with something."

Exiting from the driver's side, Lark stood up just in time to catch Sunrise, who leaped into her arms. "Hi kiddo. Nice to know that somebody missed me." She laughed and put the child down, then handed the keys to Ted. "Thanks for the loan. It drives like a dream."

Lark rummaged through bags and boxes in the back, pulled a wooden doll house from the back seat, and placed it on the flagstone.

"Wow!" Sunrise ran her fingers over the roof. "Thank you."

Lark ruffled the girl's black curls. "I thought you'd like it."

"Looks like you came home with a lot more than you left with," Chip said to Lark.

"You wouldn't believe all the bargains we found along the way. All kinds of cool shops, little roadside stands."

"Can we paint it pink like your room?" Sunrise asked Chip.

"Pink it will be," he said. He leaned forward, eyeing what remained in the car. "What's the word on the twins? Abbudin didn't brainwash them or anything, did he?"

"They're fine," Eloise grumbled, "just thoughtless like all you young people." She swiveled her legs and tried to stand, but she groaned and sank back. "Oh, my achin', achin' bones."

Coco jumped from the car and barked.

Ted came around to Eloise's side and took her hand. "Up you go."

Eloise let him steady her, then broke free. "I don't need your help." She snatched her Betty Boop lunchbox and purse, then lurched and faltered across Shinbone's mosaic of weathered stones like a mari-onette with tangled strings.

"Wait up," Lark said to Eloise. "I've got a couple bags of yours right here. We can sort through them at your house."

"That won't be necessary." Eloise struggled forward.

Lark turned to Chip. "Can you take my stuff inside? I might be a little while. She's upset because she didn't find any news of Julianna."

"She never lets anybody inside," Chip said.

"We're forming a bond, I think."

Lark strode to Eloise. Coco ran ahead. The dancer wobbled with each step. Complaining of dizziness while going up her steep stairs, Eloise had to stop several times. Lark kept a hand on her arm to steady her. Finally, they made it to the top. Out of breath, Eloise tried to unlock the door with trembling hands but could not.

"Here, let me." Lark took the key, opened the door, and a wave of rot struck her like heat from a roaring furnace. "What is that smell?" She cupped her hand over her mouth and nose and coughed.

Eloise bumped past her and stumbled into the foyer. "Does smell peculiar. Could be raccoons. They've been rummaging in the attic. Haven't been able to get rid of them, so I closed it off."

Gagging, Lark followed her. "I'll have a look. You'll probably need exterminators or something."

"You should go home. You must be tired after all that driving."

"It'll only take a minute."

Eloise sank onto her living room couch as Coco followed Lark up the stairs.

IN A BEDROOM that looked like a puppy had chomped and scattered every bit of clothing it could reach, Natalie tried but failed to close her overstuffed suitcase. Truman, who'd been hovering in the doorway, came over and pushed the lid down so she could secure the clasps.

He slid the suitcase off the bed and carried it to the front door. "Jeez, what do you have in there?"

"It's been so long since I've left for more than an hour or two." She fussed with her hair in the hall mirror, posing like a pinup queen, though she looked more like a stout Shelley Winters than the fine-boned and toned Jane Fonda.

"Did you tell Ricky we'll be gone for several days?" Truman asked.

Natalie dug through her purse and took out a tube of lipstick. "What does it matter?" She opened the tube and applied it with care, using a tissue to wipe a smudge at the corner of her thin lips.

"He's a good son." Truman watched her preen. "Look at you, getting all pretty for me."

She pressed her lips together and exhaled through her nose. "What would you know about bein' a good son or parent or anything? I wish I'd never laid eyes on that boy." She smacked her lips, closed the tube, and tossed it back into her purse.

"You're just blowin' smoke."

"I'm serious." Her skin turned a pinkish hue.

"Okay, if you say so. Let's not have a meltdown."

"Almost forgot. Got some sodas and sandwiches for lunch on the table." She darted to the kitchen, where she picked up a paper bag and returned to Truman.

"Drinks'll be hot by lunchtime." He grabbed the door handle.

"If we don't have 'em for lunch, we can put 'em on ice wherever we land at the end of the day."

"We can be wherever we want to be. We've got time." He held the door open for Natalie and followed her outside.

"Why couldn't this client of yours get a ride from someone there?" she asked, strutting to the car.

"She trusts me. I'm the only one who knows the case through and through. Except for her dad. But he's been out of commission since his stroke. You could say I'm responsible for her now."

"Why can't she drive herself?"

"If you're gonna pester me all the way there, you may as well not come."

"Person's got a right to ask questions."

"She's legally blind, okay, and feeling abandoned. Don't you remember? I've told you before." He put her suitcase on the floor of the backseat next to a beat-up duffle bag of his own. Then he opened the passenger door, bowed, and waved her in. "At your service, madame."

Inside, she fidgeted, hands in her lap. "Maybe I shouldn't go. I don't feel—"

"It'll be fun. Nice drive. Beautiful country. Time out on the road."

"A real-life, um, what's that guy? Ricky told me about him. ... Ken Kesey, yeah, it was Ken Kesey and his Merry Pranksters. We'll have a real-life Ken Kesey experience."

"I didn't think your kid was into all the psychedelic stuff." Truman turned the key, but the engine wouldn't start.

"You probably didn't have this rat trap serviced, so it'll go kaput on us in the middle of nowhere."

When Truman turned the key a second time, the engine fired up. "You worry too much."

"It's a lot of trouble you're goin' to for this so-called client of yours." Natalie sniffed and patted the purse in her lap. "What's her name anyway?"

"Ferguson. Penny Ferguson."

"A woman with money, I expect. Just your type." She pulled out a compact, looked into the mirror, and scowled.

"She's just a kid, probably not even twenty-five. I'm no cradle robber."

Natalie snapped the compact closed and tossed it back into her purse. "A sweet young thing with money."

"You got your own kind of assets, doll, worth more than a boatload a money." He backed out of the driveway and drove off.

It was the rank smell that startled Clara. The odor assaulted her nose while she knit a mauve sweater on her front porch. For Chip, it was the thin, green fog that spoiled the light for a photoshoot he and Lark had planned for *Poetry Flash*, which had requested a headshot to run alongside a feature about her work.

As for Maddy, she almost fell off her bicycle on the way home from posting flyers when a black-and-white police cruiser passed her and stopped in front of Eloise's. By the time she leaned her bike against the bay tree at Clara's, most neighbors had left their homes, despite the rancid air, to see what was going on.

All eyes were on the officers as they hurried to Lark, who waited on Eloise's front porch and prayed her knees wouldn't buckle. After greeting them, Lark opened the front door. Coco zipped outside and ran toward Clara's, ignoring Lark's pleas to come back.

Lark and the officers entered Eloise's home while the little dog leaped into Clara's lap. "Goodness me." She put down her knitting and patted the dog's back.

Ted, who'd returned to his workshop after welcoming Lark and Eloise home, strode out in time to see a police officer escort Eloise down her front stairs. She tottered, groaning every few steps and scratching at her face.

Lark followed, shuddering at the thought of what she'd just seen. Julianna, chained to a cot. Unconscious and emaciated. Translucent skin. Dull, straw-like clumps of hair where a glorious auburn mane used to be.

An ambulance pulled up as Eloise called repeatedly, "Julianna? Have you seen my Julianna?" The officer helped her into the squad car.

Lark crossed the street and fell into Ted's arms for a long hug. When they broke apart, she took in a deep breath and described, in halting speech barely above a whisper, what she'd found.

By the time an ambulance carried Julianna away, Clara and Maddy had joined a small group of neighbors gathered in front of 346—more for mutual comfort than anything else. Clara held Coco tightly to her chest. Maddy stood beside her. A few folks spoke about what sort of help Julianna might need, assuming she pulled through, but most were unable to think beyond the present moment.

None of them could fathom how Julianna had been in their midst, hovering between life and death, and nobody knew. Nobody except Eloise, that is.

"It's hard to imagine Eloise harming Julianna," Ted said.

Lark opened her mouth, then shut it again. Her voice, when it came, was reedy. "She must have just ... snapped." She paused, swallowing hard. "How else could she have—" Her throat closed. She looked away.

Chip stepped closer. "Did she say anything at all?"

After staring at the ripple tree for several anguished moments, Lark nodded slowly. "She just ... fell apart." Her voice wavered. "Kept asking about Julianna ... again and again. Like she does. Only—" She broke off, her breath catching. "Only worse."

"Eloise, Eloise, what did you do?" Clara swayed, handed Coco to Maddy, and grabbed Ted's arm.

"Steady there." Ted leaned close to Clara.

"All that beautiful dancing on the hillside Eloise and Tilda did," Clara murmured. "I wish I'd—"

"Let me help you home," Ted said. "You must not—will not—blame yourself for Eloise's actions."

The friends in front of 346 brooded quietly as Ted and Clara crossed the lane, no one ready to leave yet. They couldn't bear the sight of crime scene tape blocking Eloise's front door. They averted their eyes. So none of them detected the tiny, putrid, chartreuse particles puffing from the chimney and various gaps and crevices in her home.

"Look, we gotta take advantage of the scenery along the way," Truman said, parking his junker in front of a cafe in downtown Petaluma.

Natalie patted the purse in her lap. "We already wasted all that time walking around Sausalito. Who cares about the former egg capital of the world? Stupid tourist trap. I can see all the scenery I need on the highway."

"Petaluma's an old river town, not a tourist trap, not like Sausalito."

"We'll really have to haul ass to get up to Portland."

"We only have to get to Ashland, not all the way to Portland. A friend of Penny's brought her to the Shakespeare Festival."

"Aren't we gettin' all hoity-toity." She pursed her lips and widened her eyes, attempting to impersonate a snob. "Shakespeare, bah." She flicked her wrist at him.

"Let's get some grub, something you haven't had to cook."

The two bantered. Truman emphasized they had plenty of time to make a few stops. Natalie declared eating out was an unnecessary expense and a time-waster. He pointed to a sandwich sign near the curb that listed her favorite: tuna salad on toast.

"Bet it comes with a side of salty fries and plenty of ketchup at the table," he said.

"You remembered that I love tuna?" Natalie peeked at him from the corner of her eye and smiled.

Inside the cafe, they sat at the only empty table. Natalie fiddled with the salt-and-pepper shakers and sugar dispenser and complained they'd have to wait a long time for their food since the place was packed. Before long, though, a waitress arrived. She plunked two glasses of ice water on the table and then pulled a pad and pencil from her apron pocket. The unlikely travelers ordered tuna for Natalie, a hamburger, medium rare, for Truman. Then he asked if the cafe could make a green river.

The waitress popped the gum in her mouth and shook her head. "A green what?"

"Never mind. We'll have Coke or Pepsi, whichever you serve."

"Okay, two Pepsis then." She trotted off to the kitchen.

"Green rivers—now that really would have been a trip down memory lane," Natalie said.

Outside, characters in tie-dyed clothing, bare feet, and beads paraded by.

"Look at them hippie holdouts. They think it's still the Sixties, don't know what's up, what real values are," Natalie said.

"And I suppose you do?"

"If we wasn't so far from home, I'd walk out right now." Their table shook. Her purse fell, and her wallet, lipstick, and several papers fluttered out.

"Take a breath." Truman retrieved the purse and contents. "You don't want to make a scene here."

Natalie took a gulp of air and then guzzled her entire glass of water. The table stopped shaking.

"How did you get by all this time, afflicted as you are, without me to talk you down?" He dropped her wallet and lipstick into her purse and handed it to her.

"Funny thing about that. In all these years, I haven't heated up all that much. You just push my buttons like nobody's business." She drummed fingertips on the table.

"Now, don't go flyin' off the handle, but I wonder about this." Truman unfolded a document that had fallen out of her purse. "Looks important to me ... the last will and testament of ... is this that inheritance you mentioned at the creamery?"

She grabbed the papers, stashed them in her purse, and clutched it in her lap. Truman tried to tease her into telling him what was in the will but gave up with a shrug when their food arrived. Natalie bit into her sandwich.

"Hey, slow down. You'll get indigestion."

She finished long before he did. "Are you slow-pokin' to tick me off?"

"I'm eating like a normal person. You should, too."

Natalie heated up again in response. Truman scarfed down the rest of his lunch and left more than enough cash on the table to cover their bill.

Back in the car, Truman said, "Next stop, Avenue of the Giants."

She glowered at him. "What are you, some tour guide?"

"Don't worry, it's a long ways from here."

THE LANE WAS as restless as a wounded songbird the night after Julianna's rescue. As the air they breathed became infused with minuscule green globules leaking from Eloise's home, some people paced by their windows. Others thrashed in bed, their dreams wrenched by Eloise's sobs. A family of raccoons slunk back and forth along hedges. A possum ran up and down the trunk of the ripple tree. Unable to sleep, Maddy padded downstairs to the living room where Clara held a whimpering Coco in her lap.

"Poor Coco can't settle down. She hasn't eaten a thing. I don't know what to do. She's been pacing like those raccoons outside."

"What about milk?" the weary teenager asked. "It might help us sleep, and who knows? Maybe it would calm Coco down, too."

"Warm milk sounds good to me, but don't give her much. We don't know whether her tummy can take it,"

Maddy headed for the kitchen. Coco leaped down and followed, yipping all the way. When they returned the dog stood on her hind legs as Maddy put a tray with warm milk and coffee cake on the table. She put a small bowl of milk on the floor; the dog lapped it up. After she served Clara milk and cake, Maddy leaned down, offering a small piece of cake in her open palm. Coco snapped it up. Then, the dog circled the table a few times, curled up, grunting, at Clara's feet, and closed her eyes. Within seconds, the dog was snoring softly.

Clara looked out the window into the dark. "Eloise looked so lost when they led her away."

Maddy sat down and began sketching Clara. "Imprisoning her own daughter like that. It's really messed up, way worse than my dad blaming me for what my mom did."

"Eloise blamed me for Tilda's death, and I felt like I deserved it."

"I can't imagine you being anything other than a great mom."

"When my daughter needed me, truly needed me, I was put to the test. And I failed."

Maddy frowned and put her drawing down. "That can't be true."

"You know how plenty of single girls who become in the family way nowadays keep their babies and raise them however they can—with parents or friends, or even with the fathers, just not married—and everyone, well, maybe not everyone, but society as a whole, is more accepting? It's not something you have to hide anymore."

"I guess I haven't given it much thought."

"It didn't used to be that way. There was so much shame with having babies out of wedlock. And my Tilda made a mistake. She had a baby on the way and asked her dad and me for help. She wanted to keep the child. But Matthew insisted on sending her to an unwed mother's home here in the city. He was convinced that was the only reasonable thing to do—and quickly, before she started to show. I went along with it, and ... it killed her."

"Did she ... die in ... childbirth?" Maddy choked out the words.

"She ran away from the home a few weeks before her due date. Matthew and I had argued about it almost nonstop in the months she'd been away. That very morning, he finally came around to the idea of bringing her home. And then she called. I was thrilled to hear her voice. I said her dad and I both wanted her to come home, that we would come get her, that she could keep the baby and we'd help her. But she said she was already at a bus stop—only one ride away—and a bus was coming. I wish I'd never said it would be okay for her to take that ride." She dabbed a tissue at the corner of her eye.

With her pulse thudding in her ears, the teenager asked, "How come?"

"She never made it home." Clara's lower lip quivered as tears flowed. Coco woke up, jumped into her lap and licked Clara's cheeks and chin.

"Maybe ... maybe she ran away like I did?"

"Her body was found ten days later. ... She'd been cut open. ... No sign of the baby."

BEFORE THE GREEN malaise poisoned the air, mornings on Shinbone Lane unfolded in a sensuous way, much like a cat stretching and preening after a long, luxurious nap. Folks relished the mystery as they emerged from dreams. They lingered in the soft light of morning, loving the smell of fresh-brewed coffee, the creak of boards beneath bare feet, the refreshing splash of water. They took time dressing, enjoying the cozy feel of clothing on their skin. Once outside, they stopped to chat with neighbors before getting into their cars or walking down hill to catch the J-Church streetcar or one of the bus lines with stops close by.

Afterward, when all light and smells filtered through the horrid green muck, people stayed in bed until the last possible moment, rushed through their routines and peeled from the lane like forest animals fleeing wildfire. Most didn't hurry home at day's end. They tarried at watering holes or friends' homes, returning to the lane after dark. They sprinted indoors, where the green menace was kept at bay with various combinations of plastic sheeting, duct tape and caulking. People who worked from home did so slowly, quietly, pausing often to stare blankly at their surroundings or take a nap.

Other neighborhoods of the city were perfectly normal. News of Shinbone's affliction spread, and visitors postponed seeing their friends, the only exception being Ted's buddy Harold, a retired social worker who continued to help all who came to his door. Harold came weekly to take Ted fishing for striped bass, catfish and sturgeon in the Delta. He sometimes convinced Ted to camp for a night near Rio Vista, saying it would be good for his lungs, and they'd head back the next afternoon. Ted basked in those hours like a man standing beneath a sudden shaft of sun, providing relief that never reached his workshop, where his tools lay waiting in the poisoned hush.

Maddy left on her bicycle regularly to post flyers, enjoying the fresh air as she pedaled in neighborhoods away from the lane. When at home, she and Clara spent most of their time in Clara's living room since they could no longer comfortably pursue their projects and sip tea and lemonade on Clara's front porch. Maddy sketched while Clara crocheted or knitted, each quietly absorbed in her work. Their thoughts often went to Julianna and Eloise.

One afternoon, Clara rested an almost completed scarf in her lap and said, "Poor Julianna, near death from starvation, and Lark said dirty plates littered the filthy floor. The poor girl was chained to the bed, didn't even have a chamber pot."

Maddy looked up from her drawing. "Will Julianna recover, do you think?"

"Fortunately, her dad is now a producer in Hollywood, quite successful, and he has stepped up. He's sparing no expense on her care."

"That's good, really good."

"Meanwhile, Eloise is in Langley Porter while her brother, who is also quite well-to-do, is trying to get her released into private care."

"I suppose that's good, too, I mean, since she's obviously not living in reality. How could she face a judge and jury, lawyers, jail, all that stuff?"

The two worked on in silence. Then Clara said, "You know what we need right now?" Her expression turned impish. "Grilled cheese. Good old-fashioned."

Maddy stood up, grinning. "With potato chips and pickles on the side?"

"Anything you want, love." Clara rose from her favorite chair. "Maybe mac and cheese, too? But that could be overdoing it."

"Why not throw in some brownies while we're at it?"

The two repaired to the kitchen, each wishing someone would come up with a solution to rid Shinbone of the green muck, but they were thankful residents were spared the worst of it while inside. And for a time they found solace in singing "You'll Never Walk Alone" while preparing what they came to call their "comfort blowout."

CHAPTER

TWENTY

At Day Park, mothers and caregivers spoke in hushed tones about Eloise and Julianna. Many expressed gratitude that the muck engulfing Shinbone Lane hadn't drifted downhill to the play area they frequented daily.

On a bench, Rosie fiddled with her wedding band while keeping an eye on her children. Lucas pushed a Tonka dump truck through the sand. Heather raced with other tykes over, under, and around the wooden play structure. Ordinarily, Rosie would join in the play, sometimes pretending to be a monster chasing the children, other times pushing them in swings or bringing water to Lucas so he could fashion roads in the sand. This day, she sat, quiet as a possum.

"That woman must be a piece of work to keep her daughter chained up for all that time and starve her to boot," one mother said.

"It's a wonder the girl survived," added another.

Rosie didn't join in. None of them knew any more than she did; she saw no point in fanning speculation and gossip.

She pulled out a Tupperware container of celery sticks stuffed with peanut butter and raisins and called her children to the bench. She doled out snacks along with a small can of Hawaiian Punch, poking

211

holes in the top with a church key before handing it over for the kids to share.

On the other side of the chain-link fence surrounding the children's area, Wayne parked his truck. He tripped getting out, wobbled to the playground, and flopped down next to Rosie. "Pack up. We're goin'. I got stuff enough in the truck. The rest we kin leave."

"It's good to be in the sunshine, don't you think?" Rosie offered him a celery stick. "The kids are having fun."

He batted the container away, gooey peanut butter landing in the sand. "I said we're leavin'." His words came out in a growl, drawing attention from other adults at the playground. "We've done diz dilly-dally dance long 'nough."

"Keep it down, will you?"

"Wha d'you care? We're not gonna see deez folks again."

Heather ran up to Rosie. "Mommy? Are you okay?"

"Everything's fine. Go back and play with your friends," Rosie said.

"No ya don'." He grabbed Heather by the wrist and twisted.

"Ow! Daddy! You're hurting me!"

"Shud up!" He dragged her a few feet toward the fence.

In one smooth motion, Rosie put her bag over her shoulder, picked up Lucas, and grabbed hold of his truck. Then she threw the toy as hard as she could at Wayne, hitting the back of his neck. Knocked off balance, he cried out and let go of Heather's hand before falling backward, hitting his head against the trash container.

"Run to the sidewalk." Rosie nudged Heather and dashed past Wayne. He grabbed for the leg of her bell-bottoms and missed.

She scrambled away, belted the children into seats in the back of the truck, and got into the driver's seat. Wayne stumbled toward them. She searched her purse for the spare key. Wayne drew closer. She found the key. He banged on the door. She started the engine and lurched off, struggling to manage the gears.

"You fool!" he screamed. "You won' even get three blocks."

Rosie ground the gears as she sped to Dolores Street and turned left. She thought of Ted's close friend Harold. She and Wayne had dropped off some furniture for charity there a couple of months ago. She would recognize the home if she could only remember what street it was on. She drove around the area, improving her gear shifting, but she feared Wayne would see her circling.

She was hyperventilating when she pulled up to a red light at 24th and Guerrero. She rolled down her window and slid over to open the passenger side window, too. She could barely focus her eyes.

A knock came at the passenger door. It took Rosie a moment to recognize Lark. "Uh, Lark, hi," she mumbled.

"Hey, Rosie, what's up?" The poet asked.

Heather bobbed up and down in her seat. "Lookie, look, it's Lark."

Trembles moved up Rosie's arms.

"Hey, kiddo." Lark smiled at Heather, then said to Rosie, "You don't look so good. You're white as a whale's underbelly."

The light turned green. "I gotta—"

Lark opened the door and climbed into the passenger seat. "You shouldn't be driving right now."

"Daddy was bad," Heather said.

Lucas stirred in his seat. A car horn blared behind the truck.

"Turn right and pull over," Lark said to Rosie. "I'll take the wheel and get you home."

"Not home." Rosie turned the corner and continued driving. "We're running away."

"Wow!" Eyebrows raised, she looked Rosie over and nodded. "Okay. Where to then?" She spotted a space near Bartlett Street at pointed.

Rosie pulled in. "I thought we'd try Harold, but I can't find his home. I remember it's yellow, with those beautiful roses out front, and some cranberry trim, and his place is above the garage. I just don't know what street."

Lark opened her door. "I know where he lives." She jumped out and walked around the front of the truck while Rosie maneuvered into the passenger seat.

~

"COME ON, ADMIT IT," Truman said as he unlocked the door to a motel room in Garberville. "You liked seeing all those giant redwoods, didn't you? And we made good time." He held the door open for Natalie and then came inside.

"If you've seen one redwood, you've seen 'em all." She surveyed the bronze-and-orange bedspreads in a geometric pattern on two full-size beds. She took in the solid orange throw pillows, bronze drapes, orange paint on the walls, and a painting of miners panning for gold. "Just like motel rooms."

"You're bluffing," he said. "I can see it 'cause you're just like me. I'm a tough guy to most, threatening when I want to be, and maybe that's a real side to me, maybe even what I am most of the time, but down deep, I'm a softie. You're the same."

She sat on a bronze-colored chair in a corner by the window and kicked the pumps off her swollen feet. "I'd rather have my own room. I am an heiress, after all, just short on cash till I sell something."

"Come off it. I saw that sexy little nightie you packed." He set their bags down. "So, miss-let's-not-admit-how-much-we're-alike, which bed do you want?"

"I'll have you know I sleep best in flimsy nighties, has nothin' to do with you." She crossed a leg over her knee and rubbed her foot. "You get the one by the door, so you can pounce in case someone breaks in."

"Fair enough. I'll get the rest of our stuff."

"I've got first dibs on the shower." She picked out toiletries and a kimono from her suitcase.

From the car, Truman brought back deli items they'd bought in town. By the time Natalie returned from the bathroom—hair wrapped in a towel, the kimono draped around her—he had their sandwiches and side dishes arranged on a table. A spire of lupine blossoms rose from a motel glass at the center.

"You probably picked that bluebonnet from that planter outside."

"What does it matter where I got it?"

"Not gonna work on me this time." Natalie unwrapped the towel and fluffed up her hair. "I sure am hungry, but we shoulda just had the sandwiches I packed."

"They got all soggy, remember?"

"Yeah, yeah, if you say so."

The two dug into BLTs, potato salad, and garlic-stuffed olives washed down with Budweiser.

"Where's dessert?" Natalie asked, patting her rounded tummy.

"Oh, here it is." He dug into the deli bag and put a large peanut butter cookie on a napkin.

She broke off a piece, took a bite, and chewed slowly. "Not bad, but we shoulda bought Chips Ahoy! instead. They're not crumbly and greasy like these things made by who knows who—probably some stringy-haired floozy in a rundown kitchen with a squalling baby in a playpen nearby."

"Natalie, Natalie, there's never been anyone like you. You'll always—"

"Stop the sappy stuff. I don't buy this damsel in distress so-called client of yours for one little minute."

"She's disabled. Honest. That's why we're picking her up. Poor thing doesn't see colors. It's all shadows. And she can barely walk."

"Since when do you care about stuff like that?"

"There's a lot you don't know about me."

"Oh, like your thing with Tilda? Her and that Eloise, the two of them always thinking they're better than the rest of us with their dancing. I should have known one of them would go after you."

"I was wondering when you were gonna bring that up. Tilda wanted to help you and me."

Natalie scoffed and looked at the wilting flowers in the motel glass.

"Let me explain." Truman stretched out on the bed by the window and memories he'd blocked for years roared in like a sudden windstorm tossing his feelings around like Kmart lawn furniture. It took a few moments for his pulse to slow down. Then he described his turmoil after another argument with Natalie.

"So there I was all stirred up, and I saw Tilda walking home," he said. "I don't know why, but I snuck behind her all the way up the back stairs that led to her little attic room. You know, the place where that girl Maddy lives now?"

Natalie faced him with a withering look. "I'm supposed to care?"

He sighed, tapped his brow, and then continued, "Funny thing is, when Tilda heard me on the stairs and turned around, she wasn't scared. She asked what was wrong, and could she help. Well, the thrill of following her totally vaporized." He shrugged, palms up, as though still surprised.

"I muttered something about our fight, and she invited me in to talk about it, her eyes trusting as a newborn baby's. We talked and talked, and I felt something like hope growing inside me when I walked back down her stairs."

Natalie feigned boredom. "Whoop dee do."

"I came back the next day, and the one after that, and we never ran out of stuff to say. Then, on impulse, I leaned in and kissed her. All I can say, now, is something got the better of me. She pulled away, but she didn't say no. She didn't say anything at all. I moved in, and she gave me a push, nothing forceful, you know, and—"

"Stop!" Natalie's face flashed with heat. "I don't have to listen to this. I know very well what happened between you and Tilda. You fell in love with the beautiful dancer, and—"

"It wasn't like that. Right afterward I could see she didn't want anything to do with what we'd just done, or with me either, and I, I was wishing it had been you, not her."

"Why bring this up now? Isn't it bad enough that you left me?" Heat flared from her body. "You dumb—"

"You've got to calm down. You'll burn this place up."

Natalie polished off her beer.

Truman got up and handed her another one. "I never saw her again after that. I went looking for you, but I was hauled off for a stupid robbery that went bad up on Cortland. I didn't know my buddy had a gun. ... I didn't even know till a couple months ago that Tilda was dead, a life cut short before she'd really lived."

"Poor you."

"I'm sorry, Natalie."

"Quit your groveling. I'm not pure as the driven snow either."

WINGING HOME WITH BONBON, Stormer, and Misty, Captain suddenly dove toward a repurposed delivery truck parked on 28th Street. He landed on the vehicle's roof and paced, his gait uneven due to his artificial leg. His companions followed, their claws on metal clanging like an avant garde percussion group.

"What on earth?" Rosie said, straightening from her slouch in the passenger seat. She'd been looking at Harold's, not quite ready to rally her children for whatever might lie ahead.

The commotion above continued. Heather called for her mom.

"It's okay, hon. I'm sure it's nothing to worry about," Rosie said.

Lucas, who'd fallen asleep, opened his eyes and yawned.

Lark hopped out the driver's side and laughed at the scene on the roof. "It's a friend of ours. Come on out and see."

Captain swooped to the front and somersaulted down the windshield. Bonbon joined him. Then Stormer and Misty spun into view.

"See?" Rosie said. "It's Captain. And he has friends. They're all so beautiful. Isn't that something?"

Captain flew to a flower box outside one of Harold's office windows and pecked on the glass. The other birds flitted back to the roof. Rosie unbuckled Lucas from his carseat while Heather squeezed past her and jumped to the sidewalk. Bonbon peered at the people with the wonder of a child seeing circus clowns for the first time.

Harold came to the window, saw the visitors and headed for his stairs. Captain flew back to Bonbon and preened with her. Misty opened her mouth, and Stormer nuzzled his beak inside.

Lucas fussed in Rosie's arms until she kissed his forehead and murmured a string of nonsense words, which made him giggle. "Okay, let's go," Rosie said.

"Can we go home?" Heather asked.

"Not right now, honey."

Harold met them on the front walk. They spoke briefly before he led them upstairs. In the kitchen, a pot simmered on the stove, giving the room a hearty, spiced aroma.

"Hungry?" he asked Heather.

"Sort of," the child said.

"I must have known you were coming," he said. "I always get the yen to make chili before someone special arrives."

Rosie put Lucas down, and he toddled across the floor while Harold pulled a highchair from a pantry. When all were at the table with hands freshly washed, Lark helped Harold dish up chili for everyone except Rosie, who was too jumpy to eat. She spooned soft pieces of kidney beans to Lucas instead.

"I know a place where you can stay for a little while," Harold said. "It's south of here, not far. And then once you're safe, we can talk about next steps."

"Can you do some kind of arbitration or something?" Rosie asked. "Wayne's not a bad man. He's a regular guy until he starts drinking. Then he gets rough with me. And his paranoia is through the roof. I'm tired of the footloose life, always picking up stakes on a moment's notice, you know? Especially with two children growing so fast."

"I have friends still working in social services. They might—"

"Wayne wouldn't go for anything official. He's just so ... anti-authority. I don't even know if he'd agree to meet with you."

"Let's get you situated so you can think things over in a peaceful place." Harold picked up the wall phone and punched in a number. "Hi, yes, it's Harold. ... How are you? ... Good news, good. ... Do you have room for a few more? ... Mother and two little ones? ... Great! Sure thing. We'll be there in less than an hour."

Rosie, who had cleared the table while Harold was on the phone, ran water to wash the dishes.

"No need for that. I'll clean up later," Harold said. "We're going to Pacifica. It's often fogged in there but beautiful. ... I'll take my car, and you can follow. We can stop at the beach on the way."

Soon, Harold backed an old Saab out of his driveway and turned toward Dolores Street. With hands no longer shaking, Rosie put her key in the ignition. Lark sat in back with the children, telling them nursery rhymes. When the engine rumbled to life, Captain, Bonbon, Stormer and Misty lifted off.

CHAPTER

TWENTY-ONE

Ted finished gluing a new wig onto a 1950s-era Saucy Walker doll and set it on his workbench to dry. Beside it lay a sky-blue skirt and sweater set, along with a lime green jacket, hat, and mittens—all handmade by Clara to fit the doll. It had been Lark's favorite toy growing up, but a neighbor's dog had attacked it, leaving the doll in pieces. Still, Lark couldn't bring herself to throw it away.

After seeing the sort of magic Ted worked on damaged and discarded things, she'd asked if he could fix it—in case she ever had a daughter to pass it on to.

Ted had accepted the challenge, though he dragged along like someone stricken with mononucleosis. And it had been quite the project: the dog had chewed off the doll's nose and one of her hands, eaten an eye, torn apart the clothes, and scalped her. Bit by bit, Ted brought her back to life.

Now wheezing, he pulled a strip of white patent leather from a drawer and considered how best to cut pieces for Mary Jane shoes. He'd already finished the soles, and he had little buckles of just the right size. He paused to wipe his eyes—red and runny ever since the chartreuse haze had settled over the lane—and decided to call it a day.

He plodded to the front of his home in air that felt dead, as though the green muck had smothered the spirit of the lane. Ted sat on the front steps, removed his cap, and put his head in his hands. He breathed in. The air didn't scratch his throat. He blinked. His eyes didn't sting.

He looked across the lane. Clara's porch, which had been blurred, sharpened into view. Above him, blue patches opened in the sky. A breeze—fresh, cool—swooshed the haze away. Then: birds. Bright-colored and circling, one in front, three holding back. Is it? Could it be? Ted couldn't complete the thought. Not yet.

Then, Captain's gravelly voice made Ted's whole body hum. "What are you lookin' at, stupid man? Of course it's me."

Usually undemonstrative to the extreme, Ted whooped and did a jig. Captain alighted on his shoulder. The other three pigeons settled into the ripplewood tree. By the time they finished their introductions, the haze had dissipated much like an ordinary morning fog.

Captain filled Ted in on his travels. Ted, in turn, told the birds how Lark had found Julianna near death in Eloise's attic.

"You mean she ... she trapped Julianna? All that time, Eloise knew?" Captain nearly slipped from Ted's shoulder.

"Humans!" Stormer rasped to Bonbon and Misty.

"Amen," Bonbon muttered.

"I second that," Misty said.

"There are plenty of good ones. You'll see," Captain replied.

"So are you all staying here?" Ted asked.

"We've agreed to give it a go," Stormer said.

"Looks like I need to build you a bigger home." Ted rubbed his hands together, eager to get to work.

BAREFOOT AND CLAD ONLY in torn, rumpled shorts, Wayne stormed along Shinbone Lane, bellowing and snuffling like a wounded bull. Lights blinked on one by one as groggy residents, stirred from uneasy dreams, lumbered to their windows. He halted in front of 346, pitching as though caught in a rogue wave.

Knees knocking, he groaned and turned away, but then, as he'd done so many times since Rosie's escape, he stomped up the stairs and pounded on the door. The entire structure shuddered in protest, timbers creaking.

Chip rolled away from Dave—who stirred in bed but didn't open his eyes—and threw on his robe and slippers before trundling, half asleep, downstairs. Lark, who'd been writing down remnants of a dream that had woken her minutes before, peeked outside and saw Wayne waving a bottle of Jack Daniels.

She shot to the hall just as Dave emerged yawning, from Chip's room. She bolted down the stairs and reached the front door right after Chip opened it.

"You can't keep doin' this, man, waking everyone up like this," Chip said.

"Jus bring 'er oud, please," Wayne begged, swinging the bottle across his body.

"I don't know where Rosie is," Chip said.

Wayne leaned forward so he was nose to nose with Chip, who turned aside and coughed.

"He's right," Lark said. "We don't know where she is."

"You know it's wrong, her leavin' me, takin' the kids," he growled out, "doesn't even give a fella a chance." He held the bottle above his head and sneered.

Dave arrived and snatched the bottle from Wayne. "Pull yourself together!"

The drunkard swayed and grabbed hold of the jamb for balance. "Nobody's got a perfect marriage, doesn' mean we should splid up, but you light-in-da-loavers types wouldn' know 'bout dat."

Dave handed Chip the Jack Daniels. Their fingers touched and lingered briefly before Chip put the drink on a side table.

Lark wondered why she hadn't figured out earlier that Chip was the one who'd won Dave's heart. Her throat tightened. Heat prickled her cheeks. She struggled to keep her tone even. "She probably just needs time to sort things out," she said to Wayne.

"You been talkin' ta her?"

"I haven't a clue where she is." Lark swallowed hard at the lie.

"She could be in Timbuktu, for all we know," Chip added.

"You makin' a joke?" Slobber flew from Wayne's mouth. "You don' get it. Y'all think is funny."

"Nobody thinks that," Dave said.

"I gotta get ta her. Bad stuff is comin' I kin feel it. I know it," Wayne said.

"Rosie's solid, no pushover. Nothing bad's going to happen," Chip said to Wayne.

The drunk jutted out his chin. "So were Malcom X and Mardin Luter King." He wiped his lips with the back of his hand. "Jus lemme in, will ya? I wanna talk wid Ted. He knows somethin'."

Taking a big gulp of air and letting it out slowly, Lark stepped forward and gave Wayne a hug. "Aw, honey, Ted's asleep. You should be, too."

He burst into tears. "It's bad iz whad I'm sayin'."

"How 'bout if we walk you home?" Lark suggested. "Do you have your keys?"

Wayne fumbled through his pockets until he felt them. "Yeah."

"Let's go then." Chip joined them on the porch and took Wayne's arm.

"Hands off. I ain' no queer." Wayne slugged Chip in the mouth, knocking him into Dave.

"That's it. You're too much." Lark backed into the house. "Chip was gonna help get you home safe, and now he's bleeding"

"Be dat way. See iv I care." Wayne stumbled down the stairs, tripped, and fell to the ground.

"Maybe you can get him out of here," Lark said to Dave. "He might sleep right there if you don't."

"But Chip—"

"I'll take care of him." She escorted Chip to the kitchen and turned on the light. "Whoo, looks like he got you good. I'll fix you right up."

Chip pulled out a chair and sat down. "It's not easy being gay."

"So you and Dave are—"

"I don't know what we are," he said. "He's gonna be a star. He likes to keep his options open."

"Tell me about it," Lark said.

"I know you two have some history."

"I thought we had something, but we didn't, not even close." She blinked away tears while putting alcohol on a cotton ball. "This is gonna hurt a bit," she said.

Chip winced as she dabbed the broken skin.

"Do you really not know where Rosie and the kids went?" Chip asked.

"I know where she went the first night. But right now? No. I know who does, though." She cleaned up Chip's superficial wound, pulled a pack of frozen peas from the freezer, and handed it to him. "That's gonna be one heck of a shiner in the morning."

They chatted until they heard the front door open and footsteps going up the stairs. Yawning, the two decided to head back to bed.

Upstairs in his room, Chip found a note on his pillow by the glowing bedside lamp. He saw no words of love, no signature, only four words: "I can't do this."

NATALIE SNORED in the back seat as Truman steered the rattling Volvo onto the Golden Gate Bridge. "We're almost there," he said to Penny. "Wish you could see it in all its glory, the most famous bridge in the world."

Next to him, Penny squinted outside her window. "Things aren't as fuzzy as they were. I don't see color yet, but I can make out those birds flying, and the clouds."

"You'll see color again one day," Truman said.

"Things will light up when I have Blossom in my arms. When can we get her?"

A trickle of sweat ran from Truman's temple into his ear. He shook his head. "It won't be long."

"You said everything is in place. What's the hold up?"

"You can't just go and snatch a child."

"Why not? That's what happened to me, isn't it?"

"Just trust me," he said.

"What choice do I have?"

They rumbled toward the toll booths at the end of the bridge. The brakes screeched and squealed as Truman slowed the car.

Natalie stirred awake and sat up. "We're back in the city. Thank God." She bent over to look through a shopping bag at her feet. "Jeez, don't we have anything left to drink? Heck, no more chips either? And the red vines?"

"We polished everything off last time we stopped, remember?" Truman accelerated. "Hey, we're right by the Palace of Fine Arts, one of our finest attractions. Want to stop and have a look?"

"No way," Penny said.

"You and your stops." Natalie tapped Penny's shoulder. "It takes him five times as long to get from A to B as anyone else. That's something I never knew before."

Penny craned her neck to squint at Natalie. "I don't know why my dad took him, of all people, under his wing to learn the detective game."

"Hey, watch what you say, you two. There's a method to my madness, and I learned it from him," Truman said. "He sure left me up a creek when he had that stroke, though."

"He's starting to write." Penny faced forward again. "His first word was 'stop' but he can't explain what he means by that yet."

Natalie leaned back and stretched. "I'm no fan of the cops, but you should bring them in. What's yours is yours, after all. Should be plain as day to San Francisco's finest."

Truman made eye contact with Natalie in the rearview mirror. "Even if the fuzz saw things Penny's way, and that's a big if after years have passed," he said, "there'd be red tape stretching from here to Portland and back."

Penny leaned her elbow on the rattling passenger door and rubbed the side of her head. "What do you suppose would happen to Blossom in the meantime? A foster home? ... I've already missed too much time with her."

She looked sideways at Truman, urgency fraying her voice. "We have to get back to Portland right away. Mom was frantic when I called yesterday—practically shrieking that I should turn around and come home. I swear, she'll have a stroke if we don't bring my baby home soon."

"What if Truman's wrong?" Natalie flashed a sly smile. "Do you have a Plan B?"

"He can't be." Penny opened her purse and pulled out an old photo of her daughter. "There is no Plan B." She kissed the photo.

"I woulda thought you'd have more faith in me, Nat." Truman turned right onto Scott Street. They all felt the car strain as it struggled up the hill.

"Why in the world would I have any faith in you?" Natalie asked. "Your judgment isn't great. I mean, look at you driving us up these steep hills through Pacific Heights instead of taking 19th Avenue. Makes no sense."

"This is a scenic route," he said. "You can see how the other half lives in these mansions, and just look out the back window for that sparkling view."

Penny shook her head. "No point in sparkling views for me."

The car rolled backward several feet at a stop sign. Penny and Natalie both held their breath until Truman got it to sputter forward again.

~

A FEW DAYS after Captain's return, Lark bobbed her head in time to an Art Tatum piano solo coming from down the hall as she read pages in her journal. She circled a section for possible reworking:

She drags the chain/ one end cinched at her waist/ the other bolted to the front door/ once flung wide for boots and slickers/ for voices rising in laughter/ hopes too big to hold/ now rusted shut/ hinges thick with silence/ the garden's gone/ no salvia, no sweet peas/ no roses curling around the gate/ no silk-blade grass to welcome bare feet/ she circles the yard/ weeds bristle through broken concrete/ links clink like windblown chimes, off-key/ basement window opens a breath/ she wedges halfway in/ gropes for brittle photos/ and old bars of Fels Naphtha/ that never scrubbed away the fear/ the air is sour with longing/ she pushes, but the frame clamps her ribs/ she slides back out/ lands hard on packed dust/ groaning, stomping/ she rises, trembling/ house screaming behind her/ she bolts for the street/ chain clattering.

Lark turned the page and read on, circling another paragraph:

I am a sneaker on the sidewalk/ a comb missing half its teeth/ pie without filling/ perfume with no scent/ no wonder I am alone, a whale solo and beached/ a mockingbird that sings only one note/ My heart beats in outer space/ no one is soaring up to claim me.

She scribbled more on a fresh page, hoping for a breakthrough. Absorbed in her work, she didn't notice when the music stopped, nor did she hear footsteps in the hallway.

"Lark?"

She raised her head and saw Chip in the doorway, his curls mussed and his face haggard. The black eye from Wayne sported purple and blue hues. "What's up?" she asked.

"Do you know when Dave's coming back?"

"Are you kidding? He and I don't talk anymore."

He shook his hands as though flicking off water and shifted his weight from foot to foot. "I should go. You were working."

"Hey, I need to take a break. I've been at the desk for a couple of hours and getting nowhere." She got up and walked to her window. "Things look peaceful out there. It's so good to not see that greenish veil."

Chip leaned on the door jamb and crossed his legs at the feet. "That's for sure. ... Star Bakery's scones are selling out again. Nobody smelled them, let alone lined up to buy them when the haze was upon us."

"Those scones are the highlight of the week for everyone, except those of us trying to lose weight." She sat down on her bed and motioned for him to sit next to her. "So, about Dave. Are you guys unraveling? I was just getting used to you being together."

Chip joined her. "It's probably not fair for me to dump any of my woes on you."

"He never made me any promises. I wanted him to be somebody he's not."

"He let me down with a note. Then he wouldn't talk about it. Now, poof! He's gone. He said goodbye to Ted and to everybody else except me."

"He didn't tell me either, if that's any consolation. The word is that his grandfather in Illinois got pneumonia in the hospital after a fall. It's really dangerous when that happens."

"I heard that, too. What should I do?"

"I wouldn't trust my advice if I were you. There's still a part of me that wants him to walk in here, grab hold of me, and kiss me passionately."

"I have something similar running through my head."

"So, my advice, if I felt qualified to give it, would be to move on. But how can I tell you to move on when I haven't really done it myself?" Lark brought her hands together and cracked her knuckles. "Say, I just had a crazy idea." A smile spread across her face. "Maybe we should go dancing, you know, dance Dave right out of our dreams."

He stood up, clapping. "We could get dressed up, too."

"I've heard Minnie's Can Do Club is really fun. Let's go there."

"You're on!"

"Oh, I just got an idea for a poem. I want to riff on it while it's hot. Let's meet up after dinner." Lark darted to her desk and opened her journal.

Chip strode to the door, paused, and grinned at Lark. "I bet some of the Frogs would join us. They're probably miserable without Dave, too."

Lark nodded in agreement before imagination swept her away.

TWENTY-TWO

In his workshop, Ted finished drawing plans for an expanded loft in the backyard—one with plenty of roosting places for Captain and the three new arrivals. The birds huddled on Captain's favorite shelf and peeked down.

Ted put his pencil behind his ear and looked up at them. "I've been working on this idea since the day you all arrived. I hope you like it. Nothing's written in stone, of course. It's just my idea how to make you four comfy, cozy and safe. Come closer, have a look. I think it's palatial."

Captain dove to Ted's shoulder. The others stayed put, stretching and bobbing their heads, a feathered chorus line.

"You can tell them I won't bite," Ted said.

Captain beamed his reply. "They understand that to some degree, but remember, Stormer and Misty were captured and locked up in a cage. I don't know how long it will take them to warm up to you. For all they know, you'll cart them off, put them on display, and sell them."

"What about Bonbon?"

"She remembers people with rifles shooting at her flock."

"I understand. I do. It's the hardest thing to work through trauma." Ted tapped on the plans. He pointed out the nooks and roosts planned for the tree outside his bedroom window, as well as an expanded window ledge so Captain and his crew could tap on the glass more easily whenever they wanted to come inside. "No cat or raccoon can climb straight up to that ledge, so you'll be safe if it takes a little while for me to wake up."

"You've outdone yourself, my friend." Captain paused. "There is something else, though," the bird said.

Ted nodded for him to go on.

"How long is that guy Wayne gonna be carrying on at night? He's driving us crazy." Captain snorted in frustration. "He moans, he cries out, he talks to himself, he rails against everyone at the top of his lungs. And then he nods off in the gutter, and he snores. It's so loud that it hurts. I sold Bonbon, Misty, and Stormer on this being the best place for us, and they're seriously questioning my judgment."

"It has been annoying," Ted said. "No doubt about that."

"We're not the only ones bothered," Captain said. "Everybody's complaining."

"It'll be over soon."

"Bonbon is talking about settling back in the forest up north. And Stormer is losing feathers, just like people can lose hair from stress."

Surprised, Ted took a quick breath in. "Wayne will leave after he meets with Harold and Rosie on Wednesday. Can you wait till then?"

"You can't know that for sure." Captain tightened his grip on Ted's shoulder with his natural claw. "Bonbon needs her sleep."

"I understand that, and—"

"She's in the family way."

"That's fantastic news!" Ted turned his head to get a good look at Captain and smiled wider than he had in years. "I'd lost faith this day would ever come. I'm so happy for you."

"There must be something you can do about Wayne." The bird nipped Ted's ear.

"Hey, watch it!" Ted rubbed his ear. "I just had an idea. I'll ask the Frogs to help watch him. If we go in pairs, I bet we can keep him inside his home. It'll only be for a few more nights. It could really ease the situation."

"I wish you could blast him to the moon."

"Let's focus on what's possible for now."

RICKY WHISTLED as he walked down the hall with a bag of groceries in his arms. But when he reached the kitchen, he balked at cigarette smoke thick in the air. Ricky's mom and a strange woman sat at the kitchen table. She wore dark glasses and shivered in a wool coat despite a warm breeze coming through Natalie's open window. He stepped forward cautiously. "Uh, hi," he said. He took the bags to the counter.

"That's Ricky, my wayward son," Natalie said. "Ricky, this is Penny. She's here on a bit of business with Truman, the job you helped with."

Ricky nodded toward Penny, then grabbed a bag of mini pretzels and a package of cream cheese. "Want a snack? My roommates turned me on to this. You dip a pretzel in the cheese. It's really good."

"What do I care what you do with those roommates when you could be living here rent free?" Natalie blew a few smoke rings toward her son.

Penny stubbed out her cigarette on a saucer. "I'd like to try some."

Ricky waved his mom's smoke aside, arranged the snack on a plate and put it on the table.

Penny took a nibble. "A good combination," she said.

Truman came in from the deck, the back door banging behind him. "Somethin's up down the lane. I gotta check it out." He barged through the room, heading for the hall.

Penny grabbed his belt and yanked.

"Whoa, you're quicker than I thought." He pried her fingers off his belt. "Let go!"

"Truman." Natalie barked the words. "Have you forgotten you work for her?"

Truman tipped his fedora at Penny. "Sorry, I don't mean disrespect." He sat down, grabbed a pretzel and popped it into his mouth. Then he asked Ricky if there was beer in the fridge before he crammed several more pretzels in. His cheeks puffed out while he chewed.

Ricky's brow arched in a silent challenge. "I didn't buy any. You're going through it like gangbusters."

Truman wiped his mouth with the back of his frayed sleeve. "Thanks a lot, kid."

Penny lit another cigarette. "So, tell me. What's so important up the lane?"

"You know how Wayne's been freaking out ever since Rosie disappeared with the kids."

"That's old news," Natalie interjected.

Truman ignored her and looked straight at Penny. "Word is that they're all gonna have some kind of meeting—that's Wayne, Rosie, that guy Harold, maybe some others."

"Harold Ramsey?" Natalie asked. "The man who stole my son from me? Always gettin' into everyone else's business?"

"Do you really want to go there?" Ricky leaned against the counter and glowered at Natalie. "Do you want Truman and your new friend here to know what went down?"

"You're one mighty ungrateful kid." Natalie complained. "Never, ever worth all the trouble you caused."

Silence spread like spilled acid. Penny grimaced and ran her tongue across her lips before addressing Truman. "So, this meeting?"

"It's just a rumor, could be nothing. But Harold and Wayne turned onto the lane just now. They must be heading for 346. Maybe Rosie's already there." Truman pushed his chair away from the table and stood up. "I'll see what's up and report back."

"I'm going, too," Penny declared. "All of the kidnappers could be in one place, and you want to leave me here?"

"It's not time yet. I need—"

"You've been telling me that for months on end. I'm done waiting."

She grabbed Truman's belt again and pulled herself up. "You'll take me there right now."

"I really don't think—"

"Just get me to the car."

"Okay then, since you won't listen to reason." Truman picked her up and carried her down the hall. "Bring her chair out, will ya, kid?" he said to Ricky.

Ricky folded the wheelchair and made for the door. Natalie followed, then pushed past her son.

"I'll come, too," Natalie said to Truman. "I'm your co-conspirator now. You'll need another set of eyes and ears."

"You'll do no such thing," Truman snapped.

Natalie's face turned red. "Who are you to order me around?"

Ricky grabbed hold of her. "Come on, breathe, breathe. You're gonna lose it."

"For cryin' out loud! Just leave it," Truman said to Natalie. "This could get real messy. And God only knows what a loose cannon like you will do." He helped Penny into the car.

Ricky maneuvered the wheelchair into the back seat and closed the door. Truman backed out of the driveway and onto the street. Natalie ran down the sidewalk with Ricky chasing after her.

Rosie hurried up the stairs to 346, her breath catching with each step. She opened the door and entered the foyer, heart wild and off-beat. Familiar voices floated from the room just ahead. The floor complained beneath her feet as she approached, every creak magnifying her dread. Fear skittered up her spine—silent and inescapable.

Harold and Ted looked up and smiled in welcome. She rushed to the seat between them, bracelets clinking as she dropped down and fidgeted with her hair.

Across the room, Wayne seethed, fists clenched. "Can't a guy even see his own kids?"

"You agreed they wouldn't be here," Harold said.

"It's not right the way you're keeping them from me," Wayne said. "I'm not a threat. You haven't given me a chance—"

Harold made a slashing motion with his arm for emphasis. "You've agreed to the ground rules. You can't just lob accusations and complaints at Rosie, or this meeting won't work. You'll have to get lawyers and go to court, which, I have to add, you might need to do anyway."

Wayne looked from Harold to Ted to Rosie. "You're all on her side, thinking she's right and I'm all wrong. I can see it in your eyes."

"Give this a chance," Harold said. "All you have to lose is a little—"

Harold was interrupted by banging at the door. Ted, who had agreed to assist Harold, answered it. Truman stumbled in, slamming the door into Ted's face in the process. "Oh, sorry, old man. I slipped." He unfolded Penny's wheelchair.

Blood spurted from Ted's nose. "What the —"

In limped Penny. She tossed her walker aside and flopped into her wheelchair.

Harold shot up and stormed toward the entryway as Natalie and Ricky ran inside.

"What's going on? What are you doing here?" Harold asked Ricky.

"I'm just following my mom."

Seeing Wayne in the living room, Truman slipped past Harold while Penny wheeled after him.

"What's happening?" Wayne gripped the arms of his chair.

"It's you! It is you!" Penny cried out, waving an arm in Wayne's direction. "I'd know your voice anywhere. I've heard it over and over and over in my mind for the last three years. You told me everything would be okay."

"What?" Wayne knit his brows in confusion. "What's going on? Me and Rosie are here to sort some stuff out."

Penny turned to Rosie. "And you. How could you pretend to be Blossom's mother? How could you?"

Rosie gaped at Penny. "Who's Blossom?"

Wayne loosened his grip on the chair. "Yeah, who's Blossom and who are you?"

Penny glared at him. "I suppose you're doing drug deals here, too, ripping people off?"

Wayne narrowed his eyes. "What do you know about my drug deals?"

"You've been dealing drugs again?" Rosie asked. "I should have known."

He leaned toward her, threatening. "You never could stand by me, could you?"

"Watch it, Wayne," Harold warned.

"Get off my case, man." Wayne scoffed and looked around the room. "This is bonkers! I haven't dealt drugs since back in Arcata."

Rosie shook her head. "No wonder you've been so paranoid."

"I'm not here about drugs," Penny glared at Wayne. "Tell them. Tell everyone how you stole my Blossom. You were on Hawthorne Street the day of the explosion."

Wayne gave her a blank look. "Hawthorne Street?"

"You know damn well it's in Portland." Penny reached into her pocket.

"Lady, I don't know who the hell you are, and I've never set foot in Portland." Wayne held his arms out to Rosie. "Tell her. You know everywhere I've been."

"That's enough." Penny pulled out a snub-nose revolver and cocked it. The sharp metallic click sent a ripple of gasps through the room. "You've lied for the last time." She stood up and took aim at Wayne.

Wayne held up both hands. "No! Wait! You're making a giant mistake."

Truman grabbed her arm. "I never signed up for this."

Truman and Penny spun around in a struggle for the gun. It went off with a deafening crack, striking Natalie, who'd been standing, mouth agape, in the doorway. The acrid smell of gun powder filled the room. Natalie staggered backward and crumpled to the floor. Blood spread across her tunic.

Ricky dove toward his mother. "Mom! Mom!" He pressed trembling hands to her chest. "You shot my mom!" His voice came out raw, ragged.

Truman and Penny continued wrestling, his brawn stunted by her fury. Harold lunged toward them, knocking over a lamp that shattered upon impact. The pistol fired again, striking Ricky. He fell beside Natalie. His blood splattered the wooden floor.

Ted, holding a handkerchief to his bleeding nose, ran to the phone in the hallway to call for help. Harold and Truman finally wrenched the gun from Penny. She collapsed, sobbing, into her wheelchair. Rosie dashed to the bathroom and searched drawers and shelves for first aid supplies. Lark and several other residents came downstairs from their rooms, voices overlapping in panic. A member of the Frogs retched in a corner.

In the chaos, Wayne slinked down the hall and slipped out the back door. "Rosie judging me is one thing," he muttered, "but some lady I've never laid eyes on before comin' for me? Nothin's worth that."

He ran far down the curving path. The scent of damp earth rose as he crashed through a hedge and emerged, breathing hard, onto Billy Goat Hill. He looked over his shoulder and blinked, for he saw no trace of the hedge or Shinbone Hill. He cleared his throat and spat on the ground. "Good riddance, all of you," he called. The words faded unheard as he trotted to Mission Street and caught a bus heading south.

Back at 346, the coppery tang of blood lingered. Sirens wailed in the distance, drawing closer. The horrid haze descended again, curling through every building, path, rock, and shrub, infusing all who lived on Shinbone with a malaise unlike any they'd ever experienced.

~

REVERBERATING gunshots plunged the pigeons into chaos. Misty, who'd been napping on a branch, startled and fell toward the ground. Luckily her fall was broken by a hammock Chip had strung in the lower limbs earlier in the day. She squawked in distress because she could not stop bouncing in the fabric and thus couldn't right herself.

Bonbon, meanwhile, choked on the putrid chartreuse particles filling the air. She passed out in the nest she'd been building for the eggs she expected to lay soon. Stormer trembled like a wind-up toy and thumped around in circles.

Captain, more accustomed to disruptive human behavior, remained calm. "I'll find out what happened," he said. "I'm sure Ted can help." He flew down to his best friend, who was on the back deck catching his breath after chasing Wayne, to no avail.

Landing on a railing, Captain asked, "What happened? Guns? Since when do you people bring guns here? You must do something. You have no idea what it's done to us. Stormer, Misty, my Bonbon—they're all in distress. We need help."

Ted wiped the last of the drying blood from his nose. "Sorry, I can't help now. It's an emergency. People have been shot."

"But—"

"We'll talk later." Ted ran back inside.

Captain flew to the ripple tree out front, which drooped as though dying of thirst. An ambulance pulled to a stop on the lane for the second time within one week. People watched from porches, through windows, and on the flagstone path as EMTs brought out one person and then another on stretchers.

Bonbon awoke, grunting, and sat up in her nest to lay three cracked, undersized eggs.

Captain returned to the roost and reported that Ted was dealing with a huge emergency—people might be dying at that very moment —and Ted would check back with him later.

Misty recounted how she would never have been able to get out of the hammock if Stormer hadn't thought to dangle a string for her to bite onto. Bonbon couldn't stop shaking when she said their children were gone.

Captain faltered mid-step. "Our children? Gone?" His voice caught, brittle with shock. He lowered his head and moved close to nuzzle Bonbon.

"It's not safe here," Bonbon muttered, weeping.

"We have to leave," Stormer declared.

"That's a ... heavy decision," Captain stammered. "Let's not rush—"

"You just lost your babies!" Misty cut in.

"We both waited so long for each other, to start a family." Overcome with emotion, Bonbon turned away.

Captain inched toward her, wings trembling. "I know, love. I know, and my heart is breaking. But Ted's my best and loyal friend. He saved my life. How can I leave him after being back for such a short time? He's sworn to protect us."

"He's not protecting us now," Misty cried out.

Bonbon leaned against Captain and coughed. "I can barely breathe," she rasped. "The air is intolerable."

"Our arrival cleared it up before," Captain said. "Maybe if we give it time—"

"Who's to say it won't happen again, or something worse?" Bonbon sputtered, raw with grief. "Our lives will be filled with loss and sorrow. We'll never get back the three we lost today. I won't be able to bear it if we lose more."

The birds continued debating while the ambulance drove off. Inside the house, police apprehended Penny and told everyone else they had to remain where they were for questioning.

An hour went by. Bonbon's breathing became more labored. Frequent tremors ran through all the birds, including Captain. Their feathers took on a sickly pea green hue. The dead eggs sat in the nest, an emblem of their sorrow.

"I wonder what's keeping Ted," Captain said.

Misty ruffled her feathers and wheezed in disgust. "Obviously, he has other priorities."

The birds stood in silence as the air around pressed in thicker, deadlier.

Finally, Stormer issued an ultimatum. "It's this place and Ted or us."

With his chest swelled with grief, Captain gave in. "Okay," he said. He'd never imagined this day would come to pass, but he saw it was the way things must be. "We'll go."

The four birds lifted off and circled 346 several times before winging away. No one noticed, except Maddy. Several blocks from Shinbone, she looked up while skipping home from ArtSplash, an artist's co-op she'd just applied to join.

She recognized Captain and waved. "Captain, Captain, where ya going?"

The bird swooped down and landed in a bottlebrush tree near her, sorrow dripping from his wings. "We're going far away. We can't grow our family here."

"I'm sorry, so sorry to hear that. ... I'll really miss you."

"I'll miss you and everyone on the lane."

"I always thought we'd have a talk, you and me, you know, since you spoke to me that first day. ... I've been wanting to ask, why did you pick me?"

"Outside your childhood bedroom, the tulip tree, my girl. You understood. You're an old soul."

"How did you—"

"Some things can't be explained."

"Will you be back?"

"Please say goodbye to my dear friend Ted for me." And Captain flew up and away.

TWENTY-THREE

Coughing her way through chartreuse particles, Maddy joined Clara and a group of neighbors huddled in front of 346. People chittered like a troop of capuchin monkeys as they attempted to fit fragments of information into a coherent narrative, a challenge since the witnesses to the shooting remained inside. Curious and concerned, residents lingered until the last police officers drove off, then they gradually peeled away.

Clara and Maddy opted to look for Ted. Quiet greeted them when they stepped inside. Yellow-and-black crime scene tape blocked off part of the foyer and the entire front living room. An overturned chair balanced against a sofa. Blood stained the carpet. A handbag lay on the floor next to one scuffed black loafer.

"Where is everybody?" Maddy wondered aloud.

"Hello? ... Hello?" Clara called.

The two proceeded to the kitchen, their footsteps filling the empty space. A couple of plates with half-eaten sandwiches, cutlery askew, an open bottle of Calistoga water, and crumpled paper napkins littered the table. Finding the back door ajar, they stepped outside. Ted, Lark, Chip, Sunrise, and several other residents sat—some in lawn chairs, a few at a picnic table, others on the ground—in a very different backyard than the one they knew. Maddy froze. Clara's breath caught in her throat.

The yard now appeared shrunken, ordinary and fenced like all others in the vicinity. Gone was the expanse that revealed twists and turns as residents and friends strolled through. Gone were the yurt, the craft and music cabins built with scavenged lumber. Only a scrap of canvas and a few stray boards remained. Gone was the slender stream and path that wound along it, replaced by a lawn and small patch of strawberries. Of the former stands of oak and pine, only three trees remained. The unfinished pigeon loft sat empty.

Chip motioned for Clara and Maddy to sit by him at the picnic table. People nodded to them as they slowly made their way over. No one spoke, all words caught in a tangle of thoughts. Some people cried quietly.

Ted stood by himself, leaning against one of the remaining trees. "This isn't the end of the world," he finally said. "We are still here."

"And this is still a special place," Chip said, voice quavering.

People slowly eased back into communicating and filled Clara and Maddy in on what had happened. But why it happened eluded them like a wolverine in the wild.

The phone rang. "I'll get it." Lark ran inside, her footsteps and the ringing phone echoing in the yard.

When she returned, she said, "Um, this is a little strange, but it's that guy Truman calling from the hospital. Natalie is asking for Clara."

"Natalie?" Clara puzzled over the request. "I simply can't imagine why." She glanced upward and noticed the empty roost. "My goodness," she murmured. "Where are Captain, Bonbon, and the others?"

With creases deepening between his brows, Ted said, "I don't know. They're usually settled in by this time of day."

"Oh gosh." Maddy paused before making eye contact with Ted. "I saw Captain flying off with the others when I was walking home. I waved. He dove down to me and said to tell you goodbye. He called you his dear friend."

All conversation sputtered and died, as doubts about life without Captain dimmed hopes of recovery.

Ted had the same doubts as he took a long look around the shrunken yard and glum faces of the people he'd welcomed into his heart. Wishing he'd realized the enormity of Captain's crisis and done something, anything to help, he wanted to crumple at the foot of the tree where he stood. Instead, he made his way to Clara, put a hand on her shoulder, and said, "I'll drive you there."

CLARA AND TED PROGRESSED, arm in arm, toward Natalie's room at San Francisco General Hospital. They found her lying still, eyes closed, breath shallow, skin translucent. A monitor beeped every few seconds. Fluid in a dangling IV bag caught sunlight slanting in from the room's sole window.

"She looks asleep. Maybe we should come back another time," Clara said.

"Why don't you go in and wait? I'll mosey to the cafeteria. They're bound to have some tea." Ted nudged her gently forward. "I'll be right back."

Clara sat in a chair by Natalie's bed, leaned back and closed her eyes. Exhausted, she drifted into a catnap and was awakened by Natalie rasping.

"You gotta give him blood," Natalie mumbled, barely audible. "You're the only one."

"What did you say?" Clara leaned forward so she could hear better.

Natalie cleared her throat, which released a terrible rattle. "You gotta give him your blood," she managed to say. "You're AB negative, right?"

"How did you know that?"

"Doesn't matter now." Natalie sputtered and coughed. "Just save your grandson's life." She sank back in upon herself, struggling to breathe. Then she rallied. "I'm not gonna make it. You gotta know the truth." Natalie fixed her gaze upward. "Please, Lord, gimme the strength to do this."

"You're not making sense."

"It's about Tilda, found in a field, her body decomposing—"

"Why are you dredging this up?" Clara choked out the words.

"I ran into her that day, the day she snuck out of that unwed mother's place. With that tummy bulging like a party balloon, she didn't look the least bit ashamed. She glowed, in fact, and said she was going home to you, that you and Matthew had changed your minds about letting her keep the baby." Natalie let out a grunt and grew silent.

The monitor continued to beep. Clara fixated on Natalie's chest moving up and down.

Natalie gulped and continued, her voice weaker than before. "I tricked her, said I had a few things for the baby at my house. Why she believed me, I don't know. No street smarts, I guess. So I bring her home and get her in my bedroom and close the door, and she looks around and doesn't see any baby clothes or bottles or blankets or anything, and I say it's so strange I coulda sworn I had a little pile right here. And I pat an empty spot on my dresser, and I say maybe my mom dumped 'em, somewhere, and I laugh at that, thinkin' I'm really funny, and she's still relaxed, you know, not worried at all, and she says, oh, that's okay. It was nice of you to think of me. Maybe you can stop by when the baby's born, and I say not likely, which surprises her, you know, 'cause she senses an edge there in my voice, and she says she'd better get going, you were expecting her, and I say not so fast."

Natalie coughed several times and then continued, wheezing frequently. "I tell her we have something to sort out here, but she just looks real innocent like and asks me what's going on, and how can she help. How can she help? Oh that really makes my blood boil. Her the source of my pain thinkin' she can help me. I'm just so pissed. I don't have a plan, and there's this look between us, you know, and I can tell she's gettin' really scared, and she gets up and tries to open the door, and I grab her, yank her hair, and she slaps me hard, puts up a good fight. She's stronger than I thought and, you know, maybe three inches taller than me, too, so we struggle, but she's afraid, and I'm not, which gives me an advantage, and I stop to gloat for a sec, and she socks me real hard in the stomach, and I just slam her smack into the wall. I hear a big crack. And then she's bleeding from her head to beat the band, and she's crying, and then water gushes out from her bottom, splashing on the floor, all over our shoes, and she's screaming in pain, and there's more blood, lots of blood."

"Oh, no, no, no!" Shaking, Clara pressed both hands to her ears. "Please stop!"

"You gotta hear this before I die." Natalie managed to rise enough to lean on her elbows but then fell back down. "Tilda's awake then, still, and she begs me, 'My baby, you have to save my baby.' And then she passes out cold, and I, I panic, and I run to the kitchen, get a knife, and—"

Clara clasped her hands at her belly. "You didn't. You couldn't—'

"I cut her open and pull out the baby, who's squallin' from the get-go. ... I am so furious, I almost toss the baby out right then and there, but he's part Truman, who's in prison by then, and I have some crazy feelings overcome me like a flash flood. Then my mom comes home and—"

"You killed my daughter? Over some boy named Truman? He's, he's the father of Tilda's baby?"

"She stole him from me. I was busting all over with hatred. So, yeah, I kidnapped her. And I killed her. I did. But I didn't plan for things to go that far."

Clara bit her bottom lip to hold back her tears. "Our girl was on her way home ..."

"I just got to her first."

Their eyes met, each woman studying the other.

"How did she end up out—"

"Malachi P. Burnside, a great big mucky muck who'd never had anything to do with me—his bastard child—he took care of every-thing." Natalie coughed and then continued, sputtering and wheezing between her words. "Mom came home, saw the situation and called him, demanding help. She'd mentioned him now and again, but I never suspected he was my dad until he kicked the bucket. But he came through that day. He sent someone to clean everything up, but I guess, since the body was found in West Marin, they didn't do that good a job."

Clara's stifled tears broke free. She covered her face with her hands. "This is horrible, horrible!"

"There's more. You gotta hear it." Natalie struggled to sit up higher in the bed. "Um, Malachi forged a birth certificate for the baby and shipped me off to Sacramento as slave labor for a great aunt. He insisted I had to take the baby, too, and raise him as my own. That's what my mom said anyway. It was my punishment, a lifetime of raising a kid whose mother I'd killed."

A fit of coughs wracked Natalie, each one louder than the last. When it subsided, she lay gasping for breath. Then she groaned, took in a few breaths, and continued. "For a short while me and Ricky lived on the lane, right next to Ted and those damn pigeons. They peered through my window and watched me in the yard. I swear they saw right through me, knew exactly what I'd done. I don't know how they knew, but they saw the horror. I couldn't stand it. I sent Ricky to get rid of them, and he botched the job, got seen, didn't even kill them all."

"Ricky? The one who's sweet on Maddy?" Clara's eyes widened and more tears spilled. "He's my grandson? And he killed Captain's family?" She fumbled through her purse and pulled out a handkerchief to wipe her face.

"Don't hold it against him. He needs you now. They're all out of AB negative." With that, Natalie convulsed violently, shaking the bed and sending tremors through the room—and through Clara. Then she sank deep into her pillows and closed her eyes.

Still weeping, Clara stretched to press the call button, then sat limp in the chair.

Ted, who'd been standing at the door but hadn't walked in, fearing his presence might end Natalie's confession, said, "What a day. What a doggone day."

Battered by sorrow, Clara could barely speak. "There was something familiar about that boy ... when he came to see Maddy ... I saw Matthew in his eyes ... why didn't I piece it together?"

Ted knelt beside her and took her hand. "Oh, Clara. You couldn't have guessed."

AFTER SURGERY TO remove a bullet lodged a pinch from his heart and several harrowing days in the ICU, Ricky slept fitfully. A TV mounted on the wall was on, but silent. A stand by his hospital bed held several cards and a vase of daisies. Sitting in a chair by the bed, Harold, Ricky's old mentor, tried to read the *San Francisco Chronicle*, but his thoughts kept going over what he'd learned about Natalie and Ricky from Ted in a San Francisco General waiting area while Clara donated blood.

Ricky opened his eyes and moaned.

Harold looked up, his eyes fluttering. "There you are. Whew." He let out a long, shaky breath. "It's been all touch and go, buddy."

"How long have I been here?"

"About a week."

"And Mom? How is she?"

Harold folded the newspaper and patted it in his lap, avoiding Ricky's eyes at first. Then he faced the young man. "She didn't make it, son."

Ricky stiffened as scenes of the shooting flashed through him like firecrackers on rewind. He grabbed at the sheet. "Oh, jeez. Oh man."

"I'm so sorry."

Ricky held back a sob. "What am I all worked up about? It's not like she cared if I lived or died."

"You know what the last thing she did was?"

"What?"

"Found you a blood donor, with a little nudge from Truman."

"What did that loser think he was doing, bringing in a crazy woman with a gun?"

"He didn't know she was armed."

Ricky asked if Wayne had stolen Penny's child. Harold explained that Penny's little girl died in an explosion that severely injured Penny. Her family couldn't break the news to her when she was struggling with severe, debilitating injuries, so they said the child was missing, and the longer they waited, the harder the thought of telling her became.

Their deception knocked Ricky to a strange place between sorrow and rage. Denial disguised as kindness. Inexcusable, he thought. "That's messed up, really messed up." He stretched his arm toward a pitcher and winced in pain.

"Here, let me help." Harold stood up, filled a cup and handed it to Ricky, who grabbed it and gulped.

"Hey now, take it slow." Harold said.

"I have this awful cigarette taste in my mouth, which is crazy because I only tried smoking once when I was thirteen or fourteen at Day Park with Skeet and Bando."

"The Haley boys. One in prison, one strung out on heroin. I never could help them."

Ricky took a couple of sips. "At least they're not shooting people. How did that lunatic ever end up here?"

"Like I said, her folks couldn't tell her that her child was dead."

"And that led to this?" Ricky struggled to sit up in the bed.

Harold adjusted pillows behind him so he could lean back.

"Well, you see," Harold continued, "her dad was a private investigator. He knew how to make a pretend investigation look real, even got Truman involved. He'd taken the man on as a rehabilitation project, saw potential in him. Then he had a stroke, and things just snowballed. It's a convoluted situation."

"That's no excuse for killing my mom. She was all I had."

"What if she wasn't?"

"What's that supposed to mean?"

"Forget it. It's nothing."

"You're hiding something."

"Let's wait till you're stronger."

"Now you're getting me mad." Ricky twisted and wrenched, trying to sit even straighter. "You've got something to say. Spit it out." He coughed.

"I shouldn't have said anything."

"Yeah, but you did. You can't leave me hanging now. This isn't some party game."

Harold's eyebrows pinched together. He took hold of one of Ricky's hands and revealed a gut-punch of truth. "Natalie wasn't actually your mom, not your birth mom."

The truth pried open a long-forbidden door, all the old dust and shadows rushing out at once. "Oh." Ricky winced and leaned back on his pillows. "That sorta fits, thinking about it. ... Why were you afraid to say?"

"I just found out. It's a lot to digest." Harold scratched the tip of his nose.

"Okay, what else aren't you telling me?" Ricky struggled to breathe.

"Rest now. Let's wait until you're stronger. I don't want to cause a setback."

"Aw man." Ricky turned his head away from Harold.

"Everything will come out soon enough."

Ricky closed his eyes, letting go. "So Natalie wasn't my mom, and you know more, but you won't tell me. Is that it?"

"You're looking pale." Harold reached for the call button to buzz a nurse. "I don't want to tire you out. There'll be plenty of time for all this once you're discharged."

"Where will I go from here, huh?"

"You'll stay with me, of course, till you're fully recovered."

"I'm not a foster kid anymore, not one of your cases."

"Don't you know yet, Ricky, that you're my friend?"

~

WITH A CALM WIND at their backs and pale blue skies above, Captain, Bonbon, Stormer, and Misty winged northeastward toward Siskiyou County. When Misty and Stormer were newborn squabs living in dank pens, their parents told stories about the beauty and peace of their homeland, how they wouldn't have been kidnapped if, as rebellious adolescents, a group of them hadn't snuck off to the town of Dunsmuir and sashayed along, nibbling dropped crumbs and seeds. Feeling invincible, they forgot how much their bright-colored plumage and long wings and tails stood out.

They caught their captor's eye—a man certain he could make money by breeding them. Living in misery thereafter, the captured pigeons talked of life before in their flourishing community, putting a spark of hope in all their progeny. Misty and Stormer longed to go there.

Bonbon had no desire to return to her clan, where her missing eye had made her an outcast. Having always lived at 346, Captain knew of no alternatives. So they flew in close formation, almost as one. Raptors watched and followed. One, an eagle, drew dangerously close. Its claws hovered above Stormer, who brought up the rear. But then it shot backward, blasted away. A mother fox paced below a sturdy oak tree where they perched on their first night in the wild. A rat climbed part-way up the trunk of a sycamore, where they rested on their second night.

But none drew near enough to touch them. Each encountered powerful waves of energy that repulsed them, as though predator and their prey were like poles of magnets. The birds wondered at the phenomenon that protected them. They murmured their theories but drew no conclusions.

At rest times, Misty and Stormer told stories so vivid that Captain and Bonbon could feel the sway of the redwood limbs, hear the burbling water in streams, and smell the meadow flowers. It was as though they'd all been there. By the time Mt. Shasta came into view, they all had a sense of coming home. They flew past trees and rocks described in detail in Misty and Stormer's stories, and winged on as though by instinct, avoiding any signs of human life. They were curious about the dreaded town of Dunsmuir, but they knew better than to stop there.

At last, they came upon pigeons whose feathers were shades of golden-brown, fuchsia, purple, turquoise, and yellow. The flock nested in a sequoia that matched exactly the one Misty and Stormer's parents had described. They landed on a limb.

At first the flock was wary, but as soon as Stormer said, "I am Stormer, son of Cloudfire and Muse," they all leaned in with interest. Stormer bobbed his head toward his mate. "And this is Misty, daughter of Thunder and Melody. We were born in captivity and put on display." He then nodded to his other companions. "And this is Captain and Bonbon. Don't mind his missing foot and her missing eye. They are powerful allies who helped us escape. They are now our family."

The group stared in silent wonder. Then an elder female came close, sniffed Misty, and asked, "Did Thunder tell you stories from the California Gold Rush?"

And Misty told of ancestors who had lived for a time with an Irish woman whose husband was a trapper. She ran a boarding house, and pigeons from across the world came to her home. She welcomed them, fed them, helped the injured heal. And in her garden, they mixed and mated, creating hybrids of indelible hues.

Misty also mentioned a young man named Gunter from somewhere far away. He had a bright-colored pigeon that got along well with the other birds. The Irishwoman took to Gunter right away. They shared wisdom from their homelands and enjoyed each other's company. He showed her a flute made from a child's shinbone and said it had tremendous healing powers, but could be dangerous, too.

When he left, some of the pigeons living with the Irish woman joined him, and no one ever heard from them again.

Captain piped in at that point and said, "I'm descended from that flock, the only survivor, I'm afraid." He told of Gunter's death in the Gold Country and his entrusting the flute to Arvel, who eventually settled in San Francisco, married, and raised a family on what became known as Shinbone Lane.

"What happened to the flute?" a curious young bird asked.

"Nobody knows," Captain replied. "It is said he didn't use it wisely, though."

The birds continued to swap stories all that day and into the next. It wasn't long before it seemed the new arrivals had always been there, and all hearts were gladdened.

After Captain described the day Chip arrived on Shinbone Lane in Crazy-Wild, Ted's backyard at 346 that held different things depending on who was looking, and the fair that took place the third Saturday in July each year, one of the squabs asked, "Can we all go there someday?"

Captain longed to stand on the top shelf in Ted's workshop and watch his friend fix what others deemed beyond repair, to philosophize with him over scones more delicious than any others in the world, to see the new loft Ted had planned for Captain and his family completed, but he replied, "No, little one. Too many dangers. We're safer here."

CHAPTER

TWENTY-FOUR

Wielding a simple metal walker, Penny clanked into the jail's visiting area. Through blurry vision, she saw someone stand up, arms waving, at a table. Since no other inmate had entered the room with her, she deduced it must be her visitor. She made her way to the table and almost turned around when she drew close enough to recognize Truman. But she pushed on, thinking this might be her only chance to tell him off.

Scowling, she shoved her walker aside and sat down, demanding, "How is it you're not locked up somewhere for what you did to me?"

"I'm not the one who killed an innocent bystander and came close to killing another," he said. "Two people who did nothing but help you."

"How dare you." She snarled the words.

"Look, it was a little ruse your dad put together that went too far. Natalie and Ricky had no clue."

"My dad can't talk yet, but he has learned to write again. His neurologist never thought he would."

"He's written to you?" Truman squared his shoulders and cleared his throat.

"Don't look so surprised. He wrote to apologize. He admitted the

255

psychologist at the hospital told them to delay telling me Blossom had died, but she never suggested pretending Blossom had been kidnapped. That was all Dad and Mom. Maybe part of them couldn't accept she was gone, either. I don't know."

She stared at the blank wall behind Truman for a moment, then zeroed in on him. "Then Dad dragged you into it. He'd already hired you for real jobs, him and his help-the-downtrodden mentality, second chances and all that." She blinked repeatedly and rubbed her eyes. "He said you didn't want to get involved at first. The thing is, though, he just wrote me that before his stroke, he told you it was time to wind things down. Time to tell me the truth. He regretted starting the whole kidnapping story. But you didn't follow through."

"Listen, now, I did talk to your mom about it."

"She was so upset about Dad's stroke. Her mind was muddled—and still is."

"She wanted to keep it going for a while longer."

"Why can't you admit it? You're a grifter. You knew the right thing to do was to close the whole thing down, but you created this whole fake scenario in San Francisco, found Wayne, and convinced me he was at the scene of the bombing. You made it all so real."

"It wasn't my place to tell you the truth."

"You just wanted our money to keep rolling in. How did you think all of this would end? Did you even care?"

Truman stammered. "How... how could I have known what you'd do?"

"You make me sick!" Shaking with rage, she banged her fists on the table.

A guard strode over and said, "Miss, you'll have to settle down or this visit will end right now."

"I'm about to leave anyway. This guy's not worth my time."

Truman curled his upper lip. "You pushed me hard for results after his stroke. You wouldn't let up."

"So now it's my fault?"

"You've got to be a sicko to go in with a gun like that."

"You're a con man, through and through."

He leaned toward her, defiant. "The woman you killed was rough around the edges, but she's probably the only one who ever really loved me."

"I'm supposed to feel sorry for you?"

He stretched closer to her, started to put a hand on hers but caught the guard's eye and sat back. "I'm sorry for how it all panned out."

"I wish I'd never met you." She seized the walker, rose with the power of a cloudburst, and marched toward the exit.

"I could say the same about you," he muttered, "but I won't." He patted the wallet in his coat pocket where the last check from Mrs. Ferguson was endorsed and ready to cash.

NOT LONG AFTER THE SHOOTING, folks on Shinbone Lane eyed a moving van with Starving Scholars logo emblazoned on both sides as it belched and groaned to a stop in front of Eloise's home. A red Datsun hatchback pulled up behind it, and out came a young man with chestnut-colored curls, paisley shirt, and blue jeans.

The planning committee of Shinbone Friends halted a discussion about the need to learn the Heimlich maneuver in case any of them might have to rescue a choking victim. Some members thought the chartreuse muck they'd been breathing might make them prone to this sort of mishap. Despite the putrid air, Clara and Maddy settled into their favorite chairs on the front porch to get a good view of what was going on. Coco chewed a piece of rawhide at their feet.

The young man spoke briefly with two well-muscled workers who had arrived in the truck before he unlocked Eloise's front door and stepped inside.

"Why, that's Julianna's boyfriend, Arty," Clara said. "I must say he looks an awful lot like Julianna's dad, or the way he looked when he was young."

Maddy asked where Julianna's dad was. Clara explained that he had been restless and wanted bigger things than a wife and child on Shinbone Lane. He left when Julianna was two years old for what was supposed to be a short-term writing job in Hollywood. One assignment led to another, and another. He never returned.

"After he and Eloise divorced, he married some B-movie actress," Clara recalled. "They started a new family, and by that time he was a very successful TV or movie producer—I can't remember which. He did support Julianna, paid for private schools, took her on some fancy trips too. He wanted Julianna to move to L.A., but Eloise wouldn't hear of it."

"No surprise there," Maddy said.

For the next hour or so, the movers loaded furniture and boxes onto the truck, while Arty remained in the house. After the moving van left, Arty carried a stack of small boxes out of the house and put them in his car. Wiggling all over, Coco barked, launched herself from the porch and bounced into Arty's arms.

"Ah, little friend, so good to see you," he said, carrying the dog back to Clara's.

"Someone's sure happy to see you," Clara said to him before introducing him to Maddy. Then she asked, "How's Julianna? I do hope she's recovering well. That's the biggest concern of everyone here. We hope Eloise is getting care somewhere, too, of course."

Arty's eyes watered as he settled into a swing to the side of the women's chairs. Coco made herself at home on his lap. "Julianna is making great progress, all things considered, still frail, but gaining strength." He rubbed his eyes. "And her mom is at one of her uncle's properties, the house at Dillon Beach."

"Eloise's little brother, Joe? He was such a sweet boy," Clara said.

Arty coughed and waved his hand in front of his face.

"I'm so sorry about the air. Nobody knows how to clear it up," Clara said.

Maddy shifted her weight, preparing to stand. "Would you like some lemonade or a glass of water?"

"No thanks," he said. "I can't stay." He coughed again and then continued. "Uncle Joe's Eloise's conservator now. He pulled some strings and got her out of Langley Porter. No charges filed for stealing Julianna's life for a year and a half—and bringing her close to death. Eloise stays sedated and under 24-hour supervision. The doctors don't think she'll ever realize what she did."

"She's a force to be reckoned with," Clara said. "I could imagine her dancing on the hillside again one day."

"I guess anything's possible," Arty replied, "but Joe controls her estate now. There's not much to it. He asked if Julianna and I might want to live there when she's out of the woods, but Julianna doesn't want to set foot in there again. She asked me to pick out some of her belongings but doesn't want the furniture, dishes—nothing. Joe will put the house up for sale. He's already spoken with a realtor."

"But it's been in the family for so long," Clara lamented.

"He doesn't want to deal with renters or leave it abandoned."

Clara gazed at Eloise's empty home, a series of memories flashing through her mind. "So where will you go then, when Julianna's better?"

"In six months or a year, depending on how Julianna's doing, we'll get Eurail passes and see all of Europe. And who knows? Maybe we'll go to Asia and Australia and South America, working at odd jobs where we can. That's what we had planned to do before ... you know." Arty stood up with the dog in his arms. "Julianna wants you to have little Coco for keeps."

"Me?" Clara patted her chest. "I'm too old to be responsible for a dog more than a short time."

"Coco loves you, Clara. You have to say yes," Maddy said.

Arty put the dog in Clara's lap.

Clara scratched Coco under the jaw. "Oh, how could I resist this little gal." She shook her finger at Maddy. "You'll have to help me, though."

Maddy chuckled and said she would.

"Um, there's one more thing," Arty pulled a note from his back pocket. "This seems to be coming from left field, but Eloise wants to see you." He handed it to Clara. "That's Uncle Joe's number. He can set it up if you're willing."

"It seems everybody calls Clara when they're in trouble," Maddy said.

Clara eyed the paper as though it might poison her. "I'll think about it."

After they bid Arty farewell, Maddy and Clara went inside and resumed their respective projects.

"If I were Julianna, I don't know if I could ever forgive Eloise," Maddy said, thinking of her father.

"You know what they say about forgiveness." Clara paused her knitting. "Keeping anger and resentment in your heart only harms you in the long run."

ON AN UNBEARABLY LANGUID AFTERNOON, several weeks into the second onslaught of the chartreuse haze, Lark slumped in the kitchen of 346, dragging her spoon through ice cream that had long since melted. She drifted through memories of brighter days, lighter air. One surfaced with clarity: a healing ceremony held in the candlelit parlor of a fellow poet from San Francisco State.

The recollection was cool, spring water for the soul—bringing her first inkling of purpose in weeks. She let the spoon drop and pushed herself to her feet, limbs slow and aching, and shuffled to the nearest phone. She dialed Rosie and described the gathering. Rosie pressed her for every detail.

"It was a powerful experience, the safety of it," Lark said. "People passed a little shaker around the room, and the person holding the shaker was the only one who could talk ... yeah ... speaking one at a time, and no interruptions or cross-talk allowed. ... Beyond that, there weren't many ground rules. It was pretty simple, but people were able to really listen to each other and say things they wouldn't ordinarily say. ... I think we can do one for us here on Shinbone. ... Are you in?"

A few hours later, at 346, Chip kept watch over Heather, Lucas, and Sunrise upstairs while Rosie and Lark sat at the kitchen table, making hand-drawn invitations for every resident of Shinbone Lane and a smattering of friends beyond. Three days later, with the preschool's mats, tricycles, and climbing structures tucked away, people filled the chairs set up in The Farmhouse.

A hush of expectancy settled over the room. Grateful that Shinbone Friends had created such a fine haven for gatherings, Rosie stood at the front and lit a sage smudge stick. Smoke curled as she waved it gently, setting the tone. Lark sat on a stool nearby, coaxing a rhythm from her bongos—soft, steady, grounding. Maddy and Clara, Ted, Chip, and others from 346 filled in alongside nearly everyone invited. Some sat stiffly, uncertain of what a healing ceremony might hold, but they were too curious to stay away.

Just as Chip was about to close the double doors, several stragglers slipped in—among them, Truman, who slid into a seat in the back.

Rosie put the sage on a dish in the center of a table that held a variety of percussion instruments, most of them homemade. She turned toward her neighbors and, with quavering voice, thanked everyone for being willing to try something new. "I've never done anything like this before, but like they say, there's no time like the present to start creating the life you want."

"I hear ya," one person called out.

"Right-on sister," another one said.

Others joined in with words of encouragement.

Rosie stood a little taller and continued, her voice gaining strength as she spoke. "So anyway, we're quite a diverse group when it comes to beliefs and rites of passage. We've got Presbyterians, Unitarians, Catholics, Jews, Buddhists, Wiccans, and who knows what else right here on Shinbone Lane."

Lark kept a quiet rhythm going on her bongos while Rosie spoke.

"We wanted to find a way for all of us, despite our differences, to express ourselves and help each other heal," Rosie said. "We've seen poor Julianna held captive and almost starved to death by her own mother, Wayne and me being accused of kidnapping, a shooting that left one person dead and one wounded. Then we learned of the real kidnapping, when Natalie murdered Tilda and stole her child. And it looks like we've lost Captain and everything he brought to us. It's a series of big blows, but Lark and I think we can help each other get through. So here's our plan."

Rosie crossed to a table near Lark and picked up a plastic, egg-shaped container and shook it, making a soft pitter-patter sound. "This is our shaker. We're going to pass it from person to person, and when you're holding it, it's your turn to speak."

The thought of speaking to a group made anxiety swell throughout the room—palms turned slick, hearts beat off-kilter, and voices shriveled.

"Interesting," Clara whispered to Maddy. "Could be messy, though."

Maddy leaned close to Clara and said, "I don't think I like this."

"There are a few ground rules," Rosie added. "It's important to stick to them or it won't work."

Rosie explained that when someone has the shaker, they have the floor. Everyone else listens with respect. No interruptions or crosstalk. "The next thing is when it's your turn, you can't attack other people, and you can't comment on what others have said. You just say your truth. Try to be kind. Tell us what you've been going through."

A few people who'd noticed Truman's arrival turned their heads and scowled at him. He looked down at his lap.

"Another thing is that whatever we say, every little thing we share here today, is confidential," Rosie said. "We don't tell other people who aren't here about it. And we don't go up to someone later and comment on what they said. It's a kind of a sacred space we're creating, not that I'm taking on a religious role or anything."

Maddy raised her hand, and Rosie nodded to her. "What if you don't want to say anything at all?"

"That's your prerogative," Rosie replied. "Just pass the shaker to the next person."

"What if I only want to say bad things about someone—like Natalie?" Waddles called out. "I don't have one good thing to say about her, after hearing what she did to Clara's Tilda."

Another person called out, "Not to mention egging her son on to set that fire when he was just a kid, and Captain the only survivor, maimed for life."

"Yeah," someone else chimed in, "we don't want this to be some sort of memorial service for her."

Others voiced their agreement, and the group broke into side conversations. Two people marched out of the meeting. Lark stopped drumming. She took a cowbell from the table and rang it, which got everyone's attention.

"Listen," Lark said. "We're all a mix of good and bad qualities. For some people, the bad just takes hold for complicated reasons. I think it's helpful to look for the good in even the worst person, but nobody's asking you to turn this into some kind of memorial for Natalie, okay? But if someone wants to mention something good about her, or about Eloise for that matter, please respect their right to do so."

People sat in silence, considering that. Then Waddles said, "What if someone goes on and on and on? You know how long-winded some of us are."

"Let's see how it goes," Rosie replied. "If we need to put, say, a five-minute time limit on it, we can do that. Sound good?"

Around the room, people nodded in agreement.

"What do we do after everybody's had a chance to speak?" Waddles asked.

"Good question," Rosie said. "We brought percussion instruments so we could jam later. Or we could sing a song. It'll depend on how things go. Any more questions?" The room was silent. "Okay, who wants to go first?"

～

Rosie sat down, holding the shaker in clammy hands, and panicked. She wished she hadn't said she would speak first when no one else volunteered. But she plunged ahead. She said she understood why Penny thought Wayne had kidnapped her daughter. After all, Truman had led her to that conclusion, and Wayne apparently closely resembled someone who was on the scene the day of the bombing.

But Wayne wasn't a kidnapper, just a lost soul. She was angry with him for his drinking, drug dealing, violent temper, and for skipping out after the shooting. She was angry with herself, too, for putting up with his abuse for so long.

Then, voice quavering, Rosie divulged that Wayne wasn't Heather's father. She'd married her high school sweetheart, but he'd stepped on a landmine in Vietnam when she was pregnant. With her heart split open, she'd drifted through grief like a boat unmoored. Then Wayne came along, bringing a rough current she mistook for love. In their years together, he'd promised many times to stop dealing drugs, stop drinking, stop abusing her.

Rosie had believed him, only to be disappointed time after time. Now she didn't know how to tell her children that Wayne wasn't coming back and when to let Heather know he's not her biological dad. She passed the shaker on.

In his turn, Chip recounted the shock and sorrow of his parents' drowning in a boating accident when Sunrise was three years old. Chip was nineteen at the time, and he became Sunrise's guardian. Smothered by pity in their hometown in Oklahoma, Chip put most of their belongings in storage, hired an agent to rent out their family home, and went on the road with his sister.

They kept in touch with their grandparents, who expected them to return someday to stay, but Chip didn't want to go home, except to visit, because he had to hide his true self there.

As people took turns speaking, each voice stirred something raw—grief, fear, anger, confusion, regret, love, and tender hope surfaced in waves, unshielded and unspoken until now. Many dabbed away tears;

some stifled sobs. A few, overcome, ran to another room to collect themselves before they were able to return.

When it was Maddy's turn, she tried to speak, but her voice rebelled. She passed the shaker to Clara, who wanted to speak about Ricky. Her grandson. A child she'd presumed was long dead. But no words would come. She, too, passed the shaker on. Later, when Ted spoke of Captain, whom he was certain had left because of the violence, mourning filled every corner, as though another death had occurred.

Maddy began coughing and couldn't stop. She pushed past others in her row and fled the room. Clara stood and followed, navigating the narrow aisle with effort, her concern outweighing the stiffness in her knees.

Rosie suggested everyone take a five-minute break. Some folks left the building and did not return, but most gathered again when Lark rang the cowbell. Truman fought the urge to flee as people, in turn, took the shaker and spoke their truth or, tight lipped, passed it on. He scratched the back of his neck as people detailed how his actions had harmed others.

When Truman, at last, held the shaker, a room full of people turned in their chairs to look at him, many with fire in their eyes. Yet, from a few, he sensed compassion. He pulled out a cigarette and a lighter, but Rosie waved her hand and shook her head.

"Okay, no smokes. Fair enough." He put the cigarette and lighter away. "I can see on your faces that you all blame me for so much bad stuff that happened, starting with Tilda. I see how it is. But everything turned out bad for me, too."

Murmurs broke out among the group as Truman's voice grated on people like a buzzing horsefly banging against a window.

Ignoring the growing unrest in the room, Truman continued. "I just lost Natalie. Think on—"

A member of Dave Deely's band cried out, "Why should we listen to you? You're a rapist and thief and liar!"

"Why is he even here?" Another person asked.

Others joined in with derogatory remarks. Lark rang the cowbell. Rosie asked everyone to settle down. People quieted, many with jaws set hard and arms folded across their chests.

Then Rosie addressed Truman. "Um, you know, you weren't invited to this meeting. You are neither resident nor friend. I should have asked you to leave as soon as you walked in, but I thought you might just sit in back and listen for a while and then leave without stirring the pot. You deserve forgiveness. But this is not the time or place for it. We aren't the ones who can listen to your story. We shouldn't have to."

"Way to go, Rosie!" Lark called out.

"Tell it like it is, sister," another person said.

Ted spoke up. "You put that a lot nicer than I would have."

Others let loose with comments. All in favor of Truman leaving.

Truman locked eyes with Ricky, whose every cell exuded undisguised hostility. "There you are, my very own son, lookin' holier than thou. Well, fella, I'm not that fond of you either. I'll be gone soon enough. But get to know your grandmother, Clara. If she's even a tiny bit like her daughter, she's—"

"Oh, shut up, man," Chip blurted loud enough for everyone to hear.

Truman stood, sneering, and walked toward the door. "Sure could use a smoke about now."

"What's this about that lowlife Ricky being Clara's grandson?" Waddles asked. "Poor Clara."

A silence fell, sharp and sudden.

Harold rose slowly, his eyes fixed on Waddles. Something inside him shifted, and words flowed like steam rising from below ground. "Any of you passing judgment on this young man for something he did when he was just a kid—you need to stop now. You've got to be better than that."

Next to him, Ricky jolted up, the back-and-forth flooding his senses. "Sorry, man," he muttered to Harold. "I can't take any more of this." He sprinted from the room.

Outside, Truman leaned against the building, a Camel dangling from his lip. He smirked as Ricky stormed past. The flare of Truman's lighter briefly caught Ricky's eye. The stench of smoke and sweat made him gag—one more thing to despise about the man Ricky swore he'd never call father.

All was silent indoors for several moments. Then Lark proposed they go around the room a second time. Waddles and a couple of others bowed out, muttering about other commitments.

Those who remained passed the shaker once more. Tears fell, some accompanied by sobs loud and lonesome as foghorns. With each turn, the air grew clearer; shoulders eased, breathing softened. When the last person who wished to speak did so, songbirds alighted on the trees outside the center. Their music filtered into the room. Lark tapped a rhythm on her drum, and Rosie sang the first line of "A Little Help From My Friends." But she didn't sing it like the Beatles did. She'd been to Woodstock in '69 and seen Joe Cocker's wild rendition, and she let loose in her own untamed way.

"Far out!" called one of the founders of Moonrise Cafe. She strutted to the front of the group, fiddle in hand, and jammed with Lark and Rosie.

Neighbors picked up tambourines, cymbals, triangles, drums; a few danced freely around the room. Some stayed in their seats, swaying and singing along. Gradually, the outpouring wound down. People filed out, their spirits lighter. Outside, clouds of slimy, grimy, minuscule bubbles hovered in the air—then popped and vanished.

AT THE TAIL end of a dream, Clara rode the carousel at Playland-at-the-Beach, the world spinning by, slippery as a memory half-remembered. Astride the horse beside her, Laffing Sal, the park's famous automaton, leaned over and whispered something. But the words eluded her as reality intruded. She opened her eyes, stretched, and rose from the couch where she'd fallen asleep trying to read one of Anaïs Nin's journals. She shuffled, yawning, into the kitchen.

At the table, Maddy looked up from her sketchbook. Her backpack, so full its seams looked ready to split, sat on the floor by her feet. She grinned at Clara. "I made lasagna while you napped." She pointed to a pan on the stove. "Pulled it out of the oven a couple minutes ago. You woke up just in time." She noticed Clara eyeing her backpack and promised she wasn't about to run away this time.

"I'm sure yesterday's meeting stirred things up, but this is so sudden." Clara gripped the back of a chair to steady herself. "If I hadn't woken up—"

"I wrote you a note." Maddy ripped out a page and slid it across the table. "There's a grad student in San Rafael leaving for the East Coast at four o'clock today. I have to catch a couple of busses to get there. But he can take me all the way to Yellow Springs."

"You're going home."

"Listening to everybody at the ceremony, it hit me that the people I need to open up to right now—have it out with is more like it—are back there. Mom and Dad ... and I've been thinking of Tyler."

"Your little brother?"

"I miss him more than I could ever say. That really hit me at the meeting. I was had it bad with my parents, but Tyler ... Tyler lost his life. He was only four years old. I want to tell him how sorry I am and how much I love him, even though I'll just be talking to a headstone."

"I suppose it wouldn't help to remind you it wasn't your fault."

"I kind of know that, but I don't feel like it's true in my bones, if that makes sense." Maddy flipped to a new page in her sketchbook.

"It does, most certainly." Clara strode to the stove. "How 'bout I dish up this lasagna? It smells delicious."

"There's salad in the fridge, too."

Maddy sketched while Clara put lunch on the table. When Clara pulled out a chair and sat down, Maddy lifted her sketchbook so Clara could see the drawing.

"What a darling little boy. Tyler?"

"As well as I can recall him." She closed the book, picked up her fork and dug into the meal.

Clara took a few bites and then put her fork down. "You know, I talk to Tilda, and sometimes I can feel her listening. I think it'll help for you to talk to him."

"I hope he can hear me. I really do. But there's so much we can never really know, isn't there?"

"It seems the older I get, the less I'm sure of."

As they finished eating, Maddy pointed out that Clara hadn't spoken much at the healing ceremony either.

The elderly woman gripped the edge of the table and leaned forward, as if steadying herself against a monstrous tide. She admitted she was off kilter, still digesting what she'd learned—Tilda's last hours, Natalie's final act, the stolen baby now grown into a young man she barely knew. And then there was what Eloise had done to Julianna. Clara stood up, unable to say more, and drew solace from a quiet moment, the way some people are soothed by prayer.

After they cleared the table, Clara said, "Don't go yet. I'll be right back." She went down the hall and returned with a forest green cardigan. "I was saving this for your birthday, but I want you to have it now." She handed it to Maddy.

The teen's eyes widened. "You made this for me?"

Clara nodded. "That shade suits you. I knew it would."

"Thank you. Thank you so much." Maddy put on the sweater. "I feel like I'm not being a good friend in leaving you right now, and you're one of my favorite people in all the world." She fastened a few buttons. "I promise I'll be back soon." She bent down for the backpack.

"Wait, wait." Clara reached for her young friend. "They're not lined up." She undid the buttons, aligned the sweater's sides, fastened the bottom three, and gave Maddy a hug. "There, see?"

"What if my dad gets me locked up," Maddy's voice wobbled, "as a truant or something?"

"Get to a phone. Ted and I will be there in a heartbeat."

CHAPTER
TWENTY-FIVE

The folks living on Shinbone Lane processed what had happened in their own ways. Clarity emerged like yarn pulled from tangles, rolled into balls, and knit into something new.

Over morning coffee Waddles and Clara discussed their neighbors' lives, concluding everyone was recovering well, all things considered. Each day after Waddles left, Clara would pick up the phone and dial only part of Harold's number before hanging up. Harold knew how to reach Ricky. She was sure of that, but she couldn't get up the gumption to ask for his number.

Three weeks after the ceremony, Clara received a letter from Maddy with doodles and sketches scattered throughout. The teenager had been unable to face her father, go to Tyler's grave, or find out where her mother was institutionalized. She didn't want to return to Shinbone until she'd done that.

On the positive side, Maddy had reconnected with school friends. They told her about a rundown whale of a house with colonial revival features where residents provided twin beds in nooks and alcoves for people needing a place to crash. Maddy arrived, and there was Keeley, the one who had taken the runaway under her wing the night she'd snuck out through her bedroom window.

Keeley had broken up with the glassblower upon their return from Peru and returned to Yellow Springs. She was working toward a degree in computer science, believing it was the way of the future. She also belonged to a collective that made quilts as fundraisers for various causes and had enlisted Maddy to draw sketches for a new project. Maddy also mentioned she often sketched in a nature preserve within walking distance from her temporary digs and drew courage from the peaceful surroundings.

Weeks folded into months. Lark finished her MFA in creative writing at San Francisco State and was asked by the university to teach an undergraduate poetry class. She worked on her lesson plans in the kitchen in the middle of the night. Chip, who was also sleepless, often joined her. At first, they spoke of Dave, whose grandfather had passed away. Dave stayed on in Illinois to teach music to children in the town, as his granddad had done before him.

"I can't believe he'd give up such a promising career, can you?" Chip asked Lark.

"He and his band were going places; that's for sure, but he seemed unsettled in a way, didn't he?"

Their conversations turned to new things. She read him snippets of her poems; he showed her his latest photographs. And they celebrated each other's publishing wins, mostly local, but some national for Chip.

Rosie had planned to move in with her parents in San Diego. But she struck up a conversation with Chip one overcast Saturday at what she assumed would be one of her last sidewalk sales. While Heather and Sunrise played nearby, Chip began fantasizing about going into business with her.

"But I'm leaving soon," she told him.

"I need some extra income, but on my own, I don't think I could manage anyway," he said.

"I could show you the ropes," she offered.

They spent the rest of the afternoon brainstorming how Chip might take over Rosie's business. At the end of the day, he helped her pack up. On Sunday, they met at Moonrise Café and tossed around ideas for making sidewalk sales stand out.

By Tuesday, a sense of possibility—compelling as Star Bakery's famous scones—had taken root. Rosie shelved her plans to start over in San Diego and moved into two rooms at 346.

Sunrise and Heather enrolled in the co-op preschool, and Rosie and Chip began adding storytelling and music to the end of each Saturday sale. Rosie also signed up for a self-defense class and found a lawyer who coached her through handling her own divorce. Chip registered for photography classes at City College of San Francisco, hoping to sharpen his skills and eventually transfer to UC Berkeley for a degree.

Ricky continued his job at Bell Market and moved into a home on Hoffman—one of the properties Natalie had inherited from her father, Malachi P. Burnside, Esq., a power broker who refused to acknowledge her in life but remembered her in his will. He set about repairing the Castro Street home to ready it for rental and considered getting a real estate license.

Ricky visited Harold often, who encouraged him to get in touch with Clara. But the former foster child, feeling guilty because he felt remnants of love for Natalie, couldn't do so.

One day, while Harold and Ricky were enjoying bowls of chili in the kitchen, the doorbell rang. Harold buzzed to unlock the door and soon returned with Truman. Harold offered him chili, but he declined, saying he was heading to L.A. for a job and would be gone a long time.

"Why are you telling me?" Ricky asked. "I don't care."

"Tough guy, huh? Well, I'm gonna write you here at Harold's every now and then."

"Don't bother."

Ricky chewed slowly, his jaw tight, his gaze fixed on Harold's phone mounted on the wall. Something bitter twisted in his chest at Truman's looming desire. The man lingered, fumbling for small talk, but Ricky didn't bite—the gulf between them sharp and final. Finally, Truman turned on his heel and left.

Back at 346, Ted finished the pigeon's roost in the shrunken backyard, hoping Captain and his family would return. He tended flowers out front, which, though smaller, still had a sun-drenched quality even in the thickest fog. And in his workshop, which smelled once again of leather, sawdust, lemon oil, rose petals and weathered books, he returned to his post-retirement passion of repairing appliances, toys, and other items to give away.

At the end of each day, he frequently sat with Clara on her front porch and offered to take her to see Eloise.

"I suppose I should drive myself one of these days since the Packard is working fine right now," she told Ted.

"I do enjoy chauffeuring you, you know," he said.

"You have so much else to do."

His ears reddened. "I've loved you since kindergarten, Clara dear."

Clara dropped a stitch in her knitting and put her needles down. "You never gave any indication. You never said—"

"Matthew loved you, too, and he was my best friend."

Clara resumed knitting, and the two sat in quiet for a time before she said. "I guess we could go tomorrow, that is, if you don't have plans."

"At your service." He nodded to the flower boxes across the street. "I do believe the pansies just doubled in size."

Jogging along a trail at Glen Helen Nature Preserve, a popular feature of her hometown, Maddy heard a little girl cry out, "Daddy!" She halted and sucked in her breath. Ahead, a father and daughter navigated stepping stones crossing Yellow Springs Creek. The giggling girl sat on the man's shoulders, her little hands resting on top of his bucket hat. He leaped from stone to stone, pretending to lose his balance with each landing.

Maddy felt a wave of vertigo as a memory came loose. She was five years old, riding on her father's shoulders, traversing the same stones. Everything about that moment roared back, prickling her body and soul: the feel of his strong grip on her suntanned legs; the smell of his Old Spice aftershave; the lingering taste of chocolate milkshake they'd just shared; the sunshine, happiness and love all mixed together.

She swallowed hard as a pang of loneliness took hold. She recalled a time when her mother was withdrawn but not yet Maddy's responsibility. Her dad would wake her up with jokes and silly made-up tunes each morning and put her to bed with stories of princesses conquering all in far-off lands at night. He cooked with her, taught her to throw a ball. He went on field trips, made cupcakes for school events, took her to and from playdates. He animated her world, picking up all the slack for her mother, who sat in the kitchen sipping cold coffee, smoking cigarettes, and talking occasionally on the phone.

But after Tyler was born, he turned into Maddy's taskmaster, her jailer, expecting her to take care of her brother and mother every moment she wasn't in school.

In the preserve, Maddy's heart cracked open as she glimpsed what she'd lost. The pain was a dizzying chasm she'd blocked out until that moment.

She took off running, biting her lip, tears flying into the wind, thankful she had a hat she could pull down to hide her sorrow. She jogged the trails out of the preserve and dodged through the Antioch College campus. Head down, she flew through streets familiar to her as the shape of her own body until she turned down the most familiar block of all and slowed to a walk.

Her childhood home came into view. Her dad's rusting Rambler station wagon sat in the driveway. The hedge, overgrown, encroached on the lawn. The white siding needed paint. The black roof needed shingles. A light glowed from inside. She walked by, uncertain she could ever open the windowless wooden door again.

WHILE RUBBING his maroon pickup's body to a glossy shine in preparation for driving Clara to see Eloise, Ted heard voices out front.

He exited his workshop to find a gaggle of locals watching a belching truck and, behind it, a bus screech to a halt in front of Eloise's home. A sticker with bright red letters screaming SOLD obscured a For Sale sign in the yard.

Lark joined Ted outside. "I was wondering when the new owners would arrive. It's kind of bittersweet, the start of a new chapter."

"A new chapter. I like that," Ted said.

A bearded man in loose fitting white pants and tunic stepped from the bus onto the flagstone path. He tightened his fuchsia sash and strode toward 346.

"Oh, my gosh. It's Abbudin!" Lark cried out, remembering the encouragement he'd given her after he'd jammed with Dave and the Frogs, and how welcoming he was when she and Eloise visited his community. She ran to him and gave him a hug.

Other people piled out of the bus. Several, like their leader, wore white pants and tunics with colorful sashes. Others, however, sported metallic-looking, tight-fitting shirts paired with bell bottoms or clingy skirts, and chunky platform shoes. Several sported feathers in their hair and boas around their necks.

Two sylph-like devotees emerged. Their formerly long, almost-white hair, was short, spiky and dyed a rainbow of colors

"Goodness! The twins! What have they done to their hair?" Clara, who was watching from her porch, put down her knitting and put a hand up to her mouth.

Waddles, who'd been working away beside her, stared, dumb-struck, then exclaimed, "My God! What is the world coming to?"

It wasn't long before the entire neighborhood was crammed into Eloise's former home for an impromptu housewarming party for the newest residents of Shinbone Lane. People brought food and drink aplenty, creating a sumptuous potluck with something for everybody.

"We're expanding into new worlds, as you can see," Abbudin said to Chip and a few others standing in a half-circle around him. He opened his arms wide to the singers scattered around the room. "They are following a spirit all their own."

"Sure is gonna be cool to have you all here," Chip said.

Abbudin explained it was a stroke of good luck that the home was offered at a price they could afford because several members wanted to live in the city for inspiration to explore new directions; others, preferring to stay in a familiar groove at their country compound, thought cross-pollination between the old and the new might be beneficial.

"Aside from their wild wardrobes, what is this splinter group or offshoot, whatever you call it, doing that's new?" Clara asked.

"I've seen people dressed like that," Rosie said. "They wait in line at this dance club that opened South of Market last year. When you pass by, you can hear and feel the music booming. It's got a great beat. It's called disco, I think."

"Yes," Abbudin said, "it's not quite for me, but I've never been one to stifle creativity. Some people are saying disco is the next big thing. It does make you want to get up and dance."

"I like what you did when you were here before," Lark said.

Abbudin put an arm around Lark's shoulders. "That's not going to end. I promise."

"Yeah, it's all fluid," Bea, one of the twins, chimed in. Her sister nodded in agreement.

"So, would you care to, ah, sing and play a little?" Chip asked.

"Is Dave going to join us?" Abbudin asked. "He might like this new sound."

"He stayed in Illinois after his granddad died," Ted said. "He's teaching music there."

Abbudin's mouth turned down momentarily. Then he rubbed his chin and said, "That's splendid in its own way, isn't it? Let's dedicate this improvisation to him."

The group gathered. Some choir members made a repetitive, pulsating four on the floor syncopated rhythm with their mouths, hands and feet. Others used their voices to make sounds that uncannily mimicked electric guitar, stringed instruments, horns, electric piano, and synthesizer. The music permeated the group. Even Ted and Clara couldn't help but sway to it. They all lost track of time.

At last, exhausted, Ted and Clara exited hand in hand and agreed it was too late to visit Eloise that day. Inside, the party continued. With a glow of rapture on his face, Chip danced until he flopped onto a couch, snuggled up to someone whom Lark later said could be innovative musician David Bowie's alter ego Ziggy Stardust come to real life.

MADDY RETURNED to her childhood home several days in a row before she finally resolved that, yes, she could face her father and accept whatever happened. She walked up the four concrete porch steps and tried the door. It opened. Once inside, she almost knocked into her father. He reached for her.

"Don't!" Maddy nudged him away.

"Touchy, aren't you? Come on then." He strutted toward the living room and waved for her to follow.

She almost ran back out the door but, steeling her resolve, she followed him and sat down on the couch.

He went to an easy chair and moved a newspaper aside before settling in. He then surveyed Maddy from head to toe, as though appraising her. "Well, I'm glad you're back," he finally said. "All is forgiven."

"Whoa! You're telling me all is forgiven? That's really whacked. I shouldn't have come." She leaned forward, prepared to rise.

"Don't be like that. You're all I have left now. Your mom died on our anniversary, you know."

"What?"

"Saved up some sedatives. Nobody was watching her. I could sue the place for negligence."

Struggling to come to terms with her mother's demise, Maddy stared into her dad's eyes, which seemed soulless as marbles. "It's always somebody else's fault, isn't it, Dad? It's never you."

"If you're talking about the night Tyler died, you're making a mountain out of a molehill. A few minutes after you ran to your room, I fessed up, told them it was your mom who'd done it. One of the officers went to get you, just as a witness after the fact. But you'd already skipped out like some yellow-bellied coward."

"When was the last time you treated me like a daughter instead of an indentured servant?"

"Things were harder than you'll ever be able to imagine. I had nowhere to turn."

"I was ten when Tyler was born. Ten years old." She choked down a sob.

"You were mature for your age, reliable."

"No way was it right for you to put an end to my childhood. I've been blaming myself for what Mom did because I went for ice cream with Oliver instead of rushing home to keep an eye on her. But all along, it was you who was the problem. I was a child. You should have gotten help for mom long before. Why didn't you do anything to help her?"

"You have to understand the stress—"

"No, I don't." Maddy raised her voice. "I don't at all."

"Okay, I can see that to be blamed for drowning your brother must have been upsetting."

"Upsetting? You don't know the half of it."

"Don't get so worked up, honey." He took a sip from a Budweiser can on his cluttered end table. "Want something to drink? There's Coke in the fridge."

"You're impossible!" Maddy eyed the wall behind him, aching at the sight of details she used to love: the wallpaper with tiny yellow roses strung together on bright green stems against a cream-colored background, the potpourri smell of the room, the throw rug covering worn spots in the carpet.

"Your room's just as you left it, you know," he said.

She waved his comment off. "I saw a father and daughter the other day. He was carrying her across the stones at Yellow Springs Creek. I remembered how you carried me there, too, when I was little. And then all the things we used to do slapped me, things I'd blocked out. How much I loved you. How much you loved me. How it all evaporated after Mom fell apart."

"Postpartum psychosis, they call it. ... Into every life, a little rain—"

"More like a tsunami. The only way I could bear it was to convince myself you'd never loved me, and I never loved you. But then I saw that father and daughter, and now I'm angry, maybe for the first time in my life. I'm really mad at you. Tyler and I were on our own from the day you brought him and Mom home from the hospital."

"Parents always let their kids down in one way or another. It couldn't have been that bad."

"What about when she tried to drown me? Why didn't you get her help then?"

His eyes betrayed shock as he stammered. "You, cuh, couldn't, you, you couldn't possibly remember. You were so, smuh, small. I—"

"So it's true. ... I've had this hunch for a while now. I just don't know what to say." She rose, quivering, from the couch.

"Wait. Stay," he said, recovering his composure. "I was told it was best to pretend it never happened."

"You weren't told to put me in charge of her; I'm certain of that. How could you?"

"Okay, okay, so I made mistakes. I admit it, but you need to knuckle down, now that you're back, and finish school. You're a bright girl, and—"

"I will finish school but not here, not with you. I'm not sure I ever want to see you again."

"You did say there was a bond. We could get it back. I still love you."

"I don't want to. I just don't want to try." She walked to the front door.

He followed. "I could call the police, force you to stay."

She pulled out a sketch of Tyler from her backpack and handed it to him. "Something to remember him by."

He looked it over, wonder lighting his face. "I didn't know you could do this sort of thing."

"Where are they buried? I want to see them before I leave."

"Glen Forest Cemetery, next to Grammy and Gramps, the family plot."

She opened the door. "Don't follow me," she said, and stepped outside. After walking about half a block, she circled back to the side yard by her bedroom window. The tulip tree soothed her as she hugged its trunk and said goodbye.

~

TED PARKED in front of the Dillon Beach house that belonged to Eloise's brother, Joe, while Eloise scanned the sparkling horizon and scratched her wrists. She struggled to escape thoughts that stabbed like falling icicles.

Could she possibly have held Julianna captive in her own home? A team of doctors had forced her to concede this before they released her 24-hour-a-day nursing assistants Joe had hired. But how could that be? Julianna, barely able to speak from her hospital bed, had begged for the district attorney to not press charges. So Joe said. But was any of it true?

Ted helped Clara out of the truck. She brushed wrinkles from her lavender sweater and poked at her pink crochet hat while Ted leaned against the door, one foot on the running board, and adjusted his fisherman's cap. Then, with her purse slung over one arm, she ambled up the front walk, a slight limp in her gait.

Eloise saw her and made a note to get her former enemy a festive walking stick if she was ever permitted to go shopping again. Clara rang the bell. A male attendant answered and escorted her to the living room. She sat in a chair that, like Eloise's, faced the ocean.

"I'll bring some coffee and snacks and be out of your hair." The aide leaned down and whispered to Clara, "Daft as a loon."

"Just leave us be." Eloise flicked her wrist at the young man. "And don't go eavesdropping either."

He gave a quick smirk and nod toward Clara.

Clara ignored him and looked out the picture window. "My, what a view. Little Joey has done well to afford a place like this."

Eloise snorted. "Depends on what you mean by doing well, hmmm? He's good at lawyering, got me in a fix, though. No doubt about that."

"He always seemed like a goodhearted boy," Clara said. "I expect he has your best interests at heart."

"How Tilda and I used to tease him! He's getting back at me for all that now."

Clara flinched, and a sharp breath caught in her throat at the sound of her daughter's name.

"Joey told me about Natalie. I'd have sworn on a stack of Bibles that you'd ... driven Tilda away. ... " She gazed out the window. "The ocean, it's so vast, so unknowable."

Seeing Eloise's bottom lip quiver, Clara tried to reassure her. "So much in life is like that." Clara said.

Eloise focused again on Clara. "We weren't nice to her, Tilda and me—not that Tilda deserved ... If Natalie had called an ambulance before she ... oh ... Tilda might ... still ... be with us."

The horror of Tilda's last moments hung in the air like a giant spider web. Silence made seconds stretch beyond reason.

Finally, Clara asked, "Did you know about Truman?"

"She never said, never said, never said ... no Truman, no."

The caregiver came in with cookies and a pot of coffee. He poured a cup for each. Eloise's hand shook as she lifted hers to her mouth.

"Don't strain yourself, now," he said.

"Go away, you pest!" Eloise spat out.

The aide leaned down and whispered in Clara's ear. "Don't be surprised if your conversation fizzles. She's only lucid for short spurts." As he left the room, he pointed to a ceramic bell on the coffee table. "Jingle if you need me."

"They all think I'm going to walk down the hill, put stones in my pockets and dive into the ocean, like Virginia Woolf, I guess, but they're wrong. I've never been suicidal, but then ... what they're saying ... about me ... and my Julianna ... it would drive anyone mad."

"What do you think happened?"

"Oh, oh." Eloise moved her head from side to side, humming random notes before speaking. "I see now, I do, what you were going through, losing Tilda. ... I blamed you for so long, because you ... you sent her away. But I guess ... is it true, tell me now, was I was one who needed worrying about?"

"I think you snapped, Eloise, and you'll find forgiveness."

Eloise resumed humming, her eyes clouding. "Joey won't let me have Coco here. I miss her. He said ... he's taking her to the SPCA."

"She's with me now, well cared for. Everyone on the lane loves her."

"Coco always had a soft spot for you, much as I tried to discourage it." She rocked and hummed some more. "He's selling my home, too, selling my home, too." She leaned closer to Clara to whisper. "I heard him, I heard him talking about it when he thought I was napping. He thinks there's land enough around it to build one of those three- or four-story monstrosities with parking on the ground floor and apartments above. My guts break apart at the thought."

Clara's heart filled with sorrow at Eloise's predicament. "Didn't he tell you? He sold it to Abbudin, the Sufi who directs that chorus. They sing all kinds of music now, even something called disco."

Eloise looked up at the ceiling. "Julianna," she said. "Have you seen my Julianna?" She turned, pleading, to Clara, "Where is she? Where could she have gone?" Then she slumped forward.

Clara grabbed the bell and shook it.

The attendant swooped in. "There, there, let's go to bed, shall we?" He helped Eloise stand up and escorted her to the hallway. "I hope you don't mind seeing yourself out," he said to Clara before leading Eloise away.

"Of course not." Clara listened to their footsteps on the stairs, then made her way back to Ted. They faced the ocean together, arm in arm. Whitecaps slammed the beach. A lone surfer, perfectly balanced, rode a wave toward shore.

"Good for you," Clara called to the far-off stranger.

"Life goes on," Ted said. "One way or another, life goes on."

MADDY SAT on the living room couch in her Yellow Springs digs. With her backpack at her feet, she thumbed through a sketchbook filled with drawings.

When she reached sketches from Glen Forest Cemetery, she traced her finger along her rendering of Tyler's headstone. Text from A.A. Milne's poem "Now We Are Six" brought raw grief to the surface, as though no time had passed since he'd died. The words in stone stopped forever after the fourth line: "When I was four I was not much more." Their mother had drowned Tyler on Maddy's fifteenth birthday, two months shy of the little boy's fifth birthday.

Maddy had drawn her grandparents' grave markers, too, but didn't have much feeling associated with them because they both passed away before she was born. Her mother's grave, though, smacked her hard. The inscription her father had chosen—*"Peace, perfect peace for our loving mother and wife, now an angel with the Lord"*—made it seem like Maddy's depressed and violent mother had never existed.

On one sketch of that stone, she'd scratched an X across the page and scribbled over the words. In another drawing, she'd substituted her own words, "A restless road for our troubled mother and wife, now a phantom in our dreams."

She flipped to sketches done from memory: Tyler eating Captain Crunch cereal at breakfast; crouched in the attic behind a box of Christmas ornaments in a game of hide and seek; riding a tiny two-wheeler with training wheels; creating cardboard racetracks for his Matchbox cars on the living room carpet; tucked into bed waiting for Maddy to read *Where the Wild Things Are* to him or make up a story in which he would befriend a dragon and chase robbers up mountains with the grace of martial arts master Bruce Lee.

Rough sketches toward the end of the book depicted little known scenes from American history for a quilt project underway for the U.S. bicentennial coming up in 1976.

After many hours searching the library for inspiring images, she'd drawn Sojourner Truth, an African-American abolitionist and women's rights advocate in the early 19th century; Lowell, Massachusetts mill workers who organized the Factory Girls Association when their wages were cut; Harriet Tubman, a former slave who became a conductor for the Underground Railroad; Seminole villages in Florida where Indians and Blacks intermarried; and Eugene Debs, who went to prison for denouncing U.S. involvement in World War I.

Maddy felt a quiet flicker of pride. Maybe Clara was right. Maybe she did have potential after all. She closed the book and tucked it into her pack.

Keeley came from the kitchen carrying a brown paper lunch bag. "Here's a PBJ, apple, and chips for the road."

"Aw, thanks."

"We've got trail mix, too, if you'd like."

Maddy leaned down and patted her pack. "Already have some."

Keeley sat next to Maddy. "This time you're leaving me like I left you in Los Angeles."

Maddy chuckled. "Not exactly like that."

"You will continue with quilt sketches, won't you?"

"Of course. It's a genius idea. I want to do dozens for you to choose from. Plus, there's a fair coming up on Shinbone. I'm going to sell a few there, maybe give one away, too, and I'll include notes about the project. I think folks will really get behind the idea of celebrating forgotten people and events from our history. There should be an address where people can send in donations. ... Come to think of it, there's this poet, Lark, lives across the street from me and Clara. You should come visit, and maybe you and Lark could collaborate on a book about the quilt."

"That's an interesting idea, a sort of documentation."

A horn honked. "Oh, gosh, my ride!" Maddy gave Keeley a quick hug before gathering her belongings.

"You done with Ohio now?"

"I did what I came here to do, so yeah."

TWENTY-SIX

Shinbone came to life with the rising sun on July 19, 1975, while the fog put on what some folks said was an exceptional show. In addition to colors that swiveled, shimmered, and swirled, glittering beads of moisture formed familiar scenes: Eloise and Coco dancing on the hillside, Maddy and Lark riding bicycles, Ted rolling a shiny Schwinn to a child, Captain circling above. Others maintained that any such observations were hallucinatory and insisted talk of them was pure poppycock.

Folks didn't argue for long, tough; they all had plenty of setup to do for their annual street fair. By nine o'clock, when the biggest crowd ever flowed in, all manned their respective displays, eager for whatever the day would bring.

Determined to try something new, Lark sat at a card table with her Smith Corona portable typewriter, a stack of paper, and a sign promoting her offer to write people short poems on the spot for $1 apiece. A line had already formed in front of her by half past nine.

Next to Lark, Chip and Rosie put finishing touches on a booth they'd designed to showcase second-hand clothes, accessories and housewares, along with a selection of pastries baked that morning.

A middle-aged fairgoer bought an apricot-filled kolache. "My mom used to make these." He took a bite. "Not bad."

"It's a family recipe," Chip said, wrapping a turquoise boa around his neck.

The man swallowed a bite and said to Chip, "What are you, a boy or a girl?"

Rosie overheard the remark. "Are you trying to pick a fight?" she demanded.

"We'll have none of that here," Chip said.

"A person's one or the other," the man said. "So I want to know, are you a boy or are you a girl?"

Chip stretched up to his full height and declared, "None of your business."

The man stepped backward, shaking his head. "It's not right, goes against wholesome values."

A young woman approached the table and took the man by the arm. "Don't mind my dad," she said to Chip and Rosie. "He's doing his Archie Bunker act, trying to get a rise out of everybody." She scowled at her father. "It's not funny."

He brushed her aside and moved to a neighboring table.

"He knows down deep there's room for all of us in this beautiful world," the woman said.

"Let's drink to that." Chip poured punch for all standing at the table.

MADDY LINED up sketches and notecards depicting scenes of Shinbone Lane and Yellow Springs. She also displayed several watercolors of unsung people and events from American history. Next to those sat a stack of flyers about the quilt project planned for the U.S. Centennial in 1976.

In her free box, Maddy placed a book of poems by Kahlil Gibran; her watercolor of Harriet Tubman, an escaped slave who led scores of slaves to freedom; a calligraphy pen; and a necklace she'd made from buttons, beads, and coins. Satisfied with her table, she sat down and leafed through her portfolio folder, and blew dust from a drawing of Captain, Bonbon, and their friends Stormer and Misty.

Clara sidled over to have a look. "My, my, you give such presence to those pigeons," she said. "They seem alive."

"Thanks. I sure miss them."

Clara looked across to the ripple tree, where Captain used to observe fair preparations as though he were in charge. "Me, too." Clara patted Maddy's shoulder and moved back to her table.

"I miss Dave, too, even though I didn't know him. I mean, it was his mandolin playing that inspired the fair, and he was a rising star. He left it all behind."

"Stardom isn't for everyone, you know." Clara said, easing into her chair.

"Yeah, I get that, but it's sure hard to imagine tonight's show without him."

A woman holding a baby approached. Clara greeted her. "Good morning. Who do we have here?"

"This is Cole. Three months today! Do you have any baby clothes?"

Clara showed her a few items, including a royal blue sweater in her free box.

The woman picked up the sweater. "This is adorable. Why is it free?"

"We each give away at least one thing we love. It's part of our tradition at this fair. This looks just right for little Cole."

The young mother thanked Clara over and over as she eased her wiggling son into the sweater. At Maddy's table, a teenager with a beagle puppy tugging at its leash flipped through Maddy's drawings and, to the young artist's surprise, purchased one of Captain perched in the ripple tree. She also asked questions about the quilt project while admiring Maddy's watercolors.

The painting in Maddy's free box of Harriet Tubman caught the girl's eye. She stared at it as though in awe. "I read a book about her last week," she finally said.

"I did that based on a photo in a library book," Maddy said.

"I want to get this, too." She handed the Harriet Tubman painting to Maddy. "My great-grandmother was Black but passed for white. We just found out. I think this picture will mean a lot to my mom. How much is it?"

"It's from my free box; you can have it." Maddy wrapped the painting in tissue paper and tucked it into the bag that already held the drawing of Captain. With purchases in hand, the girl thanked Maddy and skipped off with the puppy bouncing beside her.

Over the next couple of hours, Maddy and Clara continued to make sales. Each time Maddy slipped a bill into her cash box, her mood lifted, like a kite catching a perfect breeze, and her future, a vexing question mark, nevertheless felt boundless, like the blue sky above. "At this rate, we're gonna run out of things to sell, just like Chip did last year."

"Why don't you take a little break, stretch your legs for a while. I'll keep an eye on your table," Clara suggested.

"Sure, then I'll do the same for you, okay?"

"That would be heavenly. I'd love a catnap."

Maddy walked the fair, greeting people who last year were strangers to her and now were friends. She found an empty bench close to a couple doing a puppet show with marionettes. When the show ended, she continued on and came upon Rosie straightening rows of clothing and accessories. "How's it going?" she asked the lane's most intrepid entrepreneur.

"Great, really great," Rosie gave a big smile, her red waves shining in the sun. "Chip and I have been alternating shifts between selling here and helping out in the children's area. I'm not anywhere near as tired as last year."

"I'm glad to hear that." Maddy spotted a scarf in shades of purple, cranberry, and mauve. She held it up.

"That just came in," Rosie said. "It'll be perfect to keep you warm during another un-summery San Francisco summer."

The teenager wrapped the scarf around her neck and spun around. "How much?"

"Silly girl," Rosie said. "Didn't you notice it's in my free box?"

"Wow! It's my lucky day." Maddy made her way back to relieve Clara and found her stand-in grandmother knitting a new baby sweater and humming "Good Morning Starshine" from *Hair*. "I didn't know you liked that musical."

Clara stood up, yawned, and said, "There's a thing or two you don't yet know about me, my dear."

"Probably more than a thing or two."

Clara chuckled, then grew serious. "You didn't happen to see Ricky, did you?"

"Nope, not a sign." Maddy sat down to straighten some items on the table. "When are you going to call him?"

"I'm working up to it. I did finally get his number from Harold." She kissed Maddy on the top of her head and went inside, each step weighted with the ache of time—so much lost, and yet, so much left to gain.

WHEN THE FAIR WOUND DOWN, Maddy and Clara ambled up the hillside to join the crowd waiting for the evening show to begin. The teen carried a platter of home-made pesto pizza; the elder cradled a bag of cookies.

Chip spotted them and called out, "Glad to see you made it, Clara!" He patted the empty lawn chair next to him.

"Thank you. I had a most refreshing nap." Clara sat down and handed Chip the bag. "They're store bought, not as good as the ones you bake, but every so often I have to have a Milano."

"Ooh, Pepperidge Farm. Yum." Chip opened the bag and sniffed the delicate chocolate scent.

"We made pizza, too," Maddy said. "It's still warm."

"I love pizza!" A member of the Moonrise Cafe collective held out her arms.

Maddy handed her the platter and sat in the grass.

"I hear you've made a big splash in the photography world," Clara said to Chip.

His face flushes. "Hardly a splash. I sell a photo every now and then. Not enough to support me and Sunrise. But the sidewalk sales with Rosie are booming. So I'm fine."

Others seated with the group shared news of their own: a jewelry designer had expanded her line to include bracelets and earrings made from beads she'd scored at a new warehouse South of Market; the folks who'd opened a boutique on Cortland Avenue said their flannel pajamas in bold prints inspired by Hawaiian shirts had sold out; the newest resident of 346, who dressed in flowing, diaphanous fabrics and made her living giving tarot readings, said she'd had a line all day outside of the impromptu tent she'd set up for readings; members of a glass-blowing collective who'd been studying harmonica noted that they had given up on that instrument and taken up the ukulele.

Chip mentioned he missed Dave and his music. Rosie said an actor she was a little sweet on had stopped by to say good-bye that afternoon; he was going to New York to study with a famous coach. Ted confessed he found the lane emptier without Eloise strutting about, spewing her litany of complaints. Clara wondered aloud how soon Julianna would be well enough to travel and whether she and Arty would send a postcard. Others also told of friends who'd moved away, and a bittersweet wave washed through the group.

It wasn't long before the show began with the St. Paul's primary school choir singing remarkably on key. Then, a harpist took center stage. Her nimble fingers and sweet tones captivated all. And when she told stories, everyone entered her far-away world of mists, spells, and quests.

After that, a group of teenagers who'd been studying with the

Pickle Family Circus seemed to defy gravity with their acrobatic stunts. Then, Waddles Fenton, for the first time in her eighty-plus years, got up on the makeshift stage and yodeled to cheers from one and all. Next, Lark performed without text in hand, playing bongos for some poems, dancing in rhythm to her words for others. She recited her last lines to a standing ovation that didn't stop until she left the stage and blended back into the group.

Two members of Dave Deely's former band, the Frogs, took the mic to announce they'd formed a duo called Fried Soup. They used instruments they'd made from found materials. Their harmonies were so dissonant, some folks plugged their ears.

At last, the twins, Barb and Bea, took the stage and didn't disappoint. They opened with impersonations of former U.S. Attorney John N. Mitchell and former White House aides H.R. Haldeman and John Ehrlichman—convicted felons all—planning a breakout from prison. They followed that with their own version of the hit movie *Jaws*, in which several celebrities were chased and eaten by the monster. They sang Helen Reddy's hit song "I Am Woman" while miming housecleaning in high heels, driving race cars in evening gowns, and conducting executive board meetings in wetsuits. They then changed into traditional, vibrant Sámi dress and invited people to dance to disco, the new music sweeping the country.

Most people danced along until they could barely stand. Then one of the twins pulled out a strange looking flute. "We found this in Eloise's attic, along with some other things hidden away," she said. "We think you'll like its far-out sound."

They took turns playing as a sparkling, multicolored mist enveloped the hillside. The crowd grew quiet, everyone mesmerized, peaceful, uplifted and longing for more. Clara, lulled by the sound, fell asleep with a smile. Ted lifted her in his arms to carry her home. Far away in Siskiyou County, one of Captain's offspring heard the flute, cocked his head and vowed he'd follow that sound someday.

As the moon gleamed above, people lit lanterns like they had the year before. Ricky, who'd just finished a long shift helping with inventory at Bell Market, walked up the lane and stopped at the edge of the crowd. He saw Maddy, as beautiful to his eyes as ever. She turned, smiled at him and waved him forward. He hesitated, then stepped into the glow.

ACKNOWLEDGMENTS

For coming up with "Shinbone" when I was brainstorming about what to call the fictional lane where most of this novel takes place, as well as for his patience and humor during my countless hours at the computer, my darling husband, Jim. For lifelong camaraderie and love, my sisters, Kathy and Mary Ruth; for bringing light and joy beyond measure into my life, my daughter, Moira, granddaughters, Ava and Reina, stepsons, Ryan and Jackson, and son-in-law, Roger.

For critique sessions I'll always remember fondly, Marie Judson, Amrita Skye Blaine, Patrice Garrett, and Beth Ann Mathews; for insightful manuscript evaluation, Amelia Winters. For savvy editing and boundless inspiration, Mandy Haynes; for being the best manuscript evaluator any writer could ask for, Rayne Wolfe.

For her enthusiastic and pioneering support for women writers worldwide, J.J. Wilson; for being my dear friend in life-changing story-telling adventures, Ruth Stotter. And for kinship through the years, members of Redwood Writers, the Sonoma County branch of the California Writers Club.

ABOUT LAURA

Laura McHale Holland was so captivated in the 1970s by San Francisco's gorgeous vistas and vibrant, free-spirited denizens that a planned two-week visit stretched into thirty years. It this experience that inspired Laura's second novel, Shinbone Lane, where magic blends with reality and secrets heal, haunt and transform lives. A winner of several indie publishing awards, Laura now lives fifty miles north of San Francisco. When not writing with a pot of strong black tea nearby, watching film noir with her husband, or attempting to train their goofy dog, Tucker, Laura is a determined gardener. Though by her count, half of their plants are struggling under her watch. Connect with Laura and grab a free collection of short, short stories at https:// lauramchaleholland.com.

OTHER BOOKS BY LAURA MCHALE HOLLAND

Memoir

Reversible Skirt: A memoir

Resilient Ruin: A memoir of hopes dashed and reclaimed

Fiction

The Kiminee Dream: A novel

The Ice Cream Vendor's Song: Flash fiction

Aunt Truly's Tales: Enchantment for Story Lovers

Just In Case: Twenty-one bite-sized stories

Note from Laura

Thank you for choosing to read *Shinbone Lane*. In today's crowded publishing world, every reader who takes a chance on an independently published book makes a difference. If you enjoyed the story and can spare a moment, I would be deeply grateful if you left a review on Amazon, Barnes & Noble, or any other online retailer. Reviews help books find their way to more readers—without them, many stories go unnoticed. And if you'd like to reach out with questions or comments, I'd love to hear from you at laura@WORDforest.com.